Clive Maddison is married to Samantha and has two adult children. Serving an apprenticeship with a business in the East Midlands from 1980 - 84, he worked for the company for sixteen years. In 1996 the family relocated to South Devon where Clive became self employed.

Writing has become one of many pastimes that he has enjoyed over the years, ranging from walking and cycling, to musical instrument and model making. [Examples of the electric violins that he has made are shown on the website.]

His debut novel, Caught, was published in July 2010, two excerpts of which can be seen on the **'Inside the book'** page of his website.

www.clivemaddison.com.

OTHER BOOKS BY CLIVE MADDISON

CAUGHT - ISBN: 978 1 84386 636 7

The debut novel, Caught, was published in July 2010. For more details about the author and his writing please visit his website.

www.clivemaddison.com

CAUGHT

Having lost his mother before he was old enough to know her, Andy Numan was brought up, along with his brother Carl, by his successful businessman father. His privileged life at the country estate of Durlwood House saw him want for nothing. After a chance encounter with an old friend, Andy becomes caught between two worlds, one of loyalty to family expectations and one of intrigue, mystery and danger. Attracted to the exciting life on offer, he is presented with an opportunity to realise his dreams. In the process he meets a beguiling woman who turns his world upside down. His journey is shaped by chance happenings that cross his path, the deliberate choices he makes and the devastating consequences that follow.

PURSUIT

Clive Maddison

PURSUIT

Vanguard Press

VANGUARD PAPERBACK

© Copyright 2012
Clive Maddison

The right of Clive Maddison to be identified as author of
this work has been asserted by him in accordance with the
Copyright, Designs and Patents Act 1988.

All Rights Reserved

No reproduction, copy or transmission of this publication
may be made without written permission.
No paragraph of this publication may be reproduced,
copied or transmitted save with the written permission of the publisher, or
in accordance with the provisions
of the Copyright Act 1956 (as amended).

Any person who commits any unauthorised act in relation to
this publication may be liable to criminal
prosecution and civil claims for damages.

A CIP catalogue record for this title is
available from the British Library.

ISBN 978 1 84386 872 9

*Vanguard Press is an imprint of
Pegasus Elliot MacKenzie Publishers Ltd.*
www.pegasuspublishers.com

First Published in 2012

**Vanguard Press
Sheraton House Castle Park
Cambridge England**

Printed & Bound in Great Britain

ACKNOWLEDGEMENTS

To my friends:-

Cherrill Evans for her hard work and patient guidance during the shaping of various drafts of the manuscript. The honest criticism and helpful suggestions she gave have been significant in developing a book that I can be proud of.

Elizabeth Adamson for her help in removing a substantial amount of unnecessary words. The input given has been much appreciated in my efforts to bring this project to completion.

A special thank you to my daughter, Leanne, for the excellent job she has done interpreting the novel into a fantastic book cover. I am absolutely thrilled with the finished design.

To my family

CHAPTER 1

Running down the alleyway grabbing at any opportunity that might be presented to hide from her pursuers, she puffed and panted at the exertion of her bid for freedom. The breath felt warm on her face as she ran, but it was the only warmth that she was likely to feel if she didn't get away.

She glanced behind her and could hear the sound of shoes pounding against the paved surface as the men hunting her down charged along a short distance behind her. They were out of sight, but any moment she would be in their crosshairs, leaving little chance of getting away. Suddenly, lurching to one side of the alleyway, she scurried under some industrial shelving that had been discarded and left standing outside of a concertina warehouse door. She squeezed under the bottom rail through a space only a matter of inches tall. The hard cold paving beneath her and the dirt laden bottom shelf of the racking above became the hiding place that would help in her time of desperation. Her hidden tomb that separated her from the world around that she was desperately trying to escape from.

Gulping in air, she filled her lungs and then tried to deliberately restrain her breathing, scared that any slight sound might betray her position to the approaching gang of pursuers. The urgent need of her body fought back hard against her attempts to calm herself. The throbbing in her head and chest from the blood that pumped after the run and the fear and tension of the situation exaggerated the volume of her thumping heart a thousand times. Anxiety at the prospect of being discovered and the consequences that might follow her attempted escape heightened every nerve, every feeling and every sound. The heavy footfalls echoed around the narrow alley, making it sound like an approaching horde of warriors intent on war. Shouts that moments before had seemed far away were suddenly right there, literally on top of her position. She tensed herself in an attempt to keep totally still, but the organs of her body would not submit to the demands of her panic stricken mind and her heart beat wildly in protest, her lungs ached to gasp in air.

"Where's the bitch gone now?"

There was no doubt about the aggression of her pursuers, or the intent they had toward her.

The hostility that had been submerged, while she was submissive to their will, erupted in the vitriolic language. "You and you, that way. You, down there. Find her. *NOW!*"

There was no hesitation as the men jumped to action following the yelled instructions and the clatter of running shoes hitting the ground reverberated in the space once again. The rumble of each impact seemed to shake the very floor she was stretched out on.

Tia could see the highly polished two-tone shoes of the man who barked out the orders and was mesmerised by them as she watched from her hideaway. After the panic of the run, as the other men disappeared in different directions, it suddenly seemed so quiet.

A cigarette lighter clicked making her jump slightly and she winced at the possibility that her jolt had made a sound that might betray her hiding place. The shoes turned on the paved surface of the alleyway, making a grinding noise as the grit crunched beneath them. She was paralysed with fear as she studied the shiny two-tone dark brown and cream leather, the cream colour running around the side from heel to toe.

Time stood still and the feeling of panic increased another level as she slowly filled her aching lungs, trying to satisfy the urge of her body to gasp for breath. She felt a little dizzy, but forced herself to stay as motionless as possible.

The quiet appeared to sweep around the alleyway, like a searchlight on a dark night hunting down every minute sound that dared to express itself. Tia was acutely conscious of her racing pulse, but only time would slow the beat. It seemed to her like the pounding of jungle drums shouting to all comers, 'here I am, look at me!'

The heels of the shoes were just a few feet from her hiding place, almost within touching distance. There was a temptation to just reach out. It was like the feeling you get when standing on a high point with a sheer drop only inches away, while your brain wonders what it would be like to jump.

Periodically, the smell of tobacco smoke drifted in the air as the man exhaled after drawing on his cigarette. Tia had never smoked and the stench of the fumes irritated her throat as she quietly drew in the air that her exercised body demanded. The urge to cough was immense, but one sound like that would have finished her getaway. No doubt her captors wouldn't make the same mistake a second time. Tia knew that if she was caught, she'd have no other chance of freedom.

She was suddenly alarmed as the slapping noise of shoes hitting the paving signalled the return of the group dispatched to track her down. The running slowed to a stop as they reached the man who'd sent them and they gathered around him. Four pairs of shoes became the view from Tia's floor-level bolthole.

"Well?"

"No sign of her boss," wheezed a rough voice.

Tia almost leapt out of her skin as the racking she'd slid beneath exploded in a cacophony of sound, responding to the pounding of a fist.

"*KEEP LOOKING FOR HER!*" yelled the voice menacingly. "She can't have gone that far and I want her found. Do you understand me?"

The man in charge turned to leave once grunts of acknowledgement had been given to show that they understood.

Tia could see the distinctive shoes walking away at an aggressive pace until they were out of sight.

"I don't see what the big deal is," muttered one of the remaining men once the boss was out of earshot.

"That's because you're an idiot, Don."

"What the hell do you mean, Jack?"

The reply had the tone of a man in a bar about to engage someone in a fist fight over some point of honour.

"It's no big deal to you, but she's valuable. We're being paid to get her and someone might be willing to pay well to see her safe again. Now put your big mouth back in neutral and do as you've been told. *Find her.*"

Tia could see the three pairs of shoes begin to make their way back along the alley, but in a less urgent manner.

She was starting to feel claustrophobic in the tight space and the urge to scream and burst out of her bolt-hole was growing. She squeezed her eyes tightly closed, trying to suppress the increasing desire. One wrong move and her escape attempt would be over. The sweep of emotion was like a rollercoaster. The adrenalin, fear, temptation to run again and the pressure to let go and to turn into a blubbering wreck all fought for supremacy. Tia forced herself to go silently through the words of a song in order to distract her mind from the fear and desperation that welled up from within.

The price she would have to pay for escaping the relative safety of her enclosure was too high. It gave her the will and strength to hold on as long as was necessary until the coast was clear; allowing her to slip away.

Her pursuers were gradually moving out of sight as she found it difficult to turn her head any further to follow them. The muttering grew quiet, the sound of footsteps disappeared, but Tia was not willing to leave the safety of her hiding place just yet. She wanted to be sure that the risk of being found was reduced to a minimum before making a run for it.

It was another fifteen minutes before she plucked up enough courage to test the water by edging to the side of the racking. She slowly and carefully scraped along on the hard surface until there was a clearer view in the direction the search party had taken. The alleyway looked very narrow from her view at ground level. The walls of the buildings soared skyward with a strip of blue as the ceiling.

Quickly glancing in each direction, she confirmed that the passage was as empty of people as it was of sound. There was movement at the far end, about forty yards in the distance, where it was possible to see a little of the traffic and people going about their business on the main road that the alley opened out onto. About ten yards from her hiding place there was a branch off to the right. Realising that she couldn't stay where she was forever, she decided to make a move. There was no choice but to make an assumption that the pursuit was either over or had gone some distance away. She shuffled out from under the shelving in order to make good her escape, but was reluctant to give up the hiding place that had faithfully protected her.

Checking both directions once again, she stood to her feet and tried to brush herself off, but the industrial grime was a fixed feature of her clothing, hands and face. She needed to get away and find somewhere to clean up, otherwise she would be the centre of attention in any street she went along. To be beautiful attracted much admiration, but to be so visible and covered in dirt would make her stand out in a crowd, a crowd that could contain those who wanted to force her against her will. As if the condition of her clothes was not enough after being dragged on the floor, she was also barefoot.

The high-heeled shoes she'd been wearing would have been useless for making her escape. Having left them on the floor near her guard while she went to the bathroom no doubt gave her an advantage in her attempt to break out. Who would try to get away without their shoes? But she did, through a first-floor window onto the flat roof below. It was very tight and there was no way that anyone who had been guarding her in the apartment, could have made it through the same window after her.

Holding a knife back after she'd eaten her last meal, she'd slipped it into her trouser pocket and let her loose fitting top conceal it. It was needed to carefully undo the restraining lock on the window that had been put there more to keep people from getting in, rather than keeping them from getting out. It had taken a few minutes to loosen the screws, as she frequently winced at every unusual sound made during the execution of her escape plan; a plan that had been conceived on a previous visit to the bathroom. She just needed the right tool to deal with the latch.

Her captors were lazy and made her wash the dishes after they'd eaten. 'Why do a woman's work when we've got one available?' one of them provokingly said, while holding her by the chin and staring her in the face. Tia was not going to give him another reason or opportunity to punish her for reacting to his prodding, even though that was obviously his intent.

One of the others subtly cautioned him. "Easy, Raif," he hissed, nodding toward Jack Cougar. "Don't let him see you."

Raif glanced back over his shoulder and caught a glimpse of Cougar in the other room. He turned back to face Tia and smiled menacingly then roughly released her chin as he forcefully pushed her back into the seat. There was no mistake that he intended her harm. He could see the fire in Tia's eyes mixed with a substantial dose of fear prompted by an incident a few hours earlier with the same man, leaving her with a cut lip and feeling bruised.

~

The other two guys who had been around during the last couple of days of her incarceration had left her 'prison' for some reason. The moment she'd been left alone with the one they called Raif, she immediately felt uneasy. As if the situation wasn't already frightening, the look on his face as he turned to her after the door closed was enough to unsettle Tia.

Raif smirked as his eyes scanned Tia from head to toe. She stood up and moved over to the far side of the room conscious that his eyes followed her every move. Trying not to look at him she took a seat at the breakfast bar in the kitchenette. Turning away enough to try to shield herself from his gaze, but still able to monitor his movements, she crossed her arm over herself and put her hand on her shoulder. It was as much an act of trying to comfort herself as trying to cover her shapely form from his leering gaze.

Raif slowly, but determinedly moved across the room toward her and every step made her skin crawl. She felt like the prey being hunted. Paralysed by fear about his intent, Tia remained motionless, but her heart pounded in her chest so much that she thought it could be heard. Suddenly she felt him so close behind her that she could sense his presence wrap around her before feeling his first touch. His fingers lightly touched her cheek and combed back through her long dark hair and she felt a cold chill run down her spine. What would have been pleasurable with someone she loved filled her with a sickening feeling of disgust and terror. She felt him lean in closer and heard his intake of breath as he sampled her scent.

"Just you and me now, pretty girl, and plenty of time to kill."

Tia leapt forward to put some distance between them, but he anticipated her move. Grabbing hold of her from behind, he reeled her back into his embrace and let out a sinister laugh. She struggled against his powerful grasp trying to find some way of escape, but couldn't break free.

"Get off me! Let me go!" Tia squirmed in all directions in an attempt to slip away from the vice-like hold, but felt as overwhelmed as a fly caught in a web, knowing its fate.

"Shhh." Raif attempted to pacify her pressing his cheek against hers. He brought his hand up to her other cheek to hold her against him. Tia knew she was in grave danger from this man. Over the last couple of days she'd noticed his interest. With every move she felt him eye her up and down and had, in a strange way, been thankful for the continued presence of the other two men. The moment it appeared she was to be left alone with him, panic rose quickly inside her.

He started to try to nuzzle into her neck. Tia tilted her head and brought her shoulder up to squeeze him away, but he simply increased the force.

"Don't! Leave me alone!" she protested. She had to do something to escape the embrace that swamped her, making her skin crawl. In a desperate attempt, she slammed down a well-aimed heel onto his foot and the momentary shock of the pain released his hold, allowing her to jump free as he cursed her. Not quite quick enough to get beyond his reach he grabbed her wrist bringing her to a stop and whirling her around to face him.

"You bitch!" he yelled and swiped his hand across her face. She tried to dodge the blow but was caught on the lip by the ring he wore on his third finger. She momentarily lost balance and started to reel backwards only to be grabbed by the arm and pulled forcefully into him. He lifted her clear of the floor, carrying her to the sofa where he threw her back onto it before bringing his weight on top of her. She clawed at his face in an attempt to fight him off, but he managed to pin one of her arms under his body weight as he knelt alongside the couch. As she fought with her free hand, his shoulder thumped into her cheek as he gradually subdued her. Blood filled her mouth as the impact broke the skin against her teeth. The very sensation and taste added to the panic in her desperate situation. Finally reaching beneath her back with one hand, he forced her arm down with his other until he grabbed her wrist then locked it in place by her side. With both arms solidly pinned at her sides she felt like she was being held in a straightjacket at the mercy of her tormentor. Suddenly his hand was around her throat. She froze instantly.

Her eyes wide with terror at what this man would do to her, she locked onto his face. The coldness of his stare was made more frightening by the smirk that slowly crept across his lips as they both knew he'd gained complete control. His hand remained poised on Tia's throat, but instead of applying the pressure she thought was coming he began to run his fingers up onto her chin and along her cheek. In sheer panic Tia shook her head side to side to try to knock his hand away from the intimate gestures he made. She kicked her legs out, but he had her securely locked in place.

"There now," he said condescendingly. "This is nice and cosy."

Tia screamed out, but his hand immediately clamped over her mouth. She felt smothered and gasped for breath when he lifted the pressure. The smell of his overpowering aftershave hit her as she gulped in air.

Suddenly his touch was once again light as his hand brushed her face in the way a lover would touch his partner, but Tia's revulsion gave rise to a nauseating feeling in the pit of her stomach. Questions flashed involuntarily through her mind. How had she ended up in this situation? What did these men want? More frighteningly, what did this particular man want? Would he have the time to take it?

She was abruptly back with reality as his hand slipped down to her throat again, partly encircling her slender neck. His hand moved down until his fingers reached her collarbone then moved inside her blouse almost to her shoulder. Tia squirmed at his touch and let out another cry of protest, but he shook her in warning that his hand would clamp down silencing her if she persisted. No amount of protest made him relent.

She felt the first button of her blouse loosen at his tug, then the second, exposing her bra and her shapely figure. Tia cried out once more in desperation, but his sickening laugh at the twisted pleasure he was having showed he had absolutely no regard for her feelings. She felt his hand begin to travel deliberately slowly toward her partially exposed breasts.

Suddenly a fire and overpowering outrage at the situation this man had put her in, and the liberties he was trying to take, stirred something in her that felt above and beyond her own strength. She threw her head to the side where his shoulder pressed down on her and grabbed a chunk of his shirt and flesh between her teeth. His reaction was instant and he pulled away to break her off. Tia spat at him. His face contorted in rage at her resistance. He instinctively swept his hand over his eyes to wipe his face. She took advantage of the moment and brought up her leg, planted her foot in his chest and using the back of the couch to brace herself she shoved for all she was worth. Raif was propelled across the room tumbling backward onto the floor. He landed heavily, winding himself. She jumped up and launched herself at the door, but just as she reached it she heard the rattle of keys in the lock. Suddenly the wind was taken from her sails and the brave attempt was thwarted at the last hurdle. As the door swung open, she was rooted to the spot, the two other men filling the opening. Her shoulders dropped in defeat as all eyes landed on her and Raif was suddenly looming behind. Tia became aware of the focus of the men in front of her and her hands immediately went up to the partly open blouse. Drawing it together, she fastened the buttons in a defiant and obvious manner while holding the stare of the older man. He moved his attention to Raif who was still standing behind Tia.

"You make a move like that again," Jack hesitated to make sure that Raif was listening closely, "and I swear I'll break your legs with a baseball bat and take pleasure doing it. Do you understand me?"

"It was just a bit of fun Jack…"

Jack stormed past Tia and shouted, "SHUT IT!" as he leaned close to Raif's face to make sure he understood. Tia turned to watch and saw the young man visibly shrink before his superior. Jack's hand was suddenly around Raif's throat. He began to gag at the pressure as Jack propelled him backward into the room. "I told you to watch her, not take advantage of her!"

"Okay, okay Jack," Raif choked out as he stumbled backward.

Tia was thankful that the others had returned, but her mind was already in full flow, figuring out how she was going to get out of there. The black hatred in Raif's eyes as he glanced in her direction, blaming her for how Jack was dealing with him, made her realise she couldn't wait for him to get another opportunity.

Her chance came after dinner that same evening. It was now or never and as she carefully hid the pilfered knife she tried as nonchalantly as possible to make her way to the bathroom.

As she scrambled through the open window, the three of them must have got wind of the fact something was amiss and began hammering on the bathroom door shouting for her to unlock it. There was no turning back now. She either took the opportunity or faced the wrath of her captors.

The gravel dug into her bare feet, but she felt no pain as she dropped onto the flat roof below, her mind was focused on the escape. It had been a struggle getting through the narrow window opening, but her small stature and slim frame were the assets needed to prevent her captors from following.

Tia awkwardly moved to the edge of the roof as quickly as her vulnerable feet would allow. As she glanced over the drop the sound of a splintering door frame made her immediately look back. Suddenly Raif's face appeared in the opening as he desperately tried to scramble through to follow her. His expression was thunderous as the impossibility of pursuit hit him, prompting a stream of curses that emanated from his rage-filled expression. If he'd been able to reach her she knew he would've taken vengeance for the interruption of his attempt to abuse her.

Forcing herself to look away from the bombarding insults, Tia quickly scanned around to plan her next move. The urgency was heightened by the sudden silence as her captors disappeared from the window, obviously intent on finding another way to get to her. The only option available was to leap down four or five feet onto a large waste bin and from there to drop the final distance to ground level.

Desperation forced her to jump, causing a loud thud as she landed on top of the container. It lurched away from the wall a little as it moved on its wheels and Tia lost balance toppling to the floor, catching and ripping her blouse on its hinge on the way. She landed awkwardly and felt the impact through her body. Pain from a gash in her arm and the cuts on her feet made her momentarily wince, but then she was instantly up and running, leaving no time to console herself. The advantage was with her, but would be quickly snatched away if she hesitated for a second.

Being under no illusion the three determined and angry men pursuing her were close behind, she ran faster than she ever had in her life. Fear and adrenalin gave her speed she never thought she possessed. The only plus was that they would have to round the building before they would be directly on her tail, which gave her a few precious seconds to get away. She had to find a place to hide if there was any chance of securing her break for freedom.

As she rounded a slight bend and ran toward the central junction of the alleyway, an opportunity to hide presented itself.

She took it without hesitation, urged on by the sound of her captors scrambling into the narrow entrance to the backstreet alley some distance behind her. The fact that there was more than one direction she could have taken, a side street veered off to the right, was to her advantage. She just hoped they expected her to continue running. Who wouldn't?

~

After the initial desperation of her escape was over and the hiding place had served its purpose, she knew she couldn't just stay where she was. Cautiously inching out from beneath the racking, Tia scanned the area to confirm she was alone. Aware that her pursuers could be back at any moment, she stealthily crept toward the side lane of the alleyway. She had to reveal her position in order to see along the narrow off-shoot. Her breathing deepened as she prepared to peer around the corner.

Figuring that she was less likely to be noticed if she crouched down, she dropped to her knees then quickly took a glance. The coast was clear, but she took another longer look to be sure. The only question to answer was, 'which way now?'

Conscious of her grubby appearance, the side alley seemed to be the best option, keeping away from the busy main street. With eyes darting to and fro, scanning the whole area for signs of threat, she steeled herself before slipping around the corner, quickly moving to a doorway twenty yards away.

Taking care to establish that she had not been seen, she made two more moves to concealed doorways until she reached the end of the narrow lane, which gave way to an open square in the centre of the buildings.

A few cars were parked around the space that was in the middle of the network of small lanes. The area seemed empty, but she hesitated rather than making a run for it. The dark shadows between the austere buildings could be sheltering anyone and she wanted to be sure of her direction before exposing herself in such an open arena.

"C'mon Tia. Stay focused." She whispered instruction to herself as she weighed up her options.

Scanning around, she checked each opening to the maze of back streets that led away from the central space, listening intently for signs of life while considering what to do next.

Just as she was about to commit herself, she was suddenly startled by a voice that came from a nearby doorway and instinctively drew back to hide.

"Get out of here Tom, and don't come back until you've picked up that list of materials from the merchants. We've got a job to finish so make it quick." The voice of an old man spilled out into the square.

"Okay. I heard you. I'm going, I'm going."

Tia carefully peered around the corner into the square toward the direction of the voices to try to measure the threat they posed. A young guy wearing overalls came from an open doorway to the left of her position. He unenthusiastically sauntered across to a pick-up truck and climbed into the cab. She could hear him muttering to himself and as he looked back at the doorway he'd come out of, his expression told a story. He clearly wasn't happy.

Tia had little time to consider her choices. An opportunity presented itself and she had to make the most of it. Crouching low, she quickly ran across to the truck hoping the driver hadn't seen her in the mirrors. As the engine started with a rattle and plume of black smoke, she used the noise as cover while she slid into the back alongside a security tool box that was bolted to the bed of the truck. Keeping low to avoid being seen through the rear view mirror and small window in the back of the cab, she prayed the guy would get moving.

The few seconds the vehicle stood with the engine idling were agony. As it finally began to move, Tia started to believe that she'd got the chance she needed to put some distance between herself and her pursuers.

She began to panic a little as the vehicle moved along at walking pace across the square and down one of the narrow lanes. If she was spotted, it only took a sprint for someone nearby to get to her.

Eventually the truck came to a stop, hesitating for a moment then turned out of the confined passage between the buildings onto the main road. Tia suddenly felt very exposed. The walls of the pick-up bed were little more than eighteen inches high and she had to lay flat to avoid being seen from the sidewalk. Quickly grabbing at a filthy tarpaulin that covered some of the equipment surrounding her, she pulled it over to conceal her presence. There was a tear near the point where it covered her head and she was able to see some of the surroundings as the truck moved along.

The scruffy area was lined with run-down shops. Some offered items discarded by more than one owner, others were food stalls or newspaper stands and any number of other merchants offering anything that would sell.

Suddenly a shadow was cast over her and the view obscured. Her initial inclination was to pull the tarpaulin tighter, as though it were some kind of cloaking device that made her invisible. She realised that a large truck had pulled alongside the pick-up. Thankfully the driver was focused on the traffic ahead and was too busy sounding out his frustration on the horn to take note of anything else. The blaring noise made her flinch, but eventually they were on the move again.

The vehicle must have travelled at least two or three miles, which Tia assumed would be enough to get her away from the immediate threat, but she still had to figure out what to do.

Unexpectedly the truck slowed with a piercing squeal from the brakes. It lurched to the left then came to a stop. The engine died as the ratcheting of the parking brake locked the wheels. The driver's door opened and slammed shut, shaking the body work of the old wagon. The tarpaulin was suddenly pulled away revealing Tia in her hiding place.

The shock of being exposed was as great for Tia as it was for the driver of the vehicle. He paused for a moment as he was presented with his young female stowaway, who was covered in the dirt of her escape and laid out among the tools of his trade. Neither one of them knew what to do, but Tia, squinting from the sudden blast of bright sunlight, was still wound-up from the chase. Beating the workman in her reaction, she leapt to her feet and jumped over the opposite side of the pick-up.

"Hey! Lady! What the hell are you doing in my truck?"

He made a half-hearted effort to chase and stop her, but saw no real reason to try to apprehend her, it would only cause him more trouble than it was worth. Tia, however, was in no mood to be caught, whoever was giving chase. The panic and fear of her earlier attempt to make a break for freedom was gone and she was determined to put as much distance as possible between herself and anyone who she thought posed a threat. For the time being that meant everyone.

Turning the corner into another street she was now out of sight of the driver and hastily looked for somewhere to conceal herself in case he intended to follow. About one hundred and fifty yards along the road, over on the other side, she spotted a tatty old building that was a garage repair workshop. To the side there was a space of land on which were parked a number of dilapidated vehicles that looked like they'd run the course of their useful lives. Running over, she slipped between two of the larger trucks that were furthest away from the building, but the gravel that covered the lot brought her quickly to her knees with the pain of the sharp stones under foot.

All the discomfort that had been masked by the adrenalin aiding her escape, flooded into her consciousness. Small cuts and bruises to her unshielded feet began to show as the blood flowed. There were tears in her blouse and she was covered in dirt and grime, the result of her journey, leaving her looking like she'd been working in the garage, the parking lot of which she was standing in.

Distracted by the state of her appearance while trying to soothe her swelling feet, she didn't hear the man come from behind the truck she was leaning against.

"Ma'am? Are you okay?"

Startled by the unexpected voice, Tia jumped up, her eyes wide with fright. Surprised at being discovered so quickly, her spontaneous reaction was to run, but she was partially hemmed in by the vehicles. Her eyes flashed side to side and behind as she quickly assessed her options. The exit was blocked behind by a wall that the two vehicles either side were parked up against. The man that discovered her was blocking the way she'd come in. The only alternative was to scramble underneath one of the trucks. Instantly she poised herself ready to make an escape if the guy moved any closer.

Seeing her alarm at being cornered and the fear etched on her face, the man held up his hands in an attempt to reassure Tia that he was no threat. Backing off a couple of steps, he repeated his question with an emphasised inflection of concern for her.

"*Are* you okay?"

Tia flashed her eyes up and down him trying to assess the situation and the man before her. He was a tough-looking character, with a strong, muscular physique. The hands he held up were blackened with oil and grease from his work. He was about six feet tall, in his late twenties, and the definition of his handsome face was partially hidden beneath a few days growth of stubble. His shoulder length brown hair was drawn back and held in place by a baseball cap. The grime of his overalls and the dirt of his occupation decorating his face could not hide the piercing blue eyes that immediately captured Tia's attention. There was sadness in his demeanour, but concern was clearly registered on his face. Tia hesitated as she assessed the situation. Should she run or should she trust?

"Miss, are you alright?" he calmly repeated. "Can I help you?"

She noticed him glance down at her feet then quickly back at her face as though he didn't want to be caught embarrassing her. As his eyes locked with hers, again he gave a gentle smile of encouragement.

Tia scanned around once again checking her options and noticing that she still saw his proximity as a threat, he backed off a couple more steps so that she could make an easy break for it if she wanted to. The move seemed to address her immediate alarm, so he tried once again to reassure her.

"My name is Will. Will Harris." He paused a moment, noting how her eyes were solidly fixed on his, watching his every move.

Her body was still tense as though muscles were coiled springs ready to burst into action. "I own this garage."

Will turned away and pointed to the ageing building several yards from where they were standing. Looking back at Tia, their eyes connected once more and she was momentarily captivated by the piercing blue colour of his eyes.

'Can I trust him?' She thought. She watched him for a few seconds and noted his non-threatening posture. She relaxed her defensive stance a little and Will immediately picked up on it.

"You look like you could use some help."

His deliberately emphasised non-threatening manner made her alarm drop down another notch.

"Miss, I'm going to go back to my workshop. If you need some help, you're welcome to come. I'll be inside, just through that side door, working on a truck."

He pointed to the doorway as he took a few more steps back, but hesitated a second as he held her stare, then smiled, turned and walked to the nearby building.

Tia tentatively moved to the edge of the truck so that she could watch him go across the parking lot. When Will reached the door, he glanced back to see if she was still there and waved to beckon her to take up his offer of help, then disappeared through the open door. Checking around to make sure they were still alone, Tia cautiously limped across the parking lot to the door that Will had gone through.

When she finally reached the threshold and peered inside, it took a few moments for her eyes to adjust to the relative gloom. The building was mostly taken up with vehicles that were in varying states of repair, with endless amounts of tools scattered around each one. Some looked beyond all hope. Tia stepped through the doorway onto the cool concrete floor which felt soothing to her injured feet.

"I've put the kettle on if you'd like coffee."

Her eyes locked on the location of the voice. She could just make out Will in a small office area at the back of the workshop and took a gamble by moving a little closer.

"There's only me," he shouted over the rumble of boiling water that echoed in the large workshop. "Been like that since my father…" He hesitated a second as if he'd suddenly found himself in territory he never intended to visit. "Since my father died about six months ago." Will had momentarily stopped making the drinks and seemed to vacantly stare at the two mugs he'd picked out of a cupboard.

Shaking himself from his isolated world of memory he continued, "Still finding it tough without the old fella, but you've got to carry on haven't you? At least that's what everyone tells you, without realising the pain it causes." He muttered the last comment at a lower volume, as if addressing himself rather than his guest.

Tia watched him and could see the weight of circumstances resting on the young man. He shrugged his shoulders as though attempting to separate himself from an unwelcome feeling, before resuming the task at hand.

Not wanting to leave Will in his self-imposed vulnerability, "I guess so." Tia whispered her answer, as she gathered a little confidence in his intentions.

Will glanced across and weakly smiled in response. Picking up a coffee mug, he took a few paces toward Tia and placed it on the bench that lay between them. He went back to where he'd been and took his own drink, then turned to face her.

"I'll stay here Miss, if it makes you feel better."

Tia made the five yard distance to the bench and lifted the mug.

"Thanks…" She looked like she was going to say more, but stopped herself.

"You're welcome…" He drew out the last word as an encouragement for her to offer a name, but she didn't take the hint.

The silence was awkward for a few moments and Will tried not to stare at the state Tia was in. He could see that she was shaken and the anxiousness showed in her pretty eyes as they danced continually around the place and to the exit door. Her long dark hair was a little unkempt, but there was no doubt in Will's mind that she was very beautiful and very out of place in his workshop.

"You look like you've been working on one of my trucks," he said jokingly, but she didn't make any response just sipped at her drink. "Do you need me to phone someone for you?" He smiled, trying to put her at ease.

"NO!" Tia snapped. She saw the shocked reaction in Will's face and suddenly felt sorry that she'd been so short with this man who only appeared to want to help. Will froze at the abruptness of her refusal and the awkward silence was back. Placing his coffee down on the bench, he picked up an oily rag and started to clean one of the engine parts that he'd been working on earlier.

"My father opened this garage forty seven years ago," Will began. He figured that he needed to stay away from her situation until she could understand that he meant her no harm. "Come rain or shine, he opened that door for business and loved every day of it. That's what I miss most now he's gone. He used to whistle as he worked and he never lost the joy of getting an old truck running again, even when most would send them for scrap, he always saw the possibilities." Will stood statuesque for a moment as the pleasant memory washed over him. He seemed to find momentary joy in it, but then the doubts clouded his expression. "Wish I had his staying power, but I don't know that I have." The sound of resignation filled his final comment.

Will walked over to a vehicle with the part in his hand. Picking up a spanner, he set about fitting it.

"The coffee's good," Tia said, trying to make an effort.

"Yeah?" He turned to look across at her. "Don't know if this rust bucket will ever work after I've finish with it, but one thing I'm good at is making coffee."

Will buried himself in the engine bay as he struggled to fit the piece in place. "Good coffee. That's me." His muffled voice filtered up from the front of the truck.

Will continued to mutter on about matters of complete insignificance, until he realised there was no response from his guest to anything he'd said. Surfacing from the vehicle engine bay, he turned to find out what had become of the mysterious woman. He quickly scanned the workshop, but could see no sign of her.

"Hello?" Will took a few steps toward the door. "Hello?"

He suddenly noticed Tia sitting down on her heels, leaning back against the wall. Her arms were resting on her knees while still cradling the mug in her hands and her head tilted down as though she was staring at the floor. She looked so out of place in the midst of the grimy garage and dressed in some classy clothes that told a sorry tale of her recent past.

He cautiously approached, conscious of her previous reaction to his presence.

"Miss, are you okay?" he asked quietly.

"My name is Tia." Her voice betrayed the fact she was struggling to contain her emotions. Not that she was a pushover, but the experience of being trapped and the adrenalin of her escape were wearing off. It left the reality and seriousness of what had happened beginning to register. In the middle of the situation it was all about survival, but as she considered what she'd been through she felt drained of all energy.

"Tia?" Will picked up on the small break in her defences. "*Are* you alright? Is there anything I can do to help?"

The instinct to protect this vulnerable young lady surged strongly in him as he stared at her dejected state. His character had been influenced by his 'old school', gentlemanly father whom he'd highly respected. Having spent his life looking out for his younger sister, Sophie, he'd developed a certain protective element toward those around him who needed help. Even the way Tia had positioned herself reminded him of how Sophie would act when she was in trouble.

She looked up at him and he could see the weariness in her pretty face.

"I… I need to get cleaned up a bit…" She hesitated, hinting for Will to take the lead, but he wasn't sure what to suggest and stammered a little in his response.

"There's a sink…" He turned and pointed to the room where he'd made coffee a few minutes earlier. "You could…" He turned back to look at Tia. "You could…" He stopped for a few seconds as he looked at her. He smiled as she connected with his gaze and sympathy for her situation made him change tack. "I'm just about finished up here for the day. Why don't I give you a lift to somewhere more suitable? Perhaps you could use something to eat?"

He waited for a response from Tia, but wasn't sure whether she was ready to trust anyone yet. She brushed her hair back over her ear with her fingers so that she could see Will properly. He withdrew a little at the look that tried to weigh him up. The fear that he'd first seen in those eyes had gone, but he felt very conscious that Tia was taking measure of him before giving any response. Will wondered what was going through her mind, but suddenly felt conspicuous as he stared at her and broke away feeling a little embarrassed.

"That would be good. Thank you," she whispered.

He glanced back and smiled at her. Reaching out, he took the coffee mug from her and returned them to the office, then, deliberately keeping a noticeable distance between them, he indicated that she should follow.

Stepping out through the workshop side door, he glanced behind to see that she was with him. Although he didn't make it obvious that he'd seen, he couldn't help noticing that she carefully scanned the area before stepping outside.

"The blue pick-up," he said nervously. "The blue pick-up is mine." Pulling the workshop door, it closed with a loud bang making Tia jump and immediately spin around to look. "Sorry." He smiled apologetically. "If I don't pull it hard, it doesn't lock properly."

Tia smiled weakly at him while Will rattled the door to check it was secure.

He led the way over to his vehicle and instinctively unlocked the passenger door first, pulling it open for Tia. Aware that she was very nervous around him, he stood back a little way, making his attempt to put her at ease obvious.

Tia looked at him for a moment before slipping into the cab and pulling the door shut behind her. She watched as Will walked around to the driver's side and climbed in. As he closed the door, he turned to look at her. Will noticed that Tia was leaning out toward her door with her hand resting on the latch, but tried to conceal that he was aware of it. He couldn't help wondering what had made her so suspicious.

Putting the key in the ignition, he started the engine. As it fired up, there was an explosive burst of music from the cab speakers that made them both jump. Will quickly scrambled for the volume button of the stereo to extinguish the barrage of sound and as the silence returned as fast as the explosion had come, he went a little pink in his cheeks. Staring at the dashboard in front of him, he tried unsuccessfully to restrain a laugh.

"I... err... like my music... loud."

Tia coughed as she muffled a laugh. Will looked over and saw the first glimmer of a smile briefly cross her ruby lips. She quickly put her hand to her mouth, trying to hide her amusement, and gave a sideways glance, but he could see the smile in her eyes. Her slightly olive complexion so complemented her long dark hair and pretty eyes that he unintentionally paused for a moment to wonder who she was, but quickly flashed back to his previous position, looking at the dashboard.

"Sorry, I didn't mean to stare."

"It's okay. I've gotten used to it."

Will didn't pursue her comment thinking it would seem rude, but whatever trouble Tia was in, he knew she looked as out of place as him wearing a tuxedo to work.

CHAPTER 2

The pick-up pulled away and turned onto the street heading in the direction Tia had come from when she jumped and ran away from her stowaway a little less than an hour ago. As Will neared the junction, preparing to turn the corner, he saw Tia shrink into her seat and obscure her face behind her hand. Again he made no comment, but sped up a little, which seemed to put her more at ease.

"I hope you don't mind dogs. I have a stupid, loveable hound that watches the house when I'm gone." Will wasn't particularly trying to make conversation he just tried to fill the silence to make himself feel a bit more comfortable. "It's only fifteen minutes away, just outside of town." He tried to reassure Tia, but then thought it might panic her if she thought she'd be alone with him, so he decided to keep quiet and let her talk if she wanted to.

The houses began to thin out after several minutes on the main road. Just over half a mile past the gas station, Will slowed down and turned the pick-up onto a dusty driveway that led to a clapperboard house about thirty yards from the highway. The building was well looked after and nestled in a pretty setting, with a number of aged trees giving shade from the sun. What it lacked in modern features was more than compensated for in charm, which it had by the bucket load.

Once the pick-up came to a standstill, Tia climbed out and as she glanced around at the place, Will thought he detected a favourable reaction.

A dog barked from behind the gate at the side of the house, prompting Will to go over and let him out. A beautiful Golden Retriever came bounding through the opening to greet his owner. Will made a fuss of him as the pair of them enjoyed each other's company. He pushed the dog, jokingly telling him to go away, which prompted more playful excitement. Tia smiled as she watched the routine continue.

Realising that he was ignoring her, Will introduced his friend, "Tia, meet Boost." He introduced the animal with the same sentiment a proud parent introduces a child.

Boost took the change of focus as leave to welcome the new guest and shot across to Tia without waiting for further invitation. He proceeded to offer the only greeting he knew, one of acceptance for a friend of his master. She didn't hesitate to respond to him and Will smiled as the two of them became acquainted.

With the dog still dancing around them both, Will led the way to the front door and opened it. Boost insisted on being first inside and Tia laughed at his eagerness to be with them, causing Will to notice that she'd relaxed a little since leaving the garage.

The light, airy hallway with its polished wood floor was a complete contrast to the workshop they'd come from and surprised Tia a little. The stairs, with open banister and rails, ran off to the right and glass panelled double doors to the left opened to a large comfortable living space. Will looked out of place as he stood there in his greasy overalls.

The awkwardness was suddenly there again as neither of them knew what exactly to do next, but Will was very aware that the clothes Tia was wearing were not going to be suitable to relax in.

"Some of my sister's clothes are still here in the wardrobe of the back bedroom and there's a shower room there as well. There's a lock on the bedroom door," Will hastily added, but then felt a little embarrassed. "Please, help yourself, Tia."

She smiled at his obvious attempts to put her at ease and was grateful for his efforts.

"Won't your sister mind if I take some of her clothes?"

"Sophie wouldn't have minded. Even if she was here, she wouldn't. She was like that."

Tia glanced at the focus of Will's attention.

Taking pride of place on the hallway wall was a collection of pictures. His eyes were fastened on the photograph in the middle of the group. It was him, a little younger and with short cropped hair, standing with an older man and a pretty young woman with long dark hair. The similarity between them pointed to the family connection.

Will surfaced from the momentary isolation of his thoughts and noticed Tia taking interest in what had captured his attention. She suddenly felt as though she'd intruded into his personal space. He forced a little smile and she responded, but the bright-eyed young man that she'd seen in the photograph carried sadness in his expression. She could tell he tried to hide it from her, but the mask couldn't adequately cover the pain she'd glimpsed beneath.

"Life goes on though," he said, with a sigh. "That's her in the picture. She… She…" Will stumbled over his words and shook his head as though he couldn't bring himself to speak them and wanted to cast them far away.

"Sorry." Tia wasn't sure what to say in response to him, but knew he felt uncomfortable allowing her to see some of the pain that haunted him, pain that he'd meticulously tried to bury. Putting her hand on his arm she tried to redirect the focus of their conversation. "Thank you for what you've done, helping me."

Will made light of the moment to try to shake the sombreness that had speedily descended on him, as it often did when unwanted memories forced entry into his world.

"I'll use the downstairs shower room at the back of the house to get cleaned up, then I'll make us something to eat." He turned to go through to the kitchen and Tia hesitated as she watched him for a moment, before slowly climbing the stairs.

The wall displayed a number of photographs hung in a line following the steps to the landing. They were mainly of the same people in the hallway pictures. The frame at the top of the stairs displayed an image of Will on a parade ground with several others all in dress uniform and standing to attention. The smartly turned out military man she stared at in the picture was now hidden beneath greasy overalls and long hair.

Tia thought about the conflicting messages that Will seemed to give off. On the one hand his physical appearance shouted, 'keep your distance', but he had shown compassion in her moment of need.

She was still trying to weigh him up as she stepped into the warmth of the cleansing shower spray. The comforting feeling that embraced her was like refreshing rainfall to parched ground. She felt more than just the grime washing away in the soapy water. It had been the first opportunity to shower in the almost three days she'd been cooped up with her captors and after the chase and everything that followed she felt very much in need. She relished the sheer joy of feeling some of her troubles being soothed. Her feet looked in a bad way after the punishment of the day, but the suds cleansed the dirty cuts and patches of dried blood that had stained her skin.

When she finally turned the shower off, it seemed to be over all too quickly, but she couldn't stay there forever and was conscious about taking advantage of Will's generosity.

Wrapping herself in a large towel, she went back into the bedroom and cautiously opened the wardrobe door, feeling like she was invading someone's personal things. She began to look through the clothes that were hung on the rails and folded in the drawers to find something else to wear other than her bedraggled, stained clothing.

The jeans she settled on were slightly too tight, but they were long enough and began to give a little as she wore them. The baggy fleece top was chosen more for the comfort it offered than the style. It gave the feeling of hiding away in a quilt when you just can't face getting up to deal with the day.

Sounds of movement and clanking crockery reached upstairs as Tia seated herself in front of the dresser mirror to brush her damp hair. The exercise gave her time to mentally prepare. *What would she tell Will? How could she explain the circumstances of their meeting? Could she trust him even after the concern he'd shown and the help he'd given? What was she going to do next?* She decided to try to avoid the subject, if at all possible.

Eventually she placed the brush back on the dresser and stared at her image in the mirror for a few seconds. Her recent 'adventures' had left a small scratch on her cheek that was red and slightly swollen. She touched it gently, then noticed the natural waves of her drying hair. She'd battled so hard to remove them when she was younger and now wondered why it had been such an issue.

With a heavy sigh she glanced around the room, connecting with the moment and her stomach turned. There could be no further delay, so she got up to head downstairs and face Will.

Sliding the bolt on the bedroom door, she opened it and stepped onto the landing. This time she took more notice of the place than when she'd first come upstairs, when her attention was on the need to get clean.

The wooden floors matched the lower level of the house and the rectangle landing was framed with four doors and a window at the far end, opposite the stairs. Tiptoeing to the window, as though she were an intruder in the house, she peered out over the fields edging the highway that brought them there. The hills in the distance gave the horizon an undulating edge as it joined the sky and the sinking sun painted the few clouds with a subtle hint of the evening's sunset colours to come.

Heading back to the stairs, she descended to the lower floor and felt conscious at each creak of the wooden steps. Glancing through the opened double glazed-doors to the living area, she could see the large fireplace at the opposite end of the room.

The ornate grey stone fire-surround had been made deliberately large to emphasise the importance of the feature. It beckoned people to warm themselves when coming in from the cold. She could imagine the cosy feel of the room during the winter months. For the summer it was a display area for photographs and ornaments that meant something to the occupier and intrigued their guests.

As she stood in the opening to the living room she was suddenly aware that Will was standing in the doorway of the kitchen looking in. He was staring at her. It wasn't intentional, but two things had caught his attention. The first was the sweater that Tia was wearing. It was a gift he'd bought for his sister a couple of years earlier. Seeing it on Tia resurrected mixed feelings that fought for prominence in his mind as the memories jostled.

The second was how stunning Tia looked. Her long black hair draped over her shoulders, the clarity of her skin and the perfect features of her face were pronounced now that the remnants of make-up and the dirt from her ordeal had gone. Will thought she looked fresh, untainted and very beautiful.

He suddenly realised that he was staring and quickly diverted his gaze into the living room as if to see what had caught *her* attention. Glancing back at her, he said, "I made us something to eat… if you're hungry."

"That would be very nice, thank you. I'm starving." She smiled.

Tia was equally surprised by Will's appearance, but tried not to be quite as obvious as he had been. The grimy overalls gone and the baseball cap missing, he was now clean. The informal mass of his light brown hair, still wet from the shower, was swept back over his ears. Jeans, loose-fit shirt and bare feet completed the picture of a man that liked to relax after a day at work. She reflected about how different someone could be when the surroundings and circumstances of their environment changed.

Will led the way through to the dining room that had large glass doors which he'd opened to allow the outside veranda to seem like one of the rooms of the house. A small table and chairs were positioned to gain maximum impact from the scenery. The landscape gently tumbled away from the house into the distance.

He pulled a chair from the table then left it for Tia to seat herself. "Orange juice?"

Tia nodded. She watched him pour the juice then fiddle with various things on the table, as though making sure they were properly presented for his guest.

He was a good-looking guy, but had the air of someone a little withdrawn from the surroundings, in a world of his own. Tia looked away quickly when he glanced in her direction. He didn't say anything; just took his seat and began to pick at the food and Tia followed his lead. The silence was initially pleasant, non-threatening, but as it went on it became harder to bear until Tia couldn't hold any longer.

"I..." Will immediately looked directly at her, "I just wanted to thank you. For helping me... And bringing me here." She took something else from the table and leant back in her chair. "The food is lovely."

He was having a hard time trying to figure Tia out, but was cautious about asking anything too probing after seeing her come into the garage so distressed. He hoped she might offer some explanation, saving him from feeling like he was intruding into her private affairs.

"It's my pleasure." He smiled and looked at Boost, who was laid out on the veranda trying to catch the remnants of warmth from the sinking sun. "Don't often have guests do we, Boost?" The dog's tail indicated he knew he was being addressed. Will suddenly felt a bit of a fool. He was trying to fill the silence with something, but thought it must have come across like someone being obvious that they don't have a girlfriend while talking to a pretty girl.

He quickly turned away, looking to the distant horizon and the sun's stunning aerial display of colours. Had someone been looking at the house from the other direction they might have concluded that the couple they could see were having an intimate dinner while bathing in the sunset glow. The truth was that Will felt rather uncomfortable. Not just because there was an awkwardness between them, but he'd been trying to take a good look at Tia since she'd come down from taking a shower. Each time the opportunity seemed to lend itself, he felt like he'd been caught red-handed.

She was beautiful for sure. Each snatched look added a little more to the image that was taking shape in Will's mind, like a jigsaw where every piece gradually added moved the picture closer to completion. He realised he must have been staring again, so tried to break his fascination by asking if she would like coffee.

She looked at him and nodded, putting her hand to her mouth to excuse the fact that she didn't answer because she was eating. Will held his gaze at her as long as he could without seeming rude and the snippets of her image became a whole portrait. Her beautiful dark hair was still damp from being washed and cascaded down, sweeping around her neck, over her shoulder and just over her collar bone. Her slender hands and feet betrayed her slim frame that the looseness of Sophie's baggy top tried to conceal. Her defined features, cheekbones and chin, shaped the face that complemented her hair colour with the subtle, but noticeable, olive colour of her flawless skin. '*Twenty-five at most*', thought Will, as he got up to go to the kitchen to make coffee.

As he filled the water jug for the percolator, he could see her from behind through the doorway where he stood. Her head was tipped forward and her hands were on her face covering her cheeks and nose. Will had thought that she was a little more relaxed, but the posture he saw told him that she was covering her anxiety.

A couple of minutes later he returned to the veranda. This caught Tia off guard and he clearly saw evidence of tears that she was hurriedly trying to wipe away.

Will put the coffee down on the table in front of her, but she deliberately kept her head down, rather than acknowledging him.

"Are you alright?" he asked, as he touched her shoulder.

Tia exploded from her seat and ran into the house. The sudden movement knocked the chair over in her haste to leave and Will lurched back as she disappeared from sight. The sharp bang as the seat hit the hard floor raised Boost from his basket and he immediately followed Tia, his natural curiosity drawing him to the action.

Will stood for a moment wondering how to react, and after waiting several minutes, he went into the house, half expecting to see the front door wide open and Tia gone.

The kitchen and hallway were empty and as he quietly edged toward the living area, he suddenly saw her on the sofa, leaning forward with her arms clasped around her stomach. Boost rested his head on her knee, offering the girl sympathy and comfort. As Will stepped into the room, Boost went to his side as if encouraging him to do something to help.

"Tia, I didn't mean to startle you. I'm *really* sorry."

"It's okay." Her eyes pooled with water. "You've been..."

The tears began to flow and Tia sucked in gulps of air as she tried desperately to restrain her sobs. Her shoulders shook a little as she struggled to maintain her composure, but neither of them were being fooled by her efforts. The pent-up tension from her ordeal suddenly found an outlet. Tia gave up trying to restrain it and just let go. Will went to the kitchen to fetch tissues and brought their drinks from the veranda, placing them on the coffee table between where they were seated.

"I can't help, Tia, if you don't tell me what's wrong," he pleaded. "Do you want me to contact someone?"

She shot upright her watery eyes wide and fixed on Will.

"NO! DON'T TELL ANYONE I'M HERE!"

Will held his hands up to indicate he understood and after a few seconds her rigid posture relaxed again.

"I'm sorry. Please. You mustn't tell anyone that I'm here. I just need some time to think about what I'm going to do." She took the coffee mug from the table and cradled it in her hands while she sat staring into the cup.

"I promise you'll be okay here, Tia. You must tell me something though. She returned from the world she'd been in, looked up and met his gaze. Are you in trouble with the law?"

"Not exactly."

He squinted a little at the vague answer. "I don't understand. What does, 'not exactly', mean?"

"I am in trouble... but I'm not sure why or how much. I really can't tell you anything else yet, Will. I need some time to think and get my head straight. Can I..." She slid forward from her seat to her knees and reaching over the coffee table put her hand lightly on his forearm. "You've already done so much for me, but can I stay here tonight until I decide what to do tomorrow?"

Will looked down at her hand, then into her eyes. The redness showed clear evidence of emotions close to the surface. Her cheeks were tearstained and pools of tears were waiting to fall, just clinging to her lower eyelids.

Will reasoned that he'd always been a good judge of character and he'd met many in his time; people who would lie or try to swindle, taking advantage in the hope of getting something for nothing. You don't run a repair workshop in the place he did without seeing all sorts of people, but the eyes he was looking into belonged to someone who was true, but frightened.

Will held her gaze for a few seconds before responding. "Okay, Tia."

He resisted patting her hand to assure her, worried that she might react again, so he simply nodded.

Tia moved back to the sofa, but this time relaxed back into the seat, but it was as though she were not in the room, her mind occupied in a world of her own.

Will decided to give her some space and went to the veranda to clear away the remaining food and dishes from the table. When he'd finished, he closed the outside doors and turned on a lamp as the onset of evening had made the house begin to sink into darkness.

Boost wandered into the room and Will made a fuss of him then headed to the living room. Tia was curled at one end of the couch, her knees drawn up, one cushion under her head and the other shielding her feet from the evening chill.

Will stood for a moment watching and listening to her shallow breathing in the silence of the darkened room. She reminded him of Sophie when she was a teenager. She would fall asleep watching the TV in almost the same position.

Boost went over and once again heavily planted his chin on Tia's leg. She stirred a little, but Will pulled the dog away before he woke her.

He quietly went upstairs to fetch a couple of blankets and a quilt. When he returned he gently removed the cushion at Tia's feet and carefully placed the quilt over her. Again she stirred a little in her sleep and he hesitated to allow her to settle again.

Moving the footstool over to the single chair, he threw a blanket over and settled down to make himself comfortable for the night. He lay watching Tia sleeping and wondered what she was dreaming about as she occasionally stirred.

The light faded quickly and within a short time only a faint outline of her form was visible. Will began his usual drift in and out of sleep, a pattern of broken rest that had become normal since he'd faced the family tragedy that instantly derailed his life.

CHAPTER 3

"We searched up and down those alleys and there was no sign of the bitch. She just up and vanished."

"UP AND VANISHED!" Vince Kurtis exploded in the room like a firework. "It's your brain that's up and vanished, Raif. From what I hear, you gave her good reason to run."

Raif tried to protest, but was immediately silenced by the continued barrage.

"I left her with *you* for a few hours and *you* let the girl get away. Thanks to *your* stupidity you're going to make us look like incompetent amateurs. That's what *you* are Raif and I'm going to kick your ass if you don't do something about getting her back!"

It was Vince's habit to verbally threaten people into submission. It was his way of trying to live up to his father's reputation. His smart clothes and expensive jewellery were part of the image he wanted to cultivate in an attempt to impress. He looked like his father with his black hair slicked back and dark eyes that were a little too close together. The same straight nose and square jaw-line were inherited, but one thing that was missing was the air of authority that the old man didn't have to force. When John Kurtis said "jump", the order was followed immediately and exactly. Vince used menacing language in an attempt to produce the same result, but it never could. What his father possessed was a mysterious element causing people to want to be in his presence, but made them conscious of the risk of crossing him. His demeanour instilled wariness and a need to tread carefully; the beauty of a cobra, but with venom in its bite. Vince didn't have that same character, no matter how he tried to manufacture it.

Jack Cougar had known Vince since he was a little boy. He'd worked for Vince's father for many years. If someone needed 'sorting out', it was Cougar that got the job. John Kurtis would send him with instructions about the level of pain the offender should suffer. There were never any complaints about Jack's effectiveness, but now he was working for the son who inherited the 'business' and held it because of his name rather than his ability.

Jack was standing with Raif and Don, waiting for Vince's latest performance to end as he expressed his displeasure about them losing his prize. Whilst Vince was able to intimidate the younger guys, the tactic never worked on Jack Cougar. At fifty-five years old he'd seen it all and been involved in a lot of shady things, but he never took kindly to being yelled at by a thirty-six year old spoiled brat for whom he had no respect.

Jack turned away as the focus came on Raif and sat down in a chair. He raked his fingers through his thick silver locks of hair, then reached into his pocket and pulled out a pack of cigarettes. The click of the lighter distracted Vince for a second and the annoyed look on his face didn't go unnoticed by Jack. A slight smirk crossed his face when he knew that he'd needled the pretentious prick again. It had become a frequent pastime for him of late. It seemed to go in phases as Vince tested the water to see if he was gradually breaking down Cougar's resistance to his authority. He had no idea that Jack viewed him with contempt and only tolerated the behaviour for the sake of Vince's old man and the respect he'd had for him.

Jack casually glanced around the room as though he wasn't listening and gave no response in order to deliberately irritate Vince, simply to see how he would react. It was the wise old stag outwitting the young pretender. He knew Vince was too scared to make a direct challenge toward him and smirked to himself while he watched Vince work hard to put on a tough guy show for the others.

Jack's body language gave the impression of a man in control and the two opposing forces jostled for domination of the room. As Vince's rant came to a momentary hesitation, Jack forcefully blew out a cloud of smoke which curled up toward the ceiling. The interruption threw Vince for a second before he recovered himself.

"Now get your lazy asses back down there. I don't care if you have to turn every stone in the neighbourhood and look down every sewer, I want that bitch found or I'll be knocking out what's left of your brains." Vince was inches from Raif's face as he tried to stamp his authority on the situation. "YOU HEAR ME?"

"Okay, okay Boss. I hear you," answered Raif, as he quickly glanced across at Don. They each threw a look in Jack's direction wondering what he was thinking. He was indifferently looking at the lighter he turned over and over in his hand.

The two younger men jumped to action as Vince smashed his fist on the desk for emphasis. They left the room in a hurry and were in no doubt that they had to fulfil their instructions, or pay the price for failure.

Jack continued to sit there for another thirty seconds, the lighter still the focus of his attention. Finally he looked up and locked eyes with Vince. He took a long drag on his cigarette as the two of them stared at each other. Jack's eyes narrowed and Vince momentarily gave way, glancing at the window. He was furious at the delay in following his instruction. Finally, Jack stood to his feet calmly, shook his suit jacket and fastened the buttons, then smoothed out the dark material with his hands until he was satisfied that all was up to his usually smart standard. He looked at the younger man behind his desk, locking eyes once more, but said nothing. It was Vince who again broke the stare, at which point Jack casually left the room.

Vince slumped into his chair and exhaled loudly through clenched teeth as he rubbed his hands over his face. The silent confrontations with Jack always wound him up, but the loss of his captive was paramount in his mind at that moment and all attention needed to be focused on finding her again.

The phone rang, breaking the silence. Vince reluctantly grabbed the handset, after giving it a moment longer in the hope it would stop.

"Yeah?"

When he recognised the voice, he suddenly straightened in his seat, listening to the caller for a minute before interrupting the flow.

"We've *got* the girl. You asked us to *get* the girl; we've *got* the girl. You just be ready to complete the deal and don't ever question my integrity or capability…"

The caller cut through Vince's protests, wresting control of the conversation from him. Vince listened without interruption, his face like thunder, until there was a click as the call was terminated.

He slammed the receiver down in a rage, making the items on the desk dance. Vince Kurtis was not a patient man and his very limited reserves had been exhausted seconds after Tia had disappeared through the bathroom window three hours earlier. The incompetence of Raif, Don and Jack in letting his prize catch escape had turned his day from one of order to chaos. The confrontation with Jack, albeit almost silent, and now the phone call just added to his agitation. One thing he was not about to do was let the moneyman know that he'd allowed the girl to slip his grasp. He had no intention of looking the fool, or suffering the consequences.

Pulling a cigarette from the packet he'd laid on the desk, he checked his pockets for a lighter. A sharp click provided the flame to light the fix needed to calm his nerves. He drew a lung full of smoke, held it for a few seconds then let it hiss out through his pursed lips. He rubbed his fingers on his forehead and shook his head in dismay.

Two minutes later, he stubbed out the cigarette, jumped up and snatched his jacket from the back of the chair, barging out through the door en-route to crack the whip behind the others. If they were going to find Tia, they had to do it pretty soon, before she had a chance to realise not all the authorities were in their pocket. Vince knew she'd be very cautious after the way they'd arranged to grab her, but he also knew that she would be frightened from her experience. That was likely to give them the best opportunity of tracking her down.

Beginning from the point where they'd seen Tia jump from the flat roof onto the bins, Raif, Don and Jack worked their way along the narrow lanes again, checking every window and door as they went in an attempt to discover where she'd gone. There didn't seem to be time when they were first in pursuit of her. It was just assumed that she would instinctively run and they simply did the same hoping to catch her.

As they neared the junction where the discarded shelving was standing, Raif rattled at the concertina door to the industrial unit to check if it was secure. He kicked it in frustration and letting his temper fly, releasing the pent up rage from being yelled at by Vince. Shoving over one section of the racking that stood partially over the doorway, he let his anger out.

"When we find that little whore, I'm going to ring her scrawny neck," Raif snapped, still smarting at the dressing down he got from Jack for trying to take advantage of Tia.

Don spun around to check the sound of approaching footsteps.

"Hey, Raif!" Raif looked up to see his boss closing in on them and his expression didn't look like he'd cooled down since the last encounter.

"I'm stalling the contact that wants the girl. They're expecting to collect her soon, so you had better be making progress!" he shouted. His voice betrayed the urgency of the situation. "I ain't taking the flack for this. I wasn't even in the room when she bolted." Vince's anger was boiling over as he threw out his accusations of incompetence.

He could be unpredictable when his temper took control. The rumours about his vengeance were confirmed by Jack who had known Vince for a long time. He hadn't hesitated to break a bone or two if someone crossed him… and that was just those working *for* him.

"Hey! What was the bitch wearing?" Raif called out suddenly. The others did a double take as if he'd temporarily gone mad.

"What the hell does that matter, Raif. You put your efforts into finding her or I'll bust your stupid head." Vince's face was reddening as though he was about to blow a gasket, which usually preceded a verbal outpouring.

"NO!" Raif responded with a flash of hate in his eyes that made even Jack take notice. "What the hell was that woman wearing?" He couldn't quite remember from earlier when he was more focused on what she looked like without wearing anything.

The others looked at each other while trying to recall, still unsure what Raif was up to.

"A white blouse that was loose fitting and dark trousers, I think," Don answered, eager to try to defuse the situation. "Why?"

"A bit like this?" Raif held up a piece of cloth that had snagged under the lower shelf of the racking he'd tipped over. "When we were chasing her she must have slid underneath these, the sneaky bitch. She was probably here all along, waiting for us to leave so she could slip away."

"We were covering the exits so she must have gone into a building or something," Vince suggested.

"If she'd gone down there to the main street, I would have seen her come out," Jack stated. "I was at the end all the time. There's no way I would've missed her. She must have tried to keep out of sight and gone down the side alley to avoid the busy area."

The four of them set off, turning right into the short linking alleyway and trying all the doors as they made their way to the square that sheltered a few vehicles.

When they reached the open area, Vince barked his orders. "Try every door and talk to anyone you can find!" They fanned out and began working their way around the perimeter of the small quadrangle.

Jack pushed at a door which was locked and then at the next, hammering each time to try to rouse attention. He checked a couple of securely barred windows and then another door, which gave way under the force as he pushed. As Jack stumbled into the room he almost knocked an old man in painter's overalls off his feet.

After a moment's surprise at the sudden entry, the workman threw abuse at Jack for barging in; an unwise move. "God damn it. What the hell do you think you're doing? You idiot. You could have done me a serious injury barging in like that. Who the hell are you anyway?"

Jack didn't respond to the outburst. His cold dark eyes remained sinister and staring, making the old man suddenly feel very small. He slowly pulled a pack of cigarettes from his jacket pocket and with one hand flipped the lid open, slid one proud of the packet and took it in his lips. The workman watched the deliberateness of his movements, concerned that Jack's eyes never left him. With the same unhurried motion, he brought a lighter up to the cigarette, lit it, and deposited the lighter back in his jacket pocket. He took a drag, filling his lungs, then casually blew the smoke straight at the bemused old man.

As the workman watched, Jack smiled, but it was not a friendly gesture. His eyes indicated the malicious intent underpinning the expression. The next item to emerge was much less welcome, making the old man take an involuntary step back. The black handle in Jack's grasp suddenly clicked as a slender, menacing blade appeared, as if part of a magic trick. The steel glinted in the light as Jack purposely rolled the knife side to side in a threatening manner.

"You been decorating this place long, old man?" Cougar asked the question as if he'd just bought a drink at a bar and started a casual conversation.

"Two... Two weeks. Hey, I don't want any trouble." The old man gestured defensively with his hands.

"What time d'you get here today?" The knife turned again to keep it the focus of the workman's attention.

"We've been here since six this morning."

Jack looked at the stairs behind the old man that disappeared up to the next floor then glanced down at the knife and back at the old guy, as if he might need to be reminded of its presence. He didn't. He constantly flashed from Jack's face to the knife, unsure which one looked most sinister. Fear was etched on the old man's face while he waited for the next question.

"A young lady came through this way earlier. She up and disappeared." Jack hesitated, allowing the pause to do the work for him. He was an old hand at intimidating people and had honed his skill through many situations that needed to be 'resolved'.

"A young lady…? My… My apprentice went to get something this morning… He came back with some cock and bull story about a girl hiding in the back of the truck." The old guy tried to appease Jack as best he could, but he hadn't really taken much notice of the lad when he'd come back, thinking he was just making some excuse for taking so long. "You need to ask him what he saw."

Jack stared at the old man. The look was intended to convey the fact there would be hell to pay if he was being messed around and it did its job perfectly.

"Straight up. He's upstairs right now." The old guy pointed to the staircase behind him, emphasising that he was telling the truth.

Jack flicked the catch on the knife and folded the blade back into the handle, having done its job for the moment.

"Shout the kid," he ordered.

Immediately responding to the instruction, the old man turned a little to shout up the stairs, "TOM!" but his eyes remained fixed on the knife. There was some indistinct muttering from above. The old man tried again with more urgency. "TOM, GET YOUR ASS DOWN HERE, RIGHT NOW!"

There was a thundering of steps as the boy rushed down the stairs to the entrance hall where he suddenly stopped dead, seeing his boss standing with a stranger.

The spindly young man pushed his hat back to get a better look at Jack. Looking back and forth between the two men, he finally focused on his boss.

"What's going on Ed?"

"Just shut your mouth and listen a minute."

A smirk crossed Jack's lips. The intonation in the old man's voice betrayed the fact that he was scared about what Jack would do if they didn't come up with the goods.

"This morning you went to the hardware store?"

"Yeah! So what?"

"That tall tale you told me when you got back, tell him." The old guy flicked his thumb toward Jack.

The lad looked Jack up and down.

"Why?"

Jack lurched forward and in a split second grabbed the boy by the throat and slammed him against the wall. Taking hold of his overalls, he almost lifted his feet clear off the floor.

"BECAUSE I WANT TO KNOW... BOY!"

Totally shaken by the violent response, Tom was in no doubt that asking questions was not an option.

Jack let go and he slumped down the wall, winded by the force of impact, but it didn't stop him spilling the beans through his gasping attempts to fill his lungs.

"I just went to the hardware store to get some more decorating materials." He hesitated taking a gulp of air. "I used the truck outside. Never gave it a second thought, just jumped in and went, but when I arrived at the store, I pulled the tarpaulin off and there was a girl laid down in the back, hidden away. As soon as she saw me, she jumped over the side and ran..."

"What did she look like?" Jack demanded.

"Slim, dark hair, smart clothes but covered in dirt... She had no shoes on."

Jack's eyes were fixed on the boy. He grabbed him by the collar and flung open the door, dragging him out behind as he went.

"Vince? Vince, here!"

The young lad cowered as he moved alongside Jack, petrified about what was going to happen.

The other three guys came running at Jack's call and were there in a flash, surrounding the lad.

"Raif, get the car. Now!" Raif responded to the instruction immediately, tearing off down one of the alleyways like a terrier after a rabbit.

Jack let go of the young man's collar and turned to talk to Vince, completely ignoring the fact the young man had slumped to the floor.

"She hitched a ride in the back of this guy's truck and jumped out when he found her hiding under a tarpaulin."

"Are you sure it was her?" Vince looked down at the lad cowering under his gaze.

"He says the girl had no shoes on."

There was a sound of screeching tyres as Raif threw the car around the corner and into the quadrangle. It came to a sliding halt next to them and they immediately piled into the vehicle. Vince in the front passenger seat, Jack and Don either side of the quivering wreck of a boy in the back.

As Jack got in, he shouted to the old man who was peering out from the doorway. "Keep your mouth shut old man. The kid will be back when he's... helped us."

The sentence was finalised with the thump of the rear door closing. Raif immediately had his foot on the gas, causing the car to lurch forward at speed and the roar of the engine was amplified in the confined space.

The car suddenly slowed as it came to the end of the alley that led onto the main street. Vince turned around to face the boy in the back seat. Tom was surrounded by mean, unpredictable thugs who he knew would have no hesitation doing him harm if he didn't cooperate.

"Left or right kid? Where did you go earlier today?"

"Left, I turned left. Follow the main street to the other side of town, to Marsdon Hardware." He glanced either side at the two guys who held him. Neither one took a blind bit of notice of the terrified captive. They just stared out of the windows as the car bullied its way along the busy road.

Within fifteen minutes they neared their destination.

"Turn right at the lights and the store is on the left," Tom instructed, offering the information before it was asked for, fearing what was going to happen when they finally got there.

The car pulled into a space in front of the store and they all piled out. Jack pulled at Tom's overalls, manhandling him out of the same door.

"Okay kid," Vince said, "she ran from your truck when you surprised her. Which way?"

"She jumped over that way and headed along the road..." He nervously pointed in the direction Tia had run. "...and then she turned right down that side street."

Vince turned back to look at the boy and the cold stare sent a chill down his spine.

"Raif, Don, you come with me back to the office." Vince turned to Jack, "We'll ditch the kid then I'll send Raif back with the car."

The terrified expression on Tom's face betrayed the panic induced by Vince's words. "Man, I helped you. I helped you!" His face screwed up as though he were about to burst into tears. "I helped you find where she went. I didn't know. I had nothing to do with it. I won't say anything, just let me go. I won't say anything!"

The four guys were all looking at the kid whimpering, he was almost on his knees begging.

"He thinks were gonna smoke him Boss."

They all burst out laughing. Vince's face suddenly changed back to deadly serious. "You're damn right kid, you won't say anything to anyone. If you do, I will personally cut your tongue out." Vince indicated to the others, "Put him in the back of the car. We'll throw him out at the square so he can get back to work. Lazy bastard."

The others laughed.

Vince focused his attention on Cougar. "Go down that road, Jack. Poke around and find out if anybody knows or saw anything. I'll send Raif back with the car once he's dropped us off, then I want you two to follow any lead you get. Keep in touch, you hear. This is important." Vince slapped Jack on the shoulder, got in the car and told Raif to go. Jack watched as it pulled out of the parking space and tyres screeched as it disappeared down the road.

He looked around assessing the situation then began walking toward the turning that Tom said Tia ran down. He rounded the corner and looked at the rows of tired old houses set back about ten yards from the sidewalk. They ran the full length of the road until a bend obscured the view.

Scanning everything carefully, he began to move down the street checking each house without being too obvious. You could never be sure who was watching or what their reaction to a stranger looking into the properties would be.

Jack sauntered along, until a rundown garage, set back a little from the surrounding houses, came into view.

Figuring he might find someone to talk to, he crossed the road and wandered into the parking lot, to check out the vehicles that were all well past their best. The large front sliding doors were closed, so he went to the smaller side door. Rattling at the handle, he found it locked, so he banged on it to try to rouse some response, but there was none. Checking along the side of the building he went to a barred window and peered through, but it was so dirty he couldn't see anything.

Giving up on his fruitless search, he headed back to the road. He needed to find someone he could pump for information. As he reached the entrance, he turned back to take a last look before moving on.

"Did you try the side door?"

Jack turned to see an elderly lady on the other side of the road, leaning on her sweeping brush. She'd obviously come out to clean her pathway and caught sight of him in the garage parking lot. He decided it was time for 'Jack the charmer' to make an appearance. Waiting for a vehicle to go past, he crossed to the other side and smiled at the woman as he approached.

"Yes ma'am. It appears to be locked up." Jack sighed heavily to emphasise his disappointment.

"Yeah? That's odd." The old lady scanned the garage carefully as though she might see some sign of life Jack had missed. "The boy's had it a bit tough since his daddy died. He's been trying to keep the place going, but times are changing and people don't go to places like that anymore." She gave a little shrug of resignation indicating her belief that the business was in terminal decline.

"Poor guy... How sad." Jack laid on the sympathetic sentiment.

"I can remember when his daddy opened it in 1962. Always did a good job." She was lost for a moment in the memories of time past before quizzing Jack about what he wanted. "You looking to get your car fixed?"

Jack took a few paces closer in a friendly gesture. "Yeah. The old thing's been playing me up for the last couple of days. Came to a stop on the main road," he pointed in the general direction. "Someone told me there was a shop down here. I walked down just a few minutes ago. I was hoping he might be able to help me with it so I could just get back home." Jack gave a shrug of resignation to emphasise his need.

"Another one?" The old lady laughed. "You're the second one today. Odd that he's not back yet."

Jack's interest picked up. "What do you mean? Has he gone for a late lunch or something?"

"I don't know exactly. I saw him getting into his pick-up with a young lady a little while ago." The old lady moved a little closer and tapped Jack on the forearm. She quickly glanced to the side as if to check that she wouldn't be overheard when she spilt the latest gossip. "She was dressed quite nicely, but looked like she'd been rummaging under her car hood trying to get it started." The old lady smiled. "Looked a bit of a sight, she did. I reckon she didn't expect to be going home like that."

Jack laughed and leant in a little closer. "Bet she was wearing fancy high heels as well?" he whispered.

"I don't know, couldn't see them. She got in the other side of the truck. Don't know where she came from. I must have been out back when she arrived."

"You reckon he might have gone to help her fix the car? I only ask because I don't want to wait if he's not likely to come back."

"Maybe." She shrugged and half-heartedly swished the brush along the paving. "It's unusual for him to be gone this long though. He normally tows them back here to fix. Perhaps he's decided to call it a day and gone home. It's getting late in the afternoon, I suppose." She paused a moment then added, "His daddy would never have done that."

Jack feigned disappointment and the old lady picked up on it.

"You in a hurry mister?"

"Heading home. My wife's family are coming for dinner tonight."

"Oh dear. Well I hope you get it sorted soon."

Jack knew he was losing the initiative, so decided to be a little more direct.

"I don't suppose you know where the guy lives? I mean, is it local? I just thought if it was, perhaps he would help me out. I'd have to pay him a little extra of course, for going to the trouble…"

The old lady looked Jack over and he obligingly played the part of husband in a fix.

"If he's still where his daddy lived I think it's somewhere on the outskirts of town, near the water tower at Beechfields."

As the words left her mouth, Raif turned the corner from the main road and catching sight of Jack, sped up until he came along side. He pulled up sharply and lowered the window.

"Okay Jack?"

"Yeah."

The old lady looked at Jack as if to say, 'There ain't nothing wrong with that car', but Jack just turned away and got into the waiting vehicle.

"You find anything?"

"Beechfields. Near the water tower." Jack turned and smiled at the old dear as she watched them.

Raif pulled away rapidly, leaving the old lady watching and wondering. Jack caught a glimpse of her in the rear-view mirror still staring as they rounded the bend, disappearing out of sight.

"Granny thinks she saw the guy who owns the garage giving a lift to a smartly dressed woman with dirt on her clothes. Said she looked like she'd been trying to fix her car."

"You reckon that's her?" Raif questioned.

Jack shrugged. "It's as good a lead as any. She could be miles away by now."

When they reached the Beechfield area, Jack indicated for Raif to pull in at a local store just off the highway so he could buy cigarettes. When he got to the counter, he joked with the guy about how his stupid car was playing up and he still had a distance to go before he was home.

"Say man, you don't know anybody local who might be able to just take a quick look at it?" Jack asked.

"Sorry bud, there isn't a garage in this area." The assistant took the money Jack offered for his purchase and sorted the change. Jack was just wondering what they were going to do next, but had his thoughts interrupted when the assistant continued, "But there's a guy that lives nearby who owns a garage. Sometimes stops in late in the evening on his way home, but I'd have thought he would still be at work. Lives in the last house on the right, about a half-mile along the road. If he's there you'll see his blue pick-up out front."

"Oh that's great. Thanks man." Jack pulled a twenty note from his wallet and passed it to the assistant, who was a little surprised at the gesture.

"Hope you make it back," he shouted. Jack waved in acknowledgement as he went back out to the car.

The light was beginning to fade as they left the store's parking lot and slowly drove toward the house.

"That must be it," Jack suggested, catching sight of the clapper board building at the edge of the built-up area. "Pull over where we can see it, but not too close." It was important they didn't attract undue attention.

Raif followed the instructions, setting the car in position so that they had a view through the trees to the front area of the house.

There didn't appear to be any movement, no lights on, but there was a blue pick-up outside.

"What's the plan," Raif asked, touching the gun in the holster beneath his jacket.

"Watch and wait." Jack settled himself into his seat and closed his eyes. "And you're on duty so don't screw up again."

Raif sneered at Jack as he turned away. He was getting sick of being treated like an idiot, but was cautious about making anything of it. Jack had a habit of wielding his seniority in an intimidating manner and making Raif's life a misery if he had a mind to. It was like a little power game he played for amusement, even with Vince Kurtis, but it was wearing thin.

They'd been sitting there for an hour or so as the last vestiges of daylight gradually faded, when a subtle light came on in the hallway, probably thrown from a room at the back of the house. Raif nudged Jack, who stirred immediately.

"Someone's definitely home." He pointed to the house.

Jack immediately opened the car door. "I'm going to go a little closer to take a look. Wait here. I'll be back in a minute."

He got out of the car and crossed over the road keeping out of the line of sight, using the trees to give cover. Checking the coast was clear, he headed toward the house until he was beside the pick-up out front. He was just about to move in a little more when he saw the silhouette of a dog through the hallway frosted window. He could just make out the shape of a woman sat on the couch in the front room.

Backing off, he returned to the car. As he pulled the door closed, Raif watched him for a second, but the information wasn't forthcoming quickly enough.

"Well?" He demanded.

"It's her," said Jack, confidently.

"Let's go get her."

"No. We'll wait a while, then I'll check it out when I'm ready, while *you* wait with the car."

"What's the point of waiting? Let's just grab her and go!"

"I reckon you've taken your chance at grabbing her, Raif. One sight of your ugly face and she'll be more trouble than it's worth. Anyway, what's the hurry?"

"I've got plans for tonight and it doesn't include sitting by the roadside at the convenience of that bitch!"

Jack's look killed Raif's dissenting opinion and once the point was made, he continued. "There's a dog and it'll make a fuss if we make the wrong move. They're going nowhere without us knowing about it."

Raif was always impatient and up for full-on confrontation, but Jack was a much more wily character and was willing to bide his time and get it right. "Let Vince know what's happening," Jack instructed as he turned to focus his attention on the house.

Raif reached into his pocket then paused a second before beginning an increasingly hurried search of his jacket until he finally expressed his frustration. "Shit!" Jack turned to look at him. "You got a phone with you?"

Jack raised his eyebrows as if the question was stupid. "You gotta be kidding? And give Vince the opportunity to have me on a leash like some dog." The disdain on Jack's face showed the contempt he had for the younger guys who had allowed themselves to become enslaved to their boss, jumping to Vince's every whim. "I saw a phone booth back down the road. Go call him from there." A smirk crossed Jack's lips. "I'll wait here until you get back," he said, turning his attention back to the house and dismissing his subordinate. Raif glared at Jack as he felt the anger rising, but he had no choice. The violent thud of the car door slamming shut made his opinion of Jack clear.

~

"You call me when you're in the area and I'll give you the address." Vince Kurtis was trying to sound convincing as he played for time, but he could tell the caller was not best pleased with his answer.

"You told me you had the girl, that's what I'm paying you for." The guy didn't have to be in the room for Vince to feel the threat in his voice. He'd never met the man, but from the few phone conversations knew he didn't suffer fools gladly.

"I do." Vince quickly responded with as much confidence as he could muster. "We're gonna move her to a place on the outskirts of town, out of the way. Just let me know when you're near." He dropped the receiver to terminate the call. Having given his assurance that the girl was secure, he was depending on Jack and Raif to deliver quickly. He cursed the air and momentarily leant his head in his hands. "Where the hell are they?" he growled under his breath. He glanced at his watch. It was just before eight. Jack had been on a mission to find Tia for several hours without word. Vince got up from his desk, went to the drinks cabinet and poured himself a large Scotch. He didn't hesitate, but threw it back in one shot and winced as it took effect.

The phone rang again, breaking the silence. Vince hurriedly grabbed at the receiver.

"Yeah."

"Vince, it's Raif."

"Where the hell are you? I told Jack to let me know what was happening."

"We've found her."

Vince cursed out loud in relief. "Where?"

Raif gave the location and explained the situation and his belief they should go in and get her immediately.

"If Jack says wait, you wait, and don't ever question his instructions to me again. You got that?" Raif got the message loud and clear. Vince knew he was vulnerable without Jack Cougar's support. The last thing he was about to do was allow one of the younger guys to cross Jack with his blessing. "Tell Jack the client is coming to pick her up. He's coming a distance and won't be here until about 1.30am. Tell him to make sure he's ready. I don't want another screw up." Vince hung up, leaving Raif cursing him.

CHAPTER 4

Will turned a little in his chair, trying to get comfortable, but it was never going to be like his bed. Not that that would've helped him sleep any better. The constant pattern of waking through the night had followed him for months and it didn't seem to matter where he was or how tired he might be.

He glanced over at the couch and could only just see Tia. She hadn't moved since the last time he'd checked. Her quiet, shallow breathing and the occasional noise from Boost were the only sounds that filled the room. One of the pleasures of living at the edge of a town was the peace and quiet which was exaggerated by the unpolluted darkness.

Will's mind churned over the day's events and the strange situation he now found himself in. He pondered the possibilities with regard to Tia, but it was the imagination of a sleepless night that supplied the many scenarios that came to mind.

There was a sudden murmur as Boost growled in his sleep. Will took no notice of it. He had a habit of dreaming and Will had lain awake watching him many times over recent months. The growling and pretending to run were frequent symptoms of the adventure in his dog's twilight world.

The second time Boost growled it was much more deliberate and he stirred a little as though he was listening. Will was immediately alerted at Boost's change of demeanour and was out of his seat in a flash. Grabbing Boost's muzzle, he spoke softly to quieten him, but they were both aware that something was unusual.

Will went over to Tia, and knowing there would be a shock reaction when he woke her, he clamped his hand over her mouth, while quickly pulling her to himself. At first she was like a rag doll, but within a split second she went rigid then began to struggle. Will held her tight, preventing her from screaming out and spoke calmly to her until she became conscious of where she was and who was holding her.

"Shhh, it's just me Tia," he whispered. "I'm going to let you go, okay? Please trust me and don't make a sound."

Tia's eyes were wide as she tried to look sideways at Will in the darkness. He repeated his warning to be sure that she understood and she nodded an acknowledgement. Will slowly released the pressure of his hand from her mouth and eased away, turning her toward him so that she could see his face as much as the darkness would allow. Boost was nuzzling between them as if he understood the importance of the situation.

Will put his finger to his lips and leant right into Tia to whisper. "Take Boost and go through the door under the stairs, it leads down to the basement. There's a bolt on the inside. Lock it and don't undo it until you hear me tell you to. Hold Boost close and talk quietly to him to reassure him so that he doesn't bark. Do you understand?"

Will could feel the tension in Tia and the movement of her hair brushing against his cheek as she nodded. Carefully they moved to the hallway and he gingerly opened the door. Boost followed Tia as indicated by Will and she quietly slid the bolt across after he closed the door behind her.

Tiptoeing down the few steps to the lower level, she, closely followed by Boost, tucked herself in the far corner behind some packing cases. Boost let Tia put her arms around him as he stood guard over his charge. She quickly stroked him as he rumbled a low growl of concern, but hushed to her command.

Once Will knew they were safe in the small store room beneath the house, he began to prepare himself for whatever might come. The muffled sound of cracking glass on the rear doors alerted his focus. Taking hold of a poker from the fireplace, he carefully positioned himself next to the hallway door that led to the kitchen. It was the only way to get from the back of the house to the front. With the doorway to his right and his back against the wall, he took the poker in his left hand and drew his right arm around his chest, preparing his elbow like a loaded spring. His eyes had adjusted to the dark and he was as ready as he could be without giving away the advantage of surprise that any intruder must have thought they possessed. Seconds later the door handle turned, but Will held his place, waiting for the exact moment to strike.

The door was gently pushed and slowly swung wide open. Will could see the posture of the intruder's arm as it preceded him into the room, giving away the fact that there was a gun. As the trespasser edged a little further into the room so that his shoulder was at the door frame, Will brought the poker crashing down on the extended arm. In a simultaneous movement, he unleashed his 'spring-loaded' right elbow straight into the guy's face. The gun fell to the floor, clattering as it bounced heavily on the wooden surface and the thud of the impact of Will's elbow knocked the intruder sprawling backwards onto the kitchen floor. Will quickly glanced around to confirm there was only one, then jumped on top of the dazed man slumped on the floor. Holding onto the incapacitated intruder he flipped him over and put his weight on top of him. Will pulled open the door of a nearby storage unit and dragged out the toolbox from the bottom shelf. Grabbing at its contents in the dark, he snatched out a pack of cable ties, ripped it open, drew the intruder's arms together behind him, fastening them in place. Sliding down his legs Will did the same around his ankles.

As the strap pulled tight, the man began to mutter curses as the dazed feeling cleared a little. Without a second's hesitation, Will grabbed a towel from the worktop, spun it to make a rope and whipped it around the man's mouth, gagging him.

Frisking him from head to toe, Will turned out a number of things from his pockets, including a flick knife which he hung on to. Once he confirmed the man was clean, Will sprang to his feet and recovered the gun, leaving the semi-conscious intruder flailing on the floor.

Quickly up the stairs to the front bedroom window, Will scanned the area, registering the presence of a car on the other side of the road. He fetched his binoculars and focused on the vehicle. There was enough light outside to see that there was someone in the driver's seat, leaning forwards as if anticipating something happening.

Will shot back downstairs to the kitchen and roughly planted his knee in the back of the guy on the floor, producing a muffled groan. He put the gun heavily to the side of his head so there was a clunk sound as the end of the barrel came into contact with his skull.

Leaning down close, he muttered under his breath, "Make no mistake, I'm as happy to do to you, with this as you were preparing to do to me." He gave the gun a shove to make sure there was no doubt about his meaning. I'm going to ask you a question and you're going to answer immediately, or you won't draw another breath." Will hesitated so the threat would register. "Is that your friend in the car across the road?"

Jack Cougar had rarely been intimidated in the fifty-five years of his life, but the surprise of the last few moments had shaken him. Having not been able to see who his assailant was and therefore get a measure of the person making the threat, he believed absolutely that it would be carried out as hastily as suggested. Jack nodded to indicate that his accomplice was in the car.

"Just the two of you?" Again Jack indicated that it was so.

Will checked he was securely incapacitated and once sure, was out of the back door in a flash. Dipping low, he followed the shrubbery away from the house until it reached the boundary fence. Jumping up and over to the other side, he followed the fence toward the road, using it to shield his movements. When he reached the end of the fence, he darted across to a tree, taking shelter behind the trunk and paused for a few seconds.

From his vantage point there was a view slightly to the rear of the car parked over the road. He knew there was no time to debate the possibility of being seen, so he crossed immediately to keep surprise on his side. Assuming that if one had a gun the other would too, it was a case of committing everything to the cause.

He stooped low as he shot across the road and was almost on his belly in an attempt not to be seen in the rear-view mirrors of the waiting vehicle. Once he'd reached the back of the car, he carefully looked down the passenger side to see if he could get a view of the driver through the mirror. He was conscious of the fact that if he could see the driver, the driver would be able to see him.

It was definitely a younger guy than the one in the house. Will assumed that he would not be as confident as the other as he'd been elected to stay with the car.

Will took another look and could tell the guy's attention was focused on his house across the street, rather than being aware that he was about to be ambushed. Counting to three under his breath, Will exploded down the side of the vehicle, throwing the passenger door open and launching himself inside. The driver's shock reaction to a gun in his face caused him to immediately lift his hands in surrender.

"Don't shoot! Don't shoot!" he yelled, making sure his hands were clearly visible.

"Where's your gun?" Will demanded, practically shoving the weapon in the guy's mouth, making a clacking sound as the muzzle came into contact with his teeth.

"The holster inside my jacket," was the muffled response, as he hinted with his lifted hands which side to look.

Will grabbed the gun and checked the safety catch, then pushed it in the waistband of his jeans.

"If you value your life, you'll do *exactly* as I say." Raif nodded to show he would comply. "Slowly slide over in my direction and get out of the passenger door. Not a sound or it will be the last one you make."

Raif did as he was instructed, moving deliberately and slowly to show he had no intention of giving any resistance or reason for his assailant to act rashly.

Will took a step away from the car as Raif got out. "Hold out your hands." Raif did as he was instructed. Starting a loop with a couple of ties, Will quickly slipped them over the out-stretched hands and ratcheted them tight. "Turn around *slowly* and put your hands on the car roof." Will held the gun at the ready, standing a pace back from Raif. Once he was in position, Will frisked him head to toe. Anything that was of no use, he tossed back into the car.

"Move!" Will jabbed the muzzle of the gun into Raif's side to indicate the direction and give urgency to the order. He quickly retrieved the keys from the ignition of the car and locked the doors, then marched Raif across the street and to the rear door of the house to join his friend. Working by the dim light of the night, Will threw two dining room chairs against the wall and pushed Raif into one of them. Leaving the ties around his wrists, Will put another around each elbow and secured them to the chair arms. He did the same around each ankle to make sure that Raif was going nowhere.

Dragging Jack up from the floor, amid moans of pain that Will ignored, he secured him to the other chair in a similar fashion. Roughly pulling the gag away from Jack, he moved away from the two of them.

On the veranda was a free-standing spotlight that was used for illuminating the area on a warm evening. Will dragged it into the dining area and positioned it in the archway to the kitchen. Plugging the unit in, the dining room was immediately flooded with light, like a stage under the influence of a theatre spotlight.

The two villains squinted at the ferocity of the beam bombarding them. They constantly turned their heads from side to side, trying to escape the painful needling the powerful light caused in the back of their eyes.

"You've made a big mistake son…" Jack threatened through gritted teeth, trying to reassert some kind of balance to the situation. He was not used to being outwitted and overwhelmed by the competence of someone who could defend themselves in such a capable way. Jack had perfected the art of intimidation by suggestion, but exposed in the flood of light and restrained by the ties he felt insecure and frustrated that his plan had been thwarted.

Standing behind the powerful beam, Will was hidden from them as sure as if he was behind a wall. Knowing that they couldn't see him or what he was doing, he grabbed a peach from the fruit bowl on the counter and launched it at Jack with some considerable force. It impacted the wall right next to him with a dull thud. Both guys flinched at the noise and ducked their heads at the threatening sound. The dazzling light blinded them to what was going to come next.

Will said nothing. Jack wasn't the only one who knew how to intimidate people, but now he fell under the influence of an unseen and apparently ruthless captor.

"What do you want?" Raif blurted out in desperation.

Will responded with another missile, this time on target. Raif gave out a groan as the peach slammed into his chest without warning, winding him slightly. He let out an angry growl and took a sideways glance at Jack in an appeal to do something.

Will knew he was in absolute control and taking the guns he'd retrieved, he stood directly behind the light. He slid out the magazines from each one, deliberately making as much noise as the action allowed, making sure his 'prisoners' knew exactly what he was doing.

After checking they were fully loaded, he slammed them back into place with a loud click. Raif quickly glanced at Jack, the familiar sound induced a look of fear across his face and the powerful light exposed every detail. Jack Cougar's hard expression showed what he intended to do to Will if he got the chance.

Every sound Will made was calculated to increase the confusion in the two men, heightening their concern.

He flipped the radio on that was on the counter to use as noise covering the sound of what he was about to do. He quietly went out of the kitchen into the hallway and tapped on the stair door to the lower storeroom. He heard Boost come to the other side of the door. Once he thought Tia had moved near enough to hear, he whispered, "Tia. It's Will. Carefully and quietly slide the bolt over and open the door."

There was a moment's hesitation then the door began to open. Boost tried to push his way out, inquisitive about what was going on, but Will took hold of his collar to restrain him.

The overspill of light from the kitchen lit Tia's fear-etched face. Will put a finger to his lips to indicate that she should remain quiet. He leant in close to her, almost as if he was going to kiss her and whispered. "You need to trust me, Tia. There are two of them." She drew breath a little sharply and pulled away from him to look at his face. He waited until she voluntarily came close again before continuing. "They are both tied to chairs in the dining room. I've put a floodlight on them so they won't be able to see you. It's too bright. I want you to come with me and take a look. Tell me if you know them, okay?" Will pulled away from her and she nodded to say that she understood. He then leant back into her. "I don't know if they're something to do with the reason you've been frightened and I don't know if they actually know you're here or are just in the hunt, so don't make a sound, don't do anything that will confirm your presence." Again he gave her chance to acknowledge that she understood. "Last, but this is very important and you will have to trust me, they have no idea what I'm capable of and that generates fear. That might allow me to get some information out of them. Don't react to what I do or we'll lose our grasp on the situation."

He pulled away from her to see her face. She still looked anxious, but was obviously reassured that Will was in control.

He held out his hand to Tia and she took it as she came out from under the stairs. He led her to the kitchen and noticed that she quickly put her hand to her mouth as she caught sight of them. Jack's face was a bit swollen and bloodied from Will's attack, but otherwise they seemed passive. She glanced at Will and a thought briefly crossed her mind. '*What is he capable of?*' She dismissed it immediately, knowing that she had to trust him.

Boost was still being restrained by Will, but he was not going to keep quiet for anyone. Having missed out on the initial drama, he made his feelings abundantly clear. Will didn't try to stop him barking, but held him back out of sight. Raif flinched at every bark or growl, almost as though he was expecting the dog to be let loose at any moment. Jack sneered at his lack of steel.

Tia's eyes were fixed on the younger man, so Will attracted her attention and silently mouthed a question to her, "Do you know them?"

She nodded quickly and as she did her eyes went to them and then back to Will. The alarm etched on her face spoke volumes and Will wondered about the connection between these people. She brought her hand up to her mouth as if to restrain herself from making any sound.

"It'll be okay," he mouthed, placing his hand on her shoulder and she half-smiled at him behind her hand. He got Tia to restrain Boost by his collar so he was free to deal with the situation.

Will held his hand up to Tia to warn about what was going to happen. He moved the remaining peaches to the counter in front of him, lining up the missiles to use in case he needed to reinforce the fact that he was in charge.

"Would either of you two like to explain to me what you're doing here?"

Boost barked again, punctuating the end of Will's question inducing a reaction in the men.

"Looking for valuables," Jack said, in a condescending manner.

He didn't see the peach coming, but it caught him with a glancing blow on the forehead, making him wince with pain at the impact. Tia tried to cover her surprise at Will's response to the older man, but it prompted the younger to give something away.

"It's the girl," Raif yelled. "We want the girl, that's all."

Only a few hours earlier Raif had overpowered Tia, now she watched as he was subject to Will. The justice of the switch wasn't lost on her. She had no doubt that he would have taken full advantage of her when he'd had the opportunity, but she had a little sympathy for Raif at that moment.

"Shut your mouth, boy," Jack snapped.

"What girl?" Will demanded, ignoring Jack's attempts to stop the questioning.

"The one you helped yesterday." Raif immediately clarified, much to Jack's displeasure.

"I don't like repeating myself and this is the only time I'm going to do so. *What* girl?"

Will checked the clock on the oven behind him. 1.15am.

"Just phone the police and turn us in," Jack scornfully muttered.

Tia put her hand on Will's arm, attracting his attention and vigorously shook her head to make him understand that that would be a mistake. Her experience of uniformed assistance up to that point had not been good.

Will took note of her instruction and the anxious message emanating from Tia's body language. Picking up another missile, he sent the next volley racing to its target, catching Jack square in the chest. It was more than the tethered man could stand and he went wild, at least as much as the restraints would allow him. Even Raif glanced across in surprise at his loss of control.

"If you're going to pretend you're a man and shoot us, then do it. Do it now, you low-life bastard. Instead of hiding away like a shit scared kid, why don't you act like a man?"

Will held the gun in the air, slid out the magazine then pulled the trigger so that it made a piercing click as the metal parts chimed together. He glanced at Tia. She shook her head side to side quickly to dissuade him from doing anything more serious with the weapon.

Raif was none too keen to see his days terminated and broke in the other direction to Jack, all his resolve to be tough gave way at the thought of what might be about to happen.

"No. No. Wait. We need the girl for a guy who's paying…"

Jack was not prepared to sit there and let his accomplice divulge any more information. Not after he'd just dangerously tested the water with his challenge to Will. "You shut your mouth, Raif. 'Cos if you say one more word, and we get out of this, it'll be me that puts you out of your misery, you sorry ass girl. Where's your balls, you pussy?"

Will hit Jack with one more slug in an attempt to silence him, but knew that he'd lost the initiative. If he didn't shoot one within a matter of seconds, his control over both of them was blown. He was not prepared to be so heartless without knowing why he was doing it. Not that he was weak. He'd been in military situations that required him to take a life and he hadn't hesitated for one second to do so, but he was not a murderer and that's what it would be to kill either of these two men, regardless of what they'd done. As he reasoned out the position they were in and realised that his options were running out, he glanced at Tia to find her staring at him, waiting to see what he was going to do. Taking her by the arm, he urged her out of the room, through the hallway and out onto the front porch.

Once they were outside and away from earshot, he turned to face her.

"They know that I'm not going to carry out what they first feared and you're in danger from them. We both are. They clearly think you're here, but aren't totally sure, so I think we need to leave now, or call the police to deal with the situation." Again Tia shook her head at the suggestion.

"Why don't you want to involve them?"

Tia owed Will for saving her from Jack and Raif, who would have clearly taken her and harmed anyone in their way if it had been necessary. No doubt they hadn't banked on meeting someone as capable as Will. They weren't the only ones either. Tia was just as surprised about what had happened in the last few minutes as Jack Cougar had been to be confronted with the blow that unexpectedly floored him.

She looked at Will standing on the porch in the low light of the early morning and tried to figure out why he had even helped her as much as he had. This was nothing to do with him. She'd thrown his life into turmoil and for what? He did deserve some answers, but she couldn't give them all just like that. Not there and then.

"Will," she whispered, "those two guys were part of a group of four who kidnapped me from the street three days ago. They've been holding me prisoner, locked in an apartment in the town. I managed to escape through a bathroom window by forcing the lock and climbing out onto the roof below after being terrified by that younger one. He tried to…" She didn't finish the sentence, but hugged herself as she recoiled from the memory. "I hid from them until the coast was clear and stole a lift in the back of a truck to get away. When it stopped near your garage and the driver discovered me under the tarpaulin, I ran until I hid in your parking lot. That's when you found me. That's why I was terrified when you cornered me. I don't know how they tracked me here." A look of confusion crossed her face. "I didn't think it would have been so easy." She looked intently at Will's eyes to try to read his thoughts.

"But why no police, Tia?" Will asked in exasperation.

"When they first grabbed me, I slipped free. That younger one in there got a shock when I hit him where it hurts. I guess the confusion gave me a chance to get away, but the others gave chase. I managed to get to my car and pulled away. I thought I was out of reach, but in my effort to leave them behind I was stopped by a patrol car for speeding. I can't tell you the relief I felt while I was trying to explain to the officer the reason for my haste. I mean, where could I have been safer?" She lowered her voice even further, but the venom in the words left no doubt about her anger. "Those two bastards suddenly took over, removing me from the driver's seat of my car and bundling me into the back. I freaked out and struggled, but the cop just turned away. The old one pressed a cloth over my face while the other drove my car. The next thing I knew was when I woke up in the room where they were holding me." Tia shuddered at she thought of what had happened. "God knows what they did to me while I was unconscious."

"What did they mean about someone paying?"

"I don't know." She raised her hands in frustration.

Will tilted his head and stared at her as he weighed her answer.

"You don't know why they were so keen to take you or why they have tracked you down again?"

Tia shook her head as she held his stare. Will's piercing blue eyes seemed to reach into her soul looking for answers and began to make her feel uncomfortable.

"I swear to you, it's the truth. I have no idea what's going on. I had no choice but to get away from them, for my own safety. I didn't know where I would end up." She hesitated and softened her concern-laden voice. "I ran into you…" She broke his stare and looked down at the floor for a moment before reconnecting. "I'm so sorry that you've got mixed up in this." She put both hands to her face then swept them back until they were on her cheeks. Looking back into Will's unaltered gaze she just shook her head. He put his hand on her arm to comfort her and nodded to show that he understood a little, but their communication was rudely interrupted.

"Hey, shit face." Jack's voice drifted through the hallway and Will turned to look.

"Stop it Jack! Don't provoke him." Raif showed his desperation at Jack's boldness, thinking he was putting them both in danger.

The response of Raif was like petrol to a fire. Jack raised his voice even more. "Hey, you yellow-bellied, spineless son-of-a-bitch!"

Will was staring at the kitchen door at the end of the hallway, half listening to Jack's curses. Light from the flood lamp spilled through the opening creating unusual shadows on the hallway walls. He turned back to look at Tia and she could see he was weighing up what to do. She edged away from the hallway, placing Will more definitely between her and her tormentors who seemed to be increasing in boldness.

Jack's raspy voice spilled from the dining room once more like the tentacles of some sea monster reaching from its hiding place to catch a victim.

"When I get out of this, I'm going to track you down and cut your balls off, you gutless prick!"

Tia noticed Will's face harden with a resolve to do something.

"Okay. Quietly go upstairs and take a bag from the wardrobe. Take whatever you need of Sophie's clothing and anything else you want," Will instructed. "I'll put Boost in the pick-up and get some stuff for me.

Tia did what she was asked and was back on the porch in minutes. Jack was still yelling abuse from the back room as Will came down the stairs carrying a sports bag stuffed with the things he needed. He passed it to Tia.

"Take this and go get in the pick-up." He handed her the keys.

"What are you going to do?" Concern was etched on her face.

"Don't worry. Just do as I've asked."

He put his hands on her shoulders and turned her physically in the direction he wanted her to go. Her resistance hinted at a fear of what was about to happen, but she knew she had no other option.

Will stood on the porch and watched her go as the insults from the house got ever louder and more vulgar. Once Tia and Boost were in the pick-up, Will went back into the house. Grabbing his baseball bat from inside the stair door, he slammed it into a vase that stood in the hallway. The crash of disintegrating pottery immediately put an end to the abuse flowing from the other room. Will stood for a few seconds listening in the silence, then turned and stepped into the kitchen to take a look at the two guys.

CHAPTER 5

As he slammed the driver's door, Tia nervously scanned Will for signs of what had happened in the house. He turned the ignition key and the engine roared into life then looked across at her concerned, questioning face.

"Don't worry. They're okay." He hesitated for a moment, reflecting on the turn of events then seemed to shake himself into decisive action. "We need to get you somewhere safe," he paused before continuing his sentence with deliberateness, "*then* you're going to level with me about what the hell is going on."

Tia didn't answer or question, it wasn't the time to do either, but what had just occurred had removed Will's reserve about intruding on her privacy. He wanted to know what he'd been sucked into.

The tyres spat gravel as the pick-up raced to the road and turned away from the town. Several hundred yards along the highway, Will glanced in the rear view mirror and was surprised to see headlights in the distance behind. It was a quiet road that was infrequently used by any but the locals, especially at night. As he watched, the vehicle behind suddenly turned off the road and the view behind went black.

He initially thought the bend in the road had obscured his view, but the headlights never reappeared. For several minutes he pondered why a vehicle would be out so late and why it would have stopped on the highway near his house.

After about sixty miles he pulled over at a road side store that was closed, but it had a phone booth just outside. Tia watched Will speaking to someone briefly then hang up and immediately dial again. He animatedly delivered some information to the person at the other end of the line then abruptly hung up. He stood motionless with his hand resting on the receiver for a few seconds before walking back to the driver's door and climbing into the pick-up. Tia just watched him as he put the key in the ignition. Will turned to look, having sensed her staring at him.

"Who did you call?" Tia hesitantly asked.

"A friend… and the police." The alarm in Tia's expression was obvious. An uncomfortable silence filled the cab as Tia considered if she should question further, but Will continued before there was a need to ask. "I told them I was a neighbour and thought there was something suspicious happening at the house… Can't leave those two clowns tied to the chairs forever."

He was about to look away to check the road before pulling off, but Tia motioned and caught his attention.

"I feel so awkward dragging you into this. Whatever *this* is." She shook her head as if trying to bring some clarity and understanding to the whole bizarre chain of events that had surrounded her. Will was just as confused, but he wasn't keen on discussing it while driving.

He pulled out onto the empty highway and picked up speed again.

The two travelled in uncomfortable silence for quite a while. Finally, Will cleared his throat as he prepared to say something and immediately had Tia's undivided attention.

"The friend I called, I can trust totally her. She's got a place that's out of the way and she said we could stay there a while. It'll take us at least four hours to get there. I'd rather do most of the journey in the dark, but I'm going to turn off the main road in two or three hours and follow a quieter route." He paused for a moment to make sure she was listening. "When we get there, you're going to have to bring some clarity to what's happened so that we can figure out what to do. There's a mess back home that

I'm going to have to deal with. God knows how that's going to be explained away."

Tia turned away from him feeling responsible for the predicament Will now found himself in. She leaned her head against the window and sat wondering why he didn't just ignore her and hand her over to the police.

Will glanced at her and could read the worry in her expression. He reached over to the rear seat and grabbed his jacket. Passing it to Tia, he said, "Fold that up, use it as a pillow and try to get some sleep. She smiled at his small gesture of thoughtfulness and was thankful for the opportunity to close her eyes, but there was too much going on in her head to sleep. She was plagued with concern about how Will had dealt with the intruders, but didn't want to probe about why he'd gone back into the house, sending her to the pick-up. After an hour of tossing and turning, trying to get comfortable, she decided to try and distract her mind from the more extreme imaginations. She sat up and turned to face Will. He snatched a look at her, unsure what was wrong.

"Where did you learn about guns?" she asked.

Will didn't answer immediately and she began to wonder if he'd even heard her. Finally a response came just as she was about to ask again.

"I did a stint in the army." Will gave a robotic answer while keeping his eyes firmly fixed on the road. Tia soon realised that he'd delivered all the explanation she was going to get, so she tried to prompt him further.

"How long were you in for?"

Again there was an uncomfortable delay.

"Seven years." Still his gaze was focused ahead and Tia rolled her eyes, a little frustrated at the lack of continuation. She tried once more.

"You finished because you'd had enough?"

Will sighed, as if he was annoyed at her persistence. "I came home because of a family issue."

"Your dad?" she quickly volunteered.

The moment the words came out of her mouth she began to squirm in her seat. Will looked over at his questioner, noticed her apprehension then turned his focus back to the road while he gave thought to the implications of answering.

It had been a long time since he'd talked to anyone about his past and he wasn't too sure he wanted to start now. If it hadn't been for the unusual circumstances that had thrown them together, he would definitely not have let himself end up alone with such a beguiling young woman and certainly wouldn't have tolerated the personal questions. As he baulked at responding, Tia could see that she'd hit a nerve and tried to assess Will's grim expression. She decided to try to make amends.

"Sorry." Tia's voice carried a sentiment of concern about having intruded into something where her interest was unwelcome. "I didn't mean to pry," she said apologetically. "I thought it might pass the time if we talked a little, but I guess my mouth was way ahead of my brain."

Will glanced across at her again to be greeted by a shrug and expression that emphasised her regret. As he went back to focusing on the road, Tia decided to keep her mouth shut. She had the distinct feeling Will's body language seemed to shout loud and clear that further questions were not welcome and answers would not be forthcoming.

She turned away to stare out of the car window at the passing landscape being bathed in the early morning light. The hum of the engine became the musical companion as it held a constant tone. She nervously bit her lip as she was engulfed once again with that awkward feeling that had accompanied much of their time together.

Will unexpectedly cleared his throat in a way that made it obvious he was about to say something, attracting Tia's attention. She turned to look at him in anticipation, but wondered for a moment if she'd misunderstood when he continued staring ahead.

Will snatched a look and found her watching him. "My…" He cleared his throat again and shifted uncomfortably in his seat. "My dad was killed about six months ago…" Although Tia had gathered that Will's father had passed away from the snippets she'd picked up in their sparse conversation, she caught her breath at the blunt opening statement. The way his opening line tailed off showed he was searching to find the words to explain. He seemed to be under a hypnotic effect from the passing highway and the wait for him to give more information seemed endless.

Just as she began to think he'd decided not to continue, Will glanced across again and smiled weakly at her.

"He was returning from a trip to the hospital. Sophie, my sister, was driving." Will left another long pause. Tia could see he was having difficulty trying to frame the words without seeming blasé or uncaring. There were no such words that could describe what had happened that day and he knew it, so surrendered to the meaninglessness of his terrible loss.

"Some drunk decided to take a drive home. He pulled out onto the wrong side of the road and hit their car head on." Again there was an uncomfortable pause in his explanation that Tia sensed was not left in order for her to respond. "Dad was killed instantly. Sophie and the other guy were rushed to the local hospital. He was dead on arrival and she…" His voice wavered slightly with emotion, but he cleared his throat again in an attempt to hide it. "She had a brain haemorrhage three weeks later."

He turned away for a moment, conscious of being watched, but Tia caught a look in his eye that showed the pent up anger buried just beneath the surface. "The doctors…" Will coughed again and was clearly restraining emotion. "The doctors told me she was being kept alive only by the machines." There was a long pause, too long to mistake the internal struggle going on in Will. "I had to make the decision… She slipped away…" He swallowed hard. "She slipped away while I sat helplessly in the room… watching my little sister die."

Will drew a deep breath to try to stop the surging emotion from welling to the surface. The moment he'd seen Sophie, held in this world by a life-support machine in the hospital, rage had risen in him at the injustice of the situation. As he related the facts to Tia, he could taste, smell and feel the same things he'd had to live through all over again. He'd tried to numb himself to deal with the pain of loss and of being the one left behind, but had barely managed to suppress it by not facing the truth. Despite the fact that so many things that surrounded him prompted reminders of his family, he'd deliberately avoided talking about any of it, even with friends.

Tia felt a shiver and sat uneasily with the silence and palpable aura of sorrow that engulfed Will. She understood the feeling of loss, having been separated from her father, but it didn't help her to find the words for that moment. She wondered what to say to someone who has just told you such a thing.

After a few minutes of churning over his thoughts in his own world, Will noticed that Tia was still staring at him, so he tried to lighten the atmosphere.

"Sorry. That was a bit heavy, but you did ask." She smiled apologetically at him. "I've never worked out how to say it without the awkwardness that inevitably follows. Perhaps there shouldn't ever be a way to do that. I haven't talked about it for quite a while," he turned to momentarily look at Tia. "In fact I haven't really talked at all." His tone relaxed a little, putting her more at ease. "When I get pissed off about it, which is pretty often, I take it out on the trucks at the garage. I thought about having a punch bag, but you can't use a hammer on one of those." He snorted at the image it conjured up.

"I don't really know why I keep the place. More sentimental attachment than anything, I suppose. Anyway, that's why they all stand in the parking lot looking so sorry for themselves, hoping I don't pick on them. They've all had a beating from me at one time or another, but at least they don't complain." He glanced again in Tia's direction and she acknowledged his effort with a nod.

The droning of the vehicle replaced the talk and they both sat staring through the windscreen at the distant road ahead. Several minutes passed before Tia summoned up the courage to ask what had been on her mind since they left the house.

"Earlier, back at the house, when you had the gun in your hand, what were you thinking?"

Will smirked at the question and was inclined to ignore it, but decided not to.

"I was thinking how easy it would be to waste scum like those two. People like that think it's okay to break into homes and do what they want... I see the drunk in the car that killed my family and the rage rises, but you can't do what they do. Can you?" He looked across at her. "Besides, the look of horror on your face warned me away from doing anything stupid. So thank you. I don't think I would have, but your pretty face with a shocked expression certainly helped restrain me."

Tia smiled, embarrassed at Will's backhanded compliment, but was thankful that he didn't do what the demons inside him pressured him to do. She leant across and put her hand on his shoulder for a moment, it was one of those inexplicable spontaneous gestures, but it surprised him. She slumped back against the door of the pick-up facing in toward Will, casually observing him.

The road disappeared beneath the vehicle and the constant unchanging hum of the engine was a strange kind of comfort, as it had been in the truck where she stowed away to make her escape. The monotonous noise represented increasing distance from her troubles, but a thought suddenly crossed her mind, 'they had come to find her last time she'd escaped. If it happened once, what was to stop it happening again?'

After half an hour of hearing nothing from her, Will turned to look at Tia. The disturbed night, in every sense, had taken its toll. She was resting against the door window with a folded jacket beneath her head to cushion the vibrations. He wasn't sure if she was asleep, but her eyes were closed. Considering the ordeal they, and she before that, had gone through, her spirit was remarkably resilient. Facing fears that would have caused many to cry out, she'd followed Will's instructions, restraining her natural responses when it came to identifying the two guys who broke into the house. Never once did she do anything that gave away her presence, despite what Will had intimated he would do to the intruders.

He kept an eye on the road, but frequently glanced at Tia, wondering who she was and how she'd come to need his help. The dim glow in the vehicle illuminated the exposed part of her neck and collarbone that showed as her head tilted away from him. After the third deliberate glance across at her, Will suddenly felt conscious that he was intruding on her privacy, but if she'd been awake he wouldn't have taken such a good look. Classy and beautiful, he decided.

An all-night gas station soon came into view. Will pulled off the road to re-fuel the vehicle. The bump as he left the highway onto the forecourt roused Tia from her slumber. As the pick-up came to a stop she involuntarily stretched to shake off the sleepiness. The fleece top pulled tight around her torso emphasising her shapely figure and Will suddenly felt embarrassed as she noticed him looking. He smiled sheepishly and quickly turned away to get out of the pick-up, shouting back as he did. "Getting some fuel. Do you want anything?"

Tia jumped out of the passenger door as Will came round to the same side of the vehicle to operate the pump. She breathed in the cool morning air and ran her fingers through her hair while scanning the area. The landscape was parched and flat, but in the distance the pale morning light drew the outline of hills which hinted at the interesting lay of the land ahead.

A few older cars were lined up on the forecourt with 'for sale' signs in the windscreens. They circled the fuel pumps like a defensive wagon train. A gaudy sign, that seemed out of place, welcomed travellers to the site with the promise of their 'famous' breakfast, freshly prepared. The furniture in the café looked like it had been 'freshly prepared' way back in the fifties.

"Do you think they'll do coffee to take with us?" Tia asked.

"Go check. I'll be there in a moment."

"You want one?"

"Sure."

When Will entered the pay booth he could see Tia on the far side at the coffee machine. He paid for the fuel, coffee and a bag of candies and headed out to the pick-up. A few moments later, Tia sauntered across the forecourt with the drinks. Will leant over to push the door open.

"We'd better get going again; it'll be light soon. I'll drink mine while I drive."

Tia clambered back into her seat and passed the coffee to Will. He placed the cup in the holder near the dashboard. The engine roared into life and they were on their way again.

"Do we have much further to go, Will?"

"About another hour. You want a candy?"

Tia took one from the offered bag and asked, "Who *is* this person we're going to impose ourselves on?"

Will laughed as he glanced across at her. The irony in her question wasn't lost on him. He knew that this was a long overdue 'visit', but the circumstances that drove his decision were less than ideal.

"A girl I've known for years."

Tia raised an eyebrow to prompt him to give more detail, but he completely missed the gesture, so she pressed for a bit more information.

"Girlfriend?"

Her question surprised Will and he turned to look directly at her. The smirk on her face immediately confirmed that she was light-heartedly prodding him to reveal the nature of the relationship.

"Just a friend, who *happens* to be a girl." Will caught her eye again and Tia knew it was her turn to feel a little sheepish about the question as he had about eyeballing her earlier. "Believe it or not, I've known Beth since before I joined the forces... she joined at about the same time as me." He quickly glanced across to see how Tia took the new information and just caught the surprised look on her face before it vanished. His smile let Tia know that he'd seen her expression. He turned his attention back to the road with the grin still in place and Tia realised that it was the first time she'd seen a 'full on' teeth-showing smile, but he didn't notice her watching him. She shook herself from mulling over how good-looking he was, especially when the shadow of sadness momentarily disappeared from his face.

"She's a good friend then?" Tia focused on developing the conversation, keen to know something of the person she would shortly meet.

"The best. The only one I would trust one-hundred percent."

"The *only* one? A bit…" Tia hesitated, causing Will to look across again.

"A bit what?" he prompted her to finish.

"I was going to say, a bit sad don't you think?" she offered apologetically.

"You're about as subtle as a shotgun." The inflection in his voice told her he was just joking with her. Will shrugged. "You take a few knocks in life and it teaches you not to trust."

Tia unconsciously shrugged, copying Will's gesture. "I guess." She was staring at the dashboard suddenly lost in thought.

"Penny for them?" Will interrupted.

"Umm?" Tia looked up at the comment.

"Your thoughts… penny for them?"

Tia put her hand to her mouth, nervously clicking her nail on her teeth.

"She's going to freak when she knows the trouble I've caused you."

Will didn't take his eyes off the road, but could tell from the tone of her voice that she was worried about the reaction of his *best* friend.

"Don't judge Beth Jackson before you meet her. I'll tell you this for sure. She'll give you more than enough surprises without you setting yourself up for them. I trust her and that's what we need at the moment."

He was a little forceful in his delivery, but wanted to drill it home to Tia that going to get help from Beth was a good move, not a desperate one.

CHAPTER 6

"Good morning to those of you who have just joined us on the seven a.m. bulletin. This is the breaking news. There are reports coming in of an incident that appears to have taken place on the outskirts of the town of Cordham sometime in the early hours. We have a reporter on the scene and she's been there for the last hour following the events.

"Jenny, we understand that there's been a serious incident there. Tell us what you've learned about the situation."

"John, I've been here following the investigation team since just before six o'clock this morning. The local police were apparently called to the house that you can see behind me in the early hours. The caller didn't leave his name, but reported a break-in taking place. The police have declined to give us any information regarding the caller and his whereabouts, but they can confirm that he was not at the property at the time of the call."

"Jenny, I understand that once the police arrived they were confronted with a situation that was much more serious than they had been led to believe by the caller?"

"That's correct, John. I managed to speak with one of the officers as he came out of the building earlier and this was what he had to say."

"We responded to an emergency call that came in early this morning. The caller informed us that there was a break-in taking place at the property. When the team arrived and entered the

building they found the bodies of two men, one white, aged approximately fifty-five and the other Hispanic, in his thirties. Both of them had been shot in the chest at close range."

"Officer, can you tell us what your initial impression of the scene is?"

"Neither of the men in question are owners or occupiers of the house. The circumstances in which we found them are... unusual. I can't elaborate on that at the moment, but we'll make a press release available as soon as possible. In the meantime we want to trace the occupier of the house, a Mr William Harris."

"John, at that point we were interrupted by the arrival of more officers, who moved us to our present position some distance away. It's quite clear that the police are dealing with a significant incident here. We will, of course, bring you further information once it's available. Back to you in the studio."

~

As the sun started to kiss the landscape, Will turned the pick-up down the lane that led to a dusty old farmhouse surrounded by rundown barns and other ramshackle out-buildings. A number of vehicles were scattered around the property, but few of them looked like there was any chance they would move under their own steam. Two of the wrecks had obviously been cannibalised for spare parts.

"Is this it?" There was a hope that a mistake had been made in the intonation of Tia's voice.

"This is it." Will's voice seemed to hint of thankfulness for their arrival.

The plume of dust thrown up behind the pick-up obscured the view of the mirrors back to the road they had just turned off. Huge potholes in the unmade track threw the vehicle left and right as it rocked its way towards the house.

As they swung around to the rear of the property, Tia could see a view much like the lot at the side of Will's garage. There were interesting wrecks of various vehicles, common and agricultural, scattered in no particular pattern around the rear yard, in addition to those that greeted the first sight from the road. The double doors to one of the out-buildings were wide open and as Will turned off the engine, music could be heard blaring out through the entrance like the overspill sound from a live concert. Fortunately, the neighbours were far enough away not to be in range of the blast. The flashing blue light that emanated from the 'venue' showed that someone was at work with a welder and Will gave out a knowing laugh at the sight as if it was to be expected.

"Should've guessed it!" he shouted, to no one in particular. "She doesn't live by conventional hours, nor does she do conventional things, come to that."

Boost had been agitated for the last few miles as he'd sensed that they were nearing their journey's end. He was excitedly dancing around in the back seat, whining and barking to be let out to go and explore. Will climbed out of the pick-up and Tia cautiously followed his lead, but Boost, who had spent most of the journey curled up behind the front seat, barged his way out pushing past Tia who was moving far too slowly for him, making her laugh at his eagerness to escape the confinement. He was gone like a rocket into the nearby out-building without the slightest hesitation. Seconds later the music abruptly ceased, but Boost took up the running as the sound of 'dog enthusiastically greeting and being greeted' spilled from the building.

Moments later a young woman in greasy overalls launched herself from the workshop out into the yard, throwing gloves to the ground in her wake and being chased by Boost, who was doing his level best to dance around his fast moving friend.

"Will! Great to see you!" she shouted, as she jumped into his embrace. There was not the slightest hesitation on his behalf as he responded to the welcome with an eagerness that looked like it had been a long time in the making.

The initial greeting over, she pulled away from Will to take a look at him. "It's *so* good to see you, you scruffy devil! You leave it nearly five months then just turn up out of the blue." She punched his shoulder in a friendly gesture. "And you couldn't even get a haircut before visiting me."

Will laughed freely at her taunts. "Hi, Beth." He pulled her into his embrace once again and Tia had a momentary glimpse of what he must have been like before he carried the scar of tragedy. He warmly accepted the comfort of his friend, grinning widely at her enthusiasm.

As they separated, they each took a long look at one another, lost in the world of a long established friendship.

"I'm so sorry Beth. I know I should have made more of an effort…"

She raised her hand to his mouth to stop the apology.

"You're here now, that's all that matters."

"It's *really good* to be here." He took hold of her short blonde hair either side of her head and gently pulled her to him until their foreheads touched, smiled then released her.

Tia watched the display, awkward and unsure about her place. Their relationship was obviously a strong one and she didn't want to interrupt the bonding ritual prematurely. She was still standing a little way back behind the pick-up waiting to be given her cue.

Will suddenly realised that he was being rude and putting his arm around Beth's shoulder, guided her to where Tia was patiently waiting.

"Tia, Beth Jackson. Beth, Tia…" Will stopped as he realised that he didn't know what Tia's surname was and felt a little stupid after beginning his introduction, but she immediately jumped in.

"Sharmez. Tia Sharmez." She held out her hand to Beth who shook it warmly, but her quick glance at Will didn't go unnoticed.

Beth was five feet seven tall, just a fraction shorter than Tia, but apart from that they couldn't have been more different. Beth's pale complexion and short blonde hair gave her a Nordic look. She had an athletic build and clearly loved 'hands on' activities. Her clear pale-blue eyes and warm smile lit up her handsome face and every movement displayed body language that shouted that she had a zest for life and every adventure that it offered.

There was an awkward moment when no one was sure what to do or say. Beth smiled at Tia then glanced again at Will, as if trying to prompt him to do something, but he didn't notice.

"Well..." she started, taking the initiative. "I guess you guys have been on the road a while. How about we go inside and find something for breakfast? And coffee, we must have coffee."

Will laughed at some private joke they must have been sharing, which made Tia feel a little like the outsider, but she pushed the discomfort to one side and focused on how grateful she was that she had literally run into Will. If he thought Beth Jackson was someone who was trustworthy, then she had to take his word for it. What option did she have?

There was general light-hearted banter as they went into the house and Tia trailed behind them onto the back porch, pausing at the door as she took another quick look around the backyard. Once in the kitchen, Will and Tia sat down at the table while Beth removed some of her work-clothes and set about scrubbing her hands clean. The inside of the house was a little like the outside. There were lots of things that looked like they were in the process of being fixed, or dismantled, Tia couldn't quite decide which. The open doors that led to the dining and living area showed that they were similar to the kitchen. It was as if the whole house had been given over to be used as a workshop. Will didn't seem to notice anything unusual about the sprawl around him, but Tia was trying to take in the scene without being too obvious about her interest, or shock.

Beth rinsed her forearms under the running water as she tossed a question over her shoulder.

"You get a good run down here?"

"Yeah. Nothing on the roads this time in the morning." Will answered. "We stopped a while back for fuel and a drink, but otherwise straight here."

"What time d'you leave?"

"About one-thirty this morning."

Beth turned to face them as she towelled her arms dry. The smiles had gone and she was suddenly deadly serious.

"A phone call at an unearthly hour, a cry for help and an unexpected visit." She stated the facts bluntly. "What would get you out of bed at one-thirty in the morning to bring you all the way down here?" She looked from Will to Tia and back again.

Will was a little flustered by the direct question and glanced at Tia, who immediately realised that Will had told Beth nothing about the situation.

Unsure how to begin to tell the story, Will wanted to buy some time to get his head straight after the speed of the events of the previous hours. The lack of sleep and the long drive left him feeling a bit cloudy and the last thing he wanted to do was launch into some heavy discussion straight away.

"Perhaps we could have breakfast first, Beth?" He appealed for her to cut him some slack before the inquisition.

All eyes were on Will, and Tia shifted uncomfortably in her seat. Beth shrugged.

"Sure."

Tia felt the need to get out of the room for a few moments to give herself chance to collect her own thoughts and to let the two of them have a little space.

"Beth, could I use your bathroom? I slept a little in the pick-up and could do with freshening up."

"Yeah, yeah. Go ahead. It's the door straight ahead of you when you get to the top of the stairs."

Tia stood to leave the room and Will's eyes followed her as she disappeared through the door. She could hear them talking in low whispers almost as soon as she'd gone and nearly held back to try to listen to what was being said. Instead she forced herself to keep going and headed up the stairs.

The top floor looked just the same as the lower one, continuing the chaotic theme through the building. The bathroom looked like it had remained unchanged since the day the house had been built. It was a relic from the sixties, but at least it was a place where she could have some time on her own.

She started to fill the basin and glanced in the mirror as she waited. Cupping her hands, she buried her face in the warmth of the water. Each time it offered moments of comfort and escape from the world around her. As she dried herself, she stared for a long time at her reflection and wondered at the circumstances that had brought her here.

A noise out in the backyard distracted her from the self-examination and she looked out of the partially opened window to see Beth heading into an enclosure behind one of the barns. The disrupted peace in the pen stirred up clucking sounds from resident chickens and moments later Beth was heading back to the house with a clutch of eggs cradled in the upturned hem of her shirt. She had a tomboyish look. Handsome would be the word to describe her. Definitely feminine, but handsome.

She was casually dressed in jeans that were well-worn, gym shoes and a T-shirt with the image of a machine gun emblazoned on the front. It seemed to be an abstract symbol in such a rural scene.

She suddenly grabbed at the bottom of her T-shirt to stop a couple of the eggs dropping to the floor and gave out a yell at the near miss.

"Shit, that was close!" she chided herself and Tia smiled at the outburst.

As Beth disappeared under the porch roof, Tia went back to the mirror. She thought she looked tired. She definitely felt tired. With a deep sigh she turned, unbolted the door and made her way back down to the kitchen.

"You like eggs, Tia?" Beth shouted, as she went to sit back at the table.

"Yes, that would be nice. I've never had them as fresh as that though."

Beth spun around with a quizzical look, but quickly realised why the comment.

"Oh. You saw me from the bathroom window going out to the chicken run." A smile spread across her face. "They're my girls. Excuse the pun, but you can't beat the eggs from my girls."

Tia laughed. Pointing to herself she said, "City girl I'm afraid." There was an, 'I feel like I've missed out' smile that told Beth she thought it was great.

"Don't worry about that. We've enough animal shit around here to re-educate the whole county."

Tia's expression showed that she hadn't quite got the measure of Beth's humour, but Will burst out laughing simultaneously with Beth and that eased the way for Tia. It broke the ice a little and despite her initial reservation about Beth Jackson, she found herself quickly roped into the breakfast preparations and loving every moment. It had been days since she'd been in female company and it felt good.

Tia had heard the muffled voices while she was in the bathroom and assumed that Will had given Beth some background in the minutes she was gone. Whatever had happened, Beth treated her like they'd been friends for years. Perhaps that was just her way with everyone she met?

Within minutes it was Will who seemed the odd one out as they both laughed at the silliest of experiences they'd had. It was just idle chatter, but the pleasure of talking to another girl was written boldly on Tia's face and Beth, sensing the need, was more than willing to oblige.

Breakfast was on the table before nine and together they enjoyed the peace of rural living. Beth was obviously appreciative of the company. Had it not been for the circumstances that no one was discussing yet, it would have been one of those days where great friendships were born.

"Will tells me that you and he go back a long way?"

Tia was inquisitive about the relationship and thought she could prompt something more from Beth than she had managed to get from Will.

"You make it sound like we're a couple of 'ancients'." Beth's raucous laugh filled the room. It was so infectious that it immediately drew the other two in.

"No!" Tia protested through the joviality of the noisy atmosphere. "I didn't…"

Beth waved her hand. "I'm just messing with you, girl. I guess you could say we go back a bit. His dad was a 'grease monkey'," she pointed at Will, and in a deliberately gruff voice she continued, "And I'm a girl who loves the stuff." She displayed her nails which still had traces of black beneath them. "Climbing trees, bungee jumping, dirt bikes and cars, just dirt in general, I guess." She hesitated for effect, then waving her hand to draw attention to their surroundings, said, "Take a look at my house."

"Yeah, just look at it," Will added with comic disdain, nodding vigorously at the confession of chaos.

Beth was not about to let him get away with that. "You needn't talk," she said, pointing at him. "I'll bet your garage is still in the same state it was when I last saw it?" This time it was Tia who was nodding, drawing laughs from Beth. "Oh! You've seen it have you?"

"But I don't *live* in my garage," Will protested.

Beth pulled a face at him and slapped his arm. "C'mon Tia. Let me show you my latest project." She jumped up from her seat and headed to the back door without a second thought about the dishes that lay scattered around the kitchen. "Just leave everything. We can see to that later," she yelled as she disappeared, simply assuming that everyone would follow as instructed.

Will rolled his eyes as Tia glanced at him. "Might as well. There's no stopping her now." He urged her to go after Beth without question, resigning himself to the unchangeable nature of his friend.

Outside the sun was beginning to warm the day on its journey to the high point at noon, by which time the freshness would be lost to the heat until evening.

Tia paused for a moment on the rear porch, taken again by the sight of the ramshackle scene before her. What seemed an untidy mess to her was clearly a wonderland of fun for Beth. They had a common connection in that they were both female and Beth obviously appreciated the fine things of womanhood, as Tia found out from the banter earlier as they prepared breakfast, but she had a whole other facet that Tia could hardly comprehend. 'Still', she thought to herself, 'she never would comprehend it unless she allowed someone with the enthusiasm to show her'.

Stepping down onto the dusty ground she walked with Will toward the workshop with the doors lying wide open. At the entrance to the building, Beth turned back to make sure that her audience was in tow and hesitated for them to close the gap before she went inside. Initially the bright morning left Tia and Will blinded as they looked into the relative darkness of the structure.

"This..." Beth announced with pride, "This is the latest project." She pointed to the tarpaulin-covered hulk at the rear of the workshop, as she tiptoed through endless tools, equipment and car parts scattered around the place, all the time heading toward the mystery object. Taking hold of the cover she dragged it away making a rustling sound that filled the cavernous space like the crackling of fireworks. "Ta daa!" she declared in triumphal tones.

"My god, Beth!" shouted Will, as he burst out laughing at the sight before them. Taking pride of place was the most incredible 'off road jeep'. It had the character and presence of a snorting, angry bull about to run down a Matador and anything else that got in its way.

"Wow!" Tia took a small step back in surprise.

"I've been building this for an 'off road' event next month. It's a bit like a rodeo, but with cars." Beth gave the other two a moment to take in the monster and soaked up every comment about how amazing it was.

"Fancy a spin?" The way Beth made the offer showed her excitement at the prospect and it was impossible to refuse.

She pushed the rear doors of the workshop open, making the building look like a huge tunnel. When she jumped into the driver's seat and fired up the engine the low thunderous rumble resonated so that the sound could be felt as well as heard. Pumping the accelerator a couple of times, a deafening roar filled the confined space until the engine returned to idle. The broad grin on Beth's face, as she watched Will and Tia's reaction showed that she was enjoying herself immensely.

The jeep began to roll out of the workshop and into the sunshine and the booming noise suddenly reduced in volume as it reached outside. Tia glanced at Will, who was mesmerised by the spectacle. "The noise of that thing is terrifying!" she shouted.

"It's great isn't it?"

Beth waved at them to jump aboard; she was in a hurry to give them the ride of their lives. Boost bounded over and up into the jeep, there was no way he was going to be left behind.

As soon as Tia and Will had settled into their seats, Beth hit the throttle and thundered away from the yard at a terrific pace. She didn't head for the road, but for the hills on a dirt track.

As the speed increased and a plume of dust curled into the air behind them, the occupants of the jeep clung tighter to their seats to try to compensate for the motion that wanted to throw them out.

"Yee ha!" Beth yelled over the sound of the air that whistled over the open cab. Will copied the shout, but Tia just clung on as she gradually began to appreciate the exhilaration of the experience.

A couple of sharp turns left, then right, threw the occupants around inside, but were clearly designed to increase the fun. Beth glanced over at Tia in the front passenger seat and noted the hint of terror in her eyes.

Suddenly the jeep screeched to a halt and the dust cloud that had been behind engulfed them all producing spluttering and exaggerated coughs mixed with laughter.

Beth swung around to face Tia. There was no mistaking the flash of mischievousness in her eyes and Tia raised her eyebrows to question what she was up to.

"That's what kinda gal I am! Now swap seats, it's your turn!"

"I don't know if I…" Tia stammered, surprised at the offer.

"No problem. Let *me* in there!" Will shouted from the back seat.

Beth took no notice of his appeal for selection, she was keen to let Tia have a go.

"Sure you can girl! We women are allowed to have as much fun as the guys. They need a spell in the back seat sometimes to understand what it's like for us when they hog the wheel all the time."

Will gave a loud groan at the put down and rolled his eyes in the most exaggerated way.

Beth was obviously not going to take no for an answer, so Tia gave in and clambered across while Beth stepped over her to the passenger side. She concentrated on the dashboard for a moment as though it was going to reveal some mystery about driving such a beast.

By this time they were able to see again as the dust cloud dispersed on the wind. The farmhouse was about a mile away down the gentle slope, but Beth insisted that they needed to go further up before returning home.

Tia, following instructions, took off at a gentle pace, but gradually increased the speed at Beth's urging. Within minutes she was laughing outlandishly with Beth as the jeep bounced along the rough surface. It was like the world she'd lived through over the last few days had left her completely and she began to understand the joy of escapism found in doing such things. Her life had been so ordered and clinical, but this was outright fun for the sake of it.

The halfway point was when they reached the highest escarpment that could be driven to. Beth indicated that they should stop and take in the panoramic view that lay before them on three sides. The remainder of the distance to the top, that would have given a three hundred and sixty degree view, had to be taken on foot, but they opted to give it a miss as the heat of the day was increasing rapidly.

Boost took the opportunity to explore while Beth went to the edge of the dirt track, where the terrain dropped away steeply, and stood looking through the dispersing dust cloud at the plain below.

"I love the view from up here," she declared, as she stood with hands on hips. "The house looks like a doll's house." She pointed to the cluster of buildings in the distance.

Beth turned to Tia and gently pushed her on the arm. "We're going to need hosing down by the time we get back. It's all set up ready in the little barn to the side of the house. Hope you're a tough one though, it's cold water only." Tia's eyes widened as Beth held the serious look as long as she could.

"Take no notice of her Tia, she might be rural, but she's not that mad," Will reassured.

The laugher rippled around the three of them and the casual nature of their time together suggested that it was an ordinary day, but Beth knew something was going on that she was not yet fully aware of. She was waiting on Will to spill the whole story, but didn't want to press too soon. His visits were never spontaneous affairs and it was the first time he'd been since the funerals.

"Well, it's hot up here and it's only going to get worse, so I guess we should head back," Beth suggested.

Will insisted that it was his turn to drive on the way back to the house, but Beth pretended it was not for boys. Will was having none of it, physically lifting her out of the driver's seat. She put up a half-hearted fight against the eviction, but the sense of fun that seemed to surround them was inclusive, drawing Tia in. She thought they looked and acted like brother and sister. Their company together was easy and comforting and she found the strength of the bond between them reassuring.

By the time they got back to the house it was heading toward midday. The adventure had given space to unwind a little, but they were all aware that they needed to talk. Tia cleared away the remains of breakfast with the help of Will, while Beth made the best of what food she had in ready for lunch.

"That was great fun! I've never done anything like that before. I really enjoyed it." Tia was thankful at being made to feel welcome.

"Oh, Beth drives like that all the time. Off road, on the road, through town…" Will joked. Beth stuck her tongue out at him and followed it up with a rude hand gesture.

"I think I'm going to have to have a shower after we've eaten. My hair's clogged with dust," Tia said. "You do have a shower?" she added cautiously after the joking earlier.

"Yeah, of course. I was just kidding about the hose pipe. Only mod cons here babe." With the application of a serious face she continued. "It's out in the old cowshed. There's a bucket with holes drilled in it, I made it in the workshop." Tia glanced at Will, but he was deadpan. "I fill it with water and quickly stand under it. If you want a long shower though, I'll have to get Will to stand on the steps and refill the bucket as you go. You're not shy are you?"

"No problem," added Will, in a matter of fact way.

The horrified expression on Tia's face overcame their ability to maintain the serious look and peals of laughter followed. Tia waved a hand to dismiss their sense of humour at her expense, but liked the harmless fun of it.

"I must just be gullible or something. I fall for it every time."

Beth stood up and drew her hand over Tia's shoulder as she passed by. "You'll get used to it soon. I'll go first," she added, with a note of seriousness. "Cos that hair of yours, beautiful though it is, will take you ages to wash." She winked at Tia and focused on Will. "And I don't suppose you will need to wash... as usual. A quick anti-perspirant cover-up for you I suppose?" Beth poked Will in the side making him jump.

"At least my perfume isn't called 'Grease Girl'," he shot back.

She slapped him on the head and pulled a face as she headed out of the door.

"I'll shout when I'm out, Tia."

"Thanks."

Once Beth was gone and Will and Tia were alone in the kitchen, there was a hint of the awkwardness from earlier. Tia tried to keep the atmosphere light by mentioning Beth.

"She seems a great girl. You two are good friends aren't you?"

"She's the only family I've got since..." His voice trailed away without completing the sentence. "Not been too good at keeping up my visits though. It's certainly good to see her again. It's been quite a while since we did anything like that together."

They chatted while Tia waited for the shower, but she was glad when she heard Beth yell down the stairs.

"I'll see you in a little while." She excused herself.

Will smiled at her as she left, then got up to go into the living area. He switched on the TV and slumped onto one of the couches.

Tia reached the top of the stairs to find Beth wrapped in a towel with another around her head. She behaved with the informality of a long-time college friend. Holding out a couple of folded towels for Tia, she pointed her in the right direction.

"There's shampoo in the shower room and I've put a hairdryer in the bedroom if you want it," she indicated.

Tia was interested by the change from tom-boy to girlfriend and thought it gave Beth a real charm and character that she envied.

"Thanks… You've been so good."

"Nonsense. You brought Will to see me. I've been trying to get him to come for ages. He always wriggles out of it. Sometimes I wonder if I just remind him of…" She gave a forced smile. "Anyway," she waved a hand to push the unpleasantness aside, "if you need anything, just give me a shout, okay?"

Tia nodded then headed to the shower. There was a déjà vu feeling as she looked in the mirror again, but this time she felt more relaxed than when they'd first arrived.

She undressed and stepped into the spray of water, enjoying the comfort of it. The distraction that Beth provided was good, but she was conscious that it didn't make the reality of her situation go away and Beth was still not fully aware of the circumstances, or what had prompted Will's journey.

She stretched the shower out as long as she dared, considering that Will probably wouldn't appreciate a cold one if she used all the hot water.

When she came out she could hear the muffled sound of the TV and, as she crossed the landing to the bedroom to use the hairdryer, she caught the sound of Beth and Will talking. She hesitated to listen for a second, but the sounds were too indistinct.

Closing the bedroom door behind her, she glanced around the room, which was clean and neat, a contrast to the rest of the house. A couple of framed photographs stood on the drawers nearby and taking a closer look she saw the familiar faces that had been in the pictures at Will's house. She picked up the brush Beth had left for her and began to untangle the long locks of her hair while looking out of the front window toward the road.

The house seemed lonely, standing some way from the nearest other buildings in the distance and she wondered about what made Beth choose such an isolated place.

~

"Not now Beth. I just need a while." Beth attempted to draw Will into telling the story, but he was not game. She got to her feet, leaving him still slumped on the sofa staring blankly at the TV.

"I've got to go and check on my neighbour, Mrs Drake," Beth announced. "She's eighty-four and I try to make a visit every few days just to make sure she's alright. It'll take me about ten or fifteen minutes. When I get back we *are* going to talk."

Will looked up at her and saw the determined look on her face that threw out the message, 'Don't mess me about." He grunted a response, "Okay, okay," moving his attention back to the TV.

Boost, who had been spreading himself out on the rug near the fireplace, was instantly aware there was an opportunity to get outside. Jumping up, he trotted over to Beth and nudged her for a fuss.

"Do you want to come too and leave that lazy man on the sofa?" Beth stroked him while talking like she might to a little child, which only emphasised to Boost that there was an adventure at hand.

As she left the room, Boost was not going to allow a hairsbreadth between them and followed alongside almost glued to her leg.

She crossed the yard and opened the door to her white station-wagon which had seen better days. Due to the lack of washing, it had a reddish hue from the dust that had settled all over it. Beth used it for anything from visiting the local store for groceries, to hauling the equipment and materials for building the much more important, in her eyes, off-road jeep.

Boost eagerly leapt into the driver's side and crossed over to let Beth in and within moments they were off down the drive to see Mrs Drake.

Boost jumped around with excitement at the trip, frequently putting his head out of the open window to enjoy the feel of the wind, but the outing was probably considerably shorter than he'd expected.

Beth turned into the front yard of the first house they came to and drew the vehicle up at the front entrance. Opening the driver's door, she jumped out, so closely followed by Boost that he almost ran Beth down, much to her amusement. It had been a long time since she'd seen him, but it was as though the dog remembered her from the time when he was just a puppy, a time when Will was much closer and their lives were intertwined more frequently than of late.

They both climbed the few steps to the front door and Beth arrived on the decking just as Mrs Drake got there, having seen them turn into the drive.

Beth was a good friend and Mrs Drake always enjoyed her visits, but the old lady was fiercely independent and determined to see out her last days in the house she'd inhabited for the last fifty three years. Beth got the benefit of a grandmotherly figure who took the time and interest in her that she'd lacked from her own family.

"Well, well. Who do we have here?" Mrs Drake practically ignored Beth and made her address directly to Boost as she sat down on the bench that decorated the front porch.

"This is Boost," Beth informed her, as she watched the dog lap up the attention he was getting.

Mrs Drake was 'old school', but charming. She was immaculately presented, though her dress sense was still locked in a generation gone by. She always stood ramrod straight, which hid her advancing years and her wiry frame made her seem much taller than her real height. She frequently talked of her days teaching many of the town's citizens at the local school, long before they became prominent people of importance in the community.

She fussed over Beth like she was a granddaughter, often sending her on her way with homemade cakes or biscuits, but with their significant age difference Beth had always addressed her formally. The retired school mistress never corrected her, so it continued for all the years they had known each other. There was definitely a special warmth in their relationship, but, everybody, young or old, addressed the congenial old lady the same way; 'Mrs Drake'.

Boost held back from his usual boisterous greeting as though he knew the frailty of the person before him, but the enthusiasm was still clearly expressed. There was no doubt he was happy to make a new acquaintance.

Mrs Drake laughed with joy at the chance encounter. "What a beautiful, well-behaved dog you are!" She spoke in high tones as she addressed Boost and without turning her attention away from him she asked, "Wherever did you get him from Beth?"

"He's owned by a friend of mine."

The old lady glanced up and saw the fondness for the dog in Beth's demeanour.

"Are they visiting you for a while?"

Beth felt a sudden check that she couldn't explain, but it made her wary of being totally truthful. "I'm just looking after Boost for the moment."

"How nice for you." She looked up again at Beth then back at Boost. "I expect I will see you again, Boost. We'd better find you a biscuit if we're going to be friends, hadn't we?"

Beth laughed at the one-sided conversation between them, but allowed it to run its course without interruption.

Mrs Drake stood, hugged Beth then led the way to the kitchen.

"I guess you like dogs, Mrs Drake?" Beth's inflection made it clear she was stating the obvious.

"Oh, my dear, I adore them. I've had three in my eighty-four years and every one a gem," she spoke to the dog to finish her sentence, "just like you Boost." She held out a biscuit for him, sealing their friendship. "I find that good owners have dogs that mirror the good in themselves," she reflected, adding in a mischievous tone, "so watch out for misbehaving dogs, it's the owners that are trouble!"

Turning to a tin on the counter behind her she said, "I've baked you a little cake, dear." That was a frequent sentence in their brief conversations and Beth greatly appreciated the gesture.

Although she could easily look after herself, she had no objection to being mothered. Besides, Mrs Drake's cooking was legendary in the locality. If ever there was a stall selling food to raise money for charity at some local event, her contribution was always the first to go. As with everything she turned her hand to, she was meticulous, disciplined and capable.

The conversation rounded up after a few minutes once Beth had checked that everything was okay. Boost had a farewell biscuit then reluctantly followed Beth back to the car, resuming the prime spot with his head out of the window. Mrs Drake waved them off as Beth pulled out of the drive and hooted the car horn in response.

~

Tia turned off the hairdryer and listened for a moment. She thought she'd heard a shout from downstairs. Thinking that Beth might have returned and was trying to get her attention, she went to the top of the stairs to listen.

Will suddenly let fly a stream of curse words, making Tia take a couple of steps back. His voice was sharp and carried a tone that showed he was angry.

The volume of the TV increased significantly and she could hear that it was a news programme. Cautiously she went back to the top of the stairs and quietly made her way down the first few steps to listen. All that could be heard was the noise of the TV, but she wasn't taking in what was being said. Her mind was focused on what was going on with Will. She continued on, still holding the towel that she'd been using for her hair.

Reaching the foot of the stairs, she could see through the wide archway into the front room. Will was sat on the edge of his seat, eyes fixed to the TV. He was totally unaware that Tia was behind him wondering why the high volume was necessary. Her focus drifted from what she was seeing to what she was hearing.

"The scene that confronted the officers attending the supposed break-in, can only be described as horrific. Two men,

who the police department have yet to formally identify, were found dead, tied to chairs in the back room of the house. It appears that they had been interrogated and possibly tortured. It has been confirmed that one man had a broken leg and the other a severe wound to his left hand, the probable weapon that inflicted the injuries was a baseball bat found at the scene. The men were shot with a single bullet to the chest at point blank range."

Tia clasped the towel to her mouth trying to stifle the scream desperate to be released.

"Detective Hallam, who is in charge of the investigation, made a short statement earlier."

"This crime is one that is particularly brutal and what we were confronted with was extremely shocking. We have people examining the scene at the moment and we expect them to be here for some considerable time. We have put out an all-points bulletin for the man who was renting the house, a Mr William Harris."

A picture of Will in military uniform appeared on the screen.

"We'll continue to follow this story and bring any further updates as they happen. We have been told that another statement will be made in due course. This is Jenny Russell reporting from Cordham."

The instant the town name was mentioned, the dam that restrained Tia's reaction gave way, she involuntarily yelled, "OH MY GOD! WHAT THE HELL DID YOU DO?"

Will jumped to his feet and spun around just as Beth burst through into the hallway in response to Tia shouting.

In the confusion Boost began to bark as he sensed the tension in the room. Tia's face was screwed up with fear and she backed away from Will until the outside wall at the bottom of the stairs prevented her increasing the distance between them. Her eyes flashed from Will to Beth, from the stairs to the front door, as if checking out her options of escape should it be necessary.

Beth reacted immediately to what she saw, placing herself between Tia and Will as she looked from one to the other.

"What the hell's going on?" she demanded.

"You need to ask Will!" Tia shouted. "What have you done? What have you done?" she repeated.

Will started to protest, but the volume of the TV was filling the room with too much noise to try to make his case. Suddenly he was totally overruled by the news presenter.

"We are returning to the headline story of two men found tied up and shot dead in the town of Cordham. Our reporter at the scene is Jenny Russell. Jenny, we understand that the detective in charge of the investigation at Cordam has just made a second statement."

Beth's eyes flicked between the screen and Will unable to decide where to settle.

"That's right. We've been told that there has been a development to the story. This is what Detective Hallam said just a few moments ago."

"Our preliminary investigations, with the assistance of the forensic team, have found evidence that Mr William Harris was at the scene with the two murdered men. We have not yet established whether he had an accomplice with him. We believe this man to be capable and willing to put the lives of the public at risk. Under no circumstances should anyone approach him or try to detain him."

Will's picture again came up on the screen with a police contact number underneath.

"We urge the public to report any sighting using the number shown on the screen. I repeat again that under no circumstances should the public try to apprehend this man.

"The police have moved very quickly with this situation and clearly believe that the public should be fully informed due to the risk that this man poses. Jenny Russell, Channel 2 News, reporting from Cordham."

"WHAT THE HELL HAPPENED BACK THERE WILL?" Beth exploded. Her fury shocked Tia and she flinched at the volume that overpowered the TV. Will quickly silenced the news report that had now moved to the next item and there was a surreal moment of silence before Beth continued.

"Two men murdered? I know you said you needed some help, but shit, I thought you might have meant fixing your car, not covering up a homicide. A double homicide!" she quickly added.

The look of horror etched in the faces of the two women staring at him told Will that he had better do something right away to try to convince them of his innocence.

CHAPTER 7

"It's not what you think," Will glanced back and forth between Beth, Tia and the TV. He made a move toward Tia to try to give some kind of explanation.

"Don't you come near me!" she yelled, with enough force to stop Will in his tracks.

Beth positioned herself even more deliberately between the two of them. With her back to Tia, her eyes were firmly fixed on Will, emphasising her determination to get an explanation of what she had just heard.

"What the hell is going on, Will?" she demanded again. "That report was for real."

"I swear, Beth, I don't know." The expression on Will's face was one of anger mixed with fear. He raked his fingers through his hair as he looked at the floor wondering what had happened and avoiding Beth's piercing stare.

"Well, those two men didn't tie themselves up in your house and shoot themselves, did they?" The light-hearted, fun loving Beth had changed to a forceful, confident challenger who clearly knew how to handle herself in difficult situations. "I want some answers, Will. Right now!"

Will's head suddenly flashed upright at Beth's demand, but his focus was beyond her, fixed on Tia. She instantly turned away, breaking his stare.

"Tia!" Will shouted. The sharpness in his voice made her look up, connecting with his eyes again. His expression showed determination to do something. She was thankful for Beth's protective stance between them, but she didn't keep her eyes on him for more than a second.

Will was more insistent and uncomfortably forceful. "TIA, look at me. LOOK AT ME NOW!"

Beth glanced back at Tia. Seeing the shock on her face, she decided to intervene and turned to confront Will.

"You're not helping matters, Will," she strongly cautioned, but he totally ignored her and took a step forward drawing a response from Tia.

"Don't you take one more step toward me!" she yelled. "You told me you didn't do anything stupid! You told me!" she challenged. Her fiery retort surprised Beth and made Will take a step back in response.

"Listen! Tia." He softened his tone, but made sure he had her full attention. "Did you *hear* gunshots?" he asked, making it obvious with his hand gesture that he required her to answer.

Both girls stared wide-eyed at Will as if he'd lost the plot. Will tried to make it plain what he was getting at. "When we were at the house, did you, *at any time*, hear gunshots?"

Beth turned to look at Tia and their eyes met. She saw her glance at Will then back again as she rewound the previous night's events in her mind.

"Tia?" Will was being very insistent, but needed to hear her answer his question. "You were at the house all the time I was there. You were outside. Did you ever, in all that time, hear the sound of gunshots? It was the middle of the night. It was quiet. You would have heard the shots. *Did you hear gunshots?*"

Tia stood motionless as the tension in the room increased until it was palpable and waiting to be released like a pin bursting a balloon. With Beth and Will both looking at her, a flicker of confusion crossed her face. She dropped her eyes to the floor as she thought, then suddenly looked up and shook her head. "No," she said, so definitely that they knew she was sure.

Will sighed and some of the tension seemed to leave his body, but he wasn't finished yet.

"There were two men. They each had a gun which I took from them, yes? You saw me with the two guns, didn't you? I don't own a gun. Beth will tell you. I haven't touched a gun since I left the forces." He let the new information sink in and Beth didn't move to challenge his assertion. "Both weapons are in the pick-up outside. Both magazines are full." Will took a few steps backwards and seated himself in the chair by the fireplace. Boost, sensing the tension, went and sat next to him. "Beth, go to the pick-up and fetch the guns. They're in the storage space under the steering wheel. Bring them back here and take out the magazines. Check they haven't been used." Will was very meticulous, giving his instruction clearly.

Beth had been observing Will's behaviour, weighing-up what she knew about her friend. She turned to look at Tia. There seemed to be some registering of what Will was trying to get at.

"Tia." She looked up at Beth. "Will is going to stay exactly where he is. You and I are going to the pick-up and together we'll check the guns, okay?"

Tia glanced at Will then back at Beth. She could read the concern in the eyes of her new acquaintance. Beth nodded to encourage her to go along with what she was suggesting and as she made a move, Tia followed closely. As they walked across the hall, Tia glanced again at Will before disappearing through the kitchen door. Worry was etched on his face at the gravity of the situation. Even if his friends finally believed he was telling the truth, it didn't alter the fact that two men *had* been shot dead in his home.

When Beth and Tia reached the vehicle, Beth opened the driver's door and checked the storage compartment. Tia watched as she pulled out the guns, handling the weapons with unmistakeable confidence.

She was very deliberate in making sure that Tia could see every movement so that there was no possibility of misunderstanding. They had to see whether Will was telling the truth and needed some reassurance after seeing the news report.

Putting one gun on the seat, Beth held the other out, released a catch, sliding the magazine into her waiting hand. She held it up so they could both see that there was no question the gun had a full load. Beth held the weapon to her nose and glanced at Tia as she did so.

"This hasn't been fired recently." She followed the same routine with the second weapon and got the same result.

Beth leant forward with both her hands on the pick-up front seat and was still for a moment. Her head tipped down as she blew air out through her pursed lips. The relief that showed in her body language was the most reassuring thing for Tia. Guns were not something she understood, but she was confident that Beth did, and the reaction reassured her that Beth believed Will *was* telling the truth.

Beth passed the magazines and the guns, still separated, to Tia, then climbed into the cab of the pick-up. "The first thing I need to do is hide this vehicle."

Beth was suddenly running in a different mode. She appeared to have taken stock of the curved ball that had been thrown and was immediately taking responsive action.

The engine burst into life and she drove the pick-up to the rear of the outbuilding furthest away from the house. Jumping out, she swung the doors wide open and backed the vehicle inside the building. She dragged a tarpaulin across the yard and threw it as best she could over the pick-up. Fetching a padlock from the workshop, she closed the doors and secured them.

Tia stood watching, glued to the spot, holding the guns and separated magazines as though they were toxic waste.

When Beth finished her task and returned, she took the guns from Tia and simply said, "We need time to think and to talk about what's happening here and how we are going to handle the situation." With that she spun on her heels and they both headed back to the house where they found Will still seated in the chair where they'd left him.

As they walked into the room, Beth slid a magazine into the handle of each gun and placed them on the coffee table. It appeared, to Tia, as some kind of gesture of trust in Will. A statement that she'd accepted his story and now wanted to figure out what came next.

"I've hidden the pick-up in the back of one of the out-buildings. The police are not stupid though. This is a big story and I'm sure that they'll be checking any records available to make connections to people you know. They'll come here to find me, hoping to get lucky and find you. If we run now, before they've been, we'll have no chance. The only hope is for them to see that I'm here and haven't a clue where you are. That means we need a plan when they arrive. I presume it will be the local units and I know most of them. We need to watch the drive so that we're not caught unawares and we need to find you both a bolt-hole."

Tia was listening intently to Beth's reasoning. Her inclination would have been to run immediately, but she could see what Beth was getting at. Will didn't say a word for a long time. Boost's sad eyes encapsulated the general feeling as he rested his chin on Will's knee trying to comfort his master.

"Beth."

"Don't say you're sorry, Will. You need my help and that's all there is to it. Until we understand what's going on, we do what we need to do. First we decide our plan of action. *Then* we sit and talk."

Beth shot the last comment while looking directly at Tia, before turning to see that Will understood her determination to find out the truth. She'd taken charge of the situation and Tia and Will were at her mercy, but they each separately thought, for different reasons, that there was no one they would have rather been subject to.

A suitable hiding place was located in the attic, well behind piles of storage boxes which they moved to allow access, placing one of the cases to cover the entrance once they were inside. It was tight, but the chances of anyone wanting to look there were slim.

It was decided that the front room would be constantly occupied by at least one of them so that the drive and part of the main road could be watched at all times. Beth disappeared to the local store to pick up some provisions, while Will manned the front view and Tia, unable to relax, spent the time clearing up in the kitchen and generally pacing around the place to keep occupied. She didn't go into the living room to see Will while Beth was gone, feeling awkward in his presence.

When Beth returned, Tia helped unpack the provisions, glancing through the window from time to time to break the discomfort of their self-imposed silence. The sun was setting and the sky beautiful, painted with gold, orange and red swathes of colour on the distant canvas, but their heavy hearts didn't really take full notice of the display.

The small group eventually assembled in the front room to try to piece together what had brought them all to this point and figure out how to deal with the situation.

They were just beginning a serious conversation when Will erupted from his seat at the window. "Car headlights turning into the drive!" he yelled.

He grabbed Tia by the hand and flew up the stairs with her in tow until they reached the attic. He unceremoniously bundled her through the opening they'd made and followed in close behind as they heard the faint sound of gravel crunching beneath the tyres of the arriving car. Tia was slowing her breathing to try to calm herself, but choked a little, prompting Will to put his arm around her shoulder and pull her close to him. She didn't object to his action and the complete turnaround from a few hours earlier wasn't lost on him.

"It'll be okay," he whispered, as he touched his chin on her head.

"Evening, Beth."

The thick set, stocky patrol officer touched the brim of his cap as he addressed her. He was a familiar face to Beth, having seen him call a number of times over the years. Her house, being the last one on the main road out of the town, had become a turning place for the patrol cars before returning to base. Beth had seen him do the turn so many times that when she bumped into him in the town, a few years earlier, she invited him to call for coffee any time he wanted.

They'd built up a loose friendship that revolved primarily around the work she was doing re-building cars. He'd taken a keen interest in her recent project, following the build-up to the event, which was definitely on the local calendar. The significant difference with this visit was that it was getting dark. He never called when it was too dark to take a look at the cars. Without that as the focus of their conversation, they simply had very little in common. He was old enough to be Beth's father, but their backgrounds made them virtual strangers. Beth was not in any way religious, this man most certainly was.

"Officer Madeley," Beth responded with a note of question in her voice as she stood at the rear door. "What brings you by this evening?" Suddenly she felt Boost trying to force his way past her legs, his inquisitive nature begging answers to what was going on. Beth quickly knelt down and grabbed him by the collar to hold him back and heard the tinkle of a collar tag.

As Madeley leant into his patrol car to get something, Beth took advantage of his distraction to pull hard at the tag, snapping it from its securing ring. She stood up to greet the officer as he strode the few yards to the porch and discreetly slipped the tag into her pocket.

"Got yourself a dog now, Beth?" His voice conveyed surprise. "Didn't figure you to be a pet person. I thought you were the type that likes to be free to roam when you want to."

"I picked him up the other day when I was out in the jeep. He was just wandering alone."

Madeley knelt down next to Boost, who obligingly flipped over onto his back responding to the fuss. "I don't recall seeing a report of a stray dog found." He looked up at Beth. She shrugged, but didn't answer. "Let's see here." He fussed Boost, then took hold of his collar. "Looks like his identification tag has been broken off. You haven't reported him found yet?"

"No. I haven't really had chance. Kinda liked having him around I guess."

"Yeah. They're great company. Part of God's wonderful creation for mankind to enjoy." Beth let the comment drop to the floor. She'd learned from past experience that if she gave any opening, Bill Madeley would be in the house talking for much longer than she could risk at that moment.

Will and Tia could hear the low mumble of voices reaching into their hideaway from the rear porch, but couldn't make out what was being said. As they sat motionless and tense, suddenly they heard Boost bark. Will flinched at the sound, knowing that they should have brought him upstairs with them. "Shit," he muttered under his breath, cursing his carelessness. Tia sensed his concern and taking hold of his hand she squeezed it. The fact that they weren't sure what was going on added to the suspense, their frayed nerves taking one more beating.

Officer Madeley stood to face Beth, having completed the bonding exercise with Boost and she momentarily hesitated before enquiring again, "So, what brings you by this evening?"

"I was wondering, Beth," there was a sudden seriousness in his demeanour. "Have you seen the news lately? Well, today actually?"

She gave him a quizzical look. "You've come to ask me if I've seen the news? Have I missed something?"

"They've been running this story about a terrible incident at Cordham." The officer paused deliberately looking for Beth's reaction.

"I'm sorry, Officer Madeley. I shouldn't leave you standing on the porch. Come inside. I don't know what I was thinking. Can I get you something to drink?"

"Just lemonade if you have some. Thank you."

He followed Beth into the kitchen and glanced around as she got the drink.

"I know someone who lives in Cordham," she said casually. "Ages since I've been there though. What's happened?" Beth prompted as she passed him the glass.

"Two men were murdered in a house there. Sometime late last night or early this morning."

"Oh, how awful!" Beth mimicked surprise as though it was the first she'd heard about the incident. She added to the ruse by slowly sitting down at the table feigning shock with her body language.

"Thing is Beth," Madeley leant in a little toward her to give comfort before delivering the worst of the news. "The house was being rented by William Harris."

Beth took a sharp breath and following the characteristics she'd seen in Tia's reactions earlier, put her hand up to her mouth in shock.

The officer noted her response. "You know William Harris, I believe?"

"Yes… Yes. I've known him from before we joined the forces. We joined at the same time," she explained. "Haven't seen him for several months though. Not since the funerals of his father and sister. They were killed in a car crash. We kind of lost touch a bit. I suppose I reminded him of them. His family I mean."

"He hasn't been in touch with you?"

Beth deliberately gave a wide-eyed expression before answering. "No. Do you think he's headed in this direction?"

Madeley shrugged, but didn't answer the question. "Mind if I look around?" Beth looked surprised at the request. "Just routine." Madeley hinted that he was only doing his job.

"No, go ahead."

Beth firmly took hold of Boost's collar to make sure he didn't disappear through the door and head upstairs, prompting curiosity on Madeley's part.

Madeley made a half-hearted browse of the ground floor and Beth, wanting to distract his attention, casually said, "I visited Mrs Drake earlier today."

"Oh yes, is she well?" he shouted from the hallway.

"Well enough to have been busy baking. Brought some cake back with me." Beth paused for effect. "Would you like a piece?"

Madeley suddenly appeared at the kitchen door. Mrs Drake's reputation extended to the local police department, who were enthusiastic recipients of her offerings whenever she went to town.

"She's a superb cook. It's not very good for the waistline, but boy does it make your taste buds sing."

Beth laughed as she handed him a slice of cake and he sat down at the table to enjoy it.

"I think the dog must have been a bit boisterous in the front room."

"What makes you say that?"

Beth suddenly remembered the guns she'd put on the coffee table earlier and had to suppress a feeling of panic that began to rise in her. 'They'd have been in full view', she thought to herself, 'Why wouldn't he have mentioned them straight away?'

"He must have tipped the table clean over." Madeley's response was muffled by the cake being consumed.

"Really?"

Beth jumped from her seat and quickly went to the front room. The coffee table was over on its side but the guns were not in view from the doorway so she assumed that Will had grabbed them en route to the loft. She went around the couch intending to lift the table upright. Glancing back toward the kitchen, she checked that Madeley was still occupied and as she reached the coffee table, she saw the weapons on the floor. They were so close to the couch that they'd been shielded from view while standing at the hallway door.

Letting out a relieved sigh, she was silently grateful to Mrs Drake and the cake she'd provided for saving them from a close call. Will's explosive move from the window while watching the drive must have caught the table, knocking it over. Beth was thankful for the blunder. Had it not happened there would have been two loaded guns left out in full view. That might have taken some explaining. She'd been a good actor so far, but that situation would have stretched her skills beyond credibility.

Carefully sliding the guns out of sight under the couch, she shouted, "That dog! I swear he does this sort of thing for attention!"

"That was great, thanks Beth." Madeley was standing with Boost at the door and his answer made Beth jump. "Oh, sorry! Didn't mean to surprise you."

She glanced across at him over the back of the couch from her kneeling position and pretended that she was straightening the rug and repositioning the coffee table.

"Whoever owns him needs to apply a little discipline I think," she said, as she got up and went to fuss the dog. "You can be a little rascal," she said playfully. "Can't you Boost." He barked in response to her tone, but Beth was suddenly aware that she had made a stupid error using his name. There was a tense moment as she waited for Madeley to make some comment and tried to prepare for it when it came.

He leant over once more to pat the dog and Beth realised that he'd been far too interested in the animal to have taken note of what she'd said.

"Look Beth, the reason I called is to tell you that William Harris is in some serious trouble. We need to track him down as soon as possible. If you hear anything, make sure you call us."

"You can bank on it," Beth answered, then followed him through to the kitchen and out onto the steps of the rear porch.

He turned and waved as he reached the car. "G'night."

Beth responded in kind and stood in the doorway watching as he got into his patrol car. The headlights illuminated the rear yard as the car turned to go down the drive, leaving a red glow from the tail lights as it disappeared around the side of the house.

Beth slumped down onto the top step and Boost was straight to her side. "That was too close, Boost," she said, stroking him. "Far too close." She cursed herself for being so careless.

Going into the house, she went to check that the coast was clear from the front room window and caught sight of the rear lights of the patrol car disappearing into the distance. As soon as it was gone she ran up the stairs to Tia and Will.

"Okay!" she shouted, as she climbed the narrow attic stairway. Will instantly jumped into action, removing the cover to their hideaway. Moments later they were traipsing down the stairs to the living room in a sombre convoy.

"Didn't waste any time before coming here," Beth mused out loud. She stopped near the bottom of the stairs and turned to look at them both. "That's bought us some time, Will, but it won't be long before they're looking more seriously. We're going to have to think about leaving while we've got the chance."

As the group fanned out to the seats in the living room, Boost was his usual happy self, greeting them all like they were playing a game of 'hide-and-seek'. Beth knelt down by the couch and reaching under pulled out the guns, deliberately holding them up for Will to see.

"Did you knock over the coffee table in the rush to get upstairs?"

"I don't know... Yeah, maybe." He looked alarmed. "Why?"

"If you hadn't, our friendly Officer Madeley would have walked in here to find two loaded pistols on display. That would have taken some explaining. *Yes officer, I've never liked those coffee table books of photographs. I much prefer a couple of guns,*" she said mockingly. "They landed on the floor in front of the couch. It's lucky that he couldn't see them when he came through the door." Beth smirked. "It's a good job I offered him some of Mrs Drake's cake."

There was a moment of silence before Tia spoke, as the close call they'd just had sunk in.

"Must be one hell of a cake, Beth!" They all laughed, more from relief than from humour.

Beth slipped her hand in her pocket and pulled out Boost's collar tag. "This was even closer." She tossed the brass disc onto the coffee table. "I told him that I found Boost wandering a few days ago and hadn't had chance to report it yet." Boost looked around at them as though he knew he was the subject of the conversation. "The first thing he did was look for that tag. It's got your name and address on it." That changed the atmosphere in the room again.

Beth beckoned Will and Tia to the kitchen and pointed for them to sit down. They dutifully followed and obediently took a seat at the table. She made coffee while the three of them were lost in their individual worlds of thought. They had to talk about what was happening and make some decisions as soon as possible, but no one was sure how to begin the conversation.

"Don't we need to watch the front?" Tia asked, finally breaking the silence. "I'm just concerned that we almost didn't get away with it."

"Bill Madeley will be off home for the evening," Beth answered, as she placed the drinks on the table and seated herself. "If they're only sending local police on friendly visits, it suggests that they're fishing for clues to find out what direction you, or at least, Will, has taken. They'll be back, but I doubt if it will be for a couple of days. Perhaps when they've narrowed down the options." She dropped a slice of cake onto three small plates and dealt them out on the kitchen table like cards in a game. There was no question that the cake was good, but the sweetness of the delicacy was tempered by the bitterness of the circumstance.

Beth glanced at the kitchen clock and suddenly jumped from her seat to flick on the small TV that stood on the counter. Will and Tia's attention was immediately directed to the small box waiting for it to deliver the next piece in their nightmare.

Watching the latest news report, no one said a word. The only noise was the clinking of cutlery on plates and the sound of Boost begging for cake.

Once the item was over, much of which was a repeat of earlier bulletins, Beth reached for the volume control and killed the sound. She sat back down looking at the moving pictures for a little while before speaking.

"Funny, don't ya think?" She lazily threw the comment out for the others to pick up on.

Tia and Will glanced at each other then fixed their eyes on Beth waiting for something more, but it wasn't forthcoming. She was obviously deep in thought. The light from the TV pictures created dancing shadows on her face.

"What's funny?" Will finally prompted.

"Umm." Beth looked over as though woken from a trance.

"What's funny?" Will repeated.

"All that coverage about what's taken place. The appeals for the public to turn you in; the in-depth analysis of every last detail of what could, or might have taken place. In all of it there was not a single mention of Tia." Beth paused then looked over at Tia who was staring wide-eyed. "Why do you think that is?"

Tia felt the heat rising in her cheeks as she came under what felt like some kind of interrogation. Beth noticed the change as Tia squirmed in her seat, so she clarified the question.

"What I mean is, I think someone knows much more than they're willing to admit. Surely, if the police had suspicions about another person being involved, they would've made that clear, wouldn't they?" She spun in her seat so that she was facing the other two, her attention completely off the TV and on the implications of what she was suggesting. "No offence Will, you're a good looking guy, but you don't stand out all that much in a crowd," Beth smirked and threw a joking insult, "Not with hair that looks like yours anyway... but Tia?" It was a compliment to Tia's beauty that didn't go unnoticed, but it was a serious point. "With your looks," Beth continued, "you can't easily be missed and would have certainly enticed all sorts of speculation in the media if they'd had any inkling that you were involved."

"Either they just don't know that you're involved in this," Will started speculating, "or they're deliberately withholding that information for some other reason."

"What do you think, Tia?" Beth asked.

Will looked at her, waiting to see how she would handle the direct question. Beth had held back from doing that before, but times had changed and the whole thing was much more serious than she first thought and now she was after some answers.

Tia felt slightly alarmed by the question and the determined tone of Beth's voice, but was more concerned that she didn't think she could give the answers they were after.

"Beth, I really don't understand any of what's happened to me, or why. I told Will about how I was taken against my will. I was just out shopping. It was the same as any other day, except..." Tia skipped what she was about to say, thinking it unimportant in the circumstances. "Anyway, the men who were found at Will's house *were* involved in snatching me and they *were* helped by the..." She paused while she corrected herself. "Were helped by *a* police officer. That's why I didn't go to the police when I escaped. Running into Will was not planned and no doubt he would rather it hadn't happened, considering the trouble I've caused," she smiled apologetically in his direction. "But I don't understand what this," she pointed to the TV, "what any of this is about." The other two could hear the frustration in her voice as she struggled to give further explanation.

"Your family? What about your family?" Beth asked.

Tia suddenly felt very vulnerable. She looked at Beth and then Will. Her eyes dipped to the table before she answered. "What family?" she said sorrowfully.

Will and Beth glanced at each other, but quickly focused on Tia as the tone in her voice revealed hidden hurt.

"You mean you don't have any family?" Will gently urged her to elaborate.

"I don't know," she shrugged.

"Why? What do you mean?"

Tia hesitated a moment before continuing, steeling herself for the emotional strain of talking about her past life. She'd seen the risk that her two companions had taken for her and knew that she had to lay the whole truth on the line.

Taking a deep breath, she began.

"My real name is Sarita Liatzo." Beth and Will immediately glanced at each other as though wondering what was about to come out. "When I left the guardians my father had put me with and came to the States, I changed my name and started using Tia Sharmez. It wasn't such a difference from my first name as you might imagine. Tia was what I was called by people who knew me well. It came from something silly we were doing when I was a child; mixing the letters of our names. It kind of came from the last letters of Sarita and I liked it." She dismissed her rambling by waving her hand. "Anyway, it stuck. So when I needed to change my name for good reason, that's what I used." Tia took a breath and continued. "I spent almost..."

"Wow! Hang on a minute," Beth held up her hand to stop Tia. "You needed to change your name for good reason. What good reason?"

Tia looked at her companions and gave a brief smile. "It's probably easier if I just tell you a little of my background to try to answer that question."

Beth shrugged. "Okay."

Tia looked down at the table as though she were checking the page of a book to find where she was. "I spent almost all of my early years living in a large villa in Mexico. It had gates on the driveway and a security fence that circled around the grounds. It was a big property," she looked up at Will and Beth and emphasised the point, "I mean big. I came to despise the place though. It was my prison. The people who monitored me were like my prison guards and the teachers that came to the house were like my torturers."

Tia sat for a moment staring into space as the memories surfaced. Beth glanced at Will, but neither of them wanted to interrupt unless it was necessary. Finally, Tia seemed to realise that she was lost in her own world and refocused on the moment.

"My father's name is…" Tia hesitated. "Carlos Liatzo." She smiled as she said the name out loud, but a sudden shadow crossed her face as she continued. "He was the best…"

"Was?" Will interrupted.

"In truth I don't know if I should say 'was' or 'is'. I haven't seen him for over three years." The pain of that statement was written clearly on her face. "My childhood was happy generally, except that there were always a lot of restrictions on me. There were guards at the gates and patrolling the grounds at home all the time. I never noticed it when I was younger, but when I got to my teens it became oppressive. Papa told me it was necessary for my safety, but I never really questioned why. I just assumed it was because we were well-off. Mexico can be a dangerous place."

"You are actually Mexican then?" Beth quizzed.

"Yes."

"But you don't sound Mexican, you have a perfect American accent."

"Gracias por ayudarme." The words flowed melodically from Tia's lips, then she smiled. "I was given a very good education."

"Okay," Beth shrugged. "So I was wrong, you *do* sound Mexican when you want to." She leant forward a little with interest. "What did you say?"

Tia put her hands on Beth and Will's hands and looked directly at them. "Thank you for helping me," she interpreted.

Beth took her hand and squeezed it. The genuineness of Tia's comment showed clearly in her eyes and there was a moment of acknowledgement before Beth spoke again. "Hey, we're not out of the woods yet, kiddo, but keep going with your story."

"My father was often away from home on business, sometimes for long periods. By the time I reached eighteen he was gone much more than he was at home. If it hadn't been for Midissia, she was one of the housekeepers who cared for me, she was like a mother, I would have gone mad. I used to complain constantly about the security. You'd have thought I was someone important or something. I soon stopped that after the break-in."

Beth and Will were locked on Tia as she talked.

"I wasn't in the villa at the time, but had been with Midissia staying with an acquaintance of my father. A vehicle rammed the front gates seriously injuring the two guards on duty. They managed to get into the house and took some things. They left after threatening to shoot one of the house staff if they didn't tell them where I was."

"Where *you* were? You mean they were after *you*?" The surprise in Beth's questions was obvious.

"My father was away at the time, but when he came home he became totally paranoid about my safety. I thought the restrictions were bad before, but afterwards they were intolerable. I complained at him for months afterward, until I began to realise that he really believed I was in danger."

"But why?" Will interrupted.

Tia shrugged her shoulders. "He intimated it was something to do with our wealth, but we lived in an affluent place and nobody else's children seemed to be at risk in the same way. He started to talk to me about moving to the States and I pressured him for answers. He told me that some of the risks were related to his business involvement, but it was necessary for him to stay in

Mexico. He told me I was at risk while I carried his name, Liatzo. He convinced me that it would be safest for me to move to the States and assume a different identity. I had to listen to him, he wouldn't make up such a thing. He wanted Midissia to go with me, she'd always talked about going to America and he knew someone who could get the documents that would give us a new start with a new identity." She paused a moment. "I won't try to explain how hard it was leaving him and I never would have agreed if I'd known..." Her voice wavered a little, but she didn't finish the sentence.

"What happened to your parents?" Beth asked.

Tia shrugged and her eyes filled a little, but she gave no answer for a long time while she tried to gather herself. "I never knew my mother. My father..." She fought the emotion that welled up. Beth tried to comfort her as best she could, but Tia was struggling. Finally she continued, "My father made me swear that I wouldn't go back to Mexico, no matter what. He said it would compromise my safety by exposing my true identity. He told me he would contact me as soon as it was safe."

"And you've heard nothing since?" Will asked.

Tia shook her head in response.

The three of them sat in silence for a few minutes taking in the story that Tia had related.

"What did you say your name was?" Will asked, once Tia had composed herself. Beth glanced sideways at him, wondering why the question.

"Sharmez," Tia answered without thinking.

"No. I mean your real name?"

"Liatzo. Why?"

Will shook his head and leaned back into his chair as though he wanted to make sure he'd heard correctly, but Beth knew him well enough to see something was amiss. Will continued staring at Tia. It wasn't intentional, but his mind was churning away at something that disturbed him.

"What have you been doing since you left, Tia?" Beth asked.

"I did all sorts of jobs at first, just to make ends meet. It was a bit of a shock after the luxury I'd been used to most of my life, but the freedom to do what I wanted, when I wanted, was fantastic. It compensated for the restrictions I'd lived under."

"I spent months waiting to hear from my father, but he never got in touch. I was too scared to try to contact him after the stern warnings he'd given me. I think it was the first time I ever remember seeing fear in his eyes. He'd always been so strong." Tia glanced at the table, her expression filled with concern.

"What about now?" Beth asked. "Your father *hasn't* been in touch at all?"

"No." Her answer was so definite and sharp that it seemed to jolt her out of the solemn frame of mind she'd slipped into. "I finally tried to contact him after I'd waited as long as I could. It was about two years after I left. I just needed to know something." She was almost apologising by the intonation of her voice for disobeying her father's wishes. "I didn't dare do too much digging after he'd so meticulously tried to hide my identity. I was too afraid, but I did find out the villa had been sold.

"Although he never told me clearly what it was about, it had to be serious to have made him send me away and not contact me. He would never…" Tia baulked at the end of her sentence, as though she had great difficulty finishing it, because the man she'd known would never have deserted her. Beth prompted her to finish what she was about to say.

Tia looked up and connected with the comfort that Beth tried to offer. "He would *never* just abandon me. I know he wouldn't."

"What do you think has happened?" Will asked.

Tia shrugged and there was a pause before she answered. "It's been three years now since I've heard anything from him… I can't help thinking the worst." The upset in her voice was clear. Beth signalled to Will to give them some space and he immediately took the hint. He got up and wandered to the back door and out onto the porch taking Boost out for a run in the yard. He could hear the low mumble of Beth's voice back in the kitchen as she was talking to Tia. He sat down on the steps to allow them some time alone. His mind churned over the events of the last couple of days, but it had all happened so fast that it seemed unreal, like he'd been watching a movie.

After ten minutes, he wandered back into the kitchen and took his seat at the table again. Tia looked a little brighter, but the sadness still lingered in her pretty eyes. She felt a little uncomfortable as she resumed her story.

"I made a friend while I was working at one of the first jobs I got. She was into photography and started going on about me becoming a model. When I was growing up, Midissia had always told me that I was beautiful and should be in the movies, but I never took her seriously. It was something that anyone would say to a child. Anyway, when Lisa started talking about making a portfolio and posting pictures out to agencies, I started to get interested. Nothing came of it for ages, but about five months ago I managed to get some temporary work. It was just modelling work for clothing magazines and stuff. It was such a lot of fun." She shrugged and smiled coyly. "They liked me enough to take me on full time and it paid much better than the restaurant and bar work I'd been doing."

"Have you been in anything I might know?" Beth smiled encouragingly at Tia. "Car Weekly? Four Wheel Drive? Mechanic's Monthly?" Beth winked. Tia appreciated her ability to lighten the mood with a little humour.

"Up to just recently the jobs were small, but this month I did an advertising shoot for a cosmetic company. The picture found its way into a magazine."

"Which one?" Beth sat upright in her seat.

"It's on the front cover of 'Mode'."

"Wow. I *know* that one. That's *so* cool." Beth's excitement spilled over as if they didn't have a care in the world. "Have you seen it?" she quizzed.

"Not properly. I mean, I've seen the picture, but not the finished magazine cover before it went to print. It only came out a few days ago." The increasing smile that had begun to surface on Tia's face suddenly disappeared. "I was going to pick up a copy for a friend when those guys tried to grab me."

Beth and Tia were lost in the chat, almost forgetting that Will was in the room, but he'd been watching Tia all the time she'd been speaking and his interruption cut through the conversation abruptly.

"You say the magazine has just come out?" Beth and Tia simultaneously turned to look at Will. "Only days before those two guys who followed you to my house tried to grab you?"

Tia nodded to confirm that he'd understood correctly.

"Do you think the two things are connected?"

Tia froze like a statue and Will caught a glimpse of the fear that had plagued her eyes when they first met. Beth was on the other side of Will like a mirror image of Tia, waiting for him to explain.

Will leant forward in his chair.

"Don't you think there's a bit too much coincidence in what you're telling us?" Tia's face changed to a defensive look. "No!" Will checked himself, not wanting to give any misunderstanding after what had happened earlier when the news report was on. "Listen. You've been away from," Will searched for the appropriate word after listening to Tia's description, but couldn't find one quick enough, "'home' for three years and never had any problem. You've been using a different name. But, at the same time your picture is published in a popular magazine, suddenly someone tries to kidnap you. Don't you see that the two things could be connected?" Will paused to let the girls consider what he was suggesting. "If there is a connection, and the type of people looking for you are willing to do what those two men did, and had done to them, then we need to make a move while we have the advantage. And quick."

"Why did you ask Tia what her real name was?" Beth asked.

"Don't know. It's familiar, but I don't know why." Will shrugged and got up to make a drink.

The room remained quiet for a while as they each mulled over their own thoughts, until Beth broke the silence.

"Getting back to where we started. Why isn't there something on the news about Tia, Will?" All eyes were on Beth as the question that had begun the discussion drew a blank. "We need some help from someone in the 'know'," she suggested.

"What do you mean?" Will gave her a quizzical look.

"I was thinking we should ask for help."

"From who?"

There was a hesitation before Beth answered. "Mr Google." She smiled.

"Oh god!" Will immediately blurted out. "Not Lester. I thought he was doing geeky things somewhere in a secret location for some government agency we're all told doesn't exist."

"He is. I think."

"Well how do you expect to find him?"

"I know how to find him. Anyway we're talking about Lester, Will. He never could resist an invite from me." Beth smiled mischievously.

Tia watched them bat the conversation back and forth before she broke into their private discussion. "Who's Lester? And Mr Google?"

Will sighed deeply in an exaggerated way that showed his exasperation with the mere mention of his name. "Lester, known as Mr Google, is the most annoying person you could ever wish to meet, but *he* doesn't know how annoying."

This time Beth sighed. Her body language showed her irritation at Will's attitude. It made him quickly backtrack.

"Okay, yeah, he does know his way around cyber-space… It's the real world he has difficulty with," Will muttered under his breath.

Beth leant forward and put her hand on Will's arm. The expression on her face had taken a very serious turn that grabbed his attention.

"We're going to have to leave soon, Will, if we intend to meet up with Lester, but there's a problem we need to resolve now."

"What problem?" The tone of Will's question reflected the sudden change in Beth's demeanour.

She cautiously nodded toward Boost, who was curled up on the rug near the table. Will glanced at Tia who had followed Beth's indication toward the dog. He looked down at him and back at Beth. Her eyes met his with a look that said, 'this is important'. "We can't take him with us, Will. There's no way that we can cover his enthusiasm for people; it's sure to get us into trouble."

Will was suddenly concerned about his faithful companion.

"We can't just up and leave him, Beth." Will whistled a signal. One moment Boost looked asleep, the next he was instantly at his master's side awaiting his bidding.

Beth and Tia could see it was going to be a difficult thing for Will to do, as they sat watching him fuss over his friend.

After a couple of minutes Beth offered, "I have an idea, but you're going to have to trust me."

Will dragged his attention away from Boost to hear Beth's proposal.

"My neighbour, Mrs Drake, the old lady whose cake you're eating, she absolutely loved him." She hesitated before continuing. "I think we should go early in the morning, before its light, and leave Boost on the porch with a note asking Mrs Drake to look after him until we get back."

Boost was alerted by the mention of his name and set his tail wagging as if he knew he was the centre of attention. The look in Will's eyes showed he was grateful that Boost couldn't understand what they were planning, but perhaps Beth was right.

"He'll be okay, Will. I promise." Seeing that he wasn't wholly convinced it was necessary, she pressed a little further. "It was a close call when Officer Madeley came by earlier. That could happen again at any time and if we take him with us I think we're increasing the risk."

"Alright, alright. I understand. I just wasn't expecting it that's all," Will snapped. Suddenly feeling a little embarrassed at his response, he added, "I'm sorry Beth." She smiled, but they all knew that the decision was made.

Beth set about getting in touch with Lester. It was a case of leaving him prompts to get back to them. Lester had an annoying habit of never answering anything immediately, but Beth knew they had to start heading south toward the area she knew Lester was based in. As she sent the email she was thankful for the stupid humour that they used whenever they communicated. It allowed the transmission to seem like code to anyone who didn't know them. It was a language developed by a long friendship that had left Lester with the nickname, Mr Google, which *he* took as a badge of honour.

Beth sorted the sleeping arrangements and set the alarm for them to get up at four in the morning, giving them chance to make some headway before the roads filled with traffic. She elected to take the car, rather than the off road jeep that she'd been working on, because it was more ordinary and gave the opportunity for Will to be hidden from view in the back. The car was less likely to attract attention or stand out and they needed to conceal Will's publicised face as much as possible.

Beth deliberately hung back before going to bed so that she could catch Will for a private chat without raising Tia's suspicions that something was going on behind her back.

"Will." She caught his attention as he was about to mount the stairs. Tia had gone in front of him and was heading into the bathroom. He paused and glanced up to the landing to see her about to close the door and, pretending he was following, shouted, "Call me when you're out will you Tia."

She turned to see him starting up the stairs.

"Sure."

The moment the door was shut, Will went to the kitchen to see what Beth wanted. She was sat at the table waiting for him.

"I'm not happy about this whole situation, Will. I think you have a hunch about what we're dealing with here and you just didn't want to let on with Tia in the room."

"I'm guessing as much as you are, Beth. The guys who came to the house were not just passing by hoping to get some valuables. They managed to track us down, very quickly. Tia told us that she'd hitched a lift with some unsuspecting workman to my end of town and jumped ship when he found her hiding in the back of his truck. That means they must have found the guy and got him to show them where he saw her run for it. After that, they still had to figure out that she'd come back home with me and then waited until the middle of the night before they made a move. It was lucky that I haven't been sleeping well lately." Will suddenly realised that he'd inadvertently let Beth know that he was still struggling with his own circumstances, despite the fact he always made out he was fine. He glanced at Beth and gave a brief smile as he shook his head, but she knew more than he was letting on. The turmoil was written on his face.

Will completed the train of thought he was on before stopping. "If I hadn't been awake, who knows what could have happened. It was Tia they were clearly after. I was of no importance and they were definitely willing to do anything to get her." Will raised his eyebrows as he considered the possibilities.

"The bathroom's free!" Tia shouted.

Will turned to look through the door into the hallway to check that she wasn't coming back down the stairs.

"Thing is Beth, unless we get to the bottom of what's going on here, it's me who's going to come off worse. The news has my picture all over it and the authorities have me down for murder, so I'm going to have to keep out of sight. I'm seriously screwed if they catch us before I know what's happened and why." Will rested his elbows on the table and put his head in his hands as the weight of the situation pressed down on him. He was tired from having driven through most of the previous night and the circumstances loomed large in his mind. "Even if I wanted to, I couldn't go to the police. God knows who's involved in this…"

Beth reached over and put her hand on his shoulder to reassure him, but she knew her concern would not deal with the situation they faced.

"You'll have to try to get some sleep, Will. We'll deal with tomorrow's problems when they come."

She smiled at him, but it was obvious another question was waiting to be asked, so Will prompted her to ask it.

"There's something on your mind, Beth."

"What do you think about Tia?"

"In what way?"

"Is she telling us the truth, everything she knows?"

Will shrugged as he read her eyes. "There's one thing I do know. I've seen some scared people in my time and I can tell you for sure, she looked terrified when I first found her in the parking lot at the garage. I mean seriously freaked. She took a long time before she said anything."

"Look, Will. I'm no perfect judge of character, but she seems too naïve to be holding anything back intentionally. I mean, maybe she *does* have some information that would be useful, but she just isn't aware of it. Am I making sense?"

"Kind of." Will nodded. "What do you suggest?"

"There was something about her name that triggered your interest. We need to do a bit of digging to see if it brings anything up and I suggest we keep Tia informed, just in case anything rings a bell."

"Okay." Will stood up and made a move to the door. "I'm going up to bed now. I'm conscious that Tia will know we're down here talking. I don't want any suspicions to start brewing."

Beth waved. "See you at four," but she wasn't finished yet. She left the kitchen to go into the small backroom and start the computer. Time was not a luxury they could waste. They needed answers fast and on their own it was going to be difficult. Getting in contact with Lester was now the main priority.

CHAPTER 8

Don Greer had worked with Jack Cougar for several years. First for Mr Kurtis senior and then for his son Vince. He'd been with Jack and the feisty newcomer, Raif, only a matter of hours before, trying to find the runaway girl. Now he had the unenviable task of delivering the bad news to Vince. He burst through the street level door and started up the stairs to the first floor office. The perspiration that broke through on his forehead was the result of the effort of getting there as fast as he could, but the thought of Vince's reaction didn't help the matter. Over the years he'd learned to keep his mouth shut in order to stay out of Vince's unpleasant, bullying control. After the three of them had been subjected to a verbal bombardment about their incompetence, Don didn't fancy facing something similar on his own.

His momentum carried him the remaining distance and he burst through the office door a little more forcefully than intended. Vince Kurtis, never a man to be taken by surprise easily, leapt from behind the desk and had a gun trained on Don in a flash. Once the realisation of who it was hit Vince, the initial expression of shock quickly switched to one of anger.

"You asshole!" he shouted. "I nearly blew your head off! What the hell are you doing coming in here like that?"

"Put the TV on, *NOW*!"

The force in Don's voice was so unusual that Vince didn't retaliate as he would normally. He studied the face of his 'employee' for a few seconds. After a moment's hesitation, as he continued to stare at Don, he returned the gun to its holster and stepped away from the confrontation. He walked across to the TV far too casually for Don's liking and flicked the switch. The dull daytime programme that filled the screen was nothing out of the ordinary.

Turning to look at Don he said, "The TV's on! So what?" The inference in his tone was, 'you'd better have a damn good reason for behaving the way you are'.

Don stormed forward and pushed past Vince to get to the controls. The news broadcast instantly caught the attention of both men.

As the two of them stared at the screen, the headlines played out for a couple of minutes, detailing the murder of two men on the outskirts of the city, not far from where they were. The significance of the situation escaped Vince and he was not about to tolerate Don's insubordination for another second without an explanation.

"What the hell is this about?" he yelled impatiently at the TV screen, but the comment was directed at Don, who immediately responded.

"Seb Marston called me... From the police department."

"I *know* who he *is*, Don. You think I'm a moron or something? So what?"

Vince was an impatient man at the best of times so Don was on rocky ground and bordering on the edge of receiving the full force of Vince's irritation.

"It's Jack and Raif, Vince." Don spat the words out in disgust. His face was filled with absolute horror. "The two guys who've been shot; it's Jack and Raif!"

Vince's face instantly drained of colour. He glanced at the TV, as though he was trying to absorb the unwelcome information, before turning to stare at Don. The two men stood rooted to the spot for what seemed like a long time, eyes locked on one another.

Suddenly Vince launched forward and grabbed the young man's jacket lapels running him back against the wall. Vince's face was inches from Don's. There was a wild look in his eyes that the guys had seen on many occasions. He looked ready to explode.

"This better be some kind of sick joke, Don, but I ain't laughing." He punctuated his statement by shoving Don back against the wall again.

In the heat of the moment Don submitted to Vince, but fought back at the inference that he was not being serious, something he'd never normally have dared to do. "IT'S NO JOKE VINCE!" he screamed, pushing his boss away to gain some breathing space. "JACK AND RAIF ARE DEAD! SHOT THROUGH THE CHEST AT POINT BLANK RANGE!" Don's face was red with anger and frustration at Vince's apparent inability to believe the awful truth.

Vince glanced back at the TV again as he struggled to weigh-up the enormity of the situation, before slowly edging his way over to the desk. He stood for a few seconds taking in what Don had told him, as the commentary from the TV news report continued to fill the room. Suddenly he grabbed the glass he'd been drinking from and launched it across the room at the opposite wall. It disintegrated into fragments with a piercing crash. His face was red with restrained rage which suddenly broke free as he yelled at the TV.

"I'll kill the bastard when I find him. The double crossing…"

The telephone on the desk rang, interrupting Vince's barrage of cursing. He immediately snatched the receiver.

"Yeah!" he snapped.

Don watched as Vince listened to the caller's voice on the line.

"We *didn't* let her get away…" Vince's protest was cut short. The silence in the room was intermittently broken as Vince tried to assert his authority over the caller, but it was obvious he wasn't succeeding and his already stoked anger exploded.

"Listen, you low life…"

Vince's attempt to make it clear to the caller exactly what he thought was obviously terminated before it had begun.

A look of disbelief momentarily crossed Vince's face. He looked at the handset, shocked that his outburst had been terminated without hesitation. He slammed the receiver home, shaking the desk, and let out a scream.

"I swear I'm going to finish that son-of-a-bitch if it's the last thing I do. No one crosses Vince Kurtis and gets away with it. No one! I'm going to make that bastard wish he'd never been born."

He spun around to look at Don, his face red with rage, eyes burning with a fire of pure hatred and filled the room with obscene names blindly addressed at the caller who was ignorant of the barrage.

"I'll cut his tongue out and make him sing nursery rhymes before I put him out of his misery. For Jack's sake, I'll make sure that bastard suffers badly. But first, we screw his plans by getting the girl back. Call everyone we know. Pull every favour. I don't give a shit who we have to blackmail or how much it costs, I want to know where Tia Sharmez is and I want to know *NOW!*"

Don knew it wasn't the moment to question the wisdom of pursuing the girl simply out of revenge, so he jumped to action.

As he was about to leave the room, Vince added a final instruction. "And call Brook Fenton!" he yelled. "Tell him to meet me in half-an-hour at the Blue Moon Club on First Avenue."

"Brook Fenton?" Don questioned. "That guy's a psycho."

"JUST CALL HIM!" Vince made sure Don understood it was not open to challenge.

Don hesitated a second before leaving the room. He knew it was not in his best interest to defy Vince at any time, but particularly not at that moment.

As he headed down the stairs to the exit door, Don could hear Vince turning the air blue with expletives as he liberated his rage. The guys always suspected he had a hidden regard for Jack Cougar, because he was his father's right-hand guy, but Vince would never have allowed them to see it. The loss of such a key man was going to hurt and Don figured the pain would be more than just business, despite the bravado.

Vince slumped into his chair having expended the immediate build-up of rage. He pulled a cigarette from the packet on the desk, lit it and took a long drag. As he exhaled, releasing the smoke upward, he thought he noticed the hand he was holding the cigarette with shaking. He momentarily became obsessed with watching for signs of nerves, one second thinking there was something, the next dismissing it.

The telephone rang again. He froze, watching it for a few seconds before answering.

"Yeah," he growled, as he snatched up the receiver.

"That you, Vince?"

"Yeah."

"It's Carl. I heard something on the grapevine."

"Oh?"

"They tell me Jack Cougar's dead." There was silence as Vince left the caller hanging until he felt uncomfortable and was compelled to fill the silence. "Your father and Jack did me a few favours over the years. I figured it might be time to pay something back. What do you need?"

"The name of the low-life-asshole who greased him," Vince snapped. "The police department happy to pass out information like that, or are you goin' to be as much use as usual?" he said. sarcastically.

There was a moment's hesitation as the caller tried to make sense of Vince's comment.

"Haven't you been watching the news, Vince? The guy's name has been plastered all over it since early this morning."

"Dumb ass! You think I'm that stupid?"

There was another hesitation before what was being suggested was picked up on.

"You saying it *wasn't* him?"

Vince slammed the receiver down totally dismissing the caller. It immediately rang again, but Vince just sat and watched it until the irritating sound caused him to explode from his seat. Grabbing the phone, he launched it at the same target as he had the glass. He pulled his jacket from the chair, left the office, slamming the door behind him, and headed out to First Avenue.

Ten minutes later, Vince walked up to the bar at the Blue Moon Club. He scanned the dimly lit room and acknowledged a couple of people present, but opted not to go over and engage. He had more important things on his mind. Top of the list was revenge.

He slid into a booth that was tucked away from prying eyes, ordered a drink then sat staring into the glass as he waited. His mind was occupied by his momentary loss of control of the circumstances. Every sinew of his body was focused on regaining the upper-hand and firmly stamping his authority on the situation so that people understood who they were dealing with in Vince Kurtis.

He'd struggled to keep power over the 'business' that his father had established when it was foisted on him by his father's untimely death. Jack had helped him take control, but he felt threatened by Jack's experience and, to be brutally honest, his command of any situation that arose. Jack Cougar's body was barely cold, but the loss of his backing made Vince begin to wonder how he was going to exert his influence without his right-hand man. The blackness of it all seemed overwhelming. He'd already been under pressure with other circumstances and Jack had warned him about getting involved in snatching the girl for the mystery client, but he hadn't listened. The client was out of the country when the identity of the girl had been established and needed someone to secure her for when he got back. The financial incentive was enough to entice Vince. It would've allowed him to deal with some of the things needing his urgent attention. To oil the wheels of his industry he needed some blind eyes in the law enforcement agencies and that didn't come cheap.

"Vince." The booming, deep voice brought him back to the present.

Brook Fenton slid along the leather bench-seat opposite. He was a mountain of a man. Physically pumped and his close-shaved head gave him an aggressive look that immediately intimidated. At six foot three, he towered over Vince, but the breadth of the man made him look like the statue of some mystical Greek warrior.

"Brook." Vince nodded and tried to hold a look of confidence.

"Don said you wanted to see me... *Urgently*."

Vince's eye ticked a little at the way Fenton delivered the last word. It carried a suggestion that Vince was out of his depth. There had been some friction between the two guys over a period of time. They were like two young bulls squaring up over the right to control a territory.

Vince tried to cover his annoyance. He needed Fenton's help, at least for the moment. The one thing that ran in his favour was the respect Fenton always showed Jack Cougar, so Vince played his card.

"Don tell you about Jack?" Vince waited a second for Fenton to acknowledge, but he sat motionless, staring and studying. "I need to find the guy who killed Jack Cougar…" Vince launched into why they were meeting. "He gave my father twenty years. Never a problem. Always there. Always got the job done… I want the bastard who greased him, and… I want to make him suffer."

Vince spat out the words with such venom and intensity, but he was not going to move Brook Fenton to fear. Fenton had the measure of Vince Kurtis, but people like Jack Cougar were the real power, the king-makers. Any attempt to manoeuvre into a place of authority had to be done cautiously and with their consent, otherwise the fall-out would damage everyone.

Fenton saw opportunity in the current crisis, but was prepared to let out a little rope in the hope that Vince would seal his own fate, leaving the way for a new order as Kurtis Senior's memory faded into history. Cougar had been a man to be reckoned with, but now *he* was gone too.

"Yeah, Vince. Don told me the news. I liked Jack. He was an important guy in our world." Fenton carefully covered every trace of opportunism for his own prospects that might have tried to creep into his voice. "I'll do what I can… For Jack's sake." The two men locked eyes. Each one tried to cover the distrust they had for the other. "This Harris guy on the news; he was in the forces…"

"It wasn't him." Vince was so emphatic as he cut across, it made Fenton lean back in his seat and focus intently on his counterpart. "Forget that guy, he's not who I'm after."

"How do you know it wasn't him?" said Fenton.

"We were doing a job," Vince leant closer across the table and lowered his voice a little, "just looking after a lady for this guy. He was out of the country when he found out who she was."

"Who was she?" Fenton interrupted.

The frustration at being interrupted showed on Vince's face, especially as he had no answer. He ignored the question and continued.

"She made a run for it. We tracked her down again. Jack and Raif found her over the other side of town. The plan was…" He hesitated while looking for the right word. "Let's say they were going to 'babysit' her and wait until the client turned up to 'collect'. You get my meaning?" Vince quickly scanned the bar.

"Yeah, I get your meaning, Vince," Fenton said scornfully.

Vince shifted in his seat, unhappy at having to ask this man for anything that might put him in debt, but the circumstances forced his hand.

"Well, he turned up alright, but the girl wasn't there so he…" Vince looked around uncomfortably as though someone might be listening that he didn't know was there. His eyes twitched with the discomfort of having to speak the next few words as if it showed his weakening authority. "He took his disappointment out on Jack and Raif. The bastard took pleasure in telling me." He slammed his fist on the table then immediately looked up at Fenton, who was closely observing him. "I need to find his name. I'm going to kill the son-of-a-bitch in a way that will make him wish he'd never messed with me."

Fenton stared at Vince for a few moments, the big man act was skin deep and Fenton saw it clearer than ever before. Vince was losing his grip on reality and living in a dream world of his own self-importance.

"What makes you think I can," Fenton hesitated, "or will, help you?"

"The way he talked. Some of the things he said." Vince hesitated a second as he locked eyes with Fenton. "I think he was a military man…"

"Shit." Fenton laughed and turned away shaking his head. "There's thousands of them."

Vince's face didn't move a muscle, his eyes stayed locked on the man opposite. He just waited until Fenton had had his fun.

"I think he was something special, like you were."

Fenton eyeballed Vince for a several seconds before he prompted Vince for more information. "What do you know?"

"Not much. He rings me, not the other way round. He doesn't live in this area. I think he's older…"

"You gotta be kidding me, right? You must have more than that."

A flash of anger crossed Vince's face, but he subdued it for the moment. He needed Fenton's help. The rest would have to wait until later.

"He used the name 'Hammerhead', a kind of call sign." Brook was suddenly focused and Vince thought he saw a hint of recognition in his eyes when he mentioned the name. "What do you know?"

Fenton didn't answer him, but looked away to the bar while he thought for a moment. Finally he turned back.

"I'll ask around for you, Vince, but I'm not promising anything." Brook slid out from behind the table and stood for a second looking down from his lofty height. "You sure you know what you're doing here, Vince? These people don't play games."

"What the hell does that mean?" Vince's temper gave way. "You think I'm playing games?"

"No, I'm just not sure you know *what* you're playing." Fenton smiled, winding Vince up further.

"That bastard's going to pay. I'll make sure of that if it's the last thing I do."

Fenton leant forward, his hands on the table. "If you're not careful, it might be exactly that." Their eyes stayed locked for a few seconds. Fenton stood up straight, held Vince's stare momentarily then turned and headed for the door, leaving Vince simmering at the table. He glanced back as he left the bar and a certain satisfaction settled on him about his future plans.

Vince sat with his drink for a few minutes mulling over what had passed between them then slammed his glass on the table in frustration and stormed out of the door. He hated being manipulated, especially having grown up in an environment where the word of the boss, his father, was treated like the word of God himself. But Vince was not his father and the deep-seated insecurity gnawed away at him. The harder he tried to emulate the power his father had wielded, the further it seemed to slip from his grasp.

Snatching the girl was a big paying job that would have given him some breathing space, but now it was dragging him under and he needed to salvage what he could from the mess.

Vince spent much of the day pacing the floor of his office, chain-smoking cigarettes, drinking coffee and calling anybody who owed him a favour to try to find out anything that would help. He'd just sat down at his desk again when there was a knock at the office door. It caused the same spontaneous reaction in Vince that it always had since the first day he'd set up his 'business' place. His hand went straight to the handle of the gun stored on a shelf just beneath the desktop. It allowed him to have it discreetly accessible without having to reach into his jacket.

"Come."

The door swung open and Brook Fenton stepped into the room.

"Vince." Fenton greeted him coolly.

Vince nodded acknowledgement, but said nothing, he just leant back in his seat and watched as Fenton pulled a chair across to the front of the desk and sat down. Vince released his light hold on the hidden gun and the two men eyed each other for a moment.

"If you want to find Hammerhead, *I* can't help you," Fenton paused trying to gauge Vince's reaction to the news. "You sure you want to pursue this, Vince? Because I know people who know this guy and he ain't worth messing with. You listening to me? Someone's going to wind up dead, but it might not be him."

Vince Kurtis was a man on a mission. The need to live up to the ghosts of his past pushed him relentlessly onward without regard for the possible consequences and without the back-up he'd once had in Jack Cougar.

"You telling me that I should forget about what he's done to Jack? Forget about Raif? They were *my* people." The agitation in his voice filled the room, but Fenton was unconcerned about Vince's attempt to rattle him, he knew that the substance of the man was the tail-end of his father's strength and he only sat in the chair because others respected the family name. Vince had made too many reckless decisions as a young man, stepping behind daddy's coat tails when the proverbial shit hit the fan.

Fenton reached into his jacket and proceeded to pull a paper from his pocket. He took note, with some slight amusement, when Vince flinched, looking wary of what was going to be drawn out. He placed the item on the desk and slid it across.

Vince went to take the paper, but Fenton kept his hand firmly on it.

"This is a favour, Vince. You understand that don't you?" The eyes of the two men stayed locked together. "I *will* be collecting on it."

Vince snatched at the sheet without any sign of acknowledgement and broke the stare to look at it. He looked up at Fenton.

"What the hell is this?"

Fenton slowly leaned back into his chair, pondering how much someone like Vince could continue to behave like the big man before he literally ran into serious trouble.

"You mean, what's this that you've kindly brought for me, Brook... don't you?"

Fenton's voice was calm and deliberate, like a parent correcting a child. He'd seen Jack Cougar at work and liked his ability to intimidate with the gentlest of comments that carried a dangerous undercurrent. Vince felt the eerie similarity come to bare and quickly glanced up at Fenton, as though he'd heard a whisper from the grave.

"What is it, Brook?" he repeated in a more measured tone.

Fenton was satisfied with the correction. He knew right then that the man before him was finished. Without Cougar's presence he couldn't continue to hold his command of the 'business' for much longer.

"That's the address of an 'acquaintance'. He *might* know what you're after. *But*," again Vince connected with Fenton's staring eyes, "these guys don't like stitching-up their own people. I don't appreciate you thinking I would want to get involved in something like this. You understand what I'm saying Vince. If it hadn't been for what happened to Jack, I would have told you to get lost." The two men sat like statues facing each other in a museum display, unmoved, unflinching. "I'm just warning you in advance, Vince. He might take exception to you asking."

Fenton stood up and made a move to the door, but stopped to throw in a last comment before leaving. "You mention my name, or that I gave you the contact, Vince, and *I'll* take exception to you asking. I hope we understand each other."

Fenton waited long enough to be sure that Vince knew he was being cautioned and needed to tread carefully. Without another word, he turned and left the room leaving the door swinging wide open until it came to a jarring stop as it hit the wall. It was a last act of disrespect.

Vince knew what was happening and determined that he would have to re-exert his authority to prevent the final game playing out, but first he needed to take his revenge for the lost team members. He picked up the phone, punched in the number and leant back into his chair.

~

Don Greer was thankful to be away from the lousy situation that had engulfed his day. He glanced across at his girlfriend, Karen, as she got into the passenger seat of his car. She looked absolutely gorgeous. She leant over to kiss him and he put his hand behind her neck to hold her to him longer than she would have done. She smiled to herself as she heard him taking in her perfume.

The dress she wore was designed to make a man stare at the wearer and Don's eyes were fastened to Karen as she moved back to her seat. It gave the impression that more was on show than was covered and what was covered seemed to be beneath the thinnest material imaginable.

"What are you looking at?" she questioned, cheeky grin spreading across her face.

Don smiled and couldn't resist letting his eyes follow the plunging neckline as he took advantage of the moment. She made no effort to conceal anything and enjoyed watching him reluctantly turn away as he pulled out into the stream of traffic.

"You hungry?" he asked, flashing his eyes over her again before turning his attention back to the road.

"For what?"

Don immediately glanced across again to find her looking suggestively at him. They both laughed as he pulled up at the lights.

"I'm in need of something to take my mind off today," he muttered.

"Why? What's happened?"

"You'll know soon enough, but I don't want to talk about it tonight." Karen knew better than to press him about what he did for the Kurtis 'empire'. "I just want to have a good time, okay." He ran his eyes once more over the bare skin on display.

The lights changed and the driver behind made known his impatience with a blast of the horn. Don quickly pulled away and laughed. "See what you do to me?"

Karen put her hand behind his neck and gently massaged and he made noises of enjoyment at her touch. "That feels good, baby. That's just what I need."

"You're just using me to…" She was interrupted when his mobile phone rang. Her expression changed and she instantly snatched her hand away.

Don glanced across as he slipped the phone out of his pocket, looked at the caller name and couldn't help speaking it out loud with a certain amount of loathing in his tone. "Vince. What the hell does he want now?" he muttered to himself, picking up the call.

"Yeah," he answered abruptly.

"Don, get the car and meet me at the house in twenty." Without greeting or salutation, Vince hung up having issued his orders.

Don pulled the phone away from his ear and stared at it for a split second. The thought of leaving town for pastures new spontaneously crossed his mind again, but to do what? The money he made working for Vince had always been way above anything his education would ever command. He liked being connected with people that others took note of and was dazzled by Vince's father and the aura that surrounded him. It rubbed off on all those in the organisation and Don had always milked the 'power by association' for all it was worth.

There had been a notable change after the demise of old man Kurtis, but no one openly voiced their opinions. What the effect of the loss of Jack Cougar would be, he couldn't be sure, but he had a feeling it was not going to be good.

His momentary consideration of making a new start was swept away before it had even passed the embryonic state and turning to Karen he said, "Sorry babe. I'm going to have to skip dinner tonight…"

Dressed up ready for an evening out, her expression of disdain was at odds with her attire. She cut straight through the beginnings of Don's explanation.

"Vince Kurtis… Why do you keep company with that parasite?"

Don was used to Karen's explosive outbursts, but they usually took a little time to flare up to the point from which she now started.

"He's not a parasite, Karen," Don attempted to calm the situation.

"Well he manages to suck the life out of you. Both of us! He sucks the life out of this relationship," she shouted.

"What do you mean by that?" Don snapped, biting at the challenge she threw out.

"Phone calls! Every time we're out doing something, he sticks his nose in. It amazes me that he doesn't turn up in our bed when we're having sex."

"Don't be ridiculous, woman." Don yelled.

"Me ridiculous? Have you taken a look in the mirror lately?" Don glanced across, surprised by the ferocity of Karen's voice.

"Vince shouts and *you* go running. Yes sir, no sir…" She mocked him with the tone of her voice, stirring his anger to greater reaction.

Don pulled in sharply, prompting disapproving blasts on the horns of the following vehicles. "Why do you always have to make an issue out of this, Karen?"

She barely drew breath before retaliating. "Because he's always there in the middle of our lives. The only way we can manage to go out for dinner together is if we invite him so that he's not busy and wanting you to run errands."

"Don't be so bitchy."

"Bitchy?"

Don tried to take a more measured tone. "Every time I *need* to work…"

"It never happened when Mr Kurtis ran the show," Karen snapped. The intonation in her comment showed that she had some respect for Kurtis senior but despised Kurtis junior. She turned to look out of the window.

Don was smarting at the way she'd escalated the situation and spontaneously fought back. "If you don't like it maybe you should go." The moment the words left his mouth, he knew that he'd crossed the line.

"What do you mean, GO?" The fire in her eyes burned into Don and he could see the disgust that welled up in her. Karen flung the car door open. "You little shit. Five years of crap I've taken from you, acting the big man. You're nothing more than an insignificant fool." She got out of the car and turned to look back at him. "Run along, Don. Go do your 'errand-boy' thing for Vince," she yelled. "Perhaps I should find myself a real man."

Don turned away with a smirk on his face. He'd seen Karen go ballistic many times before and had learned to take little notice. The car door violently slammed shut jolting him from his smug indifference. He spun around to see where she'd gone, then jumped out of the car shouting after her.

"Karen, come on. Where the hell are you going to go dressed like that?" She took no notice as she walked away, drawing looks from a group of guys across the street; one of them wolf-whistled at her. "KAREN! Get back in the car, before you make a fool out of both of us," he ordered.

She turned around and made a hand gesture to show her response then continued in the direction she was going. The audience of guys cheered in appreciation of the show.

Don watched her for a few seconds, until he was certain that she had no intention of ending the drama. Cursing under his breath he slowly got back into the car and shut the door just as his phone went again. It was Vince.

"Where are you, Don?"

"I'll be there in a minute, alright!" He hung up before there was opportunity to say anything else. He'd about had his fill of Vince Kurtis for the day and wasn't particularly keen to see him again. He thumped his hand on the steering wheel in frustration, started the car and pulled away sharply causing the tyres to squeal in protest.

Ten minutes later he turned into the driveway entrance and punched a code into the security pad. The gates slowly opened allowing him to drive up to the house and stop outside the front door. Vince was out in a flash. He threw a bag on the back seat and got in the front.

"Where we going?" Don quizzed.

"Just drive. We're going to see a man about settling a score."

Don continued looking at Vince, his face was fixed like flint, his eyes cold and full of intent. He hesitated too long for Vince's liking and got the edge of his tongue.

"You want a picture or something? Just do what I pay you for and drive."

As usual Don held his tongue. He set the car in motion, but inside anger was brewing and thoughts of putting Mr Kurtis Junior in his place became the focus of his entertainment as they travelled.

Vince barked out occasional instructions, but it soon became apparent that they were heading out of town, so Don tried his question again.

"Where are we going, Vince?"

"Spelton"

"What! That must be a hundred and fifty miles."
"So?"
"I haven't got a change of clothes or nothing."
"So what?" Vince's tone showed his indifference. He fixed his stare on Don, making him feel uncomfortable as he drove.

There was very little conversation for the rest of the journey until they pulled into a motel for the night. If Vince cared that Don was not a happy man, he never once let on. Little did he understand his actions were working opposite to how he assumed. No one respects a bully and everyone rejoices when the tables are turned and he gets what's coming.

Don silently took the key handed to him by the receptionist and watched Vince head off to his room without a word. Just as Vince was about to turn the corner, he stopped and looked back.

"We leave at eight-thirty. We've got a meeting at ten. Find out where we can eat nearby." Without salutation Vince continued on his way leaving Don stood at the desk.

"Friendly guy." The man at the reception desk filled the comment with sarcasm.

"You don't know the half of it," Don responded as he continued to look along the walkway where Vince had disappeared.

The following morning, as they set out to get breakfast, Vince was decked out in his finest, but Don's clothes looked tired from the day before and the driving. It rubbed salt in the open wounds and the meal was taken in stony silence. Don's face showed no expression, but inside he was seething. The night had not been a comfortable one and his mind had constantly gone over recent events regarding Jack Cougar and Raif Bale. Although he hadn't known Raif that well, it was the shock of having been with him and Jack only hours before that disturbed him. Working for the Kurtis family had instilled a sense of invincibility that had suddenly collapsed with the demise of two colleagues.

When they finally left the diner, Vince gave directions to a bar in the centre of town. He had barely spoken two words to Don beyond what was absolutely necessary.

Arriving at the establishment, he instructed Don to follow him inside and watch his back in case there was any trouble. Don preferred the idea of a knife in the back, such was his mood that morning.

As they entered the building, Don instinctively touched the holster inside his jacket, just to reassure himself that his weapon was in place and ready.

Vince stood for a moment in the doorway to the dimly lit room and scanned the tables until his eyes fell on one that was occupied on the far side of the club. Turning to Don he said, "Follow me across, but wait a little distance from the table while I see to business."

The pair of them slowly moved across the floor, but as they approached the guy seated at the table, two men stepped forward to show themselves, having previously been hidden in the shadows. The way they positioned themselves gave no doubt they were something to do with the man at the table. Vince hesitated before continuing.

Don stopped a little way back from where Vince was heading, as instructed. One of the guys that had suddenly appeared moved close to him. The two made eye contact, but said nothing.

"Mind if I sit down?" Vince asked when he reached the table.

The seated man motioned with a hand for him to take a seat and continued to finish clearing the food from his plate. Vince waited, but became a little annoyed that the guy was intent on completing his meal rather than giving him his attention.

When he'd finally done, he wiped his mouth with a napkin, tossed it on the plate and pushed it across the table. He pulled a cigarette from a packet, lit it, and drew on the stick. He held his breath for a few moments then sent a stream of smoke powering upward to the ceiling.

His close shaved head and squinty eyes, which were fastened on Vince, gave him a mean look. Large in build, he looked like he'd been a man to reckon with physically, but the definition had softened with age. His jacket was well worn and slightly too small, as if it had been bought ten years earlier when he was smaller, less rotund.

The two men sat facing each other across the table taking the measure of one another. Vince was unsure if he was being given a cue to proceed. It appeared *he* was in no hurry to start the conversation, simply watching and taking frequent drags on his cigarette, burning it quickly toward the stub.

"I'm looking for someone," Vince broke the silence. "I understand you might be able to help me."

"Yeah?" The response didn't suggest any willingness to help.

Vince slid a paper across the table until it was laid out in front of the guy. He made no move to pick it up, but his eyes broke away from Vince for a few seconds to read the only lead Vince had to follow. The man looked back at Vince, but his features betrayed nothing. No flicker of indication whether this trip had been a waste of time crossed his poker-face expression.

"Do you know who this is?" Vince motioned to the paper in an attempt to prompt some kind of response.

The guy took a long drag on his cigarette, burning it almost to the chubby fingers that held it. His eyes narrowed, almost to the point that they were closed. "What if I do?"

"I want to get some information. Real name, address…"

"And who the hell are you?"

The man spat out a piece of tobacco from the cigarette. The manner of his question clearly displayed the fact that he cared nothing for who Vince *thought* he was. Vince was nothing to him.

"Just need a name and how I can find him," Vince repeated calmly.

"You know I was in the forces, right?" Vince gave a slight nod of acknowledgement. "Someone must've pointed you to me?"

"Yeah," Vince confirmed, but he was not about to disclose who.

"You think I sell out my own to…" the guy waved his hand dismissively, "God knows who?"

"Yeah," Vince was blunt.

The fire was instantly in the man's eyes at the flippant way Vince answered him, but his attempt to bring correction was immediately arrested as Vince placed a bundle of crisp, bound, one hundred dollar bills on the table. Their eyes met, but nothing further was said. Vince held an unflinching posture, but he noted the hesitation in his counterpart. He immediately placed another bundle alongside the first. The guy shifted ever so slightly in his seat and Vince took it as an indication that the wheels were almost in motion, but he waited a little longer before making another move. Placing a third bundle on the table without taking his eyes off the guy applied the pressure. There was a long pause as the two of them played the game to see who would give way first.

"That might buy you a name..." His comment was suspended as another bundle hit the tabletop.

CHAPTER 9

When the alarm on Beth's watch started it's piercing staccato bleeping, she jumped upright and took a few seconds before she realised she'd fallen asleep leaning on the desk. The computer screensaver was busy doing its job. She rubbed her eyes and stretched to wake herself, shut down the equipment, collected the paper from the printer, and went to the kitchen to make coffee.

As the kettle started to boil, she went to the bathroom and woke Will on the way. At Tia's room, Beth knocked and opened the door. Tia was already awake, propped up on pillows and staring at nothing in particular. She turned to look as Beth entered the room.

"Did you sleep at all?"

Tia shook her head. "I spent most of the night thinking about the trouble I've caused Will. I couldn't help wondering what would have happened if I'd run in the other direction. Perhaps he would have been blissfully unaware, getting ready to go to his garage this morning." Tia's face was downcast.

"And you might not have been here." Beth bit her lip at the possible double meaning her statement carried and could see that it hadn't escaped Tia's attention. "Sorry. You know what I really meant. You might not have been here, with us."

Tia smiled at her, grateful that she was thoughtful enough to correct such an innocent mistake. Beth turned to leave the room.

"Beth." Tia called her back. "I don't know what to say to you or Will. Anyone else would have turned me in or freaked at the situation. You've both been..." Tia shrugged her shoulders as she was momentarily lost for the right words, but Beth understood the message.

"Chin up kid. We need to get moving as soon as we can. There's coffee in the kitchen when you're ready." She smiled and Tia weakly reciprocated the gesture.

When Beth entered the kitchen, Will was already there with mug in hand, reading through the papers that she'd printed off. He glanced up at her then went straight back to reading. She let him carry on, having already spent some time the previous evening trying to make sense of the material.

As Tia came down the stairs to join them a few minutes later, Will deposited the papers in one of the kitchen drawers until he'd cleared with Beth what she wanted to do with them.

Boost was full of beans and happy at the early start, so Will took him out into the yard for a run around to release some energy. He fussed him with special tenderness, knowing that they would have to leave him behind in a little while and he wasn't sure when he would see his friend again. Beth noticed Will's behaviour and gave a sympathetic smile when their eyes met as he came through the back door with Boost in tow.

Within forty minutes they'd packed the car with the necessary things, having barely spoken more than a few words to each other. Each one was preoccupied with their own thoughts about what was to come.

Boost was getting excited at all the activity, expecting to be going on a journey. Will helplessly looked on as the dog danced around getting in everyone's way. Tia moved alongside Will and glanced up at him. His expression clearly displayed what he was feeling. She leant a little into his arm as a simple comfort, making Will turn to look at her. He smiled, but it barely covered the emotion of the moment.

Beth had grabbed a length of rope to use as a long lead for Boost and tied it to his collar. They locked the house, got into the car and headed down the drive onto the main road towards Mrs Drake's house. Will secured the note that Beth had prepared to Boost's collar as they neared their destination.

A few moments later the car drew to a stop fifty yards away from the house so that the engine noise wouldn't disturb anyone. Will was about to get out, but Beth stopped him. "Let me go." The tone of her voice was decisive and deliberately meant to make Will understand that she was not giving him a choice. The decision was already taken. Will was not in the mood to question Beth and knew she was only thinking of him.

He fussed Boost one more time, but the dog was much more interested in getting out of the car to see what adventure lay ahead. Will passed the lead over to Beth and Boost immediately followed her without hesitation. As he jumped over, Will patted him then he was gone into the darkness.

Tia and Will watched as Beth and Boost's silhouette moved along the road and turned down the driveway to the house. A few minutes later Beth was getting back into the car and swinging it round one-hundred-and-eighty degrees to head away from town on the main road.

A quiet sombre air hung in the vehicle for the next hour as they travelled, no one said anything. They all felt a little guilty about leaving one of their group behind, even though they all knew that it was for the best.

~

Officer Madeley was seated at his desk in the small police station that looked out onto the sleepy main street. Although it was late-afternoon, the heavy sky was forcing the light to fade earlier than normal. He was on duty for another two hours before he could get away and it couldn't come soon enough. Going out and about in the community was what he preferred to do, but there was always the necessary paperwork to keep him tied to his desk. When it mounted up, there was a day like the one he was having. Very dull. He caught himself sighing heavily again as he set another pile of files to one side.

When the phone rang he grabbed it immediately, hoping it would take him away from the tedium of the reports that had been requested by the area division office. An excuse, any excuse.

"Hello, Officer Madeley speaking. How can I help?"

"Oh, Officer Madeley, this is Mrs Drake." The familiar melodic tones of the old lady were a welcome distraction.

"Hello, Mrs Drake. How are you today?" Madeley's response was filled with genuine warmth for the much respected member of the community.

"I wondered if you could drop in to see me this afternoon?"

"Is there a problem, Mrs Drake?" His tone hinted slight concern. She was not one to make an unnecessary fuss.

"Oh, no, at least, I don't think so. I am a little worried about something. I just wanted to talk to you. I'm sure that it won't take longer than coffee and a slice of cake."

Madeley laughed at the enticement and, while it was welcome, he would have done just about anything for Mrs Drake. As would most people who knew her.

"Okay, I just need to finish up something, it'll take me about an hour, then I'll call out to see you before I go home. How does that sound?"

"Marvellous. I'll make sure the kettle is ready. Goodbye."

Madeley chuckled to himself again as he replaced the receiver. Mrs Drake seemed able to get whatever she wanted in a way that a kindly headmistress in a school would.

Shaking himself from his musings, he continued with the forms that were spread out on the desk until the last one was completed. He threw it into a file and involuntarily sighed as the cabinet drawer clicked shut.

Pushing the compiled reports into an envelope, he marked it for the internal mail and tossed it in the post bin while heading for the door. Grabbing his jacket from the coat hook near the exit, he sauntered out to the patrol car parked outside the front of the building.

The ride to Mrs Drake's was toward the sunset and the colours were particularly stunning as the beams of light started to break under the cloud base from the horizon. Knowing that his dull day was completed, his last call was to be more pleasure than business. A chat with such an interesting person always lifted Madeley's spirits. She was always up for some conversation, wanting to know what was going on in the town, the latest news, especially official news, and then he would be off home to relax.

He turned into the driveway and swung around in the turning circle at the front of the house. As he got out of the car a large golden dog came bounding across to receive the visitor. Mrs Drake was at the door, having seen him turn in from the road.

Boost made the most of the attention that Madeley gave him. "Didn't I see this dog at Beth Jackson's house last night?" he queried as he reached the steps to the porch.

"Oh, you visited Beth yesterday? Come in Officer Madeley," Mrs Drake instructed as he reached the door. She led the way to the kitchen and he followed behind enjoying Boost's attention.

"Lovely temperament these dogs. You looking after him for long?"

"Take a seat."

Mrs Drake poured the coffee and set it down in front of Madeley, followed by a slice of cake. He smiled as it appeared and thanked her for her generosity.

"I'll have to come again," he joked.

"It's regarding the dog that I called you."

"Oh?" He glanced across the table at her and noticed her concerned face.

"He was on the doorstep this morning when I got up."

"He escaped again did he?" Madeley laughed. "He seems to be a bit of an escape artist this one." He glanced down at the dog who was giving him full attention in the hope of getting some reward.

"Whatever do you mean?" Mrs Drake queried.

"Beth said she'd found him wandering about when she was out trying that jeep she's building for the event that's coming up. Said she hadn't got around to reporting it."

"I don't understand." The questioning tone in Mrs Drake's voice caused Madeley to look at her.

"He must have got away from his owner, or got lost somehow," Madeley tried to explain.

Mrs Drake smiled and stroked Boost as he put his chin on her lap, his begging eyes showing he was aware of the delicacies on offer.

"I'm not sure we understand each other properly." The voice of a schoolmistress taking control in order to bring clarity to her pupil captured Madeley's full attention. "I found Boost on the porch this morning. He wasn't wandering free, he was tethered to the railings and had a note attached to his collar."

"A note?" Madeley was curious.

Mrs Drake pulled an envelope from her pocket and passed it across. He took it and pulled the notepaper out. Quickly scanning it, his half-hearted glance suddenly became total focus as he read it more carefully then looked up at Mrs Drake.

"When Beth says that she needed me to look after Boost for a little while, I thought she was perhaps going to an appointment, or to town for something. I didn't expect her to be gone so long."

"Mrs Drake, did you say the dog's name is Boost?" The mention of his name brought the dog alongside Madeley as he expected to get a morsel of something nice."

"Why yes."

Madeley was immediately suspicious.

"You say you didn't see Beth leave?"

"No... I'm a little worried about her. That's why I called you this afternoon."

"Did Beth name the stray?"

"Stray?" Mrs Drake looked surprised. "Why do you keep talking about a stray?"

"You're saying that he isn't?"

Mrs Drake sighed as if teaching a pupil that was slow to catch on.

"Boost is owned by a friend of Beth's. He's just staying with her for a little while, I believe. The dog I mean."

"Did Beth tell you that?"

"Sure. She came over yesterday."

"Did you, by any chance, meet Beth's friend?"

"No. She just came to see me as she usually does, but Boost came with her."

"You'll have to excuse me, Mrs Drake. I'm going to Beth's place to see what's going on."

Madeley hurriedly got up from his seat and was out of the door, leaving part of the cake still on the plate. Mrs Drake was slightly alarmed at the quick exit and went to look out of the window as the patrol car speedily pulled away and headed out onto the main road in the direction of Beth's place.

As Officer Madeley turned into the drive of Beth Jackson's house, he was immediately struck by the fact that there were no lights on in the building. It was just after seven and the dark was starting to settle.

He slowly rolled the patrol car around the back of the building, intently checking everywhere for signs of life. The vehicle that had been there the day before was gone and the only light was from the headlamps of his patrol vehicle. Away from the town there was no artificial light and the encroaching night was unabated by the moon, making the yard particularly eerie.

Madeley drew the car to a stop and flicked off the switch for the headlights. He sat for a few moments while his eyes became accustomed to the dark.

Scanning all around, there was no sign of movement. The house and outbuildings were in complete darkness. He took a torch out of the glove box and checked that it worked, then stepped out of the vehicle. Unnerved by the situation, an instinct of self-defence and his long experience made him wary. The holster securing strap for his gun made a distinct click as he released it. He touched the handle of the weapon to reassure himself it was ready for use.

The beam from the torch pierced the darkness creating a pool of light that ran over the buildings as he rotated around, scanning the area for anything unusual.

Focusing on the rear door, he went up the porch steps, turned the handle and rattled it. It was securely locked. He looked through a couple of windows, but could see nothing amiss inside. He made his way around the building, checking through the windows, until he reached the front door which was locked as well.

Heading back to the rear of the property again, having circled the building, Madeley began to check the outbuildings one by one. A couple of them were open, but were just storage and workshop facilities. The third building was obviously housing chickens. The furthest one had both front and rear doors to access it. The front doors were unlocked and again it was full of various items, mostly mechanical equipment. There was a dividing wall that separated the rear section, so Madeley went around to the back, but found the doors locked. The building was quite rickety so he managed to prise the doors apart enough to shine a beam of light into the space. It was difficult to see at first, but once he'd got the knack of holding the doors apart and the torch in position, it became obvious that the building housed a vehicle. It was definitely a pick-up; a blue pick-up.

Madeley immediately headed back to the patrol car and radioed the station, getting a response from Dave Simmons who had just come on duty.

"Dave, it's Bill Madeley. I'm out at Beth Jackson's house. Could you do a check on that vehicle that's been flagged up to us? The one owned by William Harris. Just find the registration and colour. Over."

The radio crackled. "Will do. Stand by. Over."

Madeley continued to sweep the torch around from his position by the car. The darkness heightened his hearing and he instantly flashed the beam to each minute but amplified sound.

Thirty seconds later the radio burst into life, "Bill this is Dave, do you read? Over."

"Go ahead Dave. Over."

The registration number came over the airwaves and Dave confirmed the colour of the wanted vehicle. "The pick-up is blue, repeat, blue. Over."

Putting Simmons on standby, Madeley fetched a crowbar from the nearby workshop and levered off the padlock securing the building. As the doors swung open, he focused his torch on the partly covered vehicle that looked like it had been deliberately put there to hide it. He quickly looked through the windows into the cab then ran to the patrol car, pulling his gun from its holster as he did.

"Dave, do you copy. Over."

"Go ahead, Bill. Over."

"Call in that we have found William Harris's blue pick-up hidden in an outbuilding at Beth Jackson's place. Let me know what they want me to do… and find out if he had a dog. Over."

"Just confirm that. Did you say, a dog? Over."

"Affirmative."

"Okay Bill, standby."

The darkness seemed more eerie than it had a few moments before. The man wanted for a double murder was, or had been in the vicinity. Madeley began to wonder whether he was here when he'd called the previous day. Beth must have been lying about not having seen him. If that dog belongs to Harris, then he may well have been in the house at the time.

The chill of the evening air gave Madeley a shiver, or perhaps it was the thought of the crime that had been committed by the wanted man. Either way, the wait for a response seemed to drag, even though it was only a matter of minutes.

"Bill, this is Dave. Do you receive? Over."

"Go ahead."

"The instructions given are as follows. You are to stay at the scene until the arrival of the investigating squad. No one, repeat, no one is authorised to enter the building. I repeat, you are not to enter the building. Over."

"Who on earth gave those orders?" Madeley forgot the protocol in his attempt to find out who was running the show, but quickly corrected himself, "Over."

"Headquarters patched me direct to the area concerned. They gave no details, but made it clear that it would be our heads on the block if the orders were violated in any way, Bill. Over."

"I suggest you get yourself out here, Dave. If we've got to sit this out, I don't want to be here on my own in case someone comes back and there's trouble. Who knows how long this is going to take. Bring some coffee with you. Over."

"Okay. Out."

Madeley jumped into the patrol car and swung around to head back down the drive. He manoeuvred the vehicle into position on the road so that he could monitor the situation and was put at ease a little when Officer Dave Simmons's patrol car finally pulled up behind.

The two of them sat in one vehicle, watching and speculating about what was happening, while waiting for the arrival of the mysterious 'authorities' in control.

It was almost nine-forty-five by the time a convoy of official-looking vehicles came tearing along the road and turned into the drive. Two swept immediately around to the rear of the building, the other came to a stop at the front. At least ten men immediately piled out in various directions around the house.

"Oh heck," moaned Madeley.

"What's wrong?"

"You know who we've got here, Dave?" Simmons raised an eyebrow to prompt the answer. "It's the *'we've got it covered brigade'*."

Dave snorted at the comment. They both got out of the patrol car from which they had been observing the house as two of the newly arrived men approached.

"Madeley?" The question was blunt, direct and rude.

Bill acknowledged that he was the man they wanted, but there was no reciprocal introduction. The lead guy put himself firmly and uncomfortably in Madeley's personal space. He was a good two inches taller than Madeley and was built like a weightlifter. The broad shoulders and thick-set neck being emphasised by the suit and tie he wore. Being so close to Madeley meant he had to look down at him like an intimidating, brutish headmaster about to severely reprimand a child.

"You first on the scene?"

The sharp tone and abrupt delivery added to the air of uncertainty about the man.

"Yes." Madeley quickly glanced across at Dave Simmons on the other side of the patrol car. The light that spilled from the open door of the vehicle threw shadows on the inquisitor's face, making him look very menacing as he waited without giving any response or acknowledgment.

In the discomfort of the withering stare that held fast on Madeley, he was desperate to break the impasse and reconfirmed his answer with an acknowledgement of some kind of rank.

"Yes, sir."

A deliberate hesitation before continuing, inferred the lack of recognition of authority from Madeley was totally unacceptable behaviour.

"When?" The guy continued to bear down on Madeley.

"I got here about seven o'clock... sir."

"Why?"

Madeley told him about Mrs Drake and how he'd become suspicious after reading the note.

"When I got here, I checked around and thought I could see a vehicle locked away in the furthest building so I radioed Dave... Officer Simmons, to find out the registration and colour of the vehicle that was being searched for. I broke into the outbuilding to confirm that it was the pick-up in question then radioed in for instructions."

The big guy edged a fraction closer to Madeley and lowered his voice to a deep, intimidating growl. "Weren't you sent out here yesterday to check whether Ms Jackson had been in contact with her old friend William Harris?"

Madeley shifted uncomfortably at the question, inching a little way back, but his interrogator was having none of it and moved inch for inch to maintain the uncomfortable distance between them. The inflection in the question suggested that there was a measure of incompetence on Madeley's part.

"Yes... sir." Simmons noticed the disdain in Madeley's response. "I came out here early evening yesterday."

Again that disconcerting hesitation before the next question had Madeley squirming.

"What *exactly* happened when you came here, Officer Madeley?"

A click preceded a flashlight beam that suddenly lit Madeley's face. He could feel the beads of sweat forming on his forehead and his temperature rising, defying the cold night air. He hesitated before answering, momentarily taken aback by the dazzling light.

"Well?"

The guy demanded an explanation. He stooped a little so that their faces were almost at the same height, almost touching nose to nose.

"I... I came and..."

"Did you see Ms Jackson?" The abrupt question cut across Madeley's first few words.

"Yes." The pause was painful until Madeley corrected himself. "Sir."

"AND?" The voice was raised, like the tactic of an army officer trying to unsettle a cadet and Madeley jumped at the sudden aggressive volume. He could feel a spot of spittle hit his face as the man barked at him.

"She said she hadn't heard from Harris. There was a dog here, but she told me that it was a stray she'd picked up and neglected to report. I checked the dog's collar, but there was no tag." The words poured from Madeley as he tried to appease his inquisitor with information.

"Did you check the house as you were instructed?" The inevitable question completely steamrolled over Madeley's explanation with its contemptuous tone. "I believe you *were* instructed to check the house? Informally that is."

"I checked through the downstairs."

The guy hovered over Madeley boring holes into him with his eyes.

"And upstairs?"

Madeley swallowed and in the quiet they all heard it. "No, sir," he answered. The long pause before a response came was painfully uncomfortable, but when it did Madeley found little relief in it.

"No, sir. I didn't do my job properly... *sir*." The guy mocked Madeley as he turned away and began walking toward the house. The other men that came with him were already inside the property.

"What do you want us to do, sir?" Madeley shouted after him, trying to resist the huge temptation to use the same mocking tone.

"Do what the hell you like, *Officer Madeley*. We don't need incompetent help here. We've got this covered."

Dave looked across the roof of the car. "Pricks."

"My sentiment exactly, Dave. Who do they think they are?" Simmons shrugged in response, but Madeley missed it as he watched his interrogator walk toward Beth's house. "You might as well get back to the station, Dave. I'm going to hang out here for a little while."

"You sure?"

"Yeah. I don't like jerks like them. They seem to think the law is for everyone else and they're above it. I'm not going to do anything. Just watch."

"Okay. If you're sure." Dave walked to his patrol car, parked behind Madeley's.

The road lit up as Dave started the vehicle, flicked on the lights and did a one-eighty to head back to town. Madeley stood for a few minutes then slumped into the seat of his car to watch the unfolding events.

CHAPTER 10

Once daylight had taken hold, Will was very conscious about being seen and when they passed through any built-up areas he instinctively shielded his face from any passers-by. The news coverage about the double murders rumbled on in the media. At one point, Beth, who was doing the driving, slammed the off switch of the radio, just to silence the continually repetitive coverage. Never once was there any mention of Tia and after the previous evening's discussion, they were all well aware of the fact.

When they reached the outskirts of the city where Beth knew they would find Lester, she pulled over at an internet café to log into her email and check for messages. There was one, but it simply gave a bizarre sequence of questions. Tia was seated with her and saw the list as it came up on the screen.

"What does that mean, Beth?"

"To tell you the truth, I'm not sure at the moment."

Beth hit the print button and grabbed the copy to check it was all there, then deleted the email from her account. She and Tia returned to the car where Will was concealing himself. He was a little uncomfortable sat in a parked vehicle on a fairly busy street, but they had to make contact with Lester to find out exactly where he was.

"Anything?" Will impatiently asked, as the girls got into the vehicle.

"Yeah." Beth passed the paper over her shoulder for Will to read.

He scanned it for a few moments and laughed a couple of times as he read. "I think he does this kind of thing deliberately, just to wind people up, or to show that he's got nothing better to do but play on his computer all day."

"What is it?" Tia asked, still curious to know what the techno-junkie could be up to.

"It's Lester's idea of a joke I think," Will answered.

"Will, I don't think it's a joke." Beth's tone was serious. "There's no greeting or end to that message, that's definitely not like him. If Lester was just joking around he'd make sure you knew that's what he was up to. You know enough about him to know he loves to milk any prank."

"What do *you* think it's about then?"

"I don't know, but those questions are focused on personal things that no one else would know. Perhaps if we answer them it will give us a clue."

"O-k-a-y." The tone of Will's answer showed he was not impressed.

He rolled his eyes at Tia who was turned sideways in her seat so that she could see him, but Beth caught his reaction in the rear-view mirror and spun around to face him.

"*Will*," she chastised, "We *need* his help right now, so don't get annoyed just because you think he's lost it. I know you and Lester grate against each other, but he's been a real friend to me over the years." Suddenly feeling conscious about what she'd just said, she immediately added, "As have you. Can't you just go along with this until we have sorted things out?"

Will held up his hands in surrender and Beth turned back to face the windscreen, placing her hands on the steering wheel.

Someone tapped on the window next to Beth making the three of them jump. Will instinctively shielded his face from view. Beth let the window down a fraction so she could hear what the man was saying.

"Miss, I think you left this in the café." He held up a jacket for her to see.

"No. It's not mine."

The man was a little more insistent. "But it was on the chair where you were sitting."

"I said, it's not mine, okay," she snapped.

The man pulled back a little, shocked that his good deed was treated with such rudeness, but Beth started the car and sharply pulled away, yelling back. "You think I don't know if it's my jacket?"

As the car joined the stream of traffic, Beth caught Will looking at her in the mirror. She sheepishly smiled. "I shouldn't have done that should I?"

Will pulled a face and shrugged suggesting he was as wound up as Beth.

"Sorry." She glanced across at Tia who smiled weakly.

"I can make out some of the things on this list," Will focused attention on the questions again, "but the others are a mystery to me. The last question," he began, *"'What was the present your Gran had for her golden wedding anniversary?'* that was a clock. Right?"

Beth glanced in the mirror to see Will looking back at her. He flashed an apologetic smile. "Yeah, it was a clock," she answered, their eyes locked again for a few seconds.

Tia looked from Beth to Will trying to weigh-up the situation and understand the friction that had just taken place between her travelling companions.

"Got a pen?" Will asked, moving on.

Beth pointed to the glove box and Tia jumped to action retrieving what was required. She passed it to Will, who scribbled down the answer.

"Question two is, *'Where Uncle Henry worked in the fifties?'* Wasn't that Henry Chiltern?"

Beth nodded. "Must be."

"Didn't he work on that industrial site out west somewhere?"

"Yeah, he was the shunt-train driver that shifted materials around the complex. Hesketh Industries, I think. What's question one, Will?" she asked, as he jotted down the last answer.

"*'The subject of Keltern's work?'* What the hell does that mean? The question doesn't even make sense to me." Will's expression showed a certain amount of frustration and he was just about to curse Lester again when he noticed Beth was looking at him in the rear-view mirror.

"Keltern," she began, showing irritation in her tone of voice, "was the butcher's shop in Lester's home town."

Will paused for a moment watching Beth in the mirror as she drove.

"How do you know that?" he quizzed.

"He took me there when I went to stay at his mother's house a couple of years ago."

"Lester took you to see a *butcher's shop* when you went to *visit* him? He sure knows how to show a girl a good time." A smirk crept across Will's face. Tia couldn't restrain herself and laughed at Will's jokey comment.

"You're not doing so bad yourself," Beth shot back while nodding in Tia's direction. Her acid comment hit Will like a slap in the face. "I'm beginning to wonder if you understand how serious this situation is. I nearly replied to that email, but something made me think better of it. If Lester's gone to the trouble of doing this, he must have some damn good reason. The police came to visit me remember? Perhaps he's had a visit too and is suspicious about what's going on. So cut the crap Will and help me figure out what Lester's doing with this."

The atmosphere in the car was uncomfortable and Tia squirmed in her seat as she sensed the tension. Will, realising that it was affecting Beth more than he'd thought, and feeling well chastised, put his hand on her shoulder.

"Beth, I'm sorry. I didn't mean…"

A patrol car swung around the corner twenty yards down the road from them and Will ducked down out of sight. The moment seemed to bring some gravity to the situation.

Beth pulled off the main road into a quieter side street, continuing until she came to a derelict lot that had a place to tuck the car out of sight. As the car came to a stop, Beth let out a sigh and turned her attention to the task in hand.

"The answer to the first question is 'butcher', yes?" Will asked, restarting the exercise at the signal of the parking brake being applied.

Beth shrugged. "I guess so."

"The second is Hesketh Industries."

There was a pause before Beth confirmed. "No. Wait a minute. Uncle Henry used to call the place he worked Hesketh Station; because of the trains. That's what he told us when we were kids."

Will made a correction to the paper and immediately went to the next question. "Three, '*Your neighbours with the swimming pool?*'"

"That was the Baker family," Beth answered.

"How does he know that?"

"You know what Lester's like," she shrugged her shoulders. "He remembers *everything*. I guess it was just stuff that we've talked about through the years. What's next?"

"Okay. Four, '*The place where you always told me you would buy a house if you came into money?*'"

Beth laughed as the question triggered fond memories that momentarily lifted her from the immediate situation.

"The Avenue." Beth and Will blurted out the answer at the same time. Tia was bemused by their performance and the questioning look prompted Beth to fill her in on the detail.

"It's the place where the rich people live in my home town. *Very* beautiful."

Will snorted at the thought of Beth living in such a neighbourhood. "Don't think they would appreciate a grease monkey and scrap yard in the area though."

Beth laughed. "Guess not."

Will scribbled the answer down. "One more. '*The first time you told me that you would drink me under the table. You still think I gave up at how many shots? (I still think you're wrong.)*'"

"Nine," Beth blurted out through her laughter. "Lester you jerk. Just admit it, I won," she muttered to herself. Looking up she found both Will and Tia staring at her. "Private joke." She shrugged. "Read out what we've got."

Will scribbled the answer, then went through from first to last. "A butcher, Hesketh station, The Baker family, The Avenue, Nine, A clock."

Beth turned around in her seat so that she and Tia were facing each other and could see Will. He looked up from the paper to see them concentrating on what he was saying, but got no response.

"Does that make any sense to you?" he asked.

"Read it again," Tia instructed. Will duly complied without complaint then looked at her and waited. "The last two answers read like a time. *'Nine o'clock',*" she offered.

Will looked back at the paper for a moment, shrugged and nodded in agreement. "Yes, I guess so. How about three and four? Wait!" The girls fixed on Will as he hurriedly scribbled on the paper. "Look." He blurted out, turning it so that they could both see. "Not *'The Baker Family'*, but *'Bakers'* and just *'Avenue'*. *'Bakers Avenue, nine o'clock'*. *'Hesketh station, Bakers Avenue, Nine o'clock.'* The first part is the bit that doesn't make sense. *'A butcher'*"

"Read the first question again, Will," Beth ordered.

"The subject of Keltern's work?"

Beth repeated after him. "The *subject* of his work. We're giving his job description. The subject was meat. *'Meet at Hesketh Station on Bakers Avenue at Nine o'clock'*. We need to find a street map. I'll walk along the road a little, I'm sure there was a local store we passed on the way here."

Beth was out of the car before there was any further discussion about the subject, leaving Tia and Will alone.

After a few moments she looked at Will, catching his gaze. "Sorry."

"For what?"

"For everything."

Will smiled. "I haven't had this much fun in ages."

"Don't let Beth hear you say that. She'd kill you."

Will nodded, agreeing. "She would," he sighed. "She certainly would." The silence returned until it was interrupted by Will. "But she's great though, don't you think?"

"Yes." Tia positively confirmed Will's opinion of his friend. "I like her a lot."

"You know," Will smiled at Tia, trying to look confident that what he was about to suggest would happen, "one day we'll sit at a nice café having a drink and laughing about this whole absurd situation."

Tia hesitated before answering as she looked into Will's eyes. "I would like that very much. Very much indeed," she said, but her voice was filled with desperate hope rather than the confidence Will had tried to impart.

He was caught off guard by Tia's answer and looked at her, trying to weigh-up the meaning in it, but she turned away to look out of the window, avoiding his gaze.

Suddenly Beth burst back into the car, destroying the moment and launching into her explanation about how she got the map and what she'd found out.

"There's no Hesketh Station, but there is a Bakers Avenue and there is a station on it."

She suddenly became aware that there was something amiss in the car and turned to look at Will who gave the impression that he felt awkward. She looked at Tia who was still turned toward the passenger door window. Softening her tone she asked, "You okay, Tia?"

She nodded in response, but said nothing. She continued to look out of the window away from them. Beth put her arm around Tia's shoulder and she allowed Beth to pull her close while they all sat in the silence. It was a couple of minutes before anybody said anything.

Finally, Tia stirred in her seat pre-empting her desire to say something. "What would I have done without you two?" she whispered.

Lifting away from Beth, she turned to face her and Will. Her face was flushed from the emotion of the moment. She glanced back and forth between them a couple of times, but her eyes quickly dropped back to staring at the seat.

Beth rubbed her arm to give some comfort and Tia tried to smile in response, but the burden of the situation was too much to maintain an expression that was so opposite to what she felt inside. No one said anything. They knew that they were in it together, whether by direct involvement or association, whatever happened. The chess pieces had been laid out and it was getting close to the time for their next move.

The day dragged slowly and they each tried to catch up on lost sleep caused by the early morning, but it wasn't very comfortable in the vehicle and the nagging thoughts about their circumstances were always present.

Will got out to stretch himself a couple of times, but thought it best not to go far. His frustrations were visible in his body language, though he tried to cover it for the sake of the others.

As darkness began to descend, it brought with it a kind of comfort that pushed out the vulnerability of exposure in the daylight. The night offered the opportunity to go about their 'business' in a less noticeable way and the next step was to get to their rendezvous point with Lester. The fact that he'd gone to the trouble of hiding the time and place behind such personal answers unique to Beth put them all on high alert. As Beth had continued to point out, he wouldn't have done it without good reason.

They'd been parked off the beaten track for a few hours before the darkness started to take hold. At just before eight it was time to move on, so they set off in the direction of Bakers Avenue, several miles from their current position.

With Will navigating and Tia keeping lookout, Beth followed the directions given from the backseat.

"We're coming up on Trellis Road on the right," Beth clarified.

"A few hundred yards down we pass the leisure centre, then it's second left," Will responded.

As they turned into Bakers Avenue, Tia pointed out, "There, the station's just on the left. She glanced at the clock in the car. "Ten minutes to nine. What do we do next?"

Beth slowed the car as they passed the station then sped up again. "I'm going to put the car a little way down the road. Tia, you get in the back with Will and I'll walk over to the station to see if I can find Lester." No one questioned Beth's judgement, but simply nodded in agreement.

Once the car was parked, Beth jumped out as if she was itching to find out what Lester was up to. She turned back to look at Will. "Don't go anywhere now, will you?" she said. The statement was punctuated by the car door slamming shut and Will muttering about Beth's humour. Tia moved to the back seat where she and Will sat in silence, waiting.

Beth ran across the road to the functional, drab bus-terminal building. There were few people about, except for a recently emptying coach that was issuing the luggage to disembarking passengers.

The area where the buses stopped was lit in an orange glow from several streetlights. An occasional gloomy spot was created underneath a few dysfunctional lamps. The walkway was lined with a row of shelters stretched out along the edge of the open space, offering a little protection to the travelling public from any inclement weather. One of them gave refuge for the night to a homeless man, who was busy organising his meagre belongings around the temporary accommodation.

Beth looked along the paved section which was enclosed by walls decorated with the work of illusive street artists that are the bane of officialdom's life. Apart from the final sounds of dispersing people leaving the station, towing luggage behind them, the place was quiet and empty. She glanced at her watch. Five minutes to nine.

Tucking herself away from view in a poorly lit area, she waited the remaining time away. The sound of footsteps approaching put her on edge, but it was just someone in a hurry to get somewhere. She watched as the man passed by, head down and determined, and wondered where he was heading to or coming from.

The cool air caused her breath to illuminate in a misty cloud under the harsh lighting. She was momentarily lost in a silly game of trying to make shapes as she breathed out.

Suddenly aware that someone was standing nearby, too close for comfort, she snapped her head sideways to see who it was and was confronted with a fleeting glance of a coloured man's face, partially hidden beneath a brimmed hat. The guise wasn't enough for her to miss the narrow jaw-line and slightly pointed nose of Lester's handsome face.

She would normally have given a boisterous welcome to a friend that she hadn't seen for such a long time, but instinct and circumstance restrained her response. Lester was clearly keen to monitor everything around them and, taking her arm, he moved them both further into the shadows.

"How did you get here, Beth?" he whispered as he leaned in close. His slim build was hidden by the long coat he wore and his handsome dark face that was nearly always filled with joviality was set in a deadly serious expression.

"Nice to see you too, Lester," Beth answered, a little churlishly.

"There'll be time for that later."

The emphasised seriousness in the voice of one of the most jocular men she had ever known immediately corrected her and she answered the question.

"By car. It's just over the road, a little way down one of the side streets."

"Your own or hired?"

"Mine."

"We need to stash it somewhere. It's always the car that gives you away. If it's yours and it's seen, they'll know you've been to the area. There's a place nearby where we can leave it. We'll walk back to my apartment from there."

Lester urged Beth to lead the way, which she did without question, but before they crossed the open road he took a good look in every direction.

As they neared the parked vehicle, he was so focused on everything around them that he didn't even look to see if the car was occupied, he just went for the passenger door and got in at the same time as Beth on the driver's side.

Glancing out of the passenger door window, the windscreen and then over Beth through the driver's window, Lester turned to look out of the rear window and was confronted with two figures in the back seat, sat in the darkness.

"Good god!" he shouted, lurching away from Will and Tia.

"Long time no see, Lester." Will's tone showed that he'd enjoyed scaring the life out of his 'friend'.

"BETH, ARE YOU OUT OF YOUR MIND?" he yelled, completely forgetting his attempts to conceal their presence with stealth. "THIS GUY'S WANTED FOR DOUBLE MURDER!"

Beth slammed her hand over his mouth and held it there against his initial struggles, totally shocking Lester into silence as he pressed back against the car door. His wide eyes flicked between the three of them as he tried to make sense of the situation.

"Keep your mouth shut... and listen," Beth commanded forcefully. "We need your help. What you've heard is not the truth, but we need to get some information, anything that will help us find out why Will is being set up for a fall. Do you understand what I am saying?"

Lester was about to say something when Beth immediately cut him off by reasserting pressure to the hand that covered his mouth. He locked eyes with her and seeing the seriousness they conveyed he just nodded to show he understood.

"You said the car was a liability," Beth slowly lifted her hand away from his mouth. "Where do we stash it?" She slid back into position, turned the key to start the engine then looked at Lester expecting an answer.

"What the hell are you getting me into?" Beth's look made him change his tack. "Down the road, take the first left and drive to the end."

The car pulled away sharply, causing a tyre to squeal in protest. Lester turned and looked directly at Will and the antagonism between them surfaced immediately.

"White man Will means trouble," Lester goaded him.

"I've just come to see my black brother," Will retorted.

Beth coughed deliberately and the two guys took note. Suddenly aware that Tia was closely watching them both, Lester caught her eye and smiled, but when his gaze fell back on Will, the grin immediately disappeared.

Reaching the end of the road as instructed, Lester turned to face forward and pointed to a deserted piece of ground that had a number of derelict warehouses on it.

"I'll open the gate and close it behind you. Go across to the far side then loop around the back of the last building." Lester jumped out and swung the rusting barrier open, allowing the car to pass.

Beth followed the directions given then waited for Lester to arrive. A few moments later he pulled at the sliding door to the warehouse and waved the car into the cavernous space, indicating that Beth should stow it near the side wall, beneath high level windows, so that it wouldn't be easily seen by someone trying to look in.

Once safely parked, they all got out and retrieved their bags. Lester was standing at the door waiting for them to join him. As they walked towards the exit, their footsteps echoed eerily in the empty building.

With everyone outside, Lester slid the door back in place making an uncomfortably loud bang as it hit home. Taking a padlock from his bag, he secured the building, then turned to face the three of them. Even in the low light it was obvious from his expression that he was not happy with the situation.

"Will someone tell me what the hell is going on?"

"I'm sorry Lester," Beth apologised. "I guess you were only expecting me?"

"You're damn right girl. I thought you might have wanted to see me because of the news reports about Will. I didn't expect you to have him... and his friend in tow." Lester was considerably agitated, but Will and Beth both knew he had a habit of getting excited, even in the most mundane of circumstances.

"Lester, I wouldn't have come, but Beth thought it was the best option for us to find out what we are dealing with."

"It's her fault then is it Will? She's the reason that you're wanted for a double murder I suppose?" Lester spat his words out in anger and pushed Will away to create some distance between them. He was a small man and his aggressive move was a brave one against someone much bigger, but he was definitely wound-up and ready for confrontation. "It's always someone else's fault with you, Will. Always!"

Will deliberately took a step back to try to diffuse the situation, but Lester hadn't finished. "It's always the same with the brawn of the outfit. Throw a punch, pull a gun, but now suddenly you need my help? Why the hell should *I* help *you*? Especially after that stunt you pulled."

"God damn it! Not that again?" Will's hackles were immediately up. "Can't you just let it go, Lester? For god's sake that was almost ten years ago." He turned his attention to Beth as if blanking out Lester's presence. "I knew it was a mistake to come here. I knew it would turn out the same as always." Will slammed his fist against the corrugated iron door in frustration and the sound echoed around the external and internal spaces.

"STOP IT. BOTH OF YOU!" There was fire in Beth's eyes and the other three jumped at the piercing voice that issued the command. "*Lester*, if you feel you can't help us then say the word and we'll be on our way."

Beth stared intently at him and let the question sink in. Lester looked from face to face, pausing to read the expression of each, before his gaze finally settled on Beth again. They waited in anticipation of his response and, finally, he explained what had been happening.

"I've had a visit from the authorities asking if I've had any contact with Will. I didn't lie," he immediately made it clear. "I hadn't *had* any contact at that point, but they asked me to let them know immediately if you tried to get in touch." Lester glanced at Will. "I didn't tell them that I'd had an email from you Beth. How was I supposed to know that you'd bring *him* with you? They're obviously suspicious, or just hopeful that Will is going to show up here at some point. I saw no reason to prompt their curiosity by letting them know you were coming." He threw a withering look at Will. "It's a good job I was cautious."

Lester hesitated as he looked at Tia. In the heated discussion with Beth and Will he'd neglected to ask who she was or what she was doing there with them. He became aware that the others were waiting for him to finish what he was saying, and breaking off looking at Tia, he continued.

"There's a couple of guys parked outside of my apartment at this moment. They're supposedly tracking my movements." Lester laughed. The hostility in his voice had suddenly vanished. "I went to the local shop just so that I could check. They were there when I came out, but I pretended not to notice."

Will was slightly alarmed and without thought asked the question that was begging to be answered. "Did they follow you when you came here to meet us?"

A condescending look flashed across Lester's face. "No..." Lester dragged out his mocking response, annoyed that Will thought he might be so stupid as to allow himself to be followed when he didn't want to be. Will glanced at Beth and seeing the glaring expression on her face, held his hand up as an apology for the suggestion in his question.

Lester unbuttoned his coat and pulled a small black device from his pocket. Flicking a switch, he checked an image which immediately appeared on a small screen.

"There they are," he snorted in derision. He turned it so they could all see what it showed. "All tucked up in their car, thinking they're doing a great job monitoring my movements. It's amazing how stupid some of these people can be. Used to see it all the time when I was in surveillance. Some people have no idea what that means. A mini camera, so I can watch them and a couple of timers to switch the lights on and off to make out I'm at home and they think they've got it covered."

He laughed as he indulged in his genius, completely lost in his own little techno-world. Beth nudged him as a reminder that they were still waiting for some confirmation that he would help.

Lester looked up at the small audience gathered around him and hesitated for a moment. "Ahh. Okay folks. After me."

He waved the party to follow and immediately set off across the scrub ground to the gate they'd just driven through.

"I guess he's in," Will muttered and then added an insult, "Arrogant bastard." Beth landed a sharp punch to his upper arm and threw daggers with her eyes, before turning to follow Lester.

Pausing at the boundary, Lester waited for the others to close the gap, then went out through the gate. Setting off down a track that bordered the industrial area, he led them along dingy alleyways and back lanes until they suddenly came out into a street of ugly apartment blocks that had seen better days.

The darkness and limited street-lighting threw ominous shadows across the dreary entrances, giving an unwelcoming feeling, like an uncaring institutional building from the past. A gothic aura had enveloped the austere landscape, squeezing out what little colour the daylight might have offered.

Lester checked for signs of life before moving out into the open public space. A man and woman walked away from them along the road about fifty yards further down. Their body language clearly showed the friction that existed between them, each plotting a lonely path separated from one another by an invisible chasm. Occasionally the sound of raised voices shooting comments back and forth echoed from the hard surfaces that lined the street. In the opposite direction a man walked his dog at an unnatural pace, as if trying to get to somewhere he thought was safe.

The group trailed along the road for a couple of hundred yards, following the edge of identical rundown apartments. Finally, Lester crossed the road and aimed for a couple of doorways opposite. The building was about four stories high with the character of a prison block. It was a concrete cube linked to equally ugly buildings either side, each rising like featureless monuments of uninspiring architecture.

Instead of heading up one set of steps to either of the entrances, Lester stepped into a rectangular recess between the two that was less than three feet wide and totally obscured by the darkness. With a rattle of keys, a panel, unrecognisable as a door, opened to allow him entry.

The dank fusty smell that emanated from the passageway caused Tia to blow out through her mouth and Beth wafted her hand in front of her nose to show she agreed. The three visitors baulked at the idea of going in, even though Lester had disappeared from sight into the tunnel. With a click, that seemed loud in the inky black of the passageway, a torch beam illuminated the way forward.

"Follow me," Lester commanded in hushed tones. "And close the door behind you. Make sure the lock engages."

Beth plunged forward and planted a hand on Lester's shoulder. She reached behind with her free hand and took Tia's as she was next in. Will glanced once more in each direction along the street before following his companions. He pulled the panel closed behind him and gave it a rattle to make sure that it was secure. The little light from the night sky was cut off and they were reliant on the torch beam that swung forward in the direction of travel.

Tia squeezed Beth's hand a little and felt a corresponding response that gave mutual reassurance as they began moving in time with Lester. The narrow, cramped tunnel ran for several yards beneath the buildings, making them feel like rats running through a sewer under the city.

Suddenly the passageway opened out into a small quadrangle in the centre of the structure. It was about twenty-five feet square and staring up the middle toward the night sky high above gave the feeling of looking up the centre of a chimney. At one side there was an iron staircase that ascended to a platform running around the quadrangle at each level of the building like the balconies of an old prison.

Lester immediately shot up the ladder to the first platform before looking back to make sure everyone was still in tow. He continued up three flights of stairs until reaching the final level. The only other ascent was up a ladder onto the roof.

As his three companions reached the top, the clattering of feet on metal grids slowed to a stop and they waited while Lester unlocked a door and stepped inside to a small entrance area. He glanced at the expectant faces that had obediently followed behind without question.

"Everybody okay?" he whispered.

There were nods of response, but no sound as they instinctively kept quiet, trying to go unnoticed.

Lester punched a series of numbers into a keypad and pushed at another door that opened to reveal a hallway into an apartment.

They all filed past Lester, who was holding both doors open and once they were all inside, he closed the outer door behind them. Stepping into the hallway, he then closed the inner one. Will turned around at the sound of the door slamming and found himself looking at a bookcase. It held Will's interest for a moment until he caught Lester's eye. The smile and wink showed that Lester had noticed Will's curiosity and made a simple statement about how brilliant he thought it was.

CHAPTER 11

The group noticeably relaxed once they'd reached the relative safety of the apartment. As they dumped bags and removed coats, Lester cautioned them. "There are two rooms with windows that overlook the apartment entrance. One is the bedroom through that door and the other is the living room that runs off the kitchen-dining area. That room has windows to the side street as well. I think it would be better if you all just stay out of both of those rooms. The two guys outside doing a lousy job of watching me are parked at the front." He smirked at his ingenuity. "It's not a problem if they see me through the windows, even if I wave at them, but they mustn't see anyone else," he warned sternly. He glanced around the group. "Now, you two, I know," he pointed to Beth and Will, "but you..." He hesitated for a moment while looking at Tia in the light. "You look familiar somehow, but I don't think we've met. Lester Donaldson," he held out his hand in greeting.

"Tia Sharmez." She accepted his gesture, but was a little unnerved at the continued interest in her face. Lester seemed to be searching a memory bank trying to place the image.

"Pleasure to meet you," he said slowly, as if buying more time to make an assessment.

Suddenly realising everyone was waiting for his lead, he made an apologetic gesture, "Sorry, perhaps we should get something to eat..." His face took on a serious expression. "And discuss what is going on here." The tone of Lester's voice left no doubt that he wanted answers. He turned and led the way through to the kitchen.

"Lester." He looked back at the sound of Tia's voice and again appeared to take the opportunity to scan her features, which distracted her for a second. "Why don't you let me cook for us? I seem to be trailing around after these two like a spare part. They're doing their best to help me and I feel like a hopeless case that has no use but to cause trouble."

Lester deliberately glanced beyond Tia at Will. "There's only one person here who does the trouble causing, darling and he ain't anything like as pretty as you."

Tia felt her cheeks flush and Will resisted the temptation to re-start the earlier fracas, even though he felt Lester was purposely goading him. Beth saw the risk and jumped in to stop any possible escalation.

"That would be a great help, Tia. Assuming you can cook, of course?"

Tia smiled at Beth's humour then turned her attention to the cupboards and the fridge to see what a computer geek like Lester would have in store.

The kitchen was functional, centring around an island counter. It opened out through an arch to the dining area and on through a doorway was the living room where they were forbidden to go.

To the side of the dining area was what looked like an international space station mission control. Screens littered the line of desks that ran along the wall, one of them displaying the observed 'observers' in the car outside. Various pieces of equipment whirred and lights flashed, all connected together with a mass of bundled cables. The equipment seemed to exert a magnetic pull that attracted Lester to the paraphernalia as soon as he entered the room, mesmerising him with information overload. The apartment certainly reflected the man who lived there, as much as Beth's house had the woman.

Will strategically placed himself at the furthest end of the dining table, thinking it would put some space between Lester and himself.

Once Tia had assessed the available ingredients, she complained to Lester about the limited provisions and that she needed some things. Pulling himself away from the keyboard where he was furiously tapping away, he offered to go to local shop for supplies. He seemed to relish the idea of showing his face to the men watching the building, just to comfort them that he was still in their sights and they were doing a fantastic job.

Beth excused herself and headed for the shower, after driving all day, she was ready to freshen up. She treated Lester's place like it was her own, but he didn't seem to mind.

"So, what do you want chef?" Lester's smile greeted Tia. She noted the warmth in his expression and responded in kind. He went to the hallway to grab his coat.

Taking a notepad from the counter, she began scribbling a list of items then handing it to him as he came back into the kitchen. He glanced at the paper and back at Tia, spun on his heels and disappeared, shouting back, "I won't be long."

The apartment was suddenly quiet as the entrance door slammed shut behind Lester. The quiet whirring of fans in the computer equipment and the barely perceptible sound of running water from Beth's shower were the only background noise. Tia focused on the task in hand and Will sat watching from his position in the dining area as she made preparations for the meal. It all seemed so normal. A few friends getting together to eat and enjoy themselves, but the circumstances were far from the normality of a few days previous, before he'd ever laid eyes on Tia.

She moved so gracefully around the kitchen, totally engrossed in what she was doing. It looked like a way of blocking out the reality that they were facing, if only for a little while, and she seemed at peace in her isolated world. It was the first time Will had been able to watch her without her actions being distorted by fear, or panic, or concern for how others would judge her.

She flicked her long hair back over her shoulder and tilted her head to the side while checking the quality of her work. Spinning around, she pulled open a drawer to get another knife and as she turned back, she glanced across and caught sight of Will staring at her. She paused, thinking their eyes had accidently met momentarily, but realised it was more than a passing look. She straightened up and turned square on, facing Will. He didn't change his attitude as Tia held his stare and she thought he must be deep in thought, so she prompted him.

"What?"

"Nothing," he responded with a shrug. "I'm sorry, I guess I was staring," but his eyes stayed locked on her.

"Staring at what?" she quizzed.

He hesitated before he replied. "At you."

"Why?" Her face suddenly showed the shadow of the worry that had been there for days.

Not wanting to cause alarm, Will tried to dismiss his action. "It doesn't matter," he said, diverting his gaze. He was concerned that he might make her uncomfortable and that was not his intention.

Tia stood motionless as she observed him and when he glanced up again their eyes met once more. She hesitantly asked again, "Why *were* you looking at me?"

Will felt a little embarrassed at being put on the spot. "I just thought you looked so…" Tia raised her eyebrows in anticipation and Will was the one who suddenly felt uncomfortable. "It's just that every time I've looked at you over the last couple of days, you've had a terrified expression in your eyes." He smiled nervously at her and unsuccessfully tried to break her stare. "While you were lost in what you were doing just now, you looked more… relaxed…" She smiled, but Will hadn't quite finished. "…beautiful," he stammered.

Will averted his eyes letting his gaze fall to the table top. He felt awkward at opening a window to what he was thinking.

"Thank you," Tia whispered, with unmasked emotion. Her response caused Will to look up at her again.

As their eyes met once more, Will felt there was some mutual connection between them. It lasted only a fleeting moment as the truth of their situation flooded his thoughts, crushing any opportunity that might have existed had they met in other circumstances.

Tia's body language suggested she was about to say something more, but then thought better of it. She briefly smiled then went back to what she was doing. Will continued to watch, but more discreetly. He was fascinated by her.

They both looked up at the kitchen door when the front door slammed shut. Jumping to his feet, Will went to the hallway to check that everything was okay. Lester was back with a broad grin on his face. He glanced at Will as he slipped his coat off, picked up the bags of shopping and headed into the kitchen.

"If only they knew how obvious they are. You can't believe that our taxes are wasted paying for 'professionals' like that!"

"Did they follow you?" Will asked.

"Oh yeah. They might as well of been wearing an 'A' board saying, 'secret agent'."

They both laughed.

Tia was standing behind the counter observing the two men. One moment they seemed to be at each other's throats and the next their hostilities slipped and they exchanged comments like old friends.

As Lester put the bags on the counter, he and Will noticed that they were being watched. The moment begged a question from either of them about what was of interest to Tia, but her expression gave an indication that neither of them would want to answer what she wanted to ask. The awkward silence lasted too long for comfort and the hostile atmosphere between the two guys appeared to be restored.

Lester returned to the computers where he'd been before going out and Will leaned back against the wall in the kitchen behind the nib of the arch, just out of Lester's sight-line. The rhythmic tapping of the keyboard was punctuated by short silences as Lester read what appeared on the screen, sometimes muttering incoherently to himself. He'd slipped into another world that existed beyond the apartment and beyond the complex relationships of the people who'd invaded his space. He was lost to the realities that surrounded him, until he unexpectedly spoke.

"Sorry to hear about your dad and sister, Will." Lester didn't turn from the screens in front of him and made no attempt at eye contact with Will.

Tia immediately looked at Lester and then at Will, her eyes wide, waiting for what would come next. Will shifted uncomfortably at being reminded and looked down at the floor.

"Thanks."

"Must have been rough on you." The genuine sympathy was evident in the tone of Lester's voice.

"Yeah... Life can be a bitch."

Will appreciated the offer of an olive branch and began to think perhaps he'd been a little hard on Lester when they first met at the station. They were such different people, and the antagonism had been so long established that it seemed impossible to build anything more than the loose acquaintance they had through the common bond Beth provided. If it hadn't been for her occasional attempts at bridge building, it was quite possible they would never have met again. Will thought about how hard he'd tried to push people away after the loss of his family and how hard Beth had fought to hold on to him. That same determination had been working on Will and Lester for years, but without great success.

"The list of questions you emailed Beth was a clever idea," Will offered.

Lester rolled back and spun around in his chair to take a measure of the sentiment behind Will's comment. He took a second to read the expression on Will's face and noted that he was serious and shrugged, "Didn't want Beth to walk into anything that might become a problem later."

Tia quietly continued with what she was doing, but was totally focused on the interaction between the two guys.

Will nodded, "Was good thinking." A smile momentarily crossed his lips. "Although... I didn't say that when she first showed it to me, as Tia can tell you." He and Lester both looked at her as a broad grin settled on her face. She glanced up and found herself the centre of attention, but ignored them and immediately shifted her focus back to the preparation of the food on the counter.

"Shit!" Lester blurted out. "I bet he called me every name under the sun? He did, didn't he?" Tia shrugged and kept her counsel. "I tell you girl, he *needs* his black brother to save his white ass. No mistake about that, it's the truth."

Tia suddenly looked up at the two of them, conscious of the racial implications of the comment, as she anticipated retaliation from Will. The two guys burst out laughing at her response and the smug look on Lester's face showed he'd deliberately baited her. Tia displayed a disapproving expression at the pair of them, but couldn't restrain a smile from crossing her lips.

"Haa, what a hoot!" shouted Lester, as he slowly turned back to the screens.

Will continued to watch Tia, who'd stopped what she was doing. She shook her head as though scolding him then smiled and went back to the task in hand.

By the time Beth was finished in the shower, the food was nearly ready so they all assembled around the table. A few minutes later, Tia put the plates down in front of them stating, 'Chicken fajitas'. Noises of gratefulness revealed the appreciation for something other than takeaway.

They had barely begun eating when Lester, ready to get immediately to the point, began. "Okay. I think it's time that you filled me in about what's going on, especially about your involvement, *Miss Sharmez*." He slid a printed page across the table toward Tia. She glanced down at it. "Pretty good cover girl if you ask me... and *much* better in the flesh," he added musically. Lester took a mouthful of food. "Damn, she can even cook," he added jokingly.

Will quickly took hold of the paper and scanned the image on it. It was Tia alright, in a figure hugging, quite revealing dress. "You're right about that," but Will wasn't focused on the food.

All eyes were immediately fastened on him and he instantly felt under the spotlight as he looked up from the picture. Tia caught his eye and lingered a second before looking away, the coy smile was back on her face. Will suddenly felt embarrassed, but

Lester was not lying about the image, even though he delivered it in a slightly jokey manner. Will's comment was deadpan serious and had revealed more than he'd intended to.

Beth cleared her throat and broke the awkwardness by lightly slapping Lester on the arm. "You men are all the same. A good looking girl shows some flesh and you're all drooling at the mouth." She and Tia laughed at the guy's squirming as Beth snatched the picture from Will's hand. She scanned it for a few seconds. "They're right though. It's a great picture. I wouldn't mind someone making me look that good!"

"Impossible!" Lester got his own back as he jumped from the table to avoid another slap. It was a brief light-hearted moment in the middle of a very serious situation.

"Anyway, it's Liatzo, not Sharmez, isn't it?" Will cut through the laughter with the new information.

Lester's face suddenly changed. "Say again."

"Liatzo." Will nodded toward Tia for confirmation that he was correct.

Lester focused on Tia for an explanation and she duly gave one, retelling the story she'd already told Beth and Will about her life in Mexico, the move to the States, and her name change.

They all listened as she related what had happened to her, until she'd got to the explanation of her first encounter with Will. He took over the telling from that point on so that Tia could eat.

Lester asked a few questions here and there, but his reaction to Tia's real surname was significant and noticed by the others. He avoided giving any reason when they pressed him, saying that he wanted to look at some files he'd been reviewing when the news story with Will's picture had broken.

"What files?" Beth interrupted.

"Oh, just some intelligence files," he dismissively replied.

"How did you get access to those?"

"You're joking, right?" Lester looked surprised at Beth.

"No. I'm not joking."

Lester sighed and realised she wouldn't let it rest without knowing.

"They call some of our government organisations 'Intelligence Agencies'. I'm not sure they always deserve the 'intelligence' part of the title." Will laughed at Lester's flippant comment, but Beth didn't. Lester's smile quickly disappeared as he caught the measure of Beth's concern. "I've been working for the military over the last few years as an official hacker. I test the systems to see if there are any weaknesses and then develop ways of increasing security…" He paused and looked at the three of them. "You don't know that though… The military guys had a bit of a kicking after some kid from abroad caused some significant problems. Anyway," he continued, "the civil authorities are not as vigilant in their approach, so I use it as a playground. Sort of." He laughed, but no one else did.

"And…" said Beth impatiently.

"That's it. I just want to check some files."

Lester left them wondering what he was up to, but wouldn't be drawn any further on the issue.

As they were finishing up the meal, Lester presented his plan for the moment. "It's nearly eleven. I suggest you girls sleep in the main bedroom and Will, you can have the small room. It's on the front, so don't turn the light on or go to the window. I'll sleep in here, but I have some things to do first so… I'll say goodnight."

The message was loud and clear. Lester wanted them out of his 'office' while he performed his magic tricks, so they duly obliged after clearing the dishes, leaving him in peace.

When Will came out of the bathroom as he was getting ready for bed, he listened at the closed door to the kitchen and could hear Lester talking. He presumed it was to himself, as he reasoned out what he was working on. With an involuntary shrug, he quietly moved away and went to his room for the night.

~

Tia sat on a stool in front of the long mirror brushing her hair before turning in. She wore a shirt that she'd taken from Sophie's wardrobe when they left his house to go to Beth's place.

Beth interrupted her nightly routine. "What do you think has happened to your father?"

Tia was a little surprised by the question and stopped brushing for a moment. She looked at Beth in the reflection of the mirror. "I... I don't know," Tia shrugged. "Sometimes I think I can't even remember what he looks like."

"What do you remember about him?"

Tia didn't answer for quite a long time. She just kept brushing her hair as if it was a kind of therapy that helped her with the difficult memories of the past. Beth felt conscious that she might not want to talk about it and gave an apologetic explanation for the question.

"I only ask because I don't have any memories. They told me that mine was just a bum who would've sold his grandmother for another drink."

Tia turned to face Beth. "I'm sorry."

"There's no need to be. I got over it a long time ago, but it does have an effect on us, don't you think?"

"Yes. Yes it does," Tia agreed.

She went back to brushing and Beth thought that was the end of the conversation as Tia seemed reluctant to dig up the memories. For the next minute or two there was only the sound of the brush running through her hair. Having resigned herself to the fact that the conversation had ended, Beth shook her pillow to make it more comfortable and settled down, but Tia began unexpectedly to recall a scene from long ago.

"The last time I saw him properly, I mean when we spent a long period of time together, was on my sixteenth birthday. Every time after that was very brief; a day, half a day, an hour, a short phone call. I remember he'd promised that I could have my ears pierced. I'd been begging him for months, at every opportunity when I got to see him. That probably seems odd to you, but he was funny about things like that. Anyway, he finally relented and agreed to have someone come to the villa to do the piercing for me." Tia put the brush down and momentarily paused as she noticed her reflection in the mirror. There was a smile on her face prompted by the memory of happy times. She became aware of

Beth watching her so she got up and went to sit on the bed before continuing.

"My father brought a small gift wrapped parcel that contained these stud earrings." Tia brushed her hair over her ear to expose the jewellery and leaned closer so that Beth could take a look.

"Very nice," Beth offered.

"They've never come out since that day."

"You've *never* taken them out?" Beth sounded surprised. "Since you were sixteen years old?"

Tia shook her head. "My father made me promise I would never remove them. They were specially fitted with a locking centre pin so that once they were in they would have to be cut to remove them. I never did, nor have I ever wanted to since I last saw him. They remind me of…" Tia paused as she choked a little at the sound of her own words that brought home the loss; the feeling of being alone; the frustration of not knowing what had happened to him. She was staring into the distance through the mirror as she sat on the bed near Beth. "They remind me of the happy times we had together. I miss him so much." She shook her head as though dismissing the distressing thoughts of what might have happened. Glancing at Beth, she smiled. "He called them, 'Saber gemas'."

"He what?" Beth asked. The curiosity in her voice was clear.

"He told me that they were called, 'Saber gemas'."

Beth's quizzical look was enough, but she asked the question anyway.

"What does that mean?"

"It's Spanish. It means 'knowledge gems'."

"That's the first time I've ever met someone who had earrings with a name." Beth's tongue in cheek comment lightened the mood and Tia smiled at her. Beth tried to suppress a yawn that scrambled her words, making her laugh as she repeated what she'd said. "I don't know about you, but I'm fading."

"Me too," Tia confirmed.

"I think the last couple of restless days have finally caught up with me." Beth smiled as she slid down into the bed making herself comfortable.

Tia climbed in and felt a little awkward that they were sharing a double, having only known one another for such a brief time. It made her sigh and almost laugh.

"You okay?" Beth asked.

"Yes... I just thought it strange that we're here in this bed together. Still, better us than Lester and Will!"

Beth blurted out a laugh at the thought of the guys being in such close proximity.

Tia switched the light out and a few minutes of quiet took over, only interrupted by the distant noises of the world outside.

"Beth?"

"Umm."

"What's Will like? I mean, what's he *really* like?"

Beth turned toward Tia, but could barely make out her silhouette in the darkness. She wondered about the reason for the question, but decided just to answer it instead of prying.

"There was a time when we might have got together as a couple, but our relationship was very different to that and we both became aware of it. I suppose I've been much more like a sister to him than anything else. Has he told you anything about what has happened to him recently?"

"He told me a little about it when we were travelling to your place." Tia answered.

"He was devastated when he lost his father and sister. It was so needless; tragic. It completely knocked the wind out of his sails and I don't think he's completely returned to his old self. I don't even know how you *can* return to normality after something like that. He's about as subtle as a bull in a china shop at times, but if you were in trouble..." Beth stopped at the irony of her turn of phrase. "Well, both he and Lester are the most genuine men that I've had the pleasure to know... And they both drive me absolutely nuts at times."

She laughed as she recalled the bickering and Tia joined her. There was a long silence before Beth added, "Will's hurting pretty bad, Tia and he doesn't need any more, but I will say this, he'll not rest until he's done the best he can for us. For you. I'm still unclear about how we got into this situation... I think you probably are too, but Will would never back away from someone in need. He was the perfect son and brother and has been a very good friend."

Beth waited for a few moments before continuing and Tia could sense the emotion in the atmosphere despite the darkness. "If there's one thing I hope will come good from this whole mess, it's that I'll get the Will I have always known back again."

Tia lay awake for a while thinking about what Beth had told her. While she was comforted about the character of the man who she'd thrown her troubles on to, she also felt guilty that such a man, who'd been knocked pretty hard, should have to suffer so much for something that was nothing to do with him.

~

The disruption of his life over the last few days had left Will feeling very tired. The comfort of lying on a real bed soon gave him an escape from the current troubles that had ambushed his life. His sleep was fitful and, on occasion, disrupted by disturbing snippets of dreams about being pursued by people trying to harm him, mixed with memories of tragic past events. The mundane pictures of things like taking Boost on long walks at the weekends, just to escape from real life, were punctuated by the horrors of what might become of his life if the accusations against him stood. His subconscious imagination was uncontrollably careering down a path of 'what if' scenarios that became increasingly extreme in their conclusions. A surreal world fraught with danger and menace, making every effort to convince him that this dream depiction was about to become reality. The claws of exhaustion held his physical body captive while his inner sight was force-fed a diet of unhappy possibilities matched with vivid imagery.

Will suddenly jumped from the adventures of the night and sat bolt upright. He glanced around the room trying to get a handle on where he was, until his misty mind cleared and he realised that he was at Lester's apartment.

A click in the hallway suddenly put him on full alert. Every possibility immediately cascaded through his mind. The last time he'd been abruptly woken saw him confronting two unsavoury characters who were intent on causing serious harm.

Again there was a suppressed click from outside his room. He quietly slid from the bed and went over to the door to listen closely. He could hear what sounded like the apartment door sweeping the floor as it closed, then another click.

Will held station trying to assess what was happening, but there was absolute silence. He knew that if someone had managed to get into the apartment he would have been able to hear further movement to confirm it.

He carefully turned the handle and eased the bedroom door open just enough to see along the hallway. It was very dark as the long corridor had no natural light. There was a glow coming from the direction of the kitchen, as if a television had been left playing, the bluish light occasionally dancing in intensity. His eyes adjusted to the surroundings gradually until he felt more confident. He tried to make out what had caused the noise that alerted him, but couldn't hear or see anything.

Slowly easing the door open wide enough to be able to look in the other direction, toward the entrance, he confirmed that the coast was clear and stepped into the hallway. A slight creak of the floor made him quickly glance in each direction again, checking the hallway, but nothing seemed untoward or out of place.

He tiptoed along the hallway and paused at the door to Beth and Tia's room. Listening intently he could just pick up the sound of deep breathing. Carefully opening the door, he glanced inside and could just make out the silhouette of the girls in the bed. The rhythmic patterns of breathing were the only sounds in the room, indicating the girls were asleep. He relaxed a little, thinking he'd probably been woken by a dream that had crossed to the real world.

Quietly pulling the bedroom door closed, he was about to return to his bed when a flickering glow from the kitchen attracted his attention. The door was slightly ajar and the dim light gave an eerie glow to the far end of the hallway. Thinking that perhaps Lester was still up and had inadvertently woken him, Will edged near enough to see into the kitchen. Using the light that spilled through the gap, he checked his watch, 4.50am. He was a little surprised, thinking that it was much earlier judging from the darkness. "The darkest hour... Just before the dawn," he whispered to himself as some kind of explanation for his mistake.

Tentatively pushing the kitchen door open, he checked around the room. Realising that the light was coming from Lester's workstation set up in the dining area, Will laughed to himself about his fearful suspicions and sensitivity to the slightest sound, real or imagined. The last encounter with uninvited guests was still fresh in his mind.

He wandered over to the fridge and was dazzled by the light as he opened the door. Filling a glass, he quietly pressed the door closed and sipped at his drink as his eyes worked at the adjustments needed to see again in the darkness. Taking the remaining half glass in one gulp, he turned to place the tumbler on the counter and looked back at the fuzzy computer screen where they'd observed the watchmen outside the previous evening.

It suddenly dawned on him that Lester was not in the room. At first he thought the light must have been playing a trick, but a quick check proved the point. Thinking he must have gone to the bathroom, Will went along the hallway to check, but the bathroom door was ajar and when he pushed it open he found the room empty.

Back in the dining room, Will had a cursory check of the monitor to try to see why the picture had been replaced by a snowy blizzard, but couldn't tell what was wrong. It was clearly unwise to turn on the light to make a better inspection, so he dipped low and went to the living room window that overlooked the street at the front of the building.

He knew that Lester had ordered them to stay away from the windows at the front, so he was very careful not to stand in full view, but cautiously edged into place so he could see outside. The road was lined from end to end, on both sides, with parked cars, much as it had been the evening before. The vehicle they'd been watching was still in the same place, but it was difficult to see clearly, from the higher level, whether it was still occupied.

He looked around the room to see if he could make better use of his position and caught sight of a spyglass on the coffee table. Picking it up, he returned to the window to get a better view. With the increased magnification he could see two men in the front of the car. Neither of them appeared to be focusing their attention on the apartment, but they were engaged in discussion with someone out of view in the rear seat. No matter how Will adjusted his position, he couldn't confirm that there was another person in the back of the vehicle, he only had the actions of the visible men to go on.

After several minutes of watching, he got what he was looking for. A man got out of the front of the vehicle and opened the rear door, then got back in the front. For another few moments no one emerged and Will was not sure what was happening. He re-focused the spyglass back to the windscreen to confirm that they were still engaging with someone and noticed both men turn to face forward. The spyglass was focused on the rear door just as a figure suddenly appeared. He turned back and hunched over, still in a flow of conversation with the men in the front seats. Moments later the man straightened up and forcefully slammed the door shut. There was no hiding the manner of the action or the thump of the door that reached Will's hearing as a dull thud, even at the fourth floor. The figure stood motionless for a while, head down, staring at the car in front of him. Will had the spyglass concentrating directly on him while he waited for something to happen that might expose the identity of the passenger. He quickly flicked to the windscreen to confirm the position of the others. They were forward facing, having disengaged with their guest.

Switching the sight back to the motionless figure, Will had him clear in the centre of the lens. He suddenly turned and flicked his head back, glancing up in Will's direction. With the magnification of the spyglass it seemed as though they'd made eye contact. In a flash response, Will dropped to the floor to hide his presence while assuring himself that he couldn't have been seen. The view through the glass just made him feel more exposed than he'd really been.

Whether he'd been caught was not the most urgent issue of the moment, he was occupied by something much more confusing and ominous. There was no mistaking the face he'd clearly seen, it was Lester.

CHAPTER 12

Will's mind was racing with the possibilities of what Lester had been doing and he had to resist the temptation to get bogged down in his thinking and focus on what to do.

Quickly glancing out of the window again, it was immediately obvious that Lester was en route back to the apartment. Will dipped to the floor and headed back to the dining room. As soon as he was away from the windows, he shot down the hallway to the bedroom and pulled his bag out from under the bed. Unzipping the end pouch, he retrieved a gun, the prize from his last confrontation.

Scrambling to pull his jeans and shirt on, he prepared for the imminent appearance of their host, while planning what he was going to do when he arrived. He grabbed the prepared weapon, quietly slipped from the bedroom, closing the door behind him, and went to the coat closet near the entrance door. Concealing himself inside it, he waited.

The suspense was excruciating as time seemed to drag. How long did it take to get to the fourth floor of an apartment block? Every slight noise put him on a higher alert as the moment of Lester's return drew closer. The suspense wound him like a tightening coiled spring. His heart was pounding in his chest at an uncomfortable volume and the darkness heightened every sound.

Suddenly there was a click just outside the closet where Will was concealed. He immediately recognised it as the same sound that had roused him from his broken sleep. He waited as he heard the door swing open and then back again. The confirmation of Lester's entry was in the second click as the latch returned to its locked position.

Sure that Lester was in the hallway, beyond the place where he was concealed, Will eased the closet door open slightly. He caught sight of Lester's silhouette in the darkness leaning into the door of the bedroom where he'd been sleeping only minutes before and watched as he stayed there for several seconds. The moment of confrontation had arrived and the advantage was with Will.

"I'm wide awake, Lester."

Lester jumped noticeably at the unexpected voice close by.

"Shit, Will! You scared the hell out of me."

"Something you'd like to tell me?"

Lester was about to say something, but the deliberate click of gun metal immediately stopped him. The two men tried to make out each other's features in the darkness, but it concealed all detail that could be used to assess the situation.

"Very, *very* slowly, lift your hands and turn around."

Will's words didn't need repeating, they carried a sinister warning in the tone and Lester immediately got the message. His hands travelled upward in response to the command and he turned to face down the hallway toward the kitchen.

"No sudden movements, no surprises, Lester."

"Will…" Lester's attempt at explanation was abruptly stopped.

"This is the second time in recent days that I've found someone sneaking around in the middle of the night. It makes me *very* nervous." Lester tried again to interrupt, but was stopped when Will added a warning. "We wouldn't want it to end up like the last time… *Would we?*"

Lester thought better of making a response and nodded to indicate that he understood. Will edged toward him, deliberately positioning himself for any surprise that might occur.

Using the barrel of the gun like a cattle prod, he prompted Lester's movement towards the kitchen and followed him along the hallway. Lester didn't hesitate to comply with the unuttered instructions.

"Carefully and slowly, take a seat on the chair in front of you, my friend," Will instructed, when they reached the dining table.

Once Lester had done as he was instructed, Will came close behind him. The gun just lightly kissed the skin on the back of Lester's neck as a reminder that it was still there. Lester restrained the shiver that the cold metal tried to induce.

"Now, put your hands down by your side."

Once Lester had complied, Will pulled the collar and back of his coat down over the back of the chair so that it restricted any surprise movements. He walked around the table and sat opposite Lester so that he had a view through the kitchen door and along the hallway.

"Been out somewhere, Lester?" The question had a casual tone that disguised the seriousness of the situation, the same intonation as asking a friend if they would like coffee.

"Milk. I went to get some milk," Lester offered cautiously.

Will brought the gun handle down with a thump on the table, making the cups left there from the night before rattle as they danced at the impact. Lester's eyes widened a little, but didn't flinch from Will's.

"Then where is it?"

Lester moved as if trying to get something and Will lurched over the table and grabbed him by his shirt collar, waving the gun barrel right in his face. Even in the dim light of the monitor screens the fear that painted Lester's face was visible. With the images from the news playing in his mind, Lester was not about to test the truth of them. He'd taken Beth's word about the situation and fought to dismiss the notion that the man threatening him was capable of doing what the news stories had alleged; that Beth and Tia might be wrong. Will was a questionable quantity to Lester and a volatile one at that.

"My... My left pocket," Lester shakily instructed.

The pause between his answer and the gun barrel moving away from his face was menacingly uncomfortable. As Will moved around the table to check the truth of the claim, his eyes didn't let go of Lester for one second.

Will reached into the deep pocket of the long coat and was a little surprised to pull out a carton. He hesitated a moment while he looked at it, then placed it on the table and went back to his seat opposite Lester. Will didn't make a sound, he just stared and the silence made Lester nervous.

"There's four..." Lester swallowed hard and the sound seemed to be amplified in the darkness. "Four of us. I thought we might need some more and I couldn't sleep, so I went out for a walk." He shrugged as if asking for forgiveness for having been so considerate.

Will suddenly slammed his hand on the table, part in frustration at Lester's excuse for leaving the apartment being shown to be true; part in anger at being kept in the dark about what else he'd been up to. The mugs and Lester jumped in unison at the force of the blow. There was sudden movement in the room down the hallway and seconds later Beth tumbled out into full view wearing shorts and T-shirt; disoriented and trying to make sense of the abrupt alarm call that had just woken her. She quickly came into the kitchen and did a double take, looking at Lester sat at the table, with his coat partly off, and Will seated opposite.

Tia immediately appeared behind Beth, rubbing her eyes and trying to get a fix on what was happening. Beth flicked the light on and the illumination spilled over the scene, but the two guys didn't take their eyes off one another. Once she'd adjusted to the sudden brightness, she caught sight of the gun in Will's hand; handle resting on the table; muzzle pointing straight at Lester.

She looked from one man to the other, weighing up the scene before her. Her expression was a mixture of anger, frustration and confusion. Beating off the abruptness of her rude awakening, Beth's gutsy character tried to assert some control over the situation.

"There'd better be a damn good explanation for what I can see," she forcefully demanded.

Her comment was directed primarily at Will. Her eyes were fastened on the gun, but she was distracted momentarily as Lester glanced at her. Will didn't move a muscle; eyes locked on Lester and face set like flint. He sat for a few seconds, as rigid as stone, as though he hadn't heard a word.

Suddenly Will stirred in his seat as he flashed a look at Beth. "Come in Beth, Tia, take a seat." Will's mocking manner didn't put the girls at ease, it merely underlined the obvious. Something was very wrong. "Lester was just about to explain to me where he's been this morning."

Will held out his hand in instruction to the two girls and they obediently fulfilled his expectation to comply with the request.

As Beth lowered herself slowly into her chair at one end of the table, her eyes having been fixed on Will's face, she took the opportunity to take a fleeting look at Lester. His grim expression displayed his discomfort at the situation. Tia followed Beth's lead, her body language showing equal concern. Her eyes darted from face to face.

Beth knew Lester well enough to see that he was alarmed by Will's behaviour. He was not a man that was easily scared, but he'd always opted to apply his technical skills for the authorities, rather than wanting to use weapons. He'd told Beth many times that you can fight physically, but you can do a lot of damage through the virtual world and that was where his skill lay.

Beth briefly smiled at him, but his response was weak. Tia continued to glance from one face to another, lingering on Beth more than the two men. She'd found a harbour in the storm through Beth's solid consistency in character and was reassured when she seemed to know what was happening. If anyone was going to mediate between the hostile parties, it was her, but Will's determined expression showed he had no intention of backing down.

Beth's gaze returned to Will as she waited for him to say something, her demand for explanation still hanging in the air. She sat at the end of the table like the chairman at a reconciliation meeting, trying to make a way through some intractable conflict.

"Lester's been out shopping," Will finally announced, nudging the carton on the table with the tip of the gun, "but I think he went visiting his friends on his way back... *Didn't you?*"

Beth and Tia turned their attention to Lester and he grimaced slightly under their scrutiny. Without taking her eyes away from Lester, Beth asked, "What are you talking about, Will?"

"Ask him," Will's answer was abrupt, but Beth was not going to be a push over.

"I'm asking *you*," she snapped, turning to glare at him.

"Well, you're asking the wrong person, *Beth*. Ask him!" His voice went up a notch in volume, as did the tension in the room. The irritation in his response was crystal clear.

"Ask him what?" Beth demanded in frustration.

"Where the hell he's been."

Beth reluctantly tore her eyes away from Will. "What's he talking about, Lester?"

Her friend shrank a little in his seat as the question was asked, but he declined to give a response immediately, as though testing what was known.

Lester suddenly let out a cry and grimaced as he lurched forward. Will's shoe had unexpectedly crashed into his shin, scraping down to his foot. The deliberateness of Will's action inflicted enough pain to create a significant reaction from Lester. Beth instantly blurted out a shocked response.

"WILL! WHAT ARE YOU TRYING TO DO?"

Her anger had been simmering but suddenly hit boiling point. Ignoring any protest that Will might make, she jumped up and went to assist Lester, snatching his coat up from the back of the chair so that his hands were released to nurse the injured leg.

"WHAT THE HELL AM *I* DOING?" Will replied angrily. The sarcasm in his question punched home his frustration. "WHY DON'T WE FIND OUT WHAT *YOUR* GEEKY FRIEND HAS BEEN DOING SITTING IN THE BACK OF THAT CAR WITH OUR WATCHMEN?"

The room was suddenly silent as Will's question was thrown down. There was a pause while Beth took in the implication of the accusation. Will didn't hesitate, waiting for a response, as he hadn't finished discharging his allegation. "Ask him *why* he disconnected that screen so that we couldn't see what he was doing if any of us should come into the kitchen and find him double-crossing us?"

Beth glanced over to the desk where Lester's equipment was stationed and noticed the snowy scene on the monitor which had been displaying an image of the car parked in the street below.

"They *threatened* me." Lester spat out through gritted teeth. His voice carried a reminder of the pain he still felt from Will's assault. All three of them suddenly focused on him as they anticipated a fuller explanation. Lester felt conscious of being watched and looked up from the table, pausing at each face for a moment. His eyes finally settled on his accuser. "It's *always* the same with you, Will. Shoot first and then put your brain in gear." Lester muttered a few unsavoury curse words as he continued to comfort the pain in his leg. "And I've still got the scars to prove it." Only Tia didn't understand the reference to past experience. "I couldn't sleep, so I went to get some milk. They saw me leave the front of the apartment and one of them followed me to the store down the road, as usual. When I came out he was waiting, but he obviously knew I was aware of his presence. He followed me back along the road, but as I came close to the car the other one got out and opened the rear door. They *didn't* ask if I was willing to sit and chat." Lester shot the last statement of fact directly at Will as a means of provocation knowing that his behaviour was quickly being shown as unreasonable.

"What did they want?" Beth's question carried the urgency and alarm they all suddenly felt and drew Lester's attention.

"To know if I'd seen, or had any contact with *William Harris*." His feelings were woven into the way he finished the sentence, almost spitting out Will's name, and his eyes threw a fiery glance across the table to the source of his suffering.

"What did you tell them?" Beth quizzed.

"The same as I did when the uniformed cops came to the apartment to take a look around, only this time I lied."

Will could hold his tongue no longer as Lester's explanations began to make him look stupid. He abruptly butted in, "You're telling me that the missing picture on the monitor is coincidence?"

The snide remark was meant more as a statement of doubt than a question.

Lester quickly stood up from the table making Will instantly react, jumping back and re-focus the gun on its target. Lester seemed to be emboldened with the presence of the girls and taking no notice he marched to his desk and planted a blow on the top corner of the monitor casing. The picture immediately returned to the screen and he cursed the equipment. He then turned his attention to another machine punching angrily at the buttons. The images on the display started moving backwards at high speed until Lester punched again, setting the recording to play. Suddenly the scene in question began to re-run for them all to see, displaying the evidence for his defence. Two men forcefully assisted Lester into the back of the vehicle in the street below, then both got back into the car. No one in the room made a sound as Lester let the images continue until the point where he'd got out of the car and walked off screen, heading to the apartment.

When Lester stopped the playback, Beth turned her glare at Will. She was in no mind to be messed about and put no courtesies into her next comment.

"Put that damn thing away. Now!" she ordered.

She got up from the table shoving the chair back behind her. The screeching sound was loud and piercing, but was a stand-in for what she appeared to want to shout at Will.

After hesitating long enough for the focus of her angry eyes to do their work, she turned and marched off to her room, yelling back, "I'm going to get dressed. If you can control yourself for five minutes, perhaps we can put our efforts into figuring out what we should do!"

The slamming door put the final punctuation in place and left no doubt about Beth's feelings. Tia thought she was fearless, but was impressed that she hadn't sacrificed her femininity to impress the brawny men that she'd so often come into contact with during her time in the forces. She could pack a physical punch alright, but the way that she left the room gave little doubt that she thought Will should engage his brain before acting.

His embarrassment was glaringly obvious. Even the light over the table seemed to take delight in exposing his discomfort.

Tia quietly stood and disappeared from the room without a word, leaving the two men uncomfortably alone.

~

The dingy daylight was beginning to seep into the apartment, but showed little promise for a day of good cheer. The sky, heavily overcast and foreboding, matched the feelings of confusion and sombreness that engulfed Will. He sat at the table with his head down, staring at the gun laid out in front of him. Lester had gone to his work station, occupying himself with anything to avoid having to engage with Will.

The story of their fragile relationship had been demonstrated over the few hours that they'd been together. One moment all seemed well, but without warning it exploded in hostility. Pieces would fall in all directions until someone made a move to put them back together, usually Beth, but the likelihood was that it wouldn't last. She was the bridge builder, but her companions would set light to her laboured efforts without a second thought.

Beth returned to the kitchen several minutes later, but she was in a mood that told the guys to leave her alone for the time being. She poured a glass of water and took a slice of bread for herself, but said nothing.

Sitting in a low chair, tucked into the corner of the dining room, she stared through the open living room door lost in her thoughts. The deliberateness of her position, set apart from the two guys, told them loud and clear to shut up and keep their distance. It was obvious that she was pondering the situation she found herself in and had no desire to engage with anyone until she could make some sense out of it all.

The circumstances had snowballed from a problem that was Tia's, to Will's, to her own and now involved Lester. They needed to understand what was happening, and fast.

Finally, as Tia returned to the room, Beth stirred from her meditation and moved back to the table where Will had seated himself after dispensing with the gun, as ordered.

Tia looked around at her sullen companions. The atmosphere was definitely frosty. "Coffee anyone?" She got a muted response from them all, but the history that affected them was a mystery to her. Rather than sitting to join their mood, she set about making the drinks. Anything that kept her occupied was better than the awkwardness of the moment.

For several minutes the clinking of cups, the kettle boiling and the intermittent tapping of Lester's computer keyboard, were the only sounds in the room.

As Tia placed the drinks on the table, with some pancakes she found in the cupboard, Lester and Beth joined the other two, moving from their 'outposts' to the table. Lester was aware that they had to look at their options, but his position, as far away from Will as possible, made a statement about the man with whom he'd had continual conflict.

Will cleared his throat and stumbled over his words, "Lester, I... I..."

There wasn't time to complete the sentence before Lester cut him up. "Keep your apologies and go shove your gun in someone else's face. It's you they're after. Shit, what have I got to do with this? You could have knocked those two guys off for all I know. You've certainly got the moves." Lester's irritation spilled out uncontrolled, until he was abruptly interrupted.

"STOP IT! FOR GOD'S SAKE WILL YOU TWO JUST STOP IT!"

The room was stunned to silence by Tia's outburst and the fire in her eyes threatened to follow up, unless something changed. There was a moment of uncertainty until Beth broke the stand-off.

"Go girl!"

The grin on her face showed that she approved of Tia's intervention as the two of them herded the guys back into the group like they were stray cattle making a bolt for freedom. Beth's throw away comment punctured the tension and the beaming smile that spread across her face cracked the determination in Tia's. They started to laugh and the guys, a little bewildered at the explosion from 'the quiet one', couldn't sustain their serious stance for long. She'd gone from church mouse to fog horn, provoked by their bull-headedness.

Will held his hands up in surrendered apology, but felt it best to stay silent.

When the girls finished their sniggering, Tia asked, "What do we do now? I'm the cause of this trouble. God knows why, but you didn't even know who I was before you all got dragged into it one by one. Do I just give myself up? What do I do?"

"You might have been there at the start Tia, but what's happened since means that Will has little option but to try and find out what's at the root of this. It'll be no laughing matter if the authorities catch up with him. I'm here to help a friend, and Lester…" Beth stopped mid-sentence as if she didn't know what to say about the reason Lester was being immersed in the situation, or even if he intended to continue to be of help to them.

He looked up at Beth and thought she was staring at him a little too intently for comfort.

"What?" he asked, glancing at Will and Tia who were staring at Beth waiting for her to complete her sentence.

The pregnant pause gave birth to the scraping of chair legs as Beth launched herself from her seat. In the confusion Lester flinched, not understanding what was going on. Beth closed in on the monitor that she could see over Lester's shoulder.

"Oh no!" she yelled. "WHAT'S HAPPENING DOWN THERE?"

The urgency in her voice roused the group to immediate action as they crowded around the screen. A black four wheel drive had pulled alongside the 'watchmen' below in the street. The new vehicle towered over the saloon car that had been the hide for the observers. The bulky four by four obscured the view of what was taking place, but the position of the new vehicle was unusual. It was parked on a slight angle blocking the road between the parked cars that ran along either side of the street.

Lester ran to the living room window and glanced in the opposite direction.

"Shit, there's another one further down the street in the other direction," he shouted, as he ran back into the dining room. "We need to leave. NOW!" He frantically punched at buttons on the machines that decorated his workstation. Pulling cables loose, he grabbed his laptop and scooped a number of other items into a bag he'd fetched from the hallway. The others swung into action, gathering the few things they'd brought with them in the little time afforded.

They congregated in the kitchen, waiting for Lester to finish gathering his stuff.

"THEY'RE COMING IN! AT LEAST A DOZEN OF THEM!" Beth shouted, to speed his actions.

The screen in the dining room showed several men crossing the road toward the main entrance, all carrying serious weapons. Will glanced at his watch, 5.52am. The surprise of the ambush had been foiled by the morning's events and they literally had seconds to hold on to that advantage.

Lester ran to the front entrance door and threw on every lock and catch available. "Will, help me put the table into the door!" he shouted, as he raced into the kitchen.

There was not a moment's hesitation as the two of them worked seamlessly together, launching the furniture along the hallway. A second later the table was upside down, jammed into the door lock at an angle and wedged against the opposite closet door of the narrow hallway.

"FOLLOW ME!" Lester shouted, unlocking the disguised rear exit that had been their entrance the night before. They ran in convoy down the external steel steps to the tiny courtyard below. Lester followed behind, having secured their escape route.

While he was coming down after them, he was pushing an earpiece in place and fiddling with the controls of what looked like a walkie-talkie. As Lester jumped the last few steps, Will shouted, "This isn't the time to be finding your favourite music!"

"Police radio," was Lester's brief response, as he led them along the tight alleyway toward the hidden street exit. Unlocking the door, he cautiously glanced left and right to check it was clear.

CHAPTER 13

Fifteen guys piled out of the vehicles that littered the road beneath the apartment. They created very little sound, but the urgency of their quest was clearly portrayed in their hurried but well organised actions. Guns appeared from the trunk of a couple of the cars and were liberally distributed to each man, preparing them for the task at hand.

As they quickly made the final checks, another vehicle turned the corner zigzagging between the road-block. It sped over the short distance to the entrance of the building and came to an abrupt stop near the preparations.

Out stepped a mountain of a man dressed in black, almost before the car came to a halt. At six foot five tall, he looked down on most of the others present and used his height to intimidate his subordinates. His dark, swept-back hair and the heavily shadowed face, from not having shaven, gave him a grim look. Deep lines were etched into his brow that was constantly furrowed with a scowl.

He quickly paced over to the assembled crew and focused his attention on the leader. "Matt, you take these six guys," barked Jim Castle. The indicated men immediately grouped closer so they could hear the instructions. "Go straight up the main entrance stairway. Leave one guy in the lobby near the lift. Send one to the roof."

Castle was a man of few words and expected his orders to be followed without question. His whole demeanour shouted confidence and authority. He glanced over the men to check he'd got their undivided attention. His eyes narrowed. The men before him waited on his every word as they stood ready for action like coiled springs about to be released.

"No screw-ups. You hear me? Do it, and do it right."

There was a collective grunt of recognition from the group. Castle gave a nod that initiated the operation, before turning to give instructions to the rest of the force.

The front of the apartment block had an entry buzzer allowing visitors to page the occupier who could then remotely unlock the doors. The security didn't stand a chance against a team that had overcome such obstacles many times before. The six guys gave space to Matt as he went down on one knee at the lock. He didn't skip a beat as he followed a routine that had been drilled into him through meticulous training. They were all well prepared for just such occasions.

Inserting a device in the gap between door and frame, he pulled the trigger. The hydraulic opener instantly split them apart, cracking the pane of toughened glass in the door as it gave way to the unstoppable pressure. A moment later the team flooded into the small lobby area, weapons held aggressively at the ready.

"Jed, stay here," said Matt, in hushed tones.

Instant unquestioning response showed the discipline as the group, minus one, headed quickly up the stairs. They cushioned their movements in the echo-prone stairwell, trying to maintain the advantage of surprise. As they reached the floor they were aiming for, Matt pointed to one of the men and indicated that he should continue up to the roof. He responded to the gesture immediately.

One of the men carefully eased open the landing door and the rest of them filed past him along several yards of the spacious corridor to the door at the far end. Each man moved as though someone shouted commands to control the choreography of their actions. A listening device was placed against the apartment door and for a couple of seconds the team looked on, waiting for the go ahead to be given.

Again, space was made as the entrance was about to be sprung open. The hydraulic unit did its job perfectly, splintering the polished wood as the jaws opened, prizing the door and frame apart until the lock gave out a sharp crack as it was destroyed.

Matt jumped to his feet and put his weight against the door, anticipating instant entry into the apartment. The other guys crowded behind their leader expecting to follow immediately after him.

For the first time since they'd disembarked from the vehicles into the breaking dawn light, confusion took over as they surged forward trying to confront whatever was inside. The door moved an inch then stopped dead jarring against Matt's shoulder as it came to an abrupt stop. He put his shoulder to it again, but it wouldn't give way.

The others backed off a little to give some room as Matt seized the momentum again. Keeping his weight against the door, he jammed the hydraulic opener into the small gap where the top hinge was, forcing it away from the frame. The sound of snapping screw heads rang out with another sharp crack. Pulling the machine away, he slammed it in again at the bottom hinge with the same result.

One of the other guys saw what he was up to and threw his weight against the door, helping Matt to edge the splintered panel sideways now that it was free from all its fixings. It moved several inches to the left until they could see the edge of the upturned table that prevented the door from opening.

Matt got his hand through the gap and threw the table upright allowing the door to fall away. It created enough space to let them go in one man at a time.

Moving as quickly as they could with weapons at the ready, they systematically scoured the apartment room by room, searching for signs of life. Within moments it became clear that the place was empty and the group, pumped for action, had no target for their preparation.

"The coffee's still warm," shouted one of the guys.

"Shit!" Matt slammed the flat of his hand against the kitchen door as he blew off steam at having been thwarted in their mission. The adrenalin still coursed through his body but there was no outlet, no triumph in the situation. As he stared into space, his thoughts reeling, trying to understand what had gone wrong. "Shake the place down and find out where they went," he yelled, impatiently.

He was just about to issue another instruction when he was interrupted by a voice that came from the direction of the destroyed entrance door.

"Hey! What's going on?"

Matt instantly had his gun trained on the guy, who had just stepped into the apartment. He responded by raising his hands in submission and cowering back from the threat.

"Who the hell are you?" Matt demanded.

"I... I live next door. I heard the noise and..." He answered with a tremble in his voice, his eyes fixed on the weapon in Matt's hands.

Matt relaxed his stance and walked towards the man, indicating for one of his guys to follow him. "Please leave the apartment, sir. This is a police operation."

"But..."

Matt flashed his badge and the two officers crowded the guy, forcing him back out of the door into the corridor.

"You got a warrant to do this?" the neighbour demanded, seeing that the threat from the weapons had been averted.

"Step back into your apartment, sir." The guy didn't move. "Right now!" Matt raised his voice just as the stairwell door opened and Castle appeared. Several brisk strides brought him towering over his subordinates. He completely ignored the neighbour and focused on Matt. Raising an eyebrow was all it took to be given a status report.

"The place is secure, sir. No occupants."

Castle glared at Matt, then the other officer beside him. "What do you mean, *no occupants?*" He raised his voice a little. "Did they jump through the window?"

"No, sir. We're not sure where they went at the moment. I was just dealing with the neighbour."

Castle glanced at the battered entrance, completely ignoring anything that was not part of their mission. He had no intention of engaging with any member of the public that got in the way of his 'mission'. "What's that table doing there?"

Matt glanced over his shoulder at the destruction. "It was wedged against the door. Took us a bit of effort to get in, sir."

"So how the hell did Lester Donaldson get out of here, damn it!" Castle looked at his men in a contemptuous manner. "I want to know where he and his friends went." The irritation in his voice was clear. "And send someone to fetch those two clowns who were supposed to be watching the place. GOD DAMN IT! I want to know why we missed them. That was Beth Jackson's car we found burning nearby, which means Harris is here somewhere. I WANT HIM FOUND!" Castle's voice echoed in the empty corridor as he marched into the apartment leaving a black cloud hanging over his subordinates.

Matt blew air out of his mouth in frustration and shook his head. "Go fetch Mike and Tel up here, Kev. I wouldn't want to be in their shoes when they get here."

"Sir." Kev disappeared through the door and down the stairs as ordered.

Matt glared at the neighbour, who backed away until he was safely behind the closed door of his apartment then cursed out loud in frustration at the situation.

Matt paced the corridor for a minute, thinking through the situation, while waiting for his man to return with the guys who'd been watching the apartment.

The stairwell door creaked, pulling Matt out from his reflections. The two guys who'd been stationed in the street walked through followed by Kev.

"I don't envy you two." Matt threw the comment casually as he walked past them to the end of the corridor and into the apartment entrance with the pair of them in tow.

"Where's Castle?" he asked one of the guys who was checking through the stuff in the bedrooms.

"In the Kitchen, Matt." The look on his colleague's face made him pause before heading through the building. The guy looked round then lowered his voice to give his boss warning of what to expect. "Watch yourself, Matt. He's spitting nails and foaming at the mouth." A smirk crossed Matt's face as he nodded in response then led the others to face the music.

As the three of them entered the room, Castle was leant over the equipment scattered over the desks in the dining area. The slight movement of his head indicated he knew they were behind him. He deliberately pushed a button on a machine so that they noticed and stepped back from the screen that lit up with an image of the street below. In the centre of the picture was the car that had been the hideaway of the watchmen.

As the group of them stood, eyes locked to the screen, it showed a black four-by-four pull up sharply in the street and several guys hurriedly jump out. Matt turned away and cursed under his breath as the images displayed all their preparation going on before they'd entered the building.

Castle stared at the picture for a few more seconds then turned his attention to the three men. He didn't say a word, but watched them shift uncomfortably under his glare. He walked out of the room, gesturing for them to follow.

At the off-shoot of the hallway, he paused in front of the bookshelves then slipped his hand under one of the shelves and pulled. The whole unit swung around like a door, revealing an exit to the fire escape. He turned to look at the three men and his laser eyes drilled into their faces.

"I've sent two guys out there to see where it goes." The intonation in his voice gave clear indication of the fury begging to be unleashed that simmered just below the surface. "Heads *will* roll for this," he focused on the guys who'd been tasked with watching the apartment, "and *you* two are the prime candidates."

The next few of hours were spent digging through everything in the apartment that would give any clue where the group were heading and scouring the local area. Castle made sure everyone knew he was taking note of everything being done. After missing his target he was not going to let it drop and proceeded to make life a misery.

When Matt finally had the chance to get away, he disappeared down to the third floor corridor and found somewhere he could make a call without being overheard by anyone. He pulled a mobile phone from his flack-jacket pocket. Glancing up to check he was completely alone, he punched the keys to connect. Seconds later the call was answered.

"It's Matt, Don. Vince told me to call this number if anything turned up. Is he with you?"

"Yeah. Hold on a second. He's just leaving a club. We've been doing some business."

Matt could hear faint voices as Don passed over the phone.

"Matt. What've you got for me?" Vince Kurtis was never a man for polite chat, but having just plied someone he'd only just met with bundles of money in exchange for information, his mood was very black.

"We raided the apartment this morning, but there's no one here."

Vince turned the airwaves blue with his cursing, making Matt move the phone away from his ear.

"*Was* she there?" Vince finally demanded, once he'd regained a measure of calm.

"We're sure Jackson was here, so Harris must have been with her. The girl was probably here too."

"Probably?" Vince cursed again. "You'd better find out. For the money you cost me I want solid information, not guesswork. What does Castle know about her?"

"Nothing. Don't forget it was *me* that helped you get her in the first place," Matt blurted out in reaction. "And it was *you* that couldn't hang on to her." He looked up suddenly conscious he was raising his voice, but there was no one to overhear.

"Just find out where the hell they're heading now," Vince snapped. The line went dead.

Matt stared at the phone for a second as if throwing daggers at Vince Kurtis. He'd about had his fill of the man, but was embroiled so deep that he had to be careful how he dealt with him. The FBI wouldn't treat him kindly if the truth about his involvement with Kurtis came out. Dissatisfaction with the lifestyle his job could give him had seduced him to go on Kurtis senior's payroll. Once Vince had taken over the role his father had dominated for so long, the cost began to seem more expensive than the benefit. In the past Matt had felt some respect for what he did, but Vince used people then cast them aside. It was a recipe for disaster that could suck in everyone who'd 'worked' in the Kurtis 'empire'. All it needed was one person bent on revenge to blow the whole can of worms and there were a number of disgruntled law enforcement people who had taken about as much as they were prepared to from Kurtis Junior.

CHAPTER 14

The daylight was rapidly taking hold and Will was becoming concerned that they would be very exposed if there was to be a chase. His thoughts simply mirrored those of his companions, but he felt it more keenly as the images of the authorities disembarking from their vehicles played over in his mind as though he were still watching the screen in Lester's apartment. He had to shake away the thought of what would've happened had they all still been in bed when the raid took place. Lester's quick thinking creating the barricade with the table had given them vital extra seconds as the attack started. It delayed them finding out the apartment was empty.

Three hundred yards along the street, Lester dodged right into a side lane and quickly checked that his posse was in tow. Waving them past as he held back to watch the street for signs of life, he shouted, "To the end and left through the arched gates."

No one questioned his instructions; there wasn't time for deliberation or debate. The immediate need forced them to place their absolute trust in Lester's judgement and follow his command to the letter.

The archway gates gave way to a market square where there were a multitude of people milling around as they set up for the day's trading. The three front runners instantly came to a stop thinking Lester must have made a mistake. Suddenly he burst through the gates behind them immediately switching from 'the prey being pursued' to 'man heading to work in the morning' mode.

The three of them almost casually followed his lead and not a soul paid any attention to them as they crossed the busy sprawl.

Once they reached the far side, the pace picked up again and leaving the noise behind, they slipped through a gap in a fence. The plot was instantly recognisable as the place where they'd stashed Beth's car the previous night. Reaching the unit where the vehicle had been left, they rounded the corner to get to the doors. One of the double sliding doors was open and the sight made Lester slam the brakes on. The others nearly ran him down.

"Shit. Shit. SHIT!"

Lester's abuse was interrupted by the shout of someone inside the building. In a slick move, Will unzipped the pouch of the sports bag and pulled out a gun as the bag dropped to the floor at his feet. There was no protest from the others this time. He stepped over the bag and followed the side of the building until he was outside the opening. There was a burst of laughter from inside, followed by the sound of voices talking about something that had recently happened.

"I didn't think we were gonna get away that time."

"Man, you're one mad bastard. If they manage to fix us to that car, we're gonna pay."

"Fix us to the car. How the hell they gonna do that? Didn't you see what Frosty did to it? You missed the last act of the show."

"We had ourselves some fireworks."

The peals of laughter echoed around the empty unit.

"You torched it?"

"Was a piece of shit anyway," one of the guys shouted over the general enjoyment. The comment prompted Will to interrupt their fun.

"BUT IT WAS MY PIECE OF SHIT!"

The four young guys spun around to focus on Will and their reaction was immediate when they clocked the gun. The animated joviality instantly stopped and the young men turned to stony figures. Will was standing in the entrance, allowing him to communicate with the others outside without them having to be seen by the rowdy group.

"What did I tell you? It's always the car," Lester whispered. "I'll bet that's what put the cops on my doorstep. They'll probably have run the plates and found it was Beth's. They obviously knew there was a connection between us and you. Damn it!" Lester's annoyance at being pushed into action before they had a plan coloured the intonation in his voice. "I reckon they'll have guessed you were in the apartment."

The young men were looking at one another wondering what was going on as Will's attention was momentarily distracted by Lester.

"We didn't mean to trash your car, man," one of them offered apologetically, testing the water. "We just thought it was abandoned."

Will focused on the spokesman, but said nothing in response.

"What next?" he whispered to Lester. "We need to move before there are police crawling all over this area."

Lester looked Will in the eye and saw that his 'friend' was genuinely asking for some guidance.

"We need to get out of town, the sooner the better. Ask them where they were when they torched the car."

Will looked back at the young guys. The alarm was building in their faces. "You," he pointed to the one who'd been the mouthpiece. "Move over here, but slowly. I've had a bad night and we wouldn't want my finger to twitch from tiredness."

The stocky young guy looked nervous about approaching a man waving a gun at them, especially as he was to be separated from his moral support. He glanced over to his other friends, but they looked relieved that they hadn't been chosen and urged him to obey.

"NOW!" Will yelled.

The shout put urgency into his actions and he moved closer to Will. When he was a few yards away Will said, "Turn around and walk backwards to me with your hands in the air."

"Say again?"

Will clicked the loading mechanism of the gun, which immediately proved that the young man had heard the instruction clearly. He quickly spun around, raised his hands and came to a standstill as he reversed into the gun barrel. The other guys in the warehouse were absolutely silent and the look of panic in their faces reflected that of the young man with the gun in his back.

"You torched my car?" Will said quietly.

"Man, we're sorry…" He started to grovel, but Will cut across his attempts to placate his tormentor.

"*Where* did you torch my car?"

The sudden squeal of approaching sirens filled the air and for a moment they braced themselves for the possibilities until the sound began to recede into the distance. Everyone inside and out was on edge.

Once Will was sure that the siren wasn't heading in their direction he reiterated the question, pushing the gun barrel hard into the young man's back to urge him to answer instantly.

"Where?"

The guy stuttered out his response. "Broadgate. Near the disused bus depot."

Will looked at Lester who gave him an indication that he knew the place. The information gave them the opportunity to set course in the opposite direction until a strategy surfaced.

"Go stand with your buddies and don't leave here for the next half hour. You understand?"

The relief was clear in the young man's body language as he nodded vigorously and made noises to confirm that they would do exactly as instructed.

Will slid the door closed, the screeching silenced with a thud as it ran into its stopper.

"It's lucky we were up early otherwise they would've had us," said Lester, stating the obvious.

"What now though? This is your turf, Lester. Where do we go from here?" Beth had turned back to talk with the others after keeping an eye out across the compound where they'd come in.

The perplexed look on Lester's face showed he was running through the options in his head. "We need to go somewhere and get hold of a vehicle that won't be missed for a few days." Lester tapped his forehead as if to jog some long, forgotten, memory. "Think Lester, think," he said out loud to himself. His face suddenly changed as an idea came to mind. "The graveyard!" Lester blurted the words out like they were the answer in a 'eureka moment'.

The others were slightly bemused by his outburst and glanced at each other for inspiration about the meaning.

"What? You want to steal a hearse or something," Tia said. "I thought we were trying to go unnoticed. It'll hardly help if we look like the Addams family."

Lester rolled his eyes at the sour humour and restrained his impulse to respond in the same vein.

"The graveyard, my dear girl, is the nickname for the local scrap yard where the 'rusted rollers' end up when someone does a trade to buy a new car. They've usually got rows of cars that are a little worn around the edges, but run okay. They set them aside in an area where you can go look around to see if you want to buy one for parts, or fix it up. There's no way they will miss one for a while, they're always too busy with the other section of the yard where they break the no hopers. It's on the edge of town, about two, maybe two-and-a-half miles."

"Don't they keep them locked up?" Beth quizzed.

A smirk crossed Lester's lips. "This is Lester you're talking to, darlin'. I am to locks what Harry Houdini was to handcuffs. I don't own this warehouse you know. How do you think we got your car into this place when you got here?"

"Probably the same way that these punks got it out so they could trash it, smart ass," Will muttered. The grin on Lester's face immediately disappeared. "We'd better get moving if that's our best option."

Beth raised her voice as much as she felt she could under the circumstances, leaving no doubt about her feelings. "Stop being such a blockhead, Will. If it hadn't been for Lester's quick response we wouldn't even be here, so just quit your snide comments."

"Yeah, blockhead," Lester chipped in, but the wry smile that accompanied his comment was wiped from his face as Beth glared at him. "It's this way," he quickly added, moving off in the opposite direction to the way Will had meant to set out.

Will glared after Lester as he shot across the open compound. "I swear I'm gonna…" Will paused when he met the eyes of Beth and Tia staring at him in disbelief and anger. He stooped down and slipped the gun back into his bag, ignoring the girls.

Beth turned to follow in Lester's footsteps with Tia close behind her. Once Will had finished what he was doing he trailed along in the rearguard.

They hurried down a series of back streets that were increasingly litter strewn. The grey morning light gave all the half-derelict buildings a sinister look, as if they'd jumped to another continent ruled by a regime that insisted every person and building was the same. The scene was monochrome, dirty, depressing.

Tia began to dwell on the situation as they hurried along the pathway to wherever Lester was taking them. The pounding of each footstep was matched by the drumming of the same beat in her head, each thud prompting a thought about the circumstances that surrounded her. The flashing of memories of the immediate past, the attempt of one of her captors to take advantage of her vulnerability and her subsequent escape, all vied for her attention. No matter how she tried to shake the spiral of despair that began to drag her down, every footfall hammered home the desperation she felt. It was one thing to be pursued by some unknown people intent on using her as some bargaining chip, but quite another to suddenly be running from the legitimate law enforcement agencies. She couldn't shake the fact that she'd been the beginning of the turmoil that now engulfed them all. It had been difficult to deal with the responsibility she felt for turning Will's life upside down, but the chain reaction for him was to go to Beth, who had become embroiled in the saga. She turned to Lester for help and now they were on their way to steal a car.

Tia held her place in the human chain, keeping to the rhythm and pace as she followed the directions set by Lester, but her leaden legs reflected a heavy heart. She began to lose awareness of her surroundings and where they were heading. Her mind filled with remorse for ever having tried to escape from her captivity. *Perhaps they would have let me go eventually. Maybe if I'd just waited a little longer. What possible value could I have been to them? Why me? What had I done? And now look at the situation I have created for these people who only tried to help me. Oh god...* The thoughts bombarded her like hammer blows. The sound of a siren wailed in the distance making her glance back in the direction of the sound. It signalled the onset of panic that flared up without restraint.

Tia abruptly stopped dead in her tracks. It was so unexpected that Will ran into the back of her and they almost toppled over in a heap on the ground. He struggled to retain his balance while holding onto Tia, trying to make sure she didn't end up in the gutter.

In the scuffle she called out, aware of what was happening as they were about to crash to the ground. The shout made Beth and Lester instantly stop and turn. They reversed direction to gather quickly alongside their companions.

As they rallied around Tia to check everything was okay, she suddenly felt overwhelmed with everything. Her eyes were wide as saucers as she looked at them and the three faces of her new friends looked back at her questioningly.

"What have I done to all of you?" Days of pent-up emotion that had been forcefully restrained burst out. "I'm like the curse of Jonah." The opportunist spirit that had made her take a chance to escape from her captors had deserted her. Raw emotion poured from deep within as the dam wall gave way and a flood of force crashed over her landscape.

The two guys were at a loss about how to deal with the situation. Lester glanced up at the towering buildings as though he were responding to a feeling of being watched from above. The sound of a distant siren still drifted on the air, causing him to be a little alarmed that they had halted their progress.

Beth caught his concern and was aware of the pressure they were under to continue their escape. She did what neither of the two men could've done. The palm of her hand came across with quite a crack as it connected with Tia's cheek. The shock of the sudden impact was not in the force, but in the surprise of the action. Lester looked stunned as he glanced at Will and the expression that met his eyes told him that Will was equally shocked.

Tia drew a sharp breath at the stinging impact and wide eyes full of spilling tears locked onto Beth's face as she invaded her space.

"Here and now, Tia," Beth spoke in a measured way. Her voice held authority and urgency, but was not without compassion. "We need you fully here and now. Do you understand?"

The two guys waited with bated breath for a response and the second or two before it came seemed like minutes. Tia's eyes solidly focused on Beth's as she took in what was being said and steeled herself for what had to be done. She nodded, indicating she understood. Without hesitation Beth said softly, "Good girl." She turned and pushed Lester back into his lead position, urging him to set the pace again. He initially hesitated, glancing at Tia's emotion filled face. A reddish mark was beginning to show on her cheek, which caught his attention, but Beth's prompting set him in motion again.

"You okay to go?" Beth checked.

Tia nodded and set off with Beth at her side and Will following behind.

Moments later they rounded a final corner and picked up a path that followed along a railway line. In the distance they could see the edge of the town marked by an industrial area. Lester indicated that they were near and picked up the pace a little. They all kept with him with renewed determination to make their getaway a success.

The light was increasing gradually, but in their situation it appeared to change at an alarming rate. The cover of darkness was always going to be of assistance, but that luxury was about to be snatched away.

They closed in on the edge of the compound that housed the remains of hundreds, if not thousands of wrecked vehicles. Many of them were in varying states on their way to the ultimate destination of the crusher.

Edging their way around the compound, they found a section that housed the 'good' vehicles. Lester rummaged around in his bag before producing the required tools to spring the lock. Less than thirty seconds later Will pulled the gate opened enough to allow them into the restricted area.

"I'll wait just out of sight at the gate… To swing it open when you're ready," Will called out under his breath. Lester threw up his thumb in recognition without missing a beat as he closed in to assess the cars. Turning to Beth he said, "You're the expert, babe. Which one?" As he paused to ask, she went straight past him to a dull grey long wheel based jeep that was tucked away beneath some trees at the far side of the section. The door was unlocked and she jumped straight into the driver's seat. When Lester reached her he looked at the vehicle with a certain amount of disdain.

"What the hell d'you want to pick this heap for?"

Beth's hands didn't stop moving for a second as she pulled at various panels beneath the dash and exposed some of the wiring.

"One," she turned and glanced at Lester to check she had his attention, "it's on the far side of the compound, obviously neglected. Therefore, it won't be missed. Two, I've been working with these for years so I know I can handle most of the problems we might face. Three, there's no steering lock on this model which removes one of the problems they never seem to have in the movies." She was still frantically working with the cables under the dash. "Four, it gives us the opportunity to drive on roads that most other vehicles would avoid and five, they look like shit, but are built like tanks. They go forever." She paused, and moved so that she could look Lester straight in the eye. "Any more questions?"

"Okay, okay." He shrugged and turned to Tia to see another impressed face.

Beth dipped back under the dash to continue what she was doing. There was a sudden clunk as the old wagon's engine turned over a few times. It gave a slight chug as if trying to convince a sceptical audience that there was still some life left in the old beast. Again the whirring of mechanical parts preceded a few more chugs and the smell of fuel. Beth jumped from the cab and lifted the bonnet until she could see what was beneath.

"Lester, hold this up."

She barely waited for him to get into position before leaping into the engine bay. The creeping daylight was just what she needed for the repair, but the last thing they wanted for them to make good their escape.

Beth stripped off the shirt she'd been wearing so that she was down to her T-shirt. She began cleaning frantically at the electrical leads under the bonnet. Tia and Lester felt helpless, but knew enough to keep out of Beth's way as she worked her magic.

Seconds later she was back in the driver's seat ready to try once more to rouse the sleeping giant. There was a clunk followed by a sudden roar of life. The dull thud of the hood closing and the race to scramble into the cab, gave way to the rattle of tyres spitting gravel through the boarded fence. Will appeared on cue, swinging the gate wide to allow the wagon to arc out of the compound. He jumped into the rear seat just as Lester jumped out of the front one.

"What's he doing?" Will shouted.

The gate came back to its closed position and Lester re-fastened the lock. It all seemed to take too long as their heartbeats raced, but they realised that it was the only way they would buy some time. The compound had to look undisturbed.

The vehicle took off almost the moment Lester's feet cleared the ground and he barked instructions about a back lane that skirted the valley before getting to a quiet road away from the town.

As the panic settled and the rumble of the wagon became an even hum, Beth glanced at Tia in the rear-view mirror. "How's the face?" she said, apologetically.

"I'm okay, thanks," Tia smiled.

Beth turned her attention back to the road and Will looked at Lester as he spun around in his seat to face them. The mischievous grin on Lester's face prompted a quizzical expression from Tia.

"If I ever saw a guy even try something like that, I would bust him on his ass without a second thought."

"Me too," added Will.

The laughter punctured the tension that had been building since the raid on Lester's apartment. They were all acutely aware of the gravity of their situation, but it seemed that they were one step ahead again and that brought a measure of relief.

The two guys returned to their positions looking out of the windows and watching the scenery pass by. Tia caught Beth's glance in the rear-view mirror. The smile they exchanged said more than words could ever explain, especially in the hearing of the two men, but something stronger than mere acquaintance was being forged in the heat of their experience. Tia knew she owed a debt of gratitude to the most extraordinary woman she'd ever met. Beth had surprised her as Will promised she would.

The old wagon rumbled its way along the road for several miles before they stopped for fuel at a station that was out of the way; the kind of place that is faceless and asks no questions because they're thankful for the business.

"Will," Beth caught his attention as he was discreetly hiding away in the back seat. "I'm going to ring Mrs Drake to check that she has Boost and everything is okay. I think I may need to make an apology."

"Okay."

Beth went inside the shop to find a payphone, leaving Lester filling the gas-tank. A scruffy old man who sauntered through from a tatty garage next door, directed her to the back of the shabby room. Closing herself in the little ramshackle kiosk that had been fitted to give some privacy, but had long outlasted its useful life, she dialled the number and listened to the ring tone that sounded distant down the line. There was no question that Mrs Drake would be up this early, but Beth braced herself for the questions that would follow her introduction.

There was a click as the tone changed and then the voice of the old lady.

"Hello."

Beth swallowed and started as brightly as she could.

"Hello, Mrs Drake. It's Beth."

"Oh, Beth, my dear. I've been so worried about you. Where *are* you?"

A twinge of conscience hit Beth as she heard the concern in the old lady's voice.

"I'm okay, Mrs Drake. I've had to make a trip somewhere. A little bit of an emergency. I'm so sorry; I didn't know what to do with Boost. I had to leave so early and at the last minute… I hoped you wouldn't mind."

"Mind? I'm delighted to look after Boost. He's a joy to have around, but it's you I'm concerned about. I rang Officer Madeley because I thought something must have happened."

Beth winced at the mention of Officer Madeley, knowing that it was not a good move and probably led to the drama they'd experienced.

"He seemed quite worried when I spoke to him," she continued. "There was *such* a lot of activity on the road after that; patrol cars coming and going and the like. Are you sure you're alright?"

"Yes, really, I'm fine."

"When will you be back? I can let Officer Madeley know so that he doesn't have to spend his time watching your house."

"He's watching my house?" Beth's voice gave away her unease.

"Yes. I don't exactly know why, but he seems to change with that other young man from the station. They must have been parked out on the road down there all day."

Beth was suddenly aware that the old lady was happy to sit and chat for a while, but she knew she couldn't afford the time, so she cut the conversation short.

"Is Boost okay with you?"

"Sure he is. We're having a ball, but…"

"I've got to go Mrs Drake. I'm so sorry to do this, but it is very important. I'll be in touch soon, okay?"

"Yes, but…"

"I have to go now, bye."

Beth dropped the receiver onto its holder and clasped her hands to her face. She didn't like to end the call so abruptly, but there was no way that she could explain the situation to the old lady.

She felt a little subdued as she wandered out into the early morning light. The freshness hit her as she stepped out of the fusty old shop. As she climbed back into the driver's seat, Will could tell that something weighed heavy on her mind.

"What's wrong Beth?" he asked, as he caught sight of her troubled expression in the rear-view mirror.

She sighed and waited as Lester and Tia got back into the vehicle. They'd been attending to the need for something to eat by buying the junk stuff that was available.

"I've just spoken to Mrs Drake."

Lester looked lost. "Who's Mrs Drake?"

"She's my neighbour back home," Beth explained. "When Will and Tia came to my place, Will brought his dog, Boost. We couldn't bring him with us when we came to meet up with you, for obvious reasons, so I left him with my neighbour. Boost is okay by the way, Will," Beth hesitated as she pulled out onto the road. "Mrs Drake called the police when I didn't return in the evening because she was worried that something might have happened. It looks like they figured out that it was your dog, Will. It seems there was a flurry of activity back home. Mrs Drake told me that Officer Madeley, the guy who came to the house when you and Tia hid in the attic, has been watching the house since yesterday evening. I assume they've been looking for my car since then. When those punks mashed it in public, it must have given the game away very quickly. They must have figured that we were trying to connect up with you, Lester."

"We need to get off the roads and hole up for a while where we're not going to be seen," Will suggested. "Travelling in daylight is just going to be too risky. Apart from that, does anyone know where we are actually heading?"

"I agree, Beth," Lester chimed in. "I picked up a map when we stopped," he dug in the bag of stuff and pulled it out. "We need to give ourselves some space to think and decide what we're going to do instead of just driving aimlessly."

"Okay. You'd better find us somewhere."

Lester and Will scanned the map until they settled on a place to head for and called out instructions to Beth that eventually took them down some remote roads and onto a dirt track. Within the hour they were parking beneath some trees alongside a stream in a picturesque setting. If it hadn't been for the reality of their circumstances, anyone would have thought they were on a recreational trip.

There was general agreement that they needed to take some time to plan the next step, but for that first few hours in the morning, before trying to get some rest, they took advantage of the warmth of the rising sun and the cool water, to try to soothe away some of their anxiety.

CHAPTER 15

"Listen guys." Lester had his 'I'm in charge' head on. "It's very important we get somewhere that I can connect to the internet. That's our only hope of trying to get to some information that might help us understand what's going on. We also need to figure out who we can trust and how to get in touch with them without giving ourselves away."

"What do you mean?" Will asked.

"There's no way that we're going to sort this on our own. If there's something deeper going on here, then we need to know who's in on it and who would love to bust the sorry asses of the people causing us so much trouble." Lester looked across at Will, realising the situation was particularly dire for him. "I'm going to start trawling through some of the classified stuff that I downloaded last night. I'll use the laptop, but we *are* going to need some help, or an almighty stroke of luck. So if anyone has any ideas..."

Lester grabbed his computer and bag of tricks from the back seat of the wagon and set about rigging up a lead from the car battery to keep it running for the day. As soon as he was set and made himself comfortable in the vehicle with the doors wide open, he began to play the laptop keyboard like a musical maestro demonstrating his genius on a piano. With his eyes glued to the screen, he sat there endlessly sifting and discarding, while the others left him to it. Beth occasionally glanced over at him to see if he was okay. It was as though he drew power from the equipment and once engaged in the virtual world he was lost to everything else.

The other three eventually got bored just waiting around, so they left Lester to his own devices, knowing that he would say something when he had something to tell them and not a moment before.

Tia wandered a little distance away from Beth and Will, sensing they needed to talk and knowing her presence would not give them the freedom to do so. She went and sat near the river's edge, leaning back against a rock while listening to the cascading water that danced over the boulders. She discreetly watched the pair of them as they stood facing each other. They were too far away for her to be able to hear what was being said, but she could read the body language and gestures. The link between them had obviously been strong and was only put under strain by the tragic circumstances that had snatched away precious people from them both.

After a little while they came and sat with Tia, but she didn't want to intrude on their privacy by asking what they'd been talking about. The three of them sat together, each lost in their own world of thought as they watched the endless flow of water with its entertaining sound and image. The sun was climbing and the heat rising, so eventually they moved to some nearby trees to take advantage of the shade.

The change initiated some light conversation and they settled in their new position while engaging in idle chat.

Tia was momentarily distracted causing Beth and Will to turn and look in the direction of her gaze. Lester was marching across the open space to join them, but his manner showed there was purpose in the action. His laptop was balanced on one hand like a waiter carrying a tray of drinks and he moved determinedly rather than leisurely.

Instead of waiting to find out what they were talking about so that he could join the conversation, he cut straight through with what was on his mind. There were questions he was burning to ask and launched straight into them without apology.

"Is this your father, Tia? Carlos Liatzo?" He spun the machine around to show her the picture on the screen as the other two leaned across to take a look.

Surprised to be suddenly presented with the picture, Tia was a little hesitant. "Yes… Where did that come from?"

Lester ignored her question and posed another without skipping a beat. "What does he do?"

Beth frowned at the blunt delivery that carried a demanding tone, but Lester didn't notice, his focus was on Tia's anticipated answer.

"He owns a company that does work for the government. Some kind of research, I think."

"SilverTech National?" Lester delivered the name before Tia could attempt to.

"Yes. How do you know that?"

"Well, the Security Agencies certainly know about him." Tia frowned, not understanding the inference in the statement. "I've just busted the release code on a file full of material and some of it is very interesting. Do you know a man called Steven Holden?"

"No." Will and Beth glanced at Tia as her answer carried an abrupt tone.

"How about, Nazim Akbbar?"

"No." The irritation at being interrogated was clearly surfacing in Tia's voice.

"Who the hell are these people, Lester?" Will butted in to try to find out where the questioning was going and the interruption broke the intensity.

Lester shrugged. "They're just names mentioned in various places in connection with Tia's father. It ain't that clear who, or what they are yet." He blew air out of the side of his mouth in frustration, closed the lid on the computer and settled down next to the others. "To keep digging properly, I need to get somewhere that I can search online."

"Internet café?" Beth quizzed helpfully.

"Sure, if the connection speed's okay. We need to get the information quickly and get out of there."

Lester leaned back against the tree trunk and closed his eyes. He was quiet for a few minutes and looked as though he was settling down for a snooze, but the peace didn't last long.

"You don't seem to know much about your old man, Tia." He opened his eyes to take a quick look at her, making sure she'd heard him, then went back to his previous position while waiting for a response.

"He spent a lot of time away from home. Sometimes for long periods. I think he was away most during my late teenage years. Each time seemed to be longer than the last. It was great when he was home, but I missed him so much when he was away." Her voice broke a little as she explained, hinting at the buried emotions. "He never talked about his work. I mean not ever. I never went to the company buildings." The concern grew in her voice. "Are you suggesting that he was some kind of criminal?" Lester was focused on Tia by the time she asked the question. "Something illegal?"

Lester realised he'd hit a raw nerve and tried to soften his approach. "I honestly don't know yet, Tia. It might be that he was working for the security services. I just don't know yet."

An awkwardness descended on the group momentarily until Beth tried to slightly change the subject. "Tia told me last night that she hadn't seen her dad properly since her sixteenth birthday. He bought her some studs," Beth casually added.

Lester pulled a face to suggest he had no idea what she was talking about.

"Earrings, you drip."

"Oh." Lester went back to his siesta.

"She said he named them…" Beth gave a little laugh. "What did he call them, Tia?" Beth suddenly felt a twinge of conscience that she'd perhaps said something she shouldn't.

"Saber gemas," Tia filled in the information, but felt a bit embarrassed by having to do so.

"Weird don't you think… Naming earrings? They look really nice though."

Lester was suddenly alert again and looking at the girls. "Knowledge gems."

Beth laughed out loud at his translation. "How did you know that, Lester?"

"It's Spanish, but never mind how I know. What do you mean they look nice?"

"She showed me last night," said Beth.

Lester immediately turned his attention to Tia and everyone else stared at Lester. "You mean you're wearing them?"

Tia nodded, curious about Lester's sudden interest. "Can't take them out. They're kind of permanent. At least, if I want to remove them they would have to be cut off."

Lester was still staring at Tia, but he was lost deep in thought and totally missed the conversation that followed, until Beth noticed he wasn't with them.

"H-e-l-l-o." She waved a hand in front of his face and he seemed to instantly return from his trance. "Penny for them."

"Not worth a penny," he said, dismissively. "Not yet anyway." He jumped to his feet and headed back to the jeep with his laptop in hand.

"What was that about?" Tia looked at Beth and Will.

Will waved a hand in Lester's direction. "Just let him do his stuff," he said, as he picked up a stone and threw it toward the river. "Much as it pains me to admit it, he's like a dog with a bone when it comes to things like this. He's certainly a one-off, thank goodness."

"Why is it that you have to say it like that, Will? I mean…" Tia paused, uncertain whether to continue, but taking a plunge into the unknown she got even more direct. "Why *are* you two always at each other's throats?"

Will ignored Tia's question and threw another stone. He stood up and went to lean against a nearby tree. Beth waited for a few moments before deciding that she would tell the reason, if Will wouldn't. She turned her attention to Tia.

"The whole stupid issue started when we were still very green, new soldiers. It was just after we'd completed basic training; before Lester went off to do his 'techy' thing; Will and I followed a more conventional route. We were stationed together at the training barracks and Lester, being Lester," she shrugged her shoulders and rolled her eyes as a sign of recognition that Lester's unique character was not going to be changed, "was out to have a little fun at my expense. I'd known both Will and Lester for quite some time before we all joined up, but *they* didn't cross paths until that 'infamous' evening." Beth rolled her eyes once more, but with greater exaggeration. She hesitated before continuing, throwing a glance across at Will, but he pretended he couldn't hear. Her expression suggested that the incident had been a thorn in her side ever since.

"One night," she turned her attention back to Tia, lowering her voice and trying to keep Will from hearing what was being said, "when I was out for the evening with a group of girls from the squad, Lester thought it would be funny to pretend to mug us in the street. He pulled a balaclava on and started acting like he was about to rob us, but it was all an act." Beth sniggered at the memory. "So, he pretends he's drunk and getting the whole thing wrong; pulls the balaclava on backwards so he can't see, then when he gets it straight he's holding his toy pistol the wrong way round. We're all screaming and laughing at this performance." Tia's smile grew as Beth painted the scene for her, but quickly glancing at Will, noticed that he appeared to be making an effort to listen without being seen. Catching Tia's look, Beth threw a glance over her shoulder at Will before continuing.

"So, when Lester finally gets to the part in the routine where he's organised with the balaclava and the pistol, we pretend to be giving ourselves up so that he can take the money." There was a smirk on Beth's face and she shook her head. Quietening her voice a little more, she leaned in to Tia. "It was at this point, when it must have looked quite real, that Will came around the corner. He was heading for the club he knew I was going to be at because I'd told him he needed to meet Lester, my friend." Beth burst out laughing at the irony that she'd arranged the meeting. When she regained her composure she continued, "Will sees his friend," she pointed to herself, "being mugged at gun point. Bold as you like, he charges the mugger, Lester, from behind." Beth snorted a laugh, but Tia glanced at Will wondering why he wasn't participating in the fun of the story. "Will gave Lester the beating of his life that night. He jumped him from behind, sending him crashing to the floor. It completely took Lester by surprise and he hit the deck, with Will on top of him, like a sack of potatoes. We tried to pull Will off, but it all happened so fast that the damage was done before we could stop it. Lester was in hospital for a few days with two broken ribs and concussion."

"No!" Tia put her hand to her mouth, her eyes wide with shock.

Beth punctuated her story with another laugh which she couldn't hold back, but quickly regained control.

"It was bad." She shook her head. "The fall-out from that incident was monumental. No word of a lie, the shit hit the fan, big-time. It's a wonder that the pair of them weren't kicked out of the forces. Neither one of them would accept responsibility or blame. They were as bull-headed then as they are now. It infuriated the commanding officer. He dragged their punishment out for weeks and weeks trying to get the stubborn schmucks to at least apologise, but they can be as bad as each other, as you've seen. He made them scrub everything from the barrack huts to the toilets; put them on the worst guard duty; work in the kitchens; the works. Neither of them would give way and both of them paid the price."

Beth dropped her voice to a whisper. "I can understand why Will did what he did, but it's been a point of friction ever since. There hasn't been a single meeting between these two that's passed without some reference to whose fault it was. Will accuses Lester of being stupid by pretending to mug us and Lester accuses Will of acting only because he saw what he wanted to see, a black man committing a crime. I've never found out whether Will took the time to see that the gun in Lester's hand was a fluorescent green water pistol. I suppose his back was turned to him." Beth laughed again. "The stupid thing about the whole incident, and all the hassle that followed with the military police, is that they're both too pig-headed to forgive and forget. If you ask me, I think Lester's a little intimidated by Will's stature and Will is the same about how smart Lester is. He admits it grudgingly, as you've seen."

Will suddenly spun around to face them, glaring at Beth. "I *did* what I thought was right. What if it had been a real mugger?"

He stormed off with a grim look etched on his face. Beth shook her head as she watched him go. "Impossible! They are both as impossible as each other. Fine if you meet them separately, but, putting them together, it's like petrol on a fire." She stood up and brushed off her trousers. "Sad thing is, they would absolutely get on together, I'm sure of it, but neither one wants to lose face." Beth made an exaggerated sigh. "I'm going to see what Lester's up to. Perhaps you should go babysit the other one?" Beth winked then turned on her heels and headed for the jeep.

Tia sat for a few moments watching Will wander away, wondered at the circumstances that had brought her to this place with these people. After a few minutes, she stood and looked over to the river bank to see where Will had got to. He was about a hundred yards upstream, standing by the water's edge. Tia followed in his footsteps until she came close to him. He looked downcast as he stood with his back to her, while staring at the much calmer section of the river. The noise level was substantially lower, away from the faster flow and the boulders that churned the river into white froth.

She approached slowly. Will turned to glance over his shoulder, acknowledging her presence, but said nothing.

Unsure what to do, Tia came alongside him, sat on a boulder at the water's edge and began to take her training shoes and socks off. She rolled up her jeans to above the knee then looked up at Will. "Fancy a dip?"

He gave a non-committal shrug. She smiled and waved him to join her as she stepped into the cold water, letting out a cry at the chill. A few moments later he was following her example.

Will put one foot in and screwed up his face at the temperature. He pretended that he'd changed his mind.

"Get in here, you sissy," Tia laughed, as she teased.

With a little more light-hearted goading, Will finally joined her.

The stones underfoot made walking difficult and they were constantly waving arms around trying to keep their balance. Moving along into the flow of the cool water felt good and Tia followed Will's lead a little way up stream.

Suddenly she squealed and Will instinctively threw out his hand to help. Tia grabbed hold and managed to steady herself as they both laughed at her close call.

"I was nearly flat on my back!" she shouted through the laughter and the sound of bubbling water. They waded back and forth for a few minutes, enjoying the moment. Will was conscious that they were still holding hands. He had no desire to let go and the awkwardness of keeping balance while walking in the river gave cover to his action. The comfort he felt in that intimate touch, the feeling of being connected and wanted, was very pleasing. There was sheer joy in Tia's face. It was radiant with happiness of the simple pleasure. Just for that moment the furrowed brow and nervous concern had disappeared from her beaming face. It made him smile in appreciation as he connected with her momentary freedom, but he didn't realise she'd noticed.

"Why the look?"

He felt a little embarrassed that she'd seen his reaction to her. "You just look like you're enjoying yourself."

She turned her head and looked up into his eyes. "I am." Time seemed to stop for a while. She pressed into him so that her shoulder rested on his arm. Will spontaneously squeezed her hand and felt Tia respond. They stood for a moment looking at the water, each one receiving comfort from the other's touch.

"This is such a lovely place. Why don't we seem to find time to come to places like this when everything's fine?" Will shrugged in answer to her question. "I bet it's years since someone was here. It's so out of the way."

"Mmm."

Tia turned to look at Will again and found him looking down at her. "What do you mean. 'Mmm'. It's much more than that, it's... It's beautiful."

There was a pause as their eyes stayed connected. "You're beautiful." Will brought his free hand up to touch her cheek and she tilted her face into his caress. The surprise and gentleness of his gesture made Tia smile and Will tilted his head down until their foreheads gently touched. He turned fully toward her, his hand still touching her cheek, but Tia's look suddenly changed. The smile disappeared and he felt her fractionally pull away from him. A smile flickered then she turned, let go of his hand and, quickly dipping, she flicked up a spray of water at him. Will winced as the cold droplets landed and smiled at the mischievous laugh Tia let out. In the moment of frivolity, she stumbled again. Their hands immediately linked once more as they headed back to where they'd got into the water.

Reaching the shore, they'd been so lost in the moment that they didn't notice Beth who had come looking for them. The smile on her face made Will instantly release Tia's hold, as if he had been caught doing something he shouldn't.

"Both okay?" she said suggestively.

Tia blushed and quickly turned away to seat herself on a rock while she put her shoes on.

CHAPTER 16

The day dragged for them as they waited for dusk to fall before setting out again. Lester wanted to head to a built-up area to find access to the internet so that he could continue his search for information. The nearest town of substance was about forty miles away, so they prepared to set out at seven o'clock.

While Lester was working on his computer, he'd been monitoring his scanner and a local radio station to check whether there was any risk to them after taking the jeep, but all seemed well. There were a few moments when the radio traffic between police units gave information about the incident earlier in the morning, but nothing that would help in their attempts to evade the authorities.

As they climbed into the vehicle, the ease that had descended on them when they stopped in such an isolated place, gave way to a feeling of apprehension as they prepared to re-engage with the world beyond. Each one tried to cover the feeling in their own way, a nervous laugh, a comment about something mundane, quietness, but they were all aware of the reality they were facing.

Once back on the normal road again, the vehicle settled into a sustained low hum that gently vibrated through every part of the jeep. As the miles disappeared and the silence in the cab lingered long, the darkness covered nervous faces and cloaked them on their journey.

The quiet was finally broken by a question from Will. "You need to go somewhere specific, Lester?"

"When we get to the built-up area I can check for a wireless signal. We just need one with unrestricted access. Could be outside someone's house or near a public building… We won't know until we get there."

"Looking for something in particular?"

"Yeah."

There was a pause as the others waited for a little more, but that was all Lester was going to give and Will didn't want to push him in case it ended in another unpleasant confrontation. Beth was less concerned, but knew that everyone was as inquisitive as she was.

"Would you care to tell us what?"

"Not until I can check something." Lester was giving no ground.

Tia turned and glanced at Will, but he was looking through the side window as though he was holding some comment about Lester that he thought might not be welcome. She went back to watching the road. Beth continued to follow the tarmac to their next destination.

Will suddenly threw a comment into the mix without any hint of expecting an answer. "I swear I've heard the name, Liatzo, before. It's been gnawing away at me since I first heard it, but I just can't put my finger on why it's got any significance."

Lester turned to look at Will. "You ever heard of 'Operation CAPA'?"

"That was some kind of weapon test facility wasn't it?" Beth caught Lester's eye in the rear view mirror.

"One that you shouldn't know anything about!" Lester stated emphatically.

"Just kept my ear to the ground." Beth shrugged, but the smug look on her face showed that she'd enjoyed stealing Lester's trump card.

He sat looking at her in the rear-view mirror for a moment, but soon became aware that Tia was waiting for the conversation to continue, having made no connection between her surname and the subject of discussion. The hesitation became too much for her and she urged them on.

"What has *that* got to do with my father?"

"Look," Lester shrugged his shoulders to show he was fishing in the dark. "I don't know all that much at the moment, but what I do know is that your father is not a businessman that owns a company working for the government. *He works for the government, period.* If there even is a company, I think it's just a cover. What exactly he does is not that easy to find out. I've ploughed through a lot of security barriers, but the files about him are locked up pretty tight. He's Mexican alright, but is, or has been, working for the US government for years."

All eyes were on Lester as he finished what he was saying. Even Beth was divided between the road and the rear-view mirror.

"Wait a minute," Will started. "You're telling me that there's something to do with Tia's father that made someone want to kidnap her?" Lester shrugged, but Will hadn't finished. "That the two guys killed at my place were something to do with her father?"

Tia's face displayed shock at Will's suggestion that her father was involved.

"Let me put it like this, Will. Whoever it was that killed those guys, and I know it wasn't you, they're playing hard ball because there's something big at stake here. God knows what. I can't even begin to make sense of it right now. If we're going to find out I need some time and some luck, and very soon."

The hum of the engine filled the vacant space in the conversation until the silence begged to be broken.

"When I was first taken," Tia's voice had a distinct shake in it, "I just thought they'd got the wrong person, but what you're talking about is scary."

"I don't mean to alarm you, Tia, but we have to face the truth. Whatever we're dealing with isn't just a case of convincing the police that Will didn't kill two guys who broke into his house. I doubt if the regular authorities even know what's going on, but someone definitely does, someone who appears to be restraining information from getting into the public domain. Like your involvement for example. I've been listening to all the news bulletins and there's still been nothing about you. So, either they don't know anything about you, or your involvement, which I doubt, or someone is deliberately suppressing that information for other reasons. The two names I mentioned to you earlier, when I asked if you knew them," Lester rustled through some papers, "Steven Holden and Nazim Akkbar. The connection between them and your father is mentioned in some of the files. They look like they were some kind of team or special unit."

"You said they *were*," Beth prompted Lester for an explanation.

"Holden died three years ago; Akkbar this year." Lester had the complete attention of the group. "The less secure files that mention Holden give the impression that he was accidentally killed in a random shooting in Columbia. The secure file I busted earlier…" he hesitated. "That is to say, the top secret file, reads like he was deliberately targeted, but there's no information about how, or who did it. There's no detail about Akkbar's demise in the material that I've got, except to say that he *is* dead."

The conversation started to reaffirm a suspicion that Tia had carried about her father for a long time. Her childhood years showed that he was a loving man who placed importance on his family, but his absence in her later teenage years made her wonder if something had happened to him. If the two men he'd been involved with were dead, perhaps he was too. The fact that Lester struggled to find the truth about the others showed that there was much more to Carlos Liatzo than she had ever understood.

Tia held her counsel, not wanting to voice her concerns, as though it would simply bring to reality what she'd feared. The little hope that she might see him again had been buried, but she was not willing to surrender it, even in the face of the increasing possibility that she wouldn't.

Tia's contemplation was broken when she noticed that Beth had suddenly started glancing from one door mirror to the rear-view mirror and back in an obvious way. Will took note of the movements and turned around to look through the rear windshield. He caught sight of car headlights behind them approaching at a substantial speed. They were out on deserted roads and still twenty miles from the town they were heading to. Their circumstances were enough to put them on high alert at anything that seemed suspicious, but the discussion that had been taking place exaggerated the alarm.

"That vehicle's coming up on us very fast, Will," Beth said, seeing that he'd observed the threat. "Let's hope this isn't trouble, but you'd better be ready just in case."

The sound of a zip being hastily opened was followed by the click-click of gun metal being readied for action. "Take this Lester," Will nudged him as he handed over the weapon before readying another for himself.

The two guys positioned themselves against the doors so that they could watch through the rear screen while trying to avoid the closing headlights from the car behind lighting them up like a stage spotlight.

"I'm hoping this has nothing to do with us," Beth shouted. "So, I'm going to slow down and make it easy for them to come straight past."

She edged nearer to the side of the road and eased off the gas. The jeep noticeably changed speed. The car behind was now less than quarter of a mile away and closing fast. As it approached, they braced themselves for what might happen.

"Tia, drop down in your seat so it looks like there's only a driver in the car," Will shouted. She reacted instantly to the instruction.

The car was now only a few hundred yards away, its speed and direction unchanged. It maintained its position on the road as it closed in behind them and was literally a few yards away before a violent swerve and sudden braking brought it alongside the jeep. Will and Lester had changed their position to being low down on the back seat, using Beth's commentary to keep in touch with what was happening.

The sleek black car held position beside them on the wrong side of the road. Beth could see a group of young guys in the vehicle. They were laughing at her and clearly intent on mischief. The car pulled away in front and started to hog the centre of the road. The driver deliberately punched the brakes from time to time so that Beth had to take evasive action.

"What the hell is going on, Beth?" Lester shouted.

"It's a bunch of no-brain, testosterone loaded, pimple-faced idiots out for a joy ride," she fumed. The jeep suddenly slowed again as she reacted to what was happening in front, prompting her to shout a few obscenities at them. Her anger was rising to the surface and someone was about to suffer the consequence. "You stupid punks!" she yelled in frustration. The car in front caught Beth off-guard as she was busy expressing her opinion about their antics and she reacted too slowly to prevent contact. The jeep juddered as it hit the back of the car with a loud thud. The sound of crunching body panels was clear. The other vehicle twitched side to side on the road from the unexpected impact then swerved over, slowing until it came back alongside the jeep. The windows were down and there was angry gesticulation from the occupants as though Beth was at fault. She contained her anger and simply smiled and waved at them as though she was enjoying the fun. Meanwhile she completely disregarded the concerns expressed by Lester about what was happening.

"It's time to end this."

The determined tone in her voice prompted the others to brace themselves. She allowed the jeep to lazily drift across the carriageway so that the sports car was being squeezed off the road. The panic in the eyes of the passengers turned to concerned shouts at the driver to get out of the way of the mad woman in the jeep. Having come off worse from the impact, figuring that the damage sustained was more than they wanted to carry, the car suddenly accelerated away into the distance until the rear lights disappeared and peace was restored.

"Dumb idiots!" Beth shouted the last insult after them as the vehicle vanished over a distant rise.

"Remind me never to argue with you on the road," Will laughed.

"Oh god!"

"What now?"

Lester and Will simultaneously turned to look out of the rear window.

"Not another one," Beth complained.

"That's no punk in a fast car, Beth. Not with flashing lights."

They assumed their previous hiding positions and listened to Beth narrating the approach of the patrol car. This time there was no slowing down. It just came tearing past like a train jumping a station and they all felt the jeep rock with the turbulence.

"Thank goodness for that," Beth let out a sigh. "I reckon we've had our share of excitement for the last few days."

As the flashing lights disappeared over the brow of a distant hill, the group relaxed ready to settle back into their quiet journey.

Two miles further on, they came over another rise, as the road gently curved to the right, they were greeted with an array of flashing lights lining the side of the road. Beth initially reacted by jamming the brakes on, but realised that there was no option if she wasn't to draw definite attention to the jeep, so she accelerated again to maintain the speed of approach. The others dropped down in their seats trying to hide themselves.

"What do we do?" Lester demanded.

"JUST STAY DOWN!" Beth was in no mood to argue. "WAIT…" She let out a laugh. "They've pulled in those punks I shunted."

The sports car clearly had a rear puncture and had continued until the rubber was torn from the wheel rim. Two grooves ran for a number of yards along the road surface until they ended at the stricken vehicle. Beth slowed as she neared the scene, but a traffic cop was vigorously waving her past. As the group of guys saw the jeep they started shouting abuse at Beth for putting them in their predicament. The patrol officers quickly brought the unruly crew back in line. Their fate had clearly been determined during the impact, damaging a rear tyre and forcing them to a standstill.

Beth made a rude gesture at them as she swept by and let out a raucous laugh at the justice of the situation. The laugh re-occurring several times over the next few minutes as she mused over the payback they'd received. The others couldn't help being amused by Beth's occasional snigger.

Into the final leg of their journey to the town, with the drama well behind, the cab once again was quiet. A few lonely buildings dotted along the road indicated that they were drawing close to a built-up area. The orange glow of distant lights was both welcome and intimidating, making the group feel apprehensive as they entered the outskirts of the town. Lester fired up his laptop and began searching for a usable signal to allow him to unearth some more information, having exhausted the material he'd downloaded previously.

A short distance into the suburbs, Lester suddenly shouted out, "Left! Turn left here! There's a library just near the corner of the road. They always have some kind of wireless access."

Beth followed the instruction and as Lester made promising noises about the location. She looked for somewhere inconspicuous they could park up.

Pulling into the space in front of the library, she found a road that led to a small rear parking place for the staff. It was empty, so she brought the jeep to a standstill close to the building so that it was partially hidden in the shadowed section where the streetlight didn't penetrate.

Within seconds of establishing a good signal, Lester was lost in a world of his own, tapping furiously on the computer keyboard. Will couldn't risk leaving the jeep as he was the 'celebrity' of the group, so Beth and Tia decided to go and get them all something substantial to eat. The junk stuff they'd spent the day living off was not what they needed if they were to keep themselves strong and motivated.

"We're going to take a walk back to the main street to see what we can find for supper," Beth informed the guys. There were grunts of acknowledgement from the back seat, but Lester was busy and Will was leaning over towards him to watch what he was doing.

Tia grabbed the baseball cap that Will had been using to screen his face to prevent anyone from recognising him. She twirled her hair onto the top of her head and hid it under the cap as Beth watched. "Just in case," she smiled.

Beth nodded. "Good thinking. We might turn you into a soldier yet, with the cross country driving, guns and disguise."

"No thanks, Beth. No offence, but if we ever see the end of this saga it'll be enough to last me a lifetime."

They climbed out of the jeep and started to walk along the street.

"I don't know how you all do it; any of the women who go into the forces. It would kill me. I would just faint at the *start* of an assault course, never mind the end." They both laughed at Tia's self-deprecating comment.

"Well, I must say, having you around has reminded me not to leave my femininity behind. When you spend all your spare time being a grease monkey like me, it's easy to forget to be beautiful like you." Tia stopped and turned to deliberately face Beth.

"Thank you. That's a very nice thing to say, *but*, don't put yourself down. I think we could teach each other a thing or two." There was a little hesitation before she continued, but as they made eye contact, Tia said, "I like you Beth, very much... And..." She paused.

"And..." Beth prompted.

"And I hope we can meet again, someday, in different circumstances."

Beth smiled and said nothing, but the mutual feeling was clear. She looped her hand through Tia's arm and pulled her alongside as they resumed walking along the street, just enjoying each other's company in what seemed to be a normal setting.

Picking up some takeaway Chinese food from a restaurant, the girls headed back to the car. When they got there and climbed into the vehicle, it was just as it had been when they left.

Beth nudged Tia. "I wonder if the two of them have even spoken to each other while we've been gone?"

Lester and Will didn't even register the comment, but the smell of real food roused them both from their adventures in the virtual world, bringing them quickly back to reality.

"At least they didn't kill each other," Tia offered.

"What?"

The two guys were focused on the smiling girls, wondering what they'd been talking about.

"Nothing."

Beth dismissed their ignorance and started to hand out the food, then settled in her seat to enjoy her share.

"So, Tia. What was it like doing the shoot for that magazine?" Lester asked casually, as if they were seated in a restaurant for an evening to enjoying each other's company.

Will and Beth looked at Tia, interested to hear what she had to say.

"It was…" She paused a moment to order her thoughts. "Have you ever had the feeling, when you did something for the first time; like you were born to do it? As if you had always been destined to fulfil that particular thing…" Her eyes were wide in the dim light of the vehicle, but there was no mistaking the buzz she'd felt, still felt, from the experience. "It fitted like a hand in a perfect glove."

"That good?" Lester teased, with a matter of fact tone to his comment.

"Yeah." She smiled coyly. "I thought it was good."

She resisted the temptation to make a comment about the publication of the magazine cover and the advertisement posters being the possible cause of their current circumstances. Lester sat pondering her explanation of the experience.

Waving the fork he was using in Tia's direction, he said, "You know what? I felt just like that when I first started working with computers. Couldn't get enough of them. I took them to pieces, read about them, built them, bought books and magazines about them."

"That explains why you're so weird, does it?" Beth jibed. Lester grinned in appreciation of the humour. "There's one other good thing about computers," she continued, but didn't immediately offer an explanation.

"What's that?" Tia said, taking the bait.

"You can be ugly and still be good at them," Beth laughed as she delivered the punch line.

"Ahh, don't you listen to her Lester. I don't think you're ugly. Quite the opposite," Tia said sympathetically. Beth pretended to vomit, which prompted further laughter.

Will was listening and observing his three companions, particularly Tia with her comment about Lester. "Perhaps we should carry on looking through the stuff that Lester's uncovering?" Will snatched the conversation in a rather abrupt manner, which instantly turned all eyes on him. He suddenly felt conscious about his deliberate redirection. "Sorry. I didn't mean to…" Unable to bring himself to explain his actions he just continued. "Is there any way we can look through the material you've already got, while you're still searching, Lester. Just to try to save some time?"

"I guess I could put some of it on a memory stick, but you would have to find somewhere that has a printer, or a photocopier that will print direct, or a computer. By the time you've done that though, and the amount you would have to print, I'm not sure it will be any help."

"Shit!" Will slammed his fist against the door panel making the others jump. "I just need to see something happening instead of feeling like we're being pushed from pillar to post by every wind of circumstance."

There was little anyone could say to rectify the situation. They were playing a waiting game and Lester was the key to their breakthrough.

Will opened the door and got out, slamming it behind him. He leaned back against the window.

"It's getting to him pretty bad, isn't it?" The tone of Lester's voice carried a hint of concern for Will that the girls hadn't noticed since they'd started their journey together.

Tia involuntarily glanced at the window where Will was leaning and Beth noticed the concerned expression on her face.

Putting her hand on Tia's shoulder she tried to reassure her. "He'll be okay. You do what you can, Lester, and we'll look out for Will."

He discarded the packaging from dinner and slid the laptop back onto his lap. In seconds he was back into his hidden world, trawling the secrets of the state, trying to find the answers they so desperately needed.

The boredom of the evening made the time drag slowly onward into the night and the discomfort of the situation grated on the nerves of the group, until it was rudely interrupted by Lester's sudden 'eureka' moment. After sitting in near silence, with nothing to do but listen to the taping of the laptop keys and ponder their predicament, the sudden intrusion was very welcome.

"You – are – not – going – to – believe – this!"

He dragged out his words while furiously scrolling around the screen of the laptop. The other three straightened in their seats, shaking away the drowsy feeling that was creeping in. Lester glanced up to find he was the centre of attention, everyone eager to be enlightened with the new information.

"I've found a file that has sketchy details about an operation that went badly wrong. Liatzo, Holden and Akkbar were all involved, along with another man called Joseph Charles. Apparently Charles was left behind in Columbia," Lester looked up from the screen. "He was presumed dead, a casualty of the botched operation. It appears they were never supposed to be in the country in the first place." Lester glanced nervously at Tia before continuing. "There's a suggestion that Carlos Liatzo was the cause of the difficulty, although he and the other two men refused to talk about what had happened during an investigation after the event."

Having been totally occupied by the fact he'd unearthed something of interest, it suddenly dawned on Lester that there was an implication for Tia's father. Considering the fate of the other men that they'd talked about earlier, he looked up at her to see what effect his words had had and found her staring intently at him. He paused while he tried to assess her mood, but Tia took the initiative.

"Lester, we need to know the truth, whatever it is. Don't worry about what I think, just carry on doing the good job you're doing." He smiled and held her gaze for a second, then nodded in acknowledgement and went back to the screen.

"The 'mission' was overseen by Joseph Charles; he was the field commander and is noted as the one who gave the order to cross the border. Some six months after the others had returned to the starting point in Mexico, Charles suddenly surfaced again." Lester looked up at the three pairs of eyes that were glued to him.

"What does that mean, Lester? What do we do with that information?" Will was thinking out loud for the whole group.

"There's very little other information about what went on. Charles seems to have been as tight-lipped as the other three, but they all suffered demotion or expulsion from the security service for their conduct. Principally for not giving any information about an incident in which several civilians died, and where the US government was severely embarrassed through an apparently unauthorised operation inside the border of another country.

Considering the fact that we know Holden and Akkbar are dead and Liatzo's whereabouts are unknown," Lester glanced again at Tia, "I've been searching for anything that might help us locate Joseph Charles. It's a long shot, but I figured that if we could get to him, perhaps we would make more sense of this. That's what made me shout out."

"What?" demanded Beth, urging him to get to the point.

They were all on the edge of their seats waiting for the gem of knowledge that would give direction.

"Although there was no information about his current location in the files I've seen, I had a scan going in the background searching other files, not as highly classified and one of them has just thrown up something very surprising."

Lester paused for effect before he delivered his ace, much to the annoyance of Beth.

"Les, quit trying to make it more dramatic, just tell us."

Lester smiled, enjoying his triumph after a long day of searching.

"He apparently owns a farmstead less than sixty miles from here." He paused again to let the information sink in. "I say we go pay him a visit."

"How are we going to know whether he's even there Lester? He could be halfway around the world for all we know." Beth was agitated at the simplicity of the plan and spun around in her seat to face the steering wheel, totally frustrated at what she perceived as an anti-climax. She quickly turned back at the sound of a dialling phone on the laptop speakers.

"Hello." The voice was gruff and abrupt as the call was answered.

"Good evening, Mr Charles. I'm calling from the telephone company. We've been having problems with the lines in your area and we're doing random calls just to check sections of the system. I wondered if you could just tell me if the line is clear and if you can hear me at the correct volume, sir."

Lester was suddenly 'the operator concerned for the customer's needs'.

"There's nothing wrong with the damn phone and I'm busy making calls," the angry voice chided.

"I'm sorry, sir, but..." Lester flinched at the click as the receiver went down showing the mood of the man at the other end. He smiled at Beth in a way that clearly said, 'aren't I clever'. "He's in all right, but I'm not sure I want to meet him."

Beth slowly turned back to face the windscreen and started the jeep. "So, where to smart ass?"

As they rolled out of the car park at 9:15pm, there was once again a sense of direction. They could take another step along the bizarre road they'd been travelling and bring an end to the feeling of their lives being out of control.

Lester shouted out instructions as they headed through the town and there was more than a little relief once they'd crossed to the outskirts without incident, leaving the illuminated streets behind. They were ten miles down the road before the tension lifted and Will broke the silence.

"What exactly are we going to do when we get to this guy's place?"

Lester leaned over to him and pointed to the screen of the computer. Will scanned the text that gave scant details about Joseph Charles. His file showed that he'd been dismissed from his post for disobeying a direct order. It wasn't the first time that it had happened either. The rest of the file showed him to be a maverick, the kind of man that you wanted on your side, but definitely not in opposition.

"Okay, so he's a man that doesn't play strictly by the rules. That doesn't mean he will help us. He might just turn us in for the hell of it."

"It says here that he isn't married, so we can hope he lives alone, but either way, he ain't going to lay down and roll over for us. He was a Marine before joining the service. The one plus is that he's sixty-three."

"A sixty-three year old can pull a trigger as good as a twenty-three year old," Will shot back.

"Sounded like a cantankerous, ball-busting, shoot first kind of sixty-three to me," Beth added from the front.

"Be that as it may, Beth," Will responded, "I suppose we're running out of options. I don't see what else we can do." He turned to Lester. "You've done a good job, Les. I just hope we can get something for your efforts, 'cos if we screw up, he isn't going to hesitate to get the police there and that could be the end of the road for us."

Beth and Lester were listening to what Will said, but were slightly distracted by Will's use of an abbreviated name for Lester; the one that usually came from Beth's lips. It was the first time they'd ever heard it since the two of them had turned against one another years before. Neither of them mentioned it and the significance completely passed by Tia, but it had definitely not gone unnoticed.

CHAPTER 17

As they travelled toward their rendezvous with Joseph Charles, Lester continued to check through other files. The more he read the more he felt they needed to put their situation on the table and expose their dilemma to this man. He would inevitably have to see their faces and that would expose them to the risk of being caught, if he blew the whistle. The difficulty was that Charles might want to polish his tarnished records with a good deed for the authorities and the group were about to give him just such a golden opportunity. There was no doubt, from the information they'd seen, that he knew something, maybe a lot, about Liatzo, Holden and Akkbar. Surely that meant he would have something useful for them?

It was 10:35pm when they found the signpost to the house. It was a hand-painted board fastened to the gatepost that simply read 'Charles Residence'. In the darkness it was difficult to tell if the house was near or far.

"How do we deal with this situation guys?" Will glanced from face to face. "Do we just go up, knock on the door and ask if he would answer a few questions?"

"Do you think we can risk that?" Lester asked.

"In all honesty? No." Will was blunt.

The two guys looked at Beth for some inspiration. She shrugged and declined to give any guidance.

Lester pulled something from his bag of tricks and passed it to Beth. "You two wait here in the car. If we manage to get into the house, I'll page that from the house phone. Let it signal once, then wait for a second time before you come. Okay?"

Beth nodded and caught hold of his arm. "You be careful. Both of you, do you hear?"

"Yes ma'am." Lester mockingly saluted, but it was his attempt to cover their nervousness.

"Armed?" Will asked.

"What choice?" Lester replied.

Will pulled his bag onto the seat between them and unzipped the pouch on the end. Taking out the two guns, Lester watched as he slid the magazine into the first and handed it over. The second weapon was prepared as Lester took a small torch from his bag. Flicking the switch on and off, he checked that it worked.

The two guys hesitated, looked at one another, as if to steel their anxiety, then slipped out of the car, closing the doors quietly behind them and were gone into the night.

Will set off at a steady pace, jogging along the road that led to the house; Lester fell in beside him. Their senses were on high alert and their eyes became accustomed to the darkness. The shape of a building several hundred yards along the road came into view.

"What's the plan, Will?"

"Don't shoot him." Will answered through the rhythmic breathing.

"Funny guy!"

"We'll just have to wing it and see what happens. You okay?"

"If it's a choice between bullets or breaking into secret files, I'm on my least preferred option."

Will snorted, but he knew the humour was to take their minds off what was coming. They were potentially about to add another crime to the string that set a trail across the country behind them.

Will slowed as they approached the house. There was a light on in the front ground floor room. He made a gesture to Lester that he was going to take a look.

They dipped low and edged up to the side of the building. Will slipped around the corner and glanced through the front window into the room to see a man sat watching TV. He edged back to where Lester was waiting.

"Just the old guy as far as I can tell. If we get in and take control, we can call the girls down and then see if we can get him to talk to us."

"You mean after we've given him a heart attack by breaking into his house and threatening him with guns?"

Will shrugged. "You stay here and keep a watch on him. I'm going around the back to see if I can find a way in."

Will passed by and Lester watched him go along the side of the house and disappear around the corner to the rear of the building.

Once Will was gone, Lester moved closer to the window and took a quick look inside. The room seemed empty. He took another look, but made a more detailed sweep of the room that was lined with shelves packed end to end and floor to ceiling with books. There was definitely no one in the room. He slipped back to the side of the building and called out to Will, but it was too late to stop what was going to happen.

Will reached the rear of the house and quietly edged his way to the door. There were no lights on in the back rooms, so he tried the handle. To his surprise the door was unlocked and it easily swung open as he gently pushed it.

Waiting for a few moments to listen, there was only the sound of the distant TV drifting through from the front of the house. Keeping low, he moved into the kitchen and in the dim light tried to make out the outline of things. The room seemed empty so he edged across to the door that would lead him to the 'target', but halfway across the room he was suddenly arrested in his tracks.

"Very slowly, my friend. Just place the gun on the table next to you and step carefully away."

Will hesitated, glancing toward the voice, wondering what options he would have if he relinquished his weapon. In the darkness he could see nothing that would allow him to get a handle on the man who had taken their advantage and turned it around. The voice, determined and steady as a rock, made sure Will understood the risk he was taking in delaying. "You're thinking, do I submit to the instruction or do I make a move. Let me tell you young man, I don't give a shit what you choose to do, but if you're going to make a move, it had better be good, because it *will* be your last."

"Okay, okay," Will acquiesced, realising he had no option, so immediately did exactly as instructed.

"Good boy." The patronising tone in his voice almost goaded Will to try something. "Now, I want you to shout that friend of yours who came down the drive with you and tell him the coast is clear to come in. You'd better make it sound like you've got the situation under control because your life is depending on it."

It was disconcerting the way the words flowed in a soft, undulating melody that seemed detached from the threats. Will obeyed.

"LESTER... YOU'RE OKAY... IT'S UNDER CONTROL. COME AROUND THE BACK!"

Seconds later, Lester came through the rear door, but he was off his guard as he started to cross the room.

Will caught sight of a glint of gunmetal in the half-light over on the other side of the kitchen as it refocused on Lester.

"What the hell's happening, Will?" Lester demanded.

The intimidating voice butted in to Lester's questioning, but it was as calm as a comment in a restaurant.

"What's happening is that you're going to very, *very* slowly place that gun next to *Will's* gun on the table, *Lester*. Don't go risking your life now. Dead heroes are still dead."

It unnerved the two of them that the man in control was calm enough to notice and to use their names when he addressed them.

Lester did exactly as he'd been instructed and as the gun clunked onto the table he glanced at Will. There was enough light for him to see the resigned look etched on his face.

"Let's go sit in the front room shall we gentlemen? Perhaps we can have a little discussion about the manners of young people in the country today. Didn't anybody teach you that it's rude to enter someone's home without being invited?"

The two guys glanced at each other again, unnerved by the calmness in the comment.

"Through the door to your left, guests first." They moved into the room where the TV was playing. "Take a seat, together on the couch if you'd be so kind."

The cool-headed mocking use of courteous language scarcely masked the sinister undertones. There was no question in their minds that they were dealing with a man who was not going to tolerate the slightest challenge to his authority.

As they slowly lowered themselves onto the sofa, Joseph Charles walked past them and flicked the off switch for the TV and they got their first look at him in the light. It was the same man Will had seen when he'd glanced through the window. He was tall, well-built, his muscular frame showing through his shirt. He was balding, but handsome with it. His face had a hardness that shouted a warning to all comers to be careful how they treated him. The military background they'd read about in the file was clearly written in his posture and actions. Despite his age, this man had presence. He was confident and forceful. He made no special effort to impress his captives, the intimidation just oozed from his every action. The way he stood; the way he held the gun; it was natural to him. He reminded the young guys of one of their training instructors when they'd first joined the forces. Some men have to yell to exert their control, but that particular trainer didn't need to do what was already done by the force of his character and confidence. The same kind of man was now sitting on the opposite side of the room.

The guys waited apprehensively as he settled himself in a chair as though he was on a social visit with friends for the evening. The only sinister thing was the pump-action gun that casually lay across his legs.

Once he was comfortable, he looked at the two of them and smiled. He didn't say anything initially, but looked as though he was taking stock of the men he was dealing with, which added to their discomfort. He knew it and used it effectively.

Finally he began. "Well, this is cosy." He smiled again, but it didn't put them at ease, quite the reverse. "How are we this evening my black and white friends?" He didn't wait for an answer. "I'm guessing that you left the car at the end of the drive? But is there someone else I wonder?"

"I…" Will's attempt to answer stopped when the gun pump-action loudly click-clunked. His attention was caught by being reminded of what he'd done to the intruders in his own house only days before. The smile remained on Charles's face.

"You wouldn't think about telling me a lie? Would you, Will and Lester?" The two guys glanced at each other. "So, there is someone else." Joseph Charles nodded. "And, how were you going to get them to come here when you'd done the dirty deed?"

"We didn't have any intention of harming you," Will quickly protested.

"The guns were just for…" Joseph let the sentence drift and fixed his stare on Will. The smile momentarily vanished as the true hardened face that belonged to the situation was flashed just long enough to stress the gravity of their predicament. "Just answer my question, *boy*." The venom in his put-down was wielded with the precision of a razor sharp sword.

"They've…" Lester started.

"They?" Charles immediately interrupted. "Two, three, more?"

Again the guys were instantly taken back by the sharpness of their captor.

"Two," Lester answered, before tentatively continuing. "They've got a pager."

"You were going to use the phone to signal that you were ready for them?"

"Yes."

"Once?"

"Twice," Lester corrected.

The old guy pulled the phone handset from its base and tossed it to Lester. The gun on his lap was deliberately and menacingly moved into position, pointing directly at the two of them.

Lester dialled the number and listened for the acknowledgement. He hung up and redialled. Once the task was complete, he placed the handset on the arm of the sofa and they both looked at the old guy.

"Guns?" he asked.

"Only the ones on the table in the other room," Will informed him.

He nodded and glanced away down the drive as the headlights of a vehicle came toward the house.

"Four young men to knock off one old man," he stated, as he turned back to them. "The odds are a little unfair don't you think?"

"Not... Not four men," Will corrected.

Joseph turned to look at him for a few seconds.

"Not *girls*?" The mocking tone was used again. "What is this, a laugh on a night out? Trying to impress the ladies, you little shits?" he sneered at them.

"Our intention was not to harm you. We need to talk to you," Will reiterated his earlier claim.

The jeep pulled up at the house and Joseph Charles moved to unlock the front door to let the girls in.

"The back door wasn't left unlocked was it?" Will asked, as Joseph passed them.

"Are you crazy?" he laughed. "Anybody could walk in. Even with the surveillance system I keep it locked. In fact I only just unlocked it so that you two clowns could come in."

Will and Lester felt the depth of how much they'd been outwitted.

"Come in ladies, come in!" he shouted theatrically into the darkness.

Beth and Tia were a little bewildered by the welcome of the old man carrying a gun, but made no attempt to question what had happened. They cautiously stepped through the front door into the house and caught sight of Will and Lester seated on the couch. They almost simultaneously glanced back at Joseph who was locking the door behind them.

"What's going on Will?" Beth asked, the alarm in her voice was clearly heard.

"Good question my dear," Joseph interrupted. "What exactly *is* going on?" He indicated for the girls to take a seat. "Remove that hat young lady," he directed Tia, who was still wearing Will's baseball cap. She quickly pulled it off and dropped it into her lap like someone caught inappropriately dressed at church.

Joseph did a double take as her hair fell over her shoulders. He paused and looked at Tia for a few moments making her feel very uncomfortable under his gaze.

"So," he began, as he struggled to pull his eyes away from her. "Let's introduce ourselves properly shall we." He was in control and was making sure that the whole group knew it. "I'm…"

"Joseph Charles, former employee of the United States government, trained as a Marine, served in several conflict areas, but later moved to special operations and finally to a special intelligence services covert operations unit until… retiring… from the forces." Lester's voice was a little shaky and he struggled to pick the right word to describe Charles's expulsion from the system, but he'd just bought them some room with his interruption. Joseph looked at Lester trying to weigh up the young man and seemed to deliberately take his time before responding.

"My phone line is perfectly okay… *operator*." Joseph added the last word with calculated intention.

Lester was a little surprised that Joseph was aware of the ruse to find out if he was at home. The slight gain seemed to have been swallowed once more by their interrogator's sharp mind.

Will noticed that the revelation had knocked his friend off his line of explanation so he picked up the running. "We needed to talk to you and couldn't risk making the trip if you weren't going to be here."

Joseph continued looking at Lester before acknowledging Will's comment by glancing at him. "So you know my name and a snippet of information about me, I still say that you came with dishonourable intention." The scowl on his face showed that he was not going to suffer fools gladly. "But my question is, who the hell are you?"

It was the first time that his voice showed any emotion. The anger at being disturbed in his home, by two men with guns, seeped out into his questioning.

There was an uncomfortable pause, but someone had to lay their cards on the table, "Lester Donaldson." The others looked at him then followed his lead.

"Beth Jackson."

Joseph scanned her face as if he was comparing it to a database of images held deep in his memory.

"Tia Sharmez."

Again the disconcerting attention fell on her and she squirmed in her seat. Even when Will announced his name, Joseph continued to look at Tia. She shifted in her seat under the examination, but had no option but to endure the interest.

Joseph moved his attention to Will and after staring at him for a few moments, he laughed. "You're the bastard that killed the two guys in Cordham. You'd think they would've had the brains to show a recent picture, rather than that clean cut military parade image they've been flashing around on the news. Makes more money for the networks I suppose, soldier turned murderer."

"It *is* me on the news, but I *didn't* kill them," Will blurted out defensively.

Joseph's look lingered a long time on him as Will's eyes burned with indignation at the accusation, but then he returned to Tia.

"Sharmez?" he asked, after a few seconds.

Tia nodded in response, as she once again fell under the spotlight.

"Tia Sharmez," Charles stated.

This time she didn't move a muscle and the eyes of everyone in the room were switching between her and Joseph like a courtroom battle between interrogator and accused.

"How old are you?"

Tia was a little alarmed and glanced at the others for moral support, but there was nothing they could do to help, she just had to answer the question.

"Twenty-two."

Joseph tipped his head back as he pondered something then completely took the group by surprise by turning his attention back to Will.

"Why shouldn't I just call the authorities to come here and pick you and your friends up?"

"Okay, okay. We came out here because we urgently needed to talk to you." He was listening to Will's answer, but had gone back to looking at Tia again.

Instead of just squirming under his glare, she boldly jumped in to try to help her friend as he'd helped her. "He didn't kill those men, Mr Charles."

"Please, call me Joseph, *Tia*."

She glanced at the others and found them looking at her. His tactic of hovering between friend and foe, between formal and informal was unsettling them. It was difficult to get a handle on the man; hard to know what to appeal to as the ground shifted constantly.

"He... He didn't kill those two men," she hesitated before tentatively finishing her statement, "Joseph."

"And how would *you* know that missy?"

Again he tried to knock her off balance by addressing her as though she were a child, but she was not going to be thrown quite so easily this time and immediately shot back her answer.

"I was there."

He paused a moment. "You were?" Charles raised his eyebrows to show his surprise.

"Yes."

Joseph glanced at Will, but Tia was going to put some meat on the bones and launched into a short explanation about how the situation came about.

"Those two guys were part of a group of men who abducted me from the street. I managed to get away and Will sheltered me. They turned up at his place in the middle of the night. I guess they must have found out where I'd gone. He managed to stop them, took their weapons, questioned them while protecting me, but he didn't kill them."

Joseph turned back to Will.

"Didn't do so good this time kid. It doesn't look like you managed to protect her, does it?" He fractionally shifted the gun that was laid on his lap to draw attention to it as he smiled at the two guys on the sofa.

Turning back to Tia he said, "Sharmez? Tia Sharmez?" He rolled the words around in his mouth like he was testing the flavour, the feel, the flow of them. "Doesn't suit you girly. Doesn't sound quite right."

Tia's eyes were wide as she watched the strange behaviour of Joseph. She'd endured far more attention than any of the others and was struggling to make sense of it.

"Where did you do the operator thing from, Lester? Phone booth?"

"Laptop," Lester answered.

"That where you found my address and number, my name, my details?"

"Yes."

"You got security clearance?"

"Some."

"But not enough to read the stuff you've read about me, right?"

"No."

"So, you illegally accessed the stuff."

"Yes."

"Got the laptop with you?"

"Yes. It's in the jeep."

Joseph thought for a moment. "I think we'll send *Tia Sharmez* to go get it." He smiled at her.

Tia looked nervously at her friends. Beth tried to give her a reassuring look, but could tell the attention was worrying her. She slowly rose from her seat and headed to the door.

"You'd better bring the whole bag of tricks, Tia," Lester shouted after her.

She looked at Joseph for confirmation that it was okay to do so. He nodded to her.

"Leave the front door open as you go out," he shouted, as he stood up and went to the window.

"You two look like you've been in the forces," he said to the guys on the sofa. "You too, Beth." He glanced over his shoulder at her then went back to watching Tia out of the window. "But she hasn't."

Will couldn't restrain himself any longer. "What's your interest in Tia?" he demanded.

Joseph waited a few seconds before turning to look at Will. "What's yours?"

Will was a little surprised by the response. "What do you mean?"

Joseph went back to his former position before asking another question. "What do you know about her?"

"Her father is…" Will was about to shoot out the answer without thinking it through. He was trying to dazzle Joseph with something he didn't already know, but Lester landed a well-aimed elbow in his ribs to put a stop to it. Joseph could see the two of them in the reflection of the window and didn't miss what happened, but said nothing about it. He just continued to watch Tia as she headed back into the house.

"You know more about her than you're letting on, don't you?" Beth said, in an answer-demanding tone.

"Is that why you're here, Beth?" Joseph had an uncanny habit of using their names in his questions. It was as if he'd been a friend for a long time and was as familiar with them as family.

"Partly… *Joseph*," she replied, using his name in a deliberate reaction to his tactic.

He turned and nodded at her. The wry grin showed his appreciation of her copy-cat humour.

Tia stepped back into the hallway with the holdall bag in hand. He beckoned her over and took the bag from her. Placing it on the coffee table, he unzipped the top and rifled through the contents to see what was there. Once he'd verified that everything was harmless, he placed it on the floor then pushed it over to Lester with his foot.

"Fire it up sunshine. Let's take a look at what you've been digging into."

Lester grabbed the bag. Retrieving the laptop, he set about bringing the material up on the screen. Joseph walked around to the back of the couch so he could see what was there from over Lester's shoulder. He still had the gun in his hand, but was holding it in a more relaxed way.

Once Lester had control of the keyboard, he behaved as though he'd been removed from the concern of the situation.

"Okay, let's take a look at Uncle Sam's secrets." He laughed at the ease with which he got what he wanted. He began tapping away with great enthusiasm. "Bingo." Lester glanced over his shoulder to verify he'd got Joseph's attention. "This is the really hot stuff that I filtered from piles of junk. A lot of it didn't have much meaning. Man, I tell you, there's ream upon ream of crap in the files they keep," he was talking directly to Joseph behind him, "Don't they ever clear the stuff out when it ain't no use any more?"

"You never know when things are going to be of use." There was a pregnant pause in Joseph's delivery. "That's right, isn't it Tia… Sharmez?"

Tia took a sharp intake of breath as the attention of Joseph seemed to be back on her, but she kept her eyes forward and made no comment.

"Are you just interested in what *we've* been looking at, or is there something of interest to *you*?" Beth queried.

"Lester's going to help me look at the stuff I was working on when the Service shit on me five years ago."

All four of the group turned in unison to look at Joseph who was standing behind them. As they did, he turned the weapon upside down and discharged the ammunition into his hand so that there was no doubt that the alert level had just been downgraded. He spun around and went to the kitchen, slid the magazines from the hand guns that had been left on the table, and deposited all the weapons in a cupboard out of the way.

"Coffee?" he shouted back to the group in the front room. They all looked at each other, unsure about what was happening.

When Joseph returned a few minutes later carrying a tray of drinks and a packet of cookies, they were all rooted in the same places they'd been when he left the room.

The turnaround in this hard-nosed character left them speechless and glued to their seats wondering how to respond to him. He laughed at their manner.

"Relax guys. I think we're going to be friends. Maybe I can help you, and you," he lifted a mug from the tray, "can help me."

The silence was begging to be broken with a question, as Joseph cradled the drink in his hands while watching the group. But what question? Each one had their own on the tip of their tongue.

Lester was first out of the starting gate. He jumped forward in his seat and grabbed a mug of coffee as he shot the opening salvo.

"Your name's plastered all over the files I've been looking through. You must have been very involved in something that links to what we are caught up in?"

Joseph laughed. "I don't know anything about what you're caught up in, Lester. I *was* the proverbial bull in the china shop, but the shop owners had a gun and they weren't afraid to use it. Any challenge about what should be done and how it should be done was dealt with severely."

"That's what happened to you, yes?" Beth prompted him to elaborate.

"They didn't just open a whole can of worms, they made one specially for me. Once they'd finished I'd lost everything that I'd worked for... My reputation included."

"So what's stopping you getting some credit by turning us... me in? That would get a gold star in your copy book."

The venom in Will's voice was done deliberately to try to provoke the situation. Joseph smiled at him, but ignored the question. There was no way a seasoned hand like him was going to be pushed into doing anything he didn't want to.

"Nice try sonny, but your problems are much bigger than mine. You're juggling with fire and you're too dumb to know it."

Will took the bait immediately. "You son-of-a…"

"WILL!"

Beth's shout cut across the room and stopped him in his tracks, but the anger was vividly portrayed in the expression on his face. The days of being under suspicion of murder were taking a heavy toll on him. The normal light-hearted nature had been knocked out of him months before, but the current circumstances were grinding him into the floor.

Tia was staring at Will. She felt the pain and turmoil he was in and the nagging guilt about her culpability had followed her. It was always there in the back of her mind.

The room was silent as the five of them sat looking at each other like they were at a gunslingers' convention, each waiting for the others to make the first move.

Lester coughed, breaking the deadlock and levelled another question. "Steven Holden, Nazim Akkbar and Carlos Liatzo, you know these people?"

Joseph's stare was still locked on Will, measuring the young man's pent-up anger and he was returning the same interest in the old man.

"I know them," Joseph said slowly, but he held fast on Will.

"How?" Lester continued. He glanced at Will to see what was holding Joseph's curiosity and it gave Will the opportunity to break the stare as he looked back at Lester.

"I used to work with them."

Tia had been watching the to and fro of the questions and answers, but she couldn't hold out any longer. "You knew my…" she hesitated as the other three immediately threw a look that stopped her, but Joseph Charles didn't miss the pitiful attempt to silence her.

"Yes, Tia Sharmez." She looked directly at Joseph. "I don't see a wedding band," he mocked a little. "Did you get married?" He paused while he observed her reaction and she shifted in her seat under his steely gaze. "Or should I still call you, Liatzo, Sarita, like your father Carlos named you?"

CHAPTER 18

Tia's eyes widened at Joseph's mention of her real name and there were quick glances between the others as they adjusted again to the fact that Joseph Charles obviously knew a lot more about their situation than he was willing to come straight out with. It was like he was playing a game of cat and mouse with them, testing to find out what they knew.

"You didn't think that I was being fooled by your shoddy attempt to conceal Sarita's identity, did you?" He addressed them all in a condescending tone.

"What do you know about me?" Tia shouted. She'd had enough of the stupid game that they all seemed to be playing. "You bastard, what do you know?"

She lunged forward at Joseph, but he grabbed her wrists and spun her around, restraining her in his embrace as he held her from behind. She initially struggled against him. Will sprang to his feet in alarm at the situation, but Joseph was very direct.

"SIT DOWN, SON!"

It was the first time that Joseph had raised his voice since they'd entered the building, but Will hesitated as Tia continued to resist.

"Sit down," he repeated more calmly.

As Will dropped reluctantly back into his seat, Joseph instantly let go of Tia.

"Now you please, Sarita. Or, Tia, as your friends call you."

She reluctantly complied with his request, but she did so in a manner that registered her protest at the way he'd treated her.

Once she was back in her place, he lowered himself into his seat and smiled at the group as though he were about to begin an evening class at college.

"You've told me bits about how you ended up here, but perhaps we should start from the beginning again, just so that I'm clear about it." He feigned his slowness to comprehend.

Tia stared daggers at him, but reluctantly gave way to his request as it became obvious that everyone was waiting for her to start the tale.

"I was kidnapped," she stated bluntly. The exasperated way the words came out showed her impatience at having to go through the story over again for what seemed like the umpteenth time to each of her companions and now to this man.

As she began to relate recent events, Joseph interrupted, "I know all that, but why? Why were you taken?"

"I – don't – know." Tia deliberately spat the words out through gritted teeth as her frustration surfaced at not being able to answer the often asked question.

Their attention was distracted from Tia as Lester slammed his hand onto the coffee table. He pulled it away to leave a paper he'd retrieved from his bag in full view of everyone. All eyes were fixed on it, waiting for some explanation.

"We think *that* might be the reason it started. What it has to do with anything, I don't know." He shrugged and leant back into his seat.

Joseph reached out and picked up the paper and the four of them watched as he unfolded it.

He said nothing for a long time as he stared at the image, but Tia was getting rather uncomfortable at the attention he was giving her picture from the magazine cover. Somehow it made her feel exposed that it was being studied so closely by a man old enough to be her father. When Will and Lester had looked they'd given an immediate reaction to the revealing silk dress that formed closely to her figure. Even Beth responded in a similar way, but Joseph's inspection seemed infinitely more detailed and wholly inappropriate, all the more so as the four of them watched him closely.

Suddenly he leapt from his seat and went to the desk on the far side of the room. Pulling open a drawer, he rummaged through and took out a magnifying glass. That was the limit for Tia.

"You can't see enough already?" she shouted across the room in anger.

The snide comment was so totally out of character for the girl that the others had come to know, albeit very briefly, that its tone surprised them all, but there was a measure of understanding on all their faces.

Joseph looked up at the audience watching his every move then focused on Tia.

"Young lady, you might be self-conscious about this picture, but you should have thought about that before you allowed a half-naked image of yourself to be plastered over the newspaper stands and advertising boards of America." Tia felt the discomfort of being chastised, but wondered why she should care what this man thought of her. "A good looking girl like you should never descend to this level."

"Wait just a minute," Will challenged, but Joseph ignored him and finished what he was saying.

"Elegance is one short step away from looking like a slut… and I think you might have crossed the line here."

Will was about to react to the further provocation, but Lester's more measured response overrode him.

"Shit, you don't hold no punches, Joseph. You're about as subtle as a machine gun. Give the girl a break, man. I don't see no problem with that picture."

"That *is* the problem, Lester. You don't see *no* problem." Joseph mimicked Lester's accent as he repeated his comment back to him. "You don't like my opinion? I don't give a shit."

Joseph turned his attention back to the photograph. The four of them exchanged glances and shrugs showing that they were perplexed by his actions.

Still looking at the image, he slowly walked across the room and lowered himself back into the seat he'd been in then looked up at Tia. She braced herself for what was next. It felt like she was in the middle of an interrogation session.

"The dress yours?" he asked casually.

"No." She was abrupt.

"The shoes?"

"No."

"The watch?"

"What are you trying to do? Play some sort of 'guess who owns what' game?" Tia leapt to her feet and looked like she was about to storm out of the room, but unsure where she was going to go she stayed rooted to the spot.

"The watch," Joseph repeated, with a sigh that hinted of his exasperation with young people in general.

"NO!" Tia shouted.

"How about…"

"WHAT? What do you want to know about now? My underwear? There isn't much else left that you haven't asked about." She was fuming at his questions.

"The earrings?"

Beth and Tia locked eyes and Beth shrugged to show she had no idea where this was going.

After a second to gather herself she hesitantly answered, "They're mine."

"Nice." He nodded his approval. "They still back home?"

"Why?"

Joseph restated the question in a staccato rhythm. "Are – they – still – back – home?"

Tia glanced around the room at her friends then looked directly at Joseph. She didn't say anything for a few moments, she just looked at him as if willing him to disappear. He gestured for an answer to his question. Tia simply swept her hair back over her left ear.

Joseph didn't move a muscle at first, he just looked. The slender contours of her neck and collarbone showed slightly at the opening of her top. Tia swept her hair over her other ear and waited for some response. It didn't come for a little while and the room was held in suspense, waiting to know what Joseph was doing.

"They don't come out, so if you're thinking of taking them, don't bother," Tia finally added, wondering how much longer she was to stand there waiting for somebody to say something.

He smiled. Tia could tell he was looking at the earrings rather than at her and she wondered what she'd done in revealing them. Suddenly he focused on her face.

Tia dropped back into her seat, but held Joseph's unbroken gaze.

"What the *hell* is going on here?" Will demanded.

Joseph smiled and shook his head as he recalled memories of a man that both he and Tia knew.

"Carlos Liatzo…" Joseph hesitated, "is… Was… Who knows?" he shrugged. "Carlos Liatzo *was* a friend and a good man. Whatever made him want to get involved in our business, I'll never understand, especially once he'd got family responsibilities to deal with, but he is… was," Joseph corrected himself and threw a look of apology to Tia for not knowing, "good at it. The problem for him was that he had a conscience." He paused as he judged their response. "Me…" he shook his head, "I just wanted to get the job done in whatever way I needed to."

Joseph looked at Tia and their eyes met. Hers were wide with surprise at the revelation Joseph had so 'matter-of-factly' thrown into the conversation.

Tia bit her lip in a nervous response, scared about where this story was going. She simply shook her head slowly side to side like some superstitious means of warding off unwelcome news. Beth was suddenly on the edge of her seat and about to say something out of concern for Tia, but Joseph threw up his hand to stop her from interrupting.

"We were on a covert operation. The mission was to track and stop a gang of drug runners that were somehow using a route from the place of origin in Columbia, through Central America, into and through the Mexican territories, and eventually across the US border. It was a joint US, Mexican action. That's why Carlos was so useful. He knew the language and the culture. Anyway, I'll spare you the unnecessary details. Things got a little out of hand and the result was that quite a number of people ended up dead, most of them criminals." He shrugged and added, "Who gives a rat's ass about them, right?" But the four in his audience didn't move a muscle or give any response, so he went back to his story. "When we got into the building they were using as shelter, we found a man, woman and five children. The bastards had used them as a shield, but we let loose before they'd had chance to let us know. We would've held fire if we'd known... we didn't know..." Joseph repeated, as if trying to convince himself that he would have acted differently had he been aware of the situation. He seemed lost in the past for a few seconds. "They were all dead... Carlos, your father, took it pretty bad."

The tension in the room was building as the story was told, but with that revelation it was electric.

"Sure I was choked about it, who wouldn't be? But we did what we did and had to leave the Mexican police to clear up." Joseph winced at his casual choice of words about a massacred family. "Our job was done... but not for Carlos Liatzo. He couldn't let it alone. He started throwing accusations around, blaming people, it became like an obsession. Right there in the field, he lost it." Joseph had wandered into telling the tale as though he was addressing people who were unconnected to the incident, as though Tia wasn't even in the room.

He came back to the present when Beth stood up and moved her chair closer to Tia. As she sat down again, she took hold of Tia's hand. The information was clearly having a profound effect on her as the images of a man prominent in her childhood, a man she thought she understood, were linked to the man that Joseph was describing.

Beth turned to Joseph, who had temporarily stopped while she repositioned and nodded to him to continue. He stood and walked to the window, looking out into the darkness for a while, before picking up his narrative.

"I've never seen anything like it. He completely broke down in the middle of the situation." Joseph glanced back over his shoulder, "That incident changed him."

He paused a few moments as he considered how to continue, then turned and sat on the windowsill.

"I was in command of the operation. It was my call, my responsibility." Joseph shook his head at the memory and the agitation in his voice betrayed something of his feelings about what had happened. "He pulled a gun and put it to my head. Threatened to shoot me on the spot."

Tia's wide eyes didn't leave their subject for a moment.

"Holden and Akkbar talked him down and, once the weapon was made safe, I ordered them to get back to the helicopter and take Liatzo… Well the rest doesn't matter. He never spoke to me again. There was some fall-out from the situation, but hey, what good does it do to dwell on the past. Bad stuff happens… But I *always* saw him as my friend. We weren't allowed to associate when not on a mission. It was a way of keeping our team hidden, secret, but he and I talked a lot during the hours of waiting time we spent in some pretty dire situations."

Joseph stood, looked at Tia again then left the room. The four didn't know what to say so they sat in silence until Joseph finally returned. As he re-entered the room, he paused where Tia was sitting and passed her a photograph. She looked at the image and it grabbed her attention. What she held was a picture she'd seen many, many times before. It was of her sixteenth birthday where she was proudly standing next to her father, Carlos Liatzo, in the garden of the villa in Mexico. The close-up image of their faces, cheeks touching, showed a time that had long passed, but suddenly seemed like yesterday. Along with the story she'd just heard and the picture in her hands, Tia totally lost control of her emotions. Beth did her best to comfort her, while the three men felt like they'd burst uninvited into someone's living room, intruding on a private moment.

Joseph looked at Will and Lester. "You want a beer?"

They responded positively and the three of them quietly left the room.

Beth held the shaking body of her friend, allowing her to take her time. The world that had been fixed in an acceptable order in Tia's mind, had just imploded, leaving her adrift in a sea of unresolved emotional turmoil about who she was, what was happening to her life, and what had become of her father.

It was approaching 1:00am and Beth was conscious that there was no way they should continue until Tia had had the opportunity to gather herself.

"Joseph." He immediately appeared in the doorway. "I need to get Tia somewhere she can sleep."

"Sure." He didn't argue, but waved for Beth and Tia to follow him.

He led the way to the back of the building where there was a self-contained block that would have been used for guests. Checking that they were okay and whether they needed anything, he left them alone and went back to the kitchen where Will and Lester were sat at the table. Their hushed conversation stopped the moment he entered the room.

Opening the fridge he pulled another bottle and waved it at Will, who declined the offer. Turning to Lester, he threw the beer to his waiting hand and pulled another one out for himself.

"I still don't understand," Lester said.

"Understand what?"

"The background story and everything is interesting, but what does that have to do with here and now?"

Will grunted in agreement.

"Well, gentlemen. That's just going to have to wait until tomorrow, so I suggest you two go get yourselves some sleep." Joseph turned to leave them.

"Where do we sleep?" Will asked.

Joseph shrugged as he turned back to face them. "You used to be in the forces, right? I suggest you find somewhere comfortable for the night. I'm going to my own bed. His face suddenly hardened and he edged closer to Will.

"And don't you ever make a threatening move on me again young man, because next time you *will* regret it."

The menace in his voice was as convincing as it needed to be to make Will consider how he dealt with Joseph Charles, and an instinctive, drilled-in training prompted an almost involuntary response.

"Yes, sir."

A second later Joseph was gone and the two guys were left to sort themselves out.

~

When Beth awoke the following morning it took her a few moments to realise where she was. She turned to check on Tia, but found her gone. Sitting up, she looked around the room, but it was empty and the en-suite door was open. The clock showed 5:45am. She huffed and slumped back down onto the mattress, listening to the noises of the early morning, the creaks and groans of an old house out in the sticks. After half-an-hour of trying to get comfortable again, she was unable to settle. Reluctantly she threw off the duvet, stretched and headed out to see if there was any sign of the others.

Passing a doorway en route to the kitchen, she peeked through the narrow opening to find Tia sitting in a swivel chair behind a desk. Her knees were pulled up to her chest supporting her chin, her arms wrapped around her legs. On the desk was the photograph Joseph had passed to her when the conversation ended the previous night. She was sitting motionless, staring at it.

Beth pushed the door gently and watched as it slowly swung open. It creaked making Tia look up. A pained smile crossed her lips as she saw Beth.

"Hi," she whispered.

"Hey. How are you doing?" Beth crossed the room and sat on the edge of the desk next to Tia. She touched her shoulder in a gesture of concern.

"Confused, I guess. I had it all figured out in my mind. Fathers can be heroes and villains. Mine was a hero up to the point this picture was taken, but I realise now that I resented his absence as he gradually disappeared from my life, especially as I didn't know why. Don't get me wrong, I loved to see him when he was home, but when we had the break-in at the villa he was so insistent that I move to the States and change my name." She caught a breath. "Not for one moment did I think I would never see him again, but now…" Tia didn't finish. Even the momentary thought that he might be dead was hard to bare and she felt so helpless in her efforts to find the truth, but every time she learned a little more it pointed to that unwelcome conclusion.

Beth moved behind Tia and wrapped her arms around her, resting her chin on the top of Tia's head.

"It's been quite a ride for you girl, but you're okay. You're doing okay." Beth waited a few moments then plonked a friendly kiss on Tia's head as with a child, she sighed heavily and went back to the door. "I'm going on a coffee hunt. Do you think the 'old coot' will have some?"

Tia smiled at Beth's disrespect.

"Yeah." The deep voice of Joseph boomed along the hallway. "The 'old coot's' got some. It's in the kitchen cupboard over the sink… and make me one while you're at it… *girly*." He deliberately addressed Beth with a humorous twist in his tone.

"Shit, Joseph. You scared the life out of me!" Beth was a little startled.

"You should see it from this angle. The last time two broads were running around my house dressed like that, I knew what to do about it."

The two girls laughed at the self-deprecating comment and looked at each other as Joseph went into the bathroom opposite. Beth pulled a face that said, 'Wow, what happened to him overnight'?

She scooted off to the kitchen and Tia went to pull on some clothes before joining her. She peeked into the living room to check on the guys and could hear the sound of deep breathing coming from the couch. Quietly closing the door she went back to the kitchen to talk to Beth.

Leaning against the counter, she watched the preparation as they chatted about nothing in particular. Joseph entered the room just as Beth was pouring coffee. She stopped what she was doing for a moment and looked at him. He stood opposite Tia, hovering in the doorway and gave a nod to Beth, seeing that she was on the verge of saying something.

"Tell me, Joseph Charles." He smiled at her for using his name so formally. "You liked Carlos Liatzo, didn't you?"

"I like you kid. You've got balls and that's good going for a gal that looks as good as you." Beth turned to face him and put her hands on her hips as if she were about to give him a scolding for being so forward. "I mean it," he said, trying to assuage the fire in her eyes.

She relaxed her stance a little. "I can't figure you out 'Old Coot'," Beth winked at Tia who couldn't help smiling.

"Okay, time out. If you're going to use the 'age' game, then I win against you pair added together plus some." He waved them off and fetched the milk from the refrigerator, putting it next to the mugs Beth had returned to filling.

He waited a second before going back to Beth's question.

"When I figured out who you were last night," he pointed at Tia. "Took me about thirty seconds, by the way, I thought, 'how can I use this situation to help me get back at those that hurt me'? That's me. That's who I am. That's how I think. Take the opportunity and turn it to home advantage." He held his hands up as if that was all there was to say about himself. "But Carlos Liatzo would have thought, these people are in trouble and distress, how can I help *them*? That was him."

Catching Joseph totally off guard, Tia walked across the kitchen, slipped her arms around him and hugged him tightly. It was the first time since they'd met that he seemed to flounder out of his depth. Beth stood with her mouth open and Joseph looked unable to figure out what he should do. His arms hovered awkwardly above Tia's shoulders, then he gently laid his hands on her, as if he was trying not to let her feel his touch.

"That's not all there is to you, Joseph Charles," she mumbled. "Thank you for telling me the truth."

Tia pulled away to look at him. "Thank you," she repeated. She turned, took a mug from the counter and seated herself at the table. "What's for breakfast?" The other two laughed and took a seat, just as the door opened behind Joseph.

"What's funny?" Will asked, rubbing his bleary eyes.

Joseph took the initiative. "You are kid. So get dressed and come and have a coffee before we laugh again."

Will looked bewildered at the changed character of the man seated at the table, but the girls just gave a knowing grin which added to his confusion. He wandered off to the bathroom and emerged a little less disorientated a few minutes later.

Shortly after, Lester followed the same routine, assembling the final member of the group.

"I hope you young fellas have ventilated my living room before I have to go in there?"

The comment was designed to get a laugh from the girls and it did, much to the annoyance of the guys.

Joseph stood up and put his mug in the sink. "I'm going out for a run. I'll be back in a little while, then we need to talk."

The four watched him go out through the door where Will had entered the night before and as soon as he was gone Will asked, "What do you think of him?"

"I wouldn't want to cross him, I'll tell you that for free," Lester chimed in.

"I like him," said Beth.

"So do I," added Tia. "What about you?"

Will pulled a face. "I don't think he likes me." The other three looked at him. "I'm serious. He doesn't like me."

"You're just being paranoid, Will. He just doesn't like being challenged and you were the first one into the house… And, you were carrying a gun. Cut him some slack and say thank you for breakfast. He'll be cool." Will shrugged, but took the advice from Lester.

By the time Joseph arrived back, the sun was up and the four of them were sitting in the living room. Tia had wandered around the house looking at the pictures on the walls.

Lester was engrossed in his virtual world, trying to dig deeper into the mysteries, but they were all convinced that Joseph held the keys to their progress.

Once he'd showered, Joseph joined them in the living room and sat down with purpose in front of them all.

"It's time we put some cards on the table kids. If there are going to be any answers to your situation or to what *I* want to know, we need to pool our knowledge."

Will, trying to be more amenable, asked, "What do you want to know?"

"How did Tia come to be in your company?"

Will tempered his tendency and answered the question. "Totally random meeting."

"You're sure?"

"I've never seen Tia before in my life. Unless she engineered coming to my garage for some reason, the meeting was totally random."

Tia shook her head at the possibility that she'd made a deliberate choice when she ended up in Will's company.

"Okay. How about you Beth?"

"I've known Will for years. He rang me after the incident at his house and asked if he could come over. We didn't know that the two guys who'd broken in had been murdered until he and Tia had been at my place for a while. We saw the news report."

"Tia, you say Will didn't shoot the intruders. How do you know that for sure?"

"It was very early in the morning. I was there all the time and there were no gunshots. Plus, when we got to Beth's and saw the news report, I freaked out, and she helped me check that the guns hadn't been used. The magazines were full."

Beth nodded to indicate that it was the truth.

"The guns were yours Will?"

"No. I took them from the men who were killed."

"The same guns you came in with last night?" Joseph quizzed.

Will winced at being reminded about the previous evening's humiliation, but didn't hesitate to answer. "Yes."

"They're in the kitchen cupboard near the back door. Can you bring them?"

Will was surprised, but nodded and complied with the request.

"Lester?" Joseph prompted.

Beth interrupted before he could answer. "*I* made the decision to involve Lester." She looked across at him and silently mouthed 'sorry'. "He's a genius at getting information. We needed him."

"Umm." Joseph pondered a second until Will stood beside him with the unloaded guns. He took one and meticulously turned it in all directions, looking at every detail. He did the same with the other, then passed them back to Will. "Thanks son."

Will smiled at the gentler language. He put the guns back in the kitchen cupboard and took his seat again in the living room.

"I've got a question," said Lester, with a hint of 'it's our turn to ask' in his voice.

"Shoot." Joseph relaxed back in his chair.

"You were rather interested in Tia's jewellery last night. Why?"

The attention of everyone was on Joseph. He smiled then got up out of his seat and left the room returning a moment later with the picture he'd given Tia the night before. He grabbed the magazine print and the magnifying glass that was still sat on the desk. He paused a second to fold over the cover print deliberately in front of them all, as if he was hinting at his attempt to keep Tia's dignity, then he handed everything to Lester and returned to his seat.

"Take a look."

Lester looked at the magazine print, but couldn't understand what he was meant to be seeing and looked with a blank expression at Joseph.

"The ears?"

Lester focused on the earrings on the magazine cover and then at the picture where, with the aid of the glass, it was possible to see that they were one and the same.

"I knew the photograph well," Joseph explained. "I've had that quite a few years and I remember asking Carlos what he'd got Sarita... Tia for her birthday. What surprised me was that the magazine cover image looked exactly the same. That's what I was looking at last night." He turned to Tia. "Did I hear you right when you said that they don't come out?"

"Yes." She nodded.

"I find that very strange. Is that some Mexican custom or something?" He looked at her for some explanation.

"Not that I am aware of. Father..." she hesitated for a moment. "Father made me promise that I wouldn't ever remove them. I was sixteen and he was my hero," she shrugged, "I promised. I never even thought of having them taken out until years after, when I hadn't seen him in a long time."

Joseph smiled and leaning forward he took her hand.

"Don't ever think he didn't want you. Circumstances may have conspired against him, as they did me, but he always wanted you... And, don't ever stop honouring him as your father." Joseph nodded, to make her give a response to say she understood.

Tia smiled at him as he leant back into his chair his eyes fixed on her. The silence lingered a few moments.

"Where were we?" Joseph asked as he re-engaged with the whole group.

"We were talking about Tia's weird 'Saber gemas'," Lester announced.

"'scuse me?" Joseph was intently looking at Lester.

Lester shifted in his seat and repeated what he said. "Tia's 'Saber gemas'. Her earrings."

"Why did you call them 'Saber gemas'?" Joseph looked at the floor as he thought for a moment. "Knowledge gems," he whispered to himself, but they all heard it.

"That's what *Father* called them when he gave them to me."

There was a long pause as Joseph stared at Tia. It was clear he was not focusing on her, but was deep in thought. Suddenly he reconnected.

"Did he tell you why?" Joseph queried.

"No. He just had this silly phrase, like a rhyme, that he made me repeat." She looked a little embarrassed and glanced at the others in discomfort at the admission.

"What was it Tia?" Joseph was deadly serious and his question had urgency.

Tia once again found herself the uncomfortable centre of attention. She looked up at the ceiling and mumbled a few words in Spanish then translated. "Numbers held in secret store," she mumbled again. "A light reveals, or shows, ten." Once again she muttered to herself, "N and Y complete the group, or set... To lead to the lion's den."

Lester grabbed a pen and paper. "Again," he demanded. Tia's embarrassment disappeared in a flash as Lester's interest in the rhyme was shown.

"Numbers held in secret store, a light reveals ten. N and Y complete the set, to lead to the lion's den. He made me say it in English and in Spanish. It rhymes better in English, but I like the Spanish."

"What on earth does that mean?" Beth asked.

Tia shrugged. "He made me chant it like a nursery rhyme until it was embedded in my memory. It's years since I've said it out loud, but it's still there."

Joseph got out of his seat and took the magnifying glass from Lester. He turned to Tia and asked, "Don't take this the wrong way, Tia, you're a pretty girl and I'm already in trouble for staring at your picture too closely, but would you mind if I take a closer look at your earrings?" He smiled at the way the request sounded, especially while he was holding the glass in his hand.

She raised an eyebrow and took note of his inquisitive expression before nodding tentatively. Looking across at Will, she hoped for some support, but he gave no indication that she shouldn't do what was asked, so she stood.

"Come over to the window." Joseph took her arm and guided her to where he wanted. She flicked back her hair and held it in a ponytail with her hand.

Joseph leaned into her and their faces were inches apart. Tia could smell his aftershave and feel the occasional slight brush of his hand on her cheek as he gently held her ear lobe while inspecting the gem.

Lifting away, he waved Lester over to take a look, then Beth. Finally, when Will lined up to take his turn, Tia lost her patience and shouted, "That's enough! If you need to inspect the studs this close then they will have to come out!"

Everyone in the room held station for just a second, trying to assess whether it was just a heat of the moment comment or if she meant it.

"You serious, Tia?" Joseph eventually asked.

She hesitated for a minute and looked him in the eye. "Do you think there's something more to them than we know?"

"I do. I think they may be of more importance than any of us can imagine."

"You think that they might help me to find out about my father?"

Joseph's serious look and the way he held her attention before answering made Tia understand that he was being as truthful as he could.

"Maybe there isn't anything to this that will help with regard to your father's whereabouts, but, not many people name earrings or teach their daughters a rhyme about them without it being of some importance. Can I promise you that they will lead to some answers about your father and make it alright to break the promise you made never to take them out? No. But we will never find out unless we can take a look at them properly and that can't happen until you take them out. Do I think it's worth a try... to maybe find Carlos... your father? Yes, I do. But *you* must decide."

Tia looked around the faces of those gathered, reading each expression that was frozen waiting for her to decide. She battled with many things as her mind sifted through the reasons to do something she had resisted for so long.

"Okay," she finally answered. "I'll trust you. They have to come out, but I'm not having anybody but Beth do it. It's Beth or it's not happening."

Beth smirked at the expressions of the men and gave a little laugh when they noticed the look on her face. She made a gesture that indicated girls one, boys nil, and Tia joined her laugh.

"You got any tools that might be helpful, Joseph?" asked Beth.

"Sledgehammer and a spade?" Tia punched him playfully on the arm. "I think we might find something," he added.

Lester pulled a small tool pouch from his bag that contained some fine cutters and passed them to Beth.

"I think we might need ice," she said.

Beth and Tia disappeared into the kitchen where they grabbed a bowl full of ice from the freezer then headed to the bedroom away from inquisitive eyes.

Initially, it was impossible to do the job for laughing. Every time they got into position, one or the other would crack, sending them both into uncontrollable fits of giggles. Beth would deliberately hold a straight face, but seconds later the room descended into chaos again. At one point Will knocked on the door to find out what was happening. He popped his head into the room, but this inspired greater joviality, so throwing his eyes and hands to the ceiling, he left them to it.

CHAPTER 19

It was almost an hour before the girls emerged from their hideaway at the back of the house and joined the impatient men in the front room.

"What took you so long?"

Lester's irritation at having to wait was clearly stamped on the tone of his question. He soon wished he hadn't asked when the two girls erupted into laughter again. He thrust out his hand to take the jewels, but Tia's face suddenly turned serious.

"You need to remember that these were a gift from my father and I've already broken a promise not to remove them."

"It's okay, Tia." Joseph replaced Lester in asking for the gems. "I promise they'll be okay. You can all come and watch while we try to see if there's something about them that might help us."

Their eyes stayed interlocked as Tia listened to him. She smiled, then carefully placed the studs in his open hand.

Following Joseph to the room where Tia had been sitting earlier that morning, they all filed in and surrounded a little workstation at one end. Joseph pulled out a square magnifying glass that was on a bendy support, so that it could be positioned where it was needed without the interference of handshake.

He grabbed some putty material and moulded it into a cone shape then fixed it to the work surface and pushed the stem of one of the studs into the top so that the gem was held upright. Next, he went to the desk drawer and found a small pen-torch with a minute point light.

"Right, let's see what we can find," he said, glancing around the room at the expectant faces as he leant over the subject. They all waited for some kind of declaration of discovery from him, hovering as close as they could without getting in the way, but were greeted with grunts of dissatisfaction.

Finally, he started to mumble some negative commentary as the others drifted ever closer around the gem, hoping to get a glimpse of any secrets they held.

"I'm no expert," Joseph straightened up and looked directly at Tia, "but this is not diamond." He hesitated while he thought, as the news sank in. "Why would Carlos Liatzo... You know what the villa was like... Why would he *not* buy his daughter real diamonds?" He hesitated a moment as he considered his own question as if it was an inconceivable concept for the man he'd known. "Here, Lester, you take a look and see if anything seems odd to you."

Lester took the torch from Joseph and repositioned the magnifying glass to look from another angle, as if it would reveal a different answer.

Again they waited for some revelation, but Lester gave no indication that there was anything to be seen. He straightened up, switched his attention to the other stud and went back to the examination. For several seconds he moved around at different angles before voicing his opinion.

"If these are 'knowledge gems' then they're acting dumb, if you ask me." He lifted up and held out the torch to the next 'contestant' in the competition to find answers.

Beth took it from him, but made a quick half-hearted inspection on the assumption that if there was anything, it wouldn't have passed the attention of the two before her. She duly offered it to Will, who was occupied in his thoughts elsewhere. She nudged him and he glanced down at the torch, but he declined the offer. Joseph took over and started a second inspection, but made only negative noises as he began to lose interest.

"STOP! Stop, go back."

The other four jumped at Will's explosive shout. "Where were you holding the torch?"

"What?" The expression on Joseph's face prompted clarification from Will.

"The torch? Where were you pointing it when I shouted? Show me."

Joseph tried to mimic his position as best he could remember, but wasn't sure what he was looking for. The four of them were so focused on the gem under inspection that they failed to see Will's attention was elsewhere. "Turn a little," he instructed. "No. No. The other way. Stop!"

While Joseph, Beth and Tia were still looking at the centre of attention, Lester's interest had moved to Will. He was looking at the wall next to the workstation.

"Don't move Joseph," he ordered. "What does that look like to you Lester? I said *don't* move the torch." Will raised his voice to stress the importance of remaining still.

He placed his finger on the wall and traced a faint shadow mark. There was a moment of anticipation.

"That's a number… five or a letter 'S'," Lester declared with confidence.

Will quickly went to the window and slammed the blind shut and the digit became almost as clear as if it had been written on the wall with a marker, along with several other blurry characters near it. By now all eyes were on the wall, but the steadiness of the torch caused the image to dance around too much to make sense of it.

"We need to focus the beam of light and turn the gem to see if there's anything else. If we get a stronger light source and try using the magnifying glass to focus it, perhaps we can generate something a little stronger and more directional," Beth suggested. "The reflector in a torch is designed to spread the beam outwards, but if we try to create the opposite and aim it on the gem, it might yield something more. A bit like you would with the sun through a magnifying glass to burn a piece of wood."

"There's a larger beam-light in the garage. If we cover it with a cloth and use the magnifying glass from the living room…"

Joseph was out of the door and on his way to the garage before completing his sentence. Lester went for the glass in the living room and Beth cleared the workstation top, setting both gems in the putty mound a little higher so that they would be between the light and a clear space on the wall behind. She glanced at Will, who was standing with Tia, watching the flurry of activity.

"Well done, Will. We could have missed that."

"Yeah. Well done," Joseph added, as he and Lester came back into the room just as Beth commented.

Within a matter of minutes they were ready to begin the ad-hoc experiment with no idea whether it would work. The lights went out and the beam was brought to focus on the gems one at a time, but there was nothing legible, a few markings, but nothing clear.

"Damn!" Will shouted out in exasperation.

"Wait! Hold the beam on one of the gems," Lester instructed. "Then rotate the gem so that the beam hits it at every angle."

Beth was on it in seconds as Lester tried to focus the light. Suddenly there was a row of figures moving in an arc across the wall. Beth reversed the direction until they were at the highest point and as clear as they could be. Tia grabbed a pen and paper from the desk and scribbled as Will read them out. "5D217E6Z7. Keep rotating it to make sure there isn't anything else, then try the other one," he commanded.

"I'm on it," Beth said, as the numbers disappeared and then reappeared like the sun setting and then rising again from the opposite side.

"Okay, now the other one," Will instructed.

Joseph and Lester manipulated the light to land on the other gem and Beth followed the same routine. Just as with the first gem, the rotation caused a row of figures to lift onto the wall. Will read them out again, "7Z6E712D5."

"Just complete the rotation, Beth," said Will, as he watched the wall intently.

Once they had satisfied themselves that they'd got the secret that the jewels had tried to conceal, Lester dropped the cover and the magnifying glass onto the workstation and went to flick the blinds open. The room was bathed in morning light and the group adjusted to the sudden brightness.

"Who in the world would know how to get that inside a gem?" asked Lester.

"Goodness knows," Will shrugged.

"Steven Holden." They all turned simultaneously to look at Joseph. "He was a wizard with micro-engineering. He would know how to do that."

The focus of attention was wrested from Joseph as Lester's impatience to understand the new information broke the moment. He turned to Tia who held the paper with the mystical code.

"Better read that out again."

She glanced down at the paper and read through the figures out loud.

"5 – D – 2 – 1 – 7 – E – 6 – Z – 7 and 7 – Z – 6 – E – 7 – 1 – 2 – D – 5." Tia meticulously reeled off the digits in a rhythmic sequence then looked up at the group as she completed them.

"That's a lot of numbers and letters," Will laughed.

"Not as many as you might think. It's the same sequence, but in reverse." Tia turned the paper to let them all see. "But why are they both the same?" she asked, as the group were staring at the scribbled numbers.

"In case you lost one?" Beth threw in her penny's worth with a shrug that said, 'it's my best guess'.

Lester cut in as he began reading from a paper he'd pulled from his pocket.

"Numbers held in secret store, a light reveals ten. N and Y complete the set, to lead to the lion's den." There was a moment's silence in the room as they individually meditated, working through what they were on to.

Joseph interrupted the internal deliberations. "Anybody got anything to add? Any suggestions?" He looked at Lester as if prompting the sharp mind he'd already seen glimpses of.

Lester ran his eyes over the rhyme before making comment. "They *were* secretly held numbers, or digits at least. And it *was* the light that revealed them. The only problem that immediately strikes me is... there's nine, not ten." Tia turned the page back to look at the sequence, but quickly glanced up at Lester as he continued. "And I'm sorry to tell you this Tia, but the studs... They're almost certainly crystal glass."

She didn't respond to what he was saying, but went back to the paper as if the importance or value of what the studs were made of was insignificant when compared with the slightest new connection to the man she'd lost from her life. The group focused on Tia, wondering what occupied her thoughts. She quickly gave them the answer.

"There's one more problem," she stated emphatically, looking up to find that she was the centre of attention. "Not only are there only nine numbers when the riddle suggests ten, but if the sequence is the same, just in reverse, which is the correct way?" She passed the paper to Lester to take a look. "I need coffee."

There were noises of agreement from around the room and they all traipsed off to the kitchen in procession behind Tia, assembling around the table.

While Tia rumbled around preparing the drinks, everyone else was focused on the two papers placed in the centre of the table. One displaying the riddle and the other the nine-digit sequence retrieved from the gems.

"Perhaps we missed one?" Beth suggested.

"We would've had to miss it twice," Will offered. "Once in each gem and the same digit both times."

The room fell silent again, realising how unlikely that was.

"What if we misread one of the figures?" Lester surfaced from his contemplation as they each grasped at all possibilities.

"That wouldn't explain why only nine," said Beth.

"No... It wouldn't," he conceded. "Wait. What if..." Lester looked up at the others who waited for his suggestion. He spun around the paper with the digits, so that it was the right way up for him to read it. "Look at the pattern." He waited a second to see if anyone would register it, but there were no takers. "7 – Z – 6 – E – 7 – 1 – 2 – D – 5," he read them out again. Number, letter, number, letter and so on." He ringed the number 1 with his finger. "Shouldn't that be a letter?"

Joseph cleared his throat. "Let's say you're right for a moment. We can't have misread it that badly, not twice. If it *is* a letter, there aren't all that many choices. It could be the letter 'L'…"

"But the others are capitals and that would rule it out, wouldn't it?" Beth interrupted.

"I agree," said Joseph. "So that leaves the letter 'I'."

"That doesn't help us much though, does it? There's still only nine digits, even if we did get one wrong." Lester sounded disappointed that the sequence he'd spotted seemed to be of no value.

"On the contrary."

The smug look on Tia's face showed that she'd seen something and the confident tone of her voice drew the attention of everyone. She glanced around the circle of expectant faces waiting with anticipation.

"AND?" Joseph raised his voice a little to show that she had their attention and they wanted to know what she was talking about.

"Can you count to ten in Spanish?" she asked with a grin on her face.

The four mystified listeners looked at one another and began stumbling through a sequence of numbers in the unfamiliar language. When they reached ten she immediately echoed the last number.

"Ten," she stated emphatically. "DIEZ."

Taking the paper from Lester, she said, "The number one *is* the letter 'I'. And the correct sequence is 5D2I7E6Z7." Pointing to the letters in the sequence, she landed her finger on each one as she spelled out, "D-I-E-Z… Ten."

A momentary silence settled in the room until Beth felt compelled to break it.

"I bet you're a real pain to do crosswords with."

Tia laughed, but took the comment as a compliment.

Congratulatory noises filled the room for a few moments, but Joseph brought the things quickly back to order.

"Now we just need to know what it means. It has to be more than just a puzzle for amusement and if the first half of the riddle is right, which it seems to be, we're still left needing to figure out the second."

"Okay," Lester straightened himself in his chair. "Anything you have, just throw it in. The first thing I see is that we're told to add, 'N' and 'Y', to the group to complete the set. Is that either end? In front? After?"

"I'm just thinking out loud here," Beth began. "When I see 'N' and 'Y' together it immediately infers New York. Perhaps we need to add the letters to the beginning of the sequence. I assume he didn't put them on because it would have destroyed the number letter rhythm. It could be a locker number in the New York airport lounge, or a safety deposit box in a bank?"

"Beth you get the gold star... After you Tia, that is. And you... damn it, we'll all have a gold star shall we?" There were a few chuckles at Lester's impromptu award ceremony. "That leaves us with the 'Lion's den'." Lester jumped up from his seat and headed to the living room.

"Where are you going?" Will shouted after him.

"To run 'Lion's den' through an anagram program and to check the bank and security company names in New York," he yelled back over his shoulder as he disappeared.

"You're a smart bunch of kids," Joseph said, as he got up from the table. He didn't say anything else, just went to the room where the studs were still held in position on the workstation. He removed them and placed them in a small envelope which he took from the desk drawer.

He wandered back through the kitchen and into the living room where they'd all relocated to be with Lester and went over to Tia. Holding out the envelope, he said, "You'd better put this somewhere safe. They've been with you for all these years it would be a shame to lose them now."

Tia took the packet from him and smiled. "Thanks Joseph, for everything."

He smiled, but quickly turned away. She caught a look in his eyes that was difficult to interpret. "How's that search coming on Lester?" Joseph queried, taking a seat next to him.

"I've just pulled up a list of the possible establishments in New York. I'm assuming that it *will be* New York. That would be most people's spontaneous reaction to the letters NY." He looked at Joseph. "Man, you really need to get a better connection to the internet. The stuff's coming down at the speed of a slow motion sloth."

"Never saw the need. Anyway, you're the telephone operator. Do something about it."

Lester laughed and turned his attention back to the screen and the job in hand. "I'm going to filter out all the places that don't have any of the letters in 'Lion's den', that should get rid of the definite no hopers. I'll need to use your printer." Lester looked at Joseph and hesitated before asking the question on the tip of his tongue. "You *do* have a printer?"

Joseph didn't even bother to answer the question simply rolling his eyes instead.

Two minutes later Lester was on his feet with the laptop in hand. "In the office or whatever that room was?" he queried.

"It's in the cupboard with the double doors," Joseph answered. Lester went to the living room door. "Make sure you wind it up before you ask it to print, you little schmuck."

A grin spread across Lester's face as he departed the room and the others couldn't help noticing. "You might be smart kids, but a little respect wouldn't go amiss," Joseph shouted, loud enough for Lester to hear through the kitchen to the other room.

When Lester returned with printed pages in hand, he couldn't resist another poke at Joseph. "I bet they didn't have electricity in houses like this for a long time… That's why you got a clockwork printer, isn't it?" There was a smattering of laughter.

"Wise guy."

Lester became engrossed organising what he'd printed, the others just waited until he was ready.

There was a question on the tip of Beth's tongue, but she'd been hesitating about asking it. Deciding to throw caution to the wind, she put it to Joseph.

"Steven Holden, what happened to him?"

"He died in a car crash."

"Accident?"

Joseph immediately looked at Beth, but chose not to voice an answer. He simply shrugged, but Beth wasn't satisfied with that.

"You have doubts?" she pressed.

"When you've been involved in the type of business that he and I, and your father," he nodded toward Tia, who was listening intently, "have been doing, for as long as we've been doing it, you learn to be suspicious. I don't know anything, except that I've got a gut feeling. Call it intuition if you will, but it's there and I've never been able to shake it. All I know is, at the time he was killed we'd begun to tread on some toes inside the organisation. Not everybody was happy that we were working to…" Joseph checked himself. "To deal with some discrepancies." He sat looking out of the window for a while before continuing. "A man lives, another dies, one disappears and another has his reputation torn to shreds. Who knows why each one gets treated so… But I wouldn't mind kicking the ass of the one who ordered it."

Lester suddenly rejoined the group.

"There doesn't seem to be anything that would correspond to the letters we have available. Some of them have way too many letters. There's only twenty-three left after I ruled out those that had letters that are not contained in 'Lion's den', but I can't make any sense of them." He looked around the room at the others for help.

"Why don't you print a copy of all the possible names regardless of what letters they have and give us all one each. If it isn't obvious, we must be missing something, but if we each take our own way of trying to figure it out, perhaps it will give us a better chance."

Will's suggestion was as good as any, so Lester went to produce the required reading matter for each of them. When he came back he handed them out to each one with a pencil he'd taken from the desk.

"Feels like exam time at school." Tia's wry comment drew mocking sympathetic groans.

They sat for the next few minutes, throwing in occasional suggestions and questions, eliminating names that were so far from the clues that they couldn't conceive that they were the right places. Finally the list was down to a small number of possibilities, but they all seemed to miss the mark.

Lester had gone back to the laptop, discarding the paper and leaving the others to continue the head scratching.

Will had been annoyingly tapping his paper with the pencil he was holding, but no one said anything until it got the better of Beth. "Must you do that?"

The tapping stopped for a moment as Will looked up at her. The glare was confirmation that he was in the frame.

"This is stupid!" Will barked, irritated at Beth's comment. "Maybe the 'NY' has nothing to do with New York."

"Wow!" Lester cut straight through the building friction. "The list, the list. Londen International Security in New York."

"What about it, Lester?" Will snapped at him in the heat of the moment. "I think there's a few too many letters," he said sarcastically. "It's crossed off my list anyway."

The others didn't show any disagreement with him.

"I know..." Lester looked up at the questioning faces. "But look at the way they logo their headed paper. He spun the laptop around to display the website.

'Londen' was presented in a bold confident font and the words 'Security International' were small font underlining the main name, except the first letter of each word was much larger and presented like a seal on an official document.

"Ignore the tiny letters. It makes the logo look like 'LONDEN I S'. LION'S DEN."

There were suddenly four faces crowded around the laptop, and Lester, who was grinning like the cat who got the cream.

"Whatever we've been paying you Lester, it's not enough." Beth whispered.

"You're not paying me anything."

"I know. It's not enough. We'll up it by one hundred percent." She smiled at him.

"Gee. Thanks, Beth."

"We need to get in there." Joseph sliced through the jovial talk. "We have the code and the location. We need to make an appointment for Miss Liatzo to go take a look at what's in the box."

Tia looked alarmed at the suggestion.

"It's time we made you look the part, Tia. We'd better go to town and pick up a dress. You can't go in there looking like that, you'd stand out like a sore thumb." Joseph jumped up and started issuing orders. "Will, you and Lester stay here. We can't risk *your* face being seen in town. Lester, get the number for Londen and ring to book an appointment for tomorrow at noon. Tell them that you're Miss Liatzo's P.A. and she's in town for one day only. Make sure they understand that it is very important that she gets to that box. The drive to New York is about five hours. Where did you get that car from? Is it yours?"

"Stolen," Lester chimed in. "Doubt they would have noticed yet though."

"Better not to risk it. We'll take my car. It's more likely to look the part anyway. Beth you come with us. Can't say I'm going to be much use helping choose a dress."

The flurry of activity saw Joseph and the two girls ready to go in minutes. He led them outside to the garage, threw open the doors and rolled out a huge four wheel drive motor. It was an ivory colour with dark tinted windows and cream leather upholstery. As the girls climbed in Beth let fly with a complimentary whistle.

"You like it?" Joseph asked.

"You kidding?"

Joseph smiled. As the doors closed, it was like the outside world had been separated from them. They were contained in a luxurious bubble.

Will stood at the window as the vehicle roared away down the drive. He watched until it was out of sight then turned to look at Lester. "Can't make him out."

Lester looked up then went back to the screen in front of him as he responded. "He's okay. A bit self-centred and cocky. Likes his own way." He shrugged. "Likes the ladies, but doesn't want one to own him."

"I don't know, Lester, but something's driving him at the moment. I'm going to poke around while he's out of the way." Lester looked up with concern written on his face. "Don't worry, I'm just interested. I won't touch anything I shouldn't."

Lester didn't let Will go from his stare for a few seconds, as if he was emphasising the importance of keeping Joseph on side.

CHAPTER 20

The trip into town was several miles and Tia was quiet all the way. The talk between Joseph and Beth was mostly about cars and she was out of her depth with discussions about engines and the like. Besides that, she was pondering the task that had been allocated to her for the following day at noon. They hadn't even set out for New York and she was already nervous about going into such a high security institution, especially as she didn't feel she had the right to be there. She wondered what would happen if she went and found the number wasn't really genuine. All kinds of scenarios played out in her mind, mainly ending in her arrest for fraud or something worse.

As they entered the outskirt of the small town Beth suddenly yelled out in excitement stirring Tia from her thoughts. "Well, would you look at that!"

Tia glanced in the direction of Beth's attention and caught a glimpse of the small billboard advert set off to the side of the highway and immediately felt her face flush.

"That's from the same photo shoot as the magazine cover isn't it?" Beth spun around in her seat to face her friend, expecting to be confronted with a smile. Tia's face showed concern and Beth instantly adjusted her attitude as she realised how exposed she must have felt. The worried expression related to recent events, overruling any joy at her success. She was being swept along in an uncontrolled direction toward an undetermined future.

She caught Tia's eye again as the billboard disappeared from view and gave an encouraging smile that showed she understood.

The low rumble of the huge engine could be felt through the vehicle as Joseph rolled it into a parking space in front of a small boutique. Beth jumped out of the car, keen to deal with the task at hand. Tia was less enthusiastic. Shopping for clothes was one of the delights she savoured, but this time it didn't quite have the same appeal.

As they entered the shop, the assistant took a subtle look at the three, but waited while Beth and Tia glanced along the clothing rails. Joseph stood in the centre of the open floor area like he was in the wrong place, but didn't know quite how to escape.

After a few minutes the assistant came over and introduced herself. "Hi. I'm Keisha. Is there anything I can help you with?"

"Hello." Joseph took the hand that was offered. "This is the daughter of a friend, and her friend, Tia and Beth." Joseph cleared his throat. "Tia has an important function in New York that she has to attend unexpectedly and she didn't bring any appropriate clothing with her. We thought we'd be spending our time driving around to some of the local sights, rather than dressing up for a classy meeting."

Keisha smiled at the girls. "What do you have in mind, Tia. Bold and confident, elegant and chic?"

Tia looked at Beth and then Joseph. He made a gesture to tell her to make her choice. "It's a business meeting really, but it's in a very wealthy part of the city and I'm not sure who I'm going to meet. So I guess *elegant* is best? But it's at noon, so I can't do evening wear."

"Okay. Let's take a look at the rails nearer the back. I'm sure we'll find you something. Size four?"

"Yes. How did you know?"

"I've been making dresses for twenty years. It soon becomes easy, believe me, especially when I have to put the green-eyed monster aside and dress a pretty lady like you."

Keisha smiled at the slightly embarrassed look on Tia's face and it didn't escape Beth's attention.

"Not dresses for both of you?"

"I wish," said Beth. They both laughed at the intonation in her voice, suggesting she'd never really found a reason to wear such classy clothes.

"I'm just going along the street, so I'll leave you ladies to it," Joseph shouted, as he went to the door.

"Joseph," Tia arrested his departure. "How much?"

"Sorry?"

"How much do we spend?"

He smiled as there was immediate attention on his anticipated answer. "Don't break me," he shouted, pulling the door. "And don't forget shoes. Trainers won't impress." With that, he was gone, leaving them still unsure of what to do.

"Don't worry Tia. We can find something at a reasonable price. Anyway, a car like that one shouts look at me, I've got money." Keisha deliberately glanced through the display window at the vehicle out front just to make sure they understood her meaning. The girls burst out laughing at the comment and it immediately sealed their liking of Keisha.

It was an hour before Joseph came back into the shop. The girls were just finishing up, having had a great time and the laughter spilled out through the door as soon as Joseph opened it.

"Are you laughing at me because I've no idea what's coming my way, or are you just laughing?"

"Listen," Keisha started. "If she were *your* daughter she would save you a fortune. Most daughters who come into a place like this, being left to their own devices, would milk daddy until his eyes watered."

The girls laughed again at the relentless comedy show they'd been audience to. Joseph smiled at the comment and handed over his card.

As Keisha completed the transaction and passed over the bags, she beamed at the happy shoppers. "You make sure you come again girls, you hear?"

They waved as they got into the car and again as it pulled away from the front of the shop. Keisha stood in the doorway watching them go.

"That was a laugh. I reckon she's in the wrong business. She should be on the stage," Beth said

"She was." Joseph's comment silenced the continuing rumble of chuckles.

"You're kidding?"

"No. She didn't perform, but she's dressed some very well-known people."

"Why doesn't that surprise me?" said Beth.

The journey back was a little lighter than the one to town, as the girls batted comments back and forth about their time with Keisha. Joseph barely said a word from the time they left the shop until they pulled into the drive at the house.

It was just after 2:15pm as Joseph drew the car to a stop. As they came through the rear door into the kitchen, Lester was already there to greet them. His expression was not encouraging, catching the attention of the returning group.

"What's the problem, Lester?" Joseph didn't beat around the bush.

"Londen have never heard of a Miss Liatzo. They're more difficult to get information from than the Secret Service."

Joseph was clearly not expecting there to be a problem. "Shit!" he shouted, as he slammed his fist on the counter. He suddenly looked up at Beth and Tia and felt embarrassed that he'd lost control of his emotions in front of them. Will came into the kitchen in response to the sudden outburst.

"Is there no way that you can get anything online, Lester?" Beth asked.

"The place is like Fort Knox. Even if I had an idea how to get into their system, it could take more time than we've got."

"Sharmez." All eyes were suddenly on Tia. "Did you try Sharmez?"

"Didn't you pick that name when you left Mexico?" Will asked.

"Not exactly. The man who sorted the whole thing out," she thought for a moment, "Caleb Sallam. He'd already organised all the papers. I was Tia Sharmez before I could argue about it."

"But how could that name relate to a deposit box? We got the numbers from your ear studs that your father gave you when you were sixteen."

Tia shrugged. "When you put it like that, it doesn't make much sense, but none of this makes any sense, not from the moment it all started." She suddenly felt a little foolish having made the suggestion.

"What else are we going to try?" Beth chimed in. "The whole thing we figured out with the code is convincing, but we can hardly ring up asking if the number relates to one of their security boxes, can we? Just ring and ask. The worst that can happen is that they say they don't have a Sharmez on the records either."

Lester shrugged and disappeared into the other room.

"I guess we might have to take the dress back, huh?" Beth said jokingly, as she looked across at Joseph, but he didn't respond. He seemed to be deep in thought. It was as though they weren't in the room with him.

"Joseph?" Beth tried to attract his attention.

"Umm." He looked up and found Tia, Beth and Will staring at him. "What?"

"Just wondered if you were okay?"

"Yeah... I'm okay." He pulled the door and went outside, slamming it behind him.

Will looked at Tia and Beth. "What's going on there?"

"Beats me," Beth answered.

Tia suddenly felt a little awkward at Joseph's change in behaviour. He'd been quite chatty while they were out, although he hadn't said much on the homeward journey.

Lester suddenly burst through the door from the living room. "You're not going to believe this. I've just booked an appointment for Miss Sharmez at Londen Security International at noon tomorrow."

"What?" Tia was stunned.

"You're due to meet Mr Randolf at noon tomorrow."

She'd completely ruled it out after Lester questioned how it could be possible, but the scheme was suddenly back on again. For some reason that she couldn't put her finger on, she felt unable to share the jubilation that filled the kitchen. She looked out of the window at Joseph as he crossed the yard on his way back from the garage. He opened the back door and straight away figured that something positive had happened.

"We're in, Joseph. Londen confirmed an appointment for Miss Sharmez at noon tomorrow."

"They did?" He looked as surprised as anyone.

Tia had been watching him as he came through the door to receive the news from Lester. He glanced her way and their eyes met, only for a moment, but Tia couldn't interpret the look on his face and it was gone in a flash, as though a mask quickly covered it.

The focus of attention was switched back to their preparations for leaving. New York had become the next step on an unpredictable journey. By four in the afternoon they were climbing into the vehicle with the plan set.

As they turned in the drive to leave, Joseph suddenly stopped the car. "Damn. I won't be a minute." He climbed out and ran to the house, emerging a few moments later. Will watched him through the rear door window as he crossed the few yards back to the car. He had a disturbing feeling that he was being eyeballed by Joseph. The tinted window might just have given the wrong impression, but it was a little unnerving.

Joseph slammed the car door and made a correction to the angle of the rear-view mirror that looked nothing more than an innocent move. Will caught a fraction of a second connection with Joseph's eyes and was aware that he'd deliberately used the manoeuvre to take a look at him.

Joseph slowed at the junction between the drive and the highway and hesitated a second at the sight of a car parked in an unusual place not too distant from the entrance. He studied the vehicle for a second before pulling out on to the highway and accelerated away, but made no comment.

The journey was relatively uneventful for the first hour, but Lester began to notice Joseph constantly checking the mirrors. He turned to look out of the rear windscreen. There was a car trailing a long way behind. It was neither getting closer nor being left.

As he turned back, he caught Joseph's look in the rear-view mirror. "You think we've got a problem?"

There were a few anxious glances in Lester's direction at his question.

"Just going to slow down a little to see what the car behind does," Joseph warned them.

The gap remained the same as the car behind had obviously adjusted its speed to compensate. Joseph picked up speed again, but instead of the distance between the vehicles opening the tailing car was clearly aware that they had been rumbled.

The gap between them began to close quite rapidly. Lester glanced over his shoulder again and the distance had halved since he'd last looked. Moments later, the vehicle following was at an uncomfortably close distance and Joseph was frequently checking his mirrors. The car suddenly roared as he jammed his foot on the gas. The power was incredible as it forced the huge beast and its occupants up to a terrific speed, pulling away from the vehicle behind. The trailing car responded and quickly moved back to such an uncomfortable distance for the speed they were travelling at that it looked like they were about to try to force Joseph off the road.

With little chance of out-running the pursuer and the risk of coming across a patrol car that would pull them both in and scupper the whole operation, Joseph took a different tack. Slowing back to a normal speed he indicated to turn at the next junction. The car behind copied and followed them along a minor road.

"I'm going to make a manoeuvre that you're not going to like, so brace yourselves for a sudden stop and an impact. He pressed the gas as though he was about to make an attempt to escape and the car behind followed suit, suddenly accelerating. Joseph shouted a warning and slammed his foot on the brakes. The car behind ploughed into the back of Joseph's vehicle with some force. Joseph reacted by hitting the gas and they lurched forward, separating from the crumple-nosed car which had hit them from behind. He slammed on the brakes, quickly spinning the vehicle to face the opposite direction and roared back past the mangled wreck. The occupants, dazed from the impact, struggled out of their car as steam rose from what was left of the front grill.

The thunder of Joseph's car engine, as it took off back to the main road, was the sound of escape and they breathed easy for a moment, but no one said a word.

Once back on the highway, Joseph travelled a mile or two before he pulled over and climbed out to take a look at the damage to his vehicle. Beth saw what was happening and leapt out from the other side, meeting him at the back of the car. There was surprisingly little damage from the impact. Most of the force had been taken by a sturdy chrome protective grill that wrapped around the back. The protruding tow hook had gone through the radiator of the other car like a hammer blow to an egg.

Joseph smiled and looked at Beth. He didn't say anything, but went back to his seat. Once they were both in, he pulled away, resuming their journey as if nothing had happened.

The silence only lasted for a few minutes. Will glanced at Lester and his look was returned. He couldn't just forget about the incident without comment.

"Do we need to say something about what just happened?"

Joseph deliberately turned the mirror so that he could see where the question came from. He left it hanging for a moment, frequently taking his eyes off the road to look at Will.

"We *were* being followed," he finally said, "and now we're not."

He connected again with Will before returning the mirror to its previous position, almost as an indication that the matter was closed to any further discussion. His voice carried the same menacing intonation that had been there when he confronted the guys breaking into his house the previous evening. It was like dealing with Dr Jekyll who had turned into Mr Hyde, but now the spooky version had returned. Whether the girls noticed, Will wasn't sure, but when he glanced at Lester it certainly confirmed that it hadn't gone past him. He'd been there when they were caught entering the house and had been subject to Joseph's sinister side.

The rest of the journey was uneventful and completed just after 9.00pm. Joseph pulled in at a hotel where there was parking underneath the building. He tucked the car into a hidden space and the group made their way upstairs to the reception.

On the way Will lifted the collar of his jacket and pulled a hat on. He deliberately used the others as a screen to hide his features, conscious that he was still the fugitive among them.

"I need three rooms. A double and two twins," Joseph stated.

The receptionist duly provided the keys and indicated how to get there.

"One more thing," Joseph turned back as they were about to leave. "Could you arrange for a rental car to be dropped here in the morning? We're due to be at Londen International Security at noon tomorrow."

"Certainly, sir." While issuing the keys to the rooms the man behind the reception desk seemed indifferent to the group, but suddenly appeared to take more interest. "Do you have any preference?"

"Make sure that it'll impress."

The guy at the counter smiled and nodded.

Joseph handed out the keys as they walked along the corridor. The girls had a room, Will and Lester were sharing and Joseph took the double. As Joseph reached his room, he bade the others goodnight and abruptly disappeared leaving the four of them standing in the hallway. Locating the other rooms, Lester waved Will ahead as he tugged on Beth's arm to get her attention.

"I'll come see you in a little while."

The serious look on Beth's face showed that she'd registered the concern in Lester's voice, but it was not the time to pursue it.

Once inside their room, Will couldn't wait to speak to Lester. "What the hell's going on here?" His voice carried an agitated tone. "That fiasco out on the highway, what was that about?"

Lester didn't respond. He dropped his bag onto the bed and began to rummage through it.

Having kept a lid on his concerns since they'd left Joseph's house, the rear shunt of that unknown vehicle, the way Joseph reacted to the whole situation, Will was ready to get some answers. Annoyed that Lester seemed to be ignoring him, he suddenly shot across the room like a coiled spring exploding. Grabbing at Lester, he spun him around to face him, took hold of his coat lapels and slammed him against the wall. "What the hell are you up to, Lester?" he whispered in a very menacing tone.

Lester still didn't answer, determined that he would not be bullied into anything, but was a little surprised when Will pulled him away from the wall and slammed him back against it again, as though trying to hammer home his question. "You know more than you've been letting on, don't you?"

Lester slowly raised his hands, palms facing toward Will until they were in view, holding a submissive posture. His eyes stayed locked on Will's. It was a game of 'who would break first', but the odds favoured Will who seemed to dwarf Lester in such close proximity. The heavy breathing, induced by the confrontation, hissed through Will's clenched teeth, but he was unsure what to do next. He'd resolved to get some answers and not allow Lester to be evasive any longer about what he'd found out.

"There's something that you're keeping from us. Something you've seen in those files that you're not sharing."

Lester's lack of response and Will's frustration prompted him to try bouncing Lester against the wall once more. As Will lifted the pressure, suddenly the prey became the hunter as Lester's palm crashed into Will's face. For a moment it induced a state of shock that gave an opportunity to turn the tables. Lester grabbed a wrist and twisted Will's arm behind his back, shoving him so that he crashed to the floor under the force. Instantly Will braced himself to fend off the next blow, but it never came. The figure of Lester towered above him, but remained unmoved while Will shook his head to clear the impact-induced blur.

"Don't you *ever* threaten me again, *not ever*. I'm sick of you throwing your weight around like you're the big man. Ain't so big anymore, sprawled out on the floor." Lester waited to see if there was going to be any retaliation, but when it was obvious that Will was not about to take the matter any further, he stepped over him and grabbed two beers from the mini-bar. He pulled the lids and tossed the opener back in the tray. Will scrambled up to a sitting position and leant back against the wall, checking his nose with the back of his hand to see if there was blood.

"You'll live. I hardly touched you."

Lester leaned forward and held out a bottle. Will glanced at him, hesitating at the sudden turn around then took it. For a few moments the two sat eyeing each other and adjusting their opinions of one another until Lester broke the stare and tipped his beer to his lips. Will copied him, but the question he'd posed was still hanging in the air.

"Whatever's going to happen tomorrow, it has to happen," Lester started. "I don't like it any more than you, but the girls are as safe as it's possible to be, under the circumstances."

"What do you mean, under the circumstances? Are you putting them in danger?" The fire was still well alight in Will's eyes with a hint of humiliation at having been floored by his smaller 'friend'.

"Tia has been in danger for a long time, she just didn't know it. The guy she told us about, that changed her identity and helped her and that maid get out of Mexico, I do know that it was Nazim Akkbar. No matter what she thought his name was, it was definitely Akkbar."

"How the hell would you know that? Don't tell me, you've been opening more secret files."

A smile flickered on Lester's face and he shrugged to suggest he just couldn't help himself. He wandered over to the window to check out the view. He'd never been one to put all his cards on the table freely, so Will wasn't expecting to get that much and was surprised when Lester launched into some kind of explanation.

"An operation took place about eight years ago," he began. "A four man team was sent to extract a witness from a sensitive area."

"You mean Mexico."

"I bet the authorities wish it had been," Lester snorted. "That might have been easier to deal with. The Mexican scenario that Joseph told us about did happen, but that's not what I'm talking about. Whether that one worked out the way he said, I don't know. Anyway, this was a different situation. Four went in, but the whole thing went pear-shaped. A lot of people were killed and several million dollars worth of the local currency went missing. The United States government was left with one of the messiest incidents of violating the borders of another country that it has ever been involved in. Two of the team are now dead, one I don't know for sure and the other is just a few yards down the hall."

"Joseph Charles?"

Lester nodded.

"The others being Steven Holden, Nazim Akkbar and Carlos Liatzo?"

"Correct."

"But I thought Liatzo was dead. I'm sure that's what Tia thinks."

"Don't know." Lester shrugged. "There's no information to say that he is for sure. Holden and Nazim certainly are. Both incidents seem suspicious, but again, nothing on record is conclusive about what happened. It's like there's more than one history to this group, as if…" Lester hesitated as he was thinking, "as if there's been a cover up or an attempt to create confusion so the truth is obscured."

"You've got suspicions about how those two died, haven't you? Do you think it was a government cover-up."

"I wish I knew."

"So what do we do now?"

Lester shrugged.

"What about Tia and Beth?" Will's voice carried a note of concern.

"Do we have any alternative other than to see this through? Heaven knows what's in that security box, but I guess we need to find out tomorrow."

"Well you're not the only one interested in knowing. Did you notice Joseph's reaction when he thought the plan to get into Londen was scuppered."

"Oh yes, I noticed," Lester gave solid confirmation.

"Could we all be at risk?"

Lester shrugged. "We can hardly call the authorities can we?" The moment the words left his mouth he regretted it. He smiled apologetically, realising that his friend was in the frame for much worse than the rest of them if the authorities got involved.

Will sat staring into space as he contemplated their predicament.

Lester moved away from the window and dropped heavily into a chair jolting Will from his thoughts.

"Sorry about your face by the way."

"I suppose I had it coming. Probably for quite a few years." Will smirked at the thought of Lester getting one over on him, but concern for the situation was etched in his features and Lester could clearly see it. Whatever differences he'd had with Will over the years, he had no desire to see him accused of something he hadn't done, especially something as serious as murder.

Lester stood up. "You okay?"

Will looked up at him. "Sure. I'm fine." He didn't sound very convincing. He locked eyes with Lester and found an expression that showed concern.

"I'm going to check on the girls, and Joseph," Lester said, as he moved towards the door. "I think it's best you stay here. I caught that look on Joseph's face when we left the house this afternoon. I guess he checked if there was a gun missing from the pair he took from us last night." Will's apologetic look was all he could offer, but Lester immediately put him at ease about it. "We might yet be thankful that you took it." Their eyes connected again just as the door closed behind Lester, and Will, for the first time he could remember, was glad that they were at least on the same wavelength. Joseph Charles continued to be an unknown quantity, as was Carlos Liatzo, if he was still alive.

Will was beginning to appreciate that, of all the people embroiled in the current events, the one he'd undervalued most was the one he'd never allowed himself to forgive, Lester. A pang of regret set in as he sat on the floor, staring into space. Beth's frequent attempts to smooth over the issues between himself and Lester flashed through his mind and he began to wonder why she had persisted with them both for so long.

Lester wandered along the empty hallway until he reached the girls' room. He knocked and waited for a response. Beth pulled the door slightly open, then further once she'd seen who it was.

"Y'all okay?"

"Yeah." Beth hushed her voice a little. "Tia's a bit nervous about tomorrow, but we're okay."

Tia shouted a greeting from the bathroom, having heard Lester's voice.

Lester leaned in to Beth and lowered his voice.

"Tia's new shoes, get them for me." Beth's puzzled expression begged an explanation. "Not now Beth. I'll tell you later. Just trust me and let me have them. Don't let Tia know," he warned. "I'll bring them back in ten minutes."

Beth did as she was asked and peered through the doorway as Lester quickly disappeared down the hallway with the goods. As promised he was back ten minutes later to be greeted by Beth when he knocked on the door.

Tia was in the room, but Lester distracted her as Beth returned the shoes to their place then went to the door with him as he left. She stepped into the hallway behind him.

"Everything okay?"

Lester leant in close. "Just make sure you lock this door when I'm gone," he hesitated. "And put a chair against the handle." Beth pulled away to see Lester's face properly. The questioning look was asking for a reason, but Lester was not going to be forthcoming. "Just do it, Beth. We go back a long way and I look out for you like my own. I want you to be cautious, that's all." He put his hand on her shoulder and smiled. She nodded. Lester waved her back into the room and waited until she'd pushed the door closed.

Moving along the hallway until he got to Joseph's room, he stood listening for a moment before knocking. There was a shout from inside, but the door didn't open for quite a while. Lester hesitated, unsure if he had been told to 'get lost'. Just as he was about to go back to his room, the lock rattled as it was undone and Joseph stood in the partially open doorway.

"Something wrong kid?" He seemed to be guarding the view into the room.

"No. Just checking you're okay for tomorrow."

Joseph laughed, as though he'd seen Lester's question like that of a child checking a parent was able to cross the road safely. "Don't concern yourself about me, kid." He hesitated while scanning Lester's face. "You've done a good job getting us this far, son. Don't worry about tomorrow, it'll be fine." Joseph smiled and bid him good night, but waited for Lester to walk away. As he reached his room, Lester took hold of the door handle, but hesitated before entering. He gave in to the urge to look back along the hall. Joseph was still in the doorway observing him. He waved as Lester glanced back.

There was nothing easy about that night. Both Will and Lester were sleeping on the edge. Every sound had one or the other of them on high alert and the darkest hours were plagued with unpleasant images of what might happen the following day. It was a relief when Will finally headed for the shower at 6:00am.

As he stood in the warm spray, he tried to reason through the order of events of the last few days to try to gain a better perspective of the situation. It occurred to him that Lester hadn't said much about the double-murder he was accused of.

He dressed and went back into the bedroom to find Lester up and about, waiting for his turn in the bathroom.

"Just one question." Lester turned to give Will his attention. "When you got into the car, when we first came to your place, did you know that I wasn't involved in the murder of those two men?"

"No."

"When *did* you know for sure?"

"Sometimes we need to put our trust in people. I trust Beth absolutely. You should try it, Will. We might not have seen eye to eye for a long time, but that doesn't mean I would betray you, or her. You sometimes act like I would. That stunt at the table in my apartment was just the outward expression of what I've felt from you for years. Why do you think we never got on, despite Beth's best efforts? She told me you didn't do it, so you didn't do it. That's when I knew."

Lester had made his point and wasn't about to wait for any response, but left Will thinking through the implications of what he'd said, while he took a shower. No sooner was he dressed and out of the bathroom than there was a knock on the door.

"Who is it?" Lester shouted, glancing across at Will.

"Joseph."

Lester unlocked the door and let him in.

He had barely stepped inside the room when he started issuing instructions for the day.

"I need you two and Beth to take my car and follow Tia and me in the rental car. I'll act as her chauffeur and drive her to the appointment. You tail behind and take a position somewhere across the street when I drop her off. There's only one way in and out of that place so that's where I'll stay until she's done."

Lester glanced at Will to try to reassure him before he asked the next question.

"Okay, but why do you even need us there, Joseph?"

He hoped that it might give them some insight to what he was planning.

"It's better for us to keep together," Joseph instantly countered. "It'll reassure Tia. I'll bet she's been nervous enough without being worried that she's doing it on her own. You guys just make sure she understands that you will be there right through the whole thing."

"Don't worry about that Joseph. We'll be there come what may." Will's tone made clear his intention to watch out for his friends, but Joseph seemed to react to his determination positively.

"I know you will and that's just what's needed. If Tia is to be reassured that she can do this, she needs that kind of support, Will." Joseph slapped him on the arm as a gesture of admiration for his loyalty, leaving Will perplexed at the response.

The rest of the morning dragged and Joseph periodically came and went from the group as they sat having breakfast together in one of the rooms. Tia nervously looked up at the clock every few minutes obviously concerned about the role she was about to play.

Will put his hand on hers and whispered. "Don't worry. Just try to relax." She smiled weakly at him, but his reassurance didn't help.

CHAPTER 21

At 11:15am the car was delivered to the hotel and Joseph went to sign for it. The sleek black lines of the classy machine made an impression, gaining his instant approval and fitting the bill perfectly for the task ahead.

Tia had begun to get ready and Beth, having expelled the others from the room, fussed over her like it was her wedding day. When all was complete, she positioned Tia in front of the full-length mirror and made a complimentary whistle that raised a brief smile to her lips. Beth stood behind her and pulled Tia close as she squeezed her in a hug.

"You're going to do great kid," she whispered over Tia's shoulder. "One day we'll laugh about this."

"I hope so, Beth. I really hope so, because right now my stomach's in knots and I just want to be sick."

The two of them stepped out into the hallway just after Joseph knocked on the door at 11:35am. Apart from the magazine cover, it was the first time any of the men had seen her dressed to impress and their appreciation was clearly displayed. The sleek dark blue dress stopped just above the knee, capped sleeves showed the smooth definition of her arms from the shoulders down. She clutched a matching purse and wore high heeled shoes that lifted her a few inches above her real height, exaggerating her slender frame. Her hair spilled over the back of the dress covering the nape of her neck and she was sporting film star sunglasses to complete the image. She looked a million dollars.

Joseph called them to order and indicated that they should follow him. He set off with them in tow like a group of tourists trailing behind a guide. As they reached the parking level, the group split, making their way to the separate vehicles. They were all on edge and it was evident in every movement and every word, except for Joseph, who strolled to the black car with Tia as casually as going on a shopping trip.

He seemed to be made of unbending steel and looked the part dressed in a suit he'd packed when they left the house. He opened the rear door of the car and Tia slipped into the sumptuous leather interior as the others watched her while getting into Joseph's vehicle.

Two minutes later the cars emerged from the underground parking area and swept out of the entrance to the hotel.

The two vehicles negotiated the city traffic as the seconds slowly ticked by toward the appointed time, each one increasing Tia's nervousness as they approached their destination. She switched her attention between the passing buildings and the clock so frequently that it provoked comment from Joseph.

"Breathe long and deep, it helps with the nerves."

Tia smiled as she caught his eye in the rear-view mirror and deliberately tried to follow the advice.

The car smoothly turned into the road where Londen S. I. was located. A few minutes later they drew up outside the impressive building and Tia's stomach knotted at the sight of the sign and the entrance.

Lester brought the other car to a stop on the opposite side of the road, just a little way back. The eyes of all three friends were glued to the scene across the street, waiting for Tia to emerge and enter the building.

Joseph spun around in his seat to look at Tia and smiled. He nodded to indicate that it was time to go and she involuntarily glanced across the road to where her friends were sat watching. When she turned back, Joseph was still looking at her. She glanced out of the darkened side window of the car at the people busy en route to various destinations, living lives that took no account of this rollercoaster ride she was living. She felt she'd been shaken until all the inner strength she possessed had been tested to the limit and beyond. Now she needed to dig deep, look confident and enter the doors of Londen International Security like someone who owned things of enough value that they would be kept in such a place.

She turned back to Joseph and nodded, "Okay, here goes."

The door clunked as Joseph pulled the latch and leant slightly against it. There was a momentary sound like the hissing of air from a sealed container and the noise of the outside world suddenly flooded inside the vehicle. He went to the rear door and opened it for Tia. She slid from the leather seat and her high heeled shoes clicked as they hit the sidewalk. Turning again, she took a last look through the rear window at the others across the street, before leaving her sanctuary for the real world.

Stepping out of the vehicle, she immediately saw her reflection in the plush glass-faced entrance of the building in front of her and wished she felt as confident as she looked. Taking a deep breath, she set off to cover the small distance to the start of the unknown. Joseph watched her go as he pushed the rear door of the car closed and returned to the driver's seat.

Several security personnel were dotted about the entrance area. Some near the door, clearly marked by uniforms announcing their function. Others, just as observable, but without any indication that was so gregarious, stationed at various places further inside. She smiled at one of the guards as she pulled off her sunglasses and took the final few steps to be greeted by the glass doors automatically sliding apart to give her access. She stepped over the threshold into the establishment and the glass doors closed behind, separating her from her friends and the world outside. She was now on her own.

The reception reminded her of an expensive hotel lobby, a little sparser in its furnishings, but with extremely high ceilings that made her feel small and insignificant. A wide open floor space drew the visitors to a desk set well back into the area. Behind the reception desk were seated a man and a woman, smartly dressed but distinctly different to the statue-like security staff. The back light from the computer screens built into the facility, threw a slight glow onto their faces. On the wall behind them was the giant logo that had given them the breakthrough when the group were searching for the identity of the organisation she was now standing in. Large gold letters in a confident font spelled the word 'LONDEN' with the letters 'S', 'I', in an outline text as a background. The display caught her attention as she walked across the open space, reminding her of the previous day's events.

"Good morning madam, how may I be of assistance?"

The helpful tone of the receptionist's voice broke into Tia's thoughts. She momentarily glanced to her left, as if looking for the person that was being addressed. Realising that it was her, she cautiously responded. "Oh!" She hesitated a second as she remembered her lines. "I have an appointment at twelve o'clock. Could you inform Mr Randolf that I have arrived please?"

"Certainly." She paused a moment before continuing. "Who should I say is here?"

Tia immediately felt stupid for forgetting to introduce herself as they had rehearsed that morning.

"Sharmez. Miss Sharmez."

"Very good, Miss Sharmez." The woman tapped at the keypad in front of her, picked up the telephone on the desk and briefly spoke to someone. Replacing the receiver, she said, "If you would like to take a seat in the lounge area to your right, Miss Sharmez, Mr Randolf will be with you shortly."

Her efficient smile struck Tia as more mechanical than meaningful, but she wondered how dull it could be waiting on the whim of the rich and famous.

"Thank you."

Tia walked over to the place indicated and settled into one of the comfortable red leather seats that gave a flash of vibrant colour to the otherwise subdued area. She had a commanding view through the entrance doors and out onto the street beyond and found some comfort in being able to see the two cars, containing her friends, close at hand.

The place seemed empty apart from employees, emphasising her discomfort at being there. The digital clock on the wall showed 11:56am. It had a smaller digital panel where the numbers indicated the seconds ticking by, but they seemed to move too slowly as she watched them counting closer to the appointed time. The three and a half minutes left felt like they would never end, but she couldn't take her eyes away from the relentless, mesmeric counting of the seconds.

"Miss Sharmez?" Her eyes focused on the clock that stated 12:00pm exactly. Randolf stood for a second observing the young lady seated before him, but she didn't respond to his prompting. He coughed deliberately and repeated himself. "Miss Sharmez?" he stated more emphatically.

"Yes…" Tia shook the daydream state from her mind and quickly stood to greet Randolf, a little startled by his presence. "I'm so sorry," she flustered. Watching the seconds tick by had had the same effect as a hypnotist's swinging watch.

"I am Conrad Randolf, the operations manager of this establishment." He held out his hand.

The subtle flavour of an accent gave away the South African origin of the tall bespectacled man. His suit was pristine, as if set on a mannequin in a high-class shop window. It shimmered as he moved under the lights.

"I hope you had a pleasant journey here?" he asked.

"Yes… Thank you, yes," she lied. The chances of Mr Randolf understanding the kind of journey that had brought Tia to this appointment were remote, to say the least.

He pointed in the direction they needed to go as they reached the edge of the reception area. "If we go through here to the elevator in the other section please, Miss Sharmez." Mirrored dividing doors slid quietly apart, anticipating the timing of their arrival perfectly. "The vault is the equivalent of four floors down, but it is very elegant and comfortable," Randolf continued. "There is no need to worry." He followed the script of his well-worn routine.

Behind them the mirrored doors closed. Tia glanced back and was surprised to be able to see into the reception area through to the entrance and the street beyond.

The elevator doors were already open, waiting to take them to the underground world. They walked straight in and Randolf pressed a button prompting the doors to close silently. The movement was almost undetectable as the descent began. Tia felt a slight sensation of panic, as though she were trapped against her will. It reminded her of that awful moment, only days before, when she'd been abducted from the street. A feeling of helpless loss of control over one's destiny seemed to parallel the two moments. She shook her head slightly, trying to dispel the unpleasant sensation, but Randolf didn't miss a thing in the mirrored reflection of the elevator walls. He smiled at Tia as she caught his eye.

"It's something you get used to, eventually." He hesitated a moment. "Some of our clients find the motion very strange, but it is essential to have such a deep vault for the security of what we keep here."

Tia nodded, but was relieved when a second later the doors slid open and they stepped out into a room about thirty feet square. Randolf immediately issued instructions to a guard that manned the desk. He sprung to action to fulfil the request.

"I will enter my security clearance code in the keypad on the left of the doors and you will need to enter your passcode in the keypad on the right of the doors, Miss Sharmez. The display you will see above the keypad is positioned so that only the keypad operator can see the code. Simply press 'enter' when you have checked that it is correct. The matching codes will release the door and allow only your box to be taken from the safe room behind." Again he smiled, terminating his instructions.

The access door to the vault that stood between them shouted, 'high security', in its construction. It was clearly designed to give comfort to the wealthy clients, guarding their privacy and valuables.

He went to his position on the left and Tia mirrored his actions as she went to the position on the right, several feet away. Randolf quickly tapped the keys then stood back from the terminal and waited for Tia.

She struggled to calm herself as she began to punch the buttons. The slight tremor in her hand betrayed her nervousness as she entered each digit, 5,D,2,I,7,E,6,Z,7. The speed of her entry was influenced by concern that she got it right first time as she battled to keep at bay the thoughts of what would happen if it didn't work.

She flinched when the door clunked and began to move as she hit the enter button. All the other doors they had come through had swiftly opened at the presence of someone wanting to enter, but this door moved slowly and meticulously, making those wishing to pass through wait for a little while.

When the security door finally stopped moving, Randolf swept inside and drew out a beautifully made box from lines of similar ones, all clearly numbered.

"Please follow me, Miss Sharmez."

He led the way into a side room where the lighting was bright and the burgundy decor rich. In the centre, standing on the plush carpet, was a leather-topped table and two matching chairs.

Placing the box carefully onto the desk, he stepped back from it and drew out a chair, waiting until Tia had taken up his invitation to sit. He slid the chair back so that she was seated comfortably, as if he were a waiter in a restaurant.

"Should you need any further assistance, or when you are finished, simply press the button on the edge of the desk here." He indicated the place.

"Thank you, Mr Randolf."

Randolf nodded slightly to acknowledge her thanks then turned and left the room.

Tia looked around the small but exquisitely presented space. Although it was dressed to make people who were wealthy feel comfortable, she felt very out of place. She had known a level of luxury in her life, but these surroundings intimidated her and the fact she felt like an imposter nagged constantly.

She glanced at the clock, 12:06pm.

Tia turned the box squarely in front of her on the table, moving it minutely a couple of times, like someone straightening a picture on a wall. She glanced around the room again, as though conscious that someone could be watching her. It was an eerie feeling that made her shiver slightly.

Undoing the latches, she lifted the lid and placed it to one side. Inside was a hinged cover with an ornate gold handle. She grasped hold of it, took a deep breath, and cautiously lifted it.

"My god!"

The clang of the lid being dropped shut made her jump as she snatched her hand away. It seemed to echo, and she glanced around the room again feeling conspicuous, but there was no one to see or hear. Her hand shook as she went to lift the lid again. As it opened it revealed more money than she'd ever seen in her whole life. The container was packed with wads of US one-thousand-dollar bills which were perfectly bound and in pristine condition, along with several other bundles of mixed bills.

On top of the stack was an envelope, with a hand written note across the front. She immediately recognised the writing of her father and drew breath at the sight. Again it was in pristine condition, as though it had been retrieved from some ancient tomb, untouched by decay or human interference. The scrolling letters gave the instruction, '*Open now*'!

Tentatively she took the letter, tore open the envelope and removed two handwritten pages.

Darling Sarita,

The intimacy of the personal salutation and the fact that her real name was used took her by surprise, but then she wondered why it should. Her father had always loved her name and had taken great delight in telling her that it meant 'Princess'.

First of all, I want to say that you have always been the most important person to me, the love of my life, but the circumstance that brought you to me was not one that I would ever have wished. What I must tell you is very difficult for me to write, but I may never have another chance to do so. Please forgive me that it has been left to a letter to break this news to you, but our lives were turned upside down and what happened was necessary in order to secure your safety.

The opening paragraph struck Tia as being very odd. She hadn't seen her father for such a long time and yet it seemed strange to find him writing as if he'd been apart from her only for a matter of weeks. She re-read the line about having to break some difficult news and wondered why he would write that it might be his only chance to tell her. Her thoughts were so distracted; what news? When did he write this? What about the money? Did this mean he was alive or had the letter been here for a long time?

Tia shook her head as if trying to dispel the thoughts that swamped her mind and focused on the letter.

I never thought there would be a time when I would have to tell you the truth, but I know that I was deceiving myself. I guess it was an attempt to pretend that you were more closely connected to me than you actually are. You are not my natural daughter, but more accurately my adopted daughter.

The words hit Tia like a sniper's bullet out of the blue. The letter was unexpected, but that line delivered total shock, arresting her reading for a few moments as her mind tried to comprehend how this could be true. There had been times when she was growing up when she'd asked about her mother, but her father had told her very little except that she'd died. It didn't take long for her to understand that the questions were not welcome because they caused her father pain. She stopped asking when she was old enough to see the tortured look that crossed his face when confronted with another attempt to find out.

Again Tia pushed away the thoughts to return to the letter.

To me there is no difference, but it is important that I finally tell you about how you came to me. It will answer a question that you have asked many times as a child and I avoided for so long; the reason you never knew your mother.

I was involved in a joint secret security operation for the Mexican and US governments that went very badly wrong. The consequence of which, and I take my responsibility for what happened, was that your real father, mother and four siblings, were killed, leaving you as an orphan.

Tia gasped at the words, but now her eyes were glued to the page as she hastily read on.

It pains me to have to tell you of this, in truth, I had hoped that it would never be necessary, but it is right that I do so now. From the very moment that I held you in my arms, in the middle of the tragic loss of your family, as I attempted to comfort a distraught, bewildered child, I knew that our destinies had been intertwined. I fought long and hard against the authorities who wanted to put you in an institution, their 'normal' solution for orphans, so that I could give you the security that I was instrumental in removing. I can only ask that you forgive me for my part in what happened and for withholding the truth from you for so long.

Circumstances seemed to conspire against my being able to offer you more than protection from the outside forces that would so readily have harmed you. I was unaware of just how isolated you felt in the villa in Mexico during my absence. The difficulties you lived under only came to my attention when I heard from Midissa about how much you struggled with the restrictions. I swear that what I did was to protect you, but my skills as a father were coloured by the dangerous world that has been the arena of my occupation for so many years.

When the break-in happened I realised that you were at increased risk because of me and that it was important that your identity was hidden. I arranged, in conjunction with Midissa, to organise a new life for you that would set you free from the ties that held you, due to your carrying my name, Liatzo. My good, and much missed friend, Nazim Akkbar, using the name Caleb Sallam, organised all the documentation and transportation to the United States, issuing you and your guardian with new identities. I tell you this so that you can measure the sincerity and truth of this letter.

The plan was good and would have relieved you of much of the risk by giving you anonymity from the world that is mine and those that would harm you to get to me. The pain that accompanied my decision to 'free' you was only eased by the knowledge that you would be safer without me. I am unsure what will be the future now, but it must play out to the end of the circumstances that you find yourself in whatever that may be.

Tia broke off from reading as the tears in her eyes overwhelmed her, obscuring the writing on the page, as she involuntarily sobbed at the pain that the words carried. Breathing deeply a few times to assuage the emotion, she tried to steady herself to continue, but had to take a few minutes before it was possible.

I only ever wanted the best for you, my darling child, and would have gladly done anything to make sure you were safe and happy.

Finally, my angel, whatever happens this day, and in the future, I wish you well and only ask that you live an honourable life. The money contained in the box is compensation that I made the US government pay for the accidental killing of your family, though it is little comfort for your loss. Every dollar that was given has been set aside for the day you would need it. If you are reading this note, that day has arrived. I hope that it will give you the chance to start again.

It is my dearest wish to see you just once more and, to that end, I put my life at risk and reveal to you that I will be at 1220 Delaware Road New York until the evening of 8 July 2001. If you decide to come you must do so alone and be very careful that nobody knows where you are going or why. THIS IS VERY IMPORTANT!

My love forever
Carlos Liatzo

Tia glanced at the clock on the wall opposite displaying time and date. 12:25pm – 7 July 2001. She felt the shock of reading his whereabouts and her hands spontaneously came up to her cheeks as the paper fell to the desk. It was the first concrete confirmation she had seen that he was alive since she'd left Mexico. She battled the turmoil that raged inside as she swung between fear, elation and trepidation about what this all meant. As tears pooled in her eyes, questions about the letter flooded her mind. When was it written? How did it get here? Had her father been here recently? What had stopped him finding a way to get this information to her before now? A horrible sense of foreboding suddenly seized Tia and her hand went to her throat as though she were guarding against invisible claws that tried to close in and choke her. Her eyes dropped to the letter laid on the desk in front of her and she swept her hand over her face trying to clear her vision to read the final line.

PS. You looked beautiful on the magazine cover.

Tia quickly stood up knocking the chair to the side and backed away to the wall of the room, as her sobs got ever more violent. She knew she had to restrain them at all costs, but each convulsion knotted her insides and felt like someone punching her in the stomach. She embraced herself in an effort to find comfort in her lonely underground cell.

It took Tia another ten minutes before she had calmed herself sufficiently to remove some money from the box, memorised the address, and replace the letter. A couple of deep breaths, a moment to prepare herself, and she pressed the button that summoned Mr Randolf.

He was as efficient as ever, carrying the box back to its place and escorting Tia to where they could watch the vault close. She felt conscious that she was wearing her sunglasses to cover her reddened eyes, but Randolf gave no indication that there was anything unusual. He focused meticulously on his job, which was to offer the client every courtesy.

The elevator ride back to the entrance lobby went unnoticed by Tia, who was still buried in the text of her father's letter. It turned on its head many things that she had thought about him over the last few years, primarily, her assumption that he must be dead. She ached inside in a way that she last remembered only months after the last time she'd seen him. It was an ache that begged to see a man whom she had loved, but she knew she couldn't let anyone know his whereabouts. If she was to see him, she had to do it the way he insisted, without the others.

Randolf escorted her to the glass entrance doors. Turning to Tia, he held out his hand which she shook, but before she let go she said, "Mr Randolf. I wonder if I could ask you something?"

"Certainly."

"Could you tell me if…" Tia hesitated, unsure if she should ask, but Mr Randolf was willing her to complete the question so that he might be of assistance. "Has anyone else been to check my security box recently?"

Randolf hesitated for a moment as the unexpected question was delivered. He smiled, glanced at the security desk and leaned in a little closer to Tia. "Miss Sharmez." His voice was gentle and reassuring. "I'm sure that you will understand when I tell you that I cannot give any information about visits made by our clients." Tia thought she sensed a desire to tell her something in the intonation in his voice, but immediately dismissed it. He smiled again. "It wouldn't do our reputation any good if I were to tell you."

"Of course," Tia smiled at him. "I'm so sorry, Mr Randolf. Please forgive me."

He resumed his upright posture and business demeanour. "Do have a pleasant afternoon, Miss Sharmez."

"Thank you, Mr Randolf."

He instantly turned on his heel and headed back to the 'hideaway' where he'd been when Tia arrived.

She watched him march across the reception and disappear through the doorway they had just come from. Glancing down at the floor, she momentarily pondered the things she'd learned, then turned and took a couple of paces toward the front entrance. The glass doors slid effortlessly apart exposing her to the rumble of the outside world again. Joseph spotted her emerging from the building, so he started the car and jumped out to open the rear door for her.

The three friends were watching the entrance of the building intently from across the street, awaiting Tia's appearance. As she emerged, she looked like a film-star coming from her hotel to a waiting car.

"What's *he* doing?" Will's question carried a note of alarm.

Will leant forward in the rear seat to get a better view of a man who suddenly picked up speed, running along the sidewalk toward Tia and Joseph. Beth and Lester latched onto what had captured his attention.

Will threw open the door and shouted an urgent warning to Joseph, who had his back turned to the approaching man. Joseph's reaction was instant as he glanced back over his shoulder. Tia was bundled into the car and the door slammed closed. Once she was safe, he spun around and leapt forward to meet the assailant just as he was about to level a gun. Joseph grabbed hold of him and forced his arm away. The gunshot echoed from the walls of the enclosed space along the busy street and a second floor window in the building opposite disintegrated, raining pieces of glass down onto the sidewalk. People scattered in all directions as the two men grappled with each other.

Joseph threw a punch catching the side of the assailant's head and received a similar response that he tried to evade. Again he landed a blow and the two of them fell heavily to the ground. A second shot rang out as Joseph slammed the attacker's wrist on the floor, sending the weapon scuttling across the sidewalk. The security staff piled out of the adjacent building to assist Joseph, whom they'd seen driving one of their clients. This caused both men to disengage and jump to their feet. Joseph leapt into the waiting car and pulled away with the wheels squealing in protest, before the guards had chance to make sense of the situation. Their confusion gave a few seconds for the other man to make it to a car that screeched to a stop alongside to pick him up.

Lester was on the case like lightening, roaring out into the street to follow Joseph and Tia, while blocking the car of the attacker. He deliberately swung the huge four wheel-drive vehicle around the road to cut off any attempt to get past in pursuit. Rubber squealed in protest at the punishment, but Joseph was getting away as Lester commanded the road holding back the pursuer.

The sound of gunshots filled the air as the rear window of their car crashed into pieces, spraying the inside of the vehicle with shards of glass. Will dropped down onto the back seat to try to avoid being maimed as he prepared his gun for action. Lester was watching the mirrors and blocking all attempts to pass. He was determined to give Joseph and Tia the best possible chance to get away, but a door opened unexpectedly on a parked car only yards in front of them. The violent swerve to avoid the obstruction pitched the car almost on two wheels and in attempt to compensate the front end came around and caught the corner of another vehicle, spinning the car through one-hundred-and-eighty degrees.

There was a thunderous thud as it slammed broadside into another parked car. The following vehicle that had been haranguing them to get past, snatched the opportunity and managed to avoid the drama, slipping through a gap alongside.

Will was out of the door before their car had hardly finished moving. He brought the gun up and reacted instantly. The sound of two shots echoed from the buildings as it took out the rear window of the disappearing vehicle which lurched left then right trying to avoid being hit.

Will stood for a split-second taking aim then thought better of letting more bullets fly in such a public place. He lowered the gun and watched the car vanish from view around a distant corner in pursuit of their escaping friends. As he stood looking at the empty road, he heard Lester shout.

"Shit!" Lester began to curse himself for allowing them to be thrown and turned the key to try to restart the engine, but steam was rising from the hood. "Damn it." He slammed his hands on the steering wheel then noticed Beth's distressed breathing, her chest rising and falling rapidly.

"WILL, HELP ME!" Lester yelled.

He ripped Beth's jacket and shirt open exposing a blood soaked T-shirt beneath. Her face was filled with a grimace of pain as she screwed her eyes closed every few seconds.

"Beth you stay with me!" Lester shouted. "Stay with me!" He leapt over her, pulling the door latch and kicking it open. "CALL 911!" he yelled out to anyone who would listen. "CALL 911!"

He quickly lifted Beth from the car as carefully as he could and with Will's help, laid her on the sidewalk.

Lester was leaning over Beth pressing his hand against her chest where the wound was oozing blood. "Stay with me girl. YOU HEAR ME? DON'T YOU LEAVE ME!"

A guy came tearing across the street, having seen what was happening, and barged Lester out of the way without apology or hesitation. His actions were those of someone who knew exactly what he was doing.

Lester followed the instructions yelled out by the 'medic' as he threw his jacket under Beth's head to cushion her. Lester glanced at Will and their eyes locked as they shared concern for Beth.

Lester looked at Beth then back at Will as he assessed the situation. "Get out of here, Will. Grab my bag and go. GO! GO!" Lester motioned with his hand, imploring Will to leave before it was too late.

The sound of distant sirens reached their ears and rapidly increased in volume as they closed in on their location. Will hesitated, looking with concern at Beth, but Lester lashed out at him, desperate to send his friend on his way before it was too late. When he looked back, Beth caught his eye.

"Both of you." She put as much effort into her whispered instruction as she could. "Tia, help Tia. Both of you."

The two guys looked at their fallen friend and were in a dilemma about the right thing to do, but she raised her voice even more. In her condition the effort was monumental.

"NOW! FOR GOD'S SAKE, BOTH OF YOU GO!"

Lester grabbed the bag from the vehicle and in the confusion the two of them slipped away through the milling crowd. They ran into a side street that led away from the busy area leaving behind their friend and the shouts of people trying to stop them leaving before the authorities arrived.

No sooner had they turned the corner than a police car screeched to a halt at the scene they'd just left. The proximity of the blaring sirens gave urgency to their steps as they ran at full speed.

As they put some distance between themselves and the mayhem, Lester looked at his hand that carried the blood of his friend and a surge of rage leapt into his efforts. Both Will and he were bound together as they never had been before, in concern for their mutual friend.

Bursting out into another busy area, they ran past the open entrance of a seedy club. Stopping, Lester shouted Will back. They ran inside, barging past all attempts to slow them down and went into the rest room where Lester washed his hands as he barked instruction to Will.

"GET THE LAPTOP OUT."

Will didn't question why, he just did what he was told.

Lester dried his hands and took command of the computer. He began tapping frantically at the keyboard. Will could stand it no longer.

"What the hell are you doing, Lester?"

"She's tagged."

"She's what?"

"Tia. She's tagged. I put a tracking device in her shoe last night."

"You did what?"

Lester ignored the distraction of answering and seconds later, he had the location of Tia on the screen.

"They're nearly back at the hotel," he shouted. "It looks like Joseph's taking her back to the hotel." He slammed the lid closed and they were off again.

CHAPTER 22

Joseph swung the car into the hotel car park and went down to the lower level, pulling into a space next to one of the support pillars to restrict any prying eyes. Snatching the keys from the ignition, he jumped out and opened the door for Tia. She was shaken by the frantic race back and the stress of the preceding hours.

Joseph crouched down so that he was almost eye to eye with her.

"You okay, Tia?" She nodded, but her eyes told a different story. "We're going to get out and go to the room. If I know anything about the others, they'll guess that we've come back here and follow on shortly. Lester did a good job of giving us some space to get away. He won't come here until he knows that he's shaken them off."

"Shaken who off? What's happening? Every time we try to resolve this mess it just gets worse. More and more people get involved. I don't understand what's happening here."

Joseph held his hand up to encourage Tia to cool down. "First, let's get back to the room then we can talk about what's happening."

Joseph took her hand, urging her to get out of the car. When she eventually did, she stood upright and straightened her dress, using the hesitation to try to calm her nerves. Joseph slipped his arm behind her and guided her in the direction of the reception.

"There'll be people around, so be ready," Joseph warned her. She smiled weakly at him.

As they walked up through the reception, Joseph tried to shield her from view as they passed by the desk. The guy sitting there was about to say something, but he read Joseph's body language and thought better of it. When they reached the room, Joseph unlocked the door and let Tia go in first, then quickly followed, closing it behind him.

"Is there any way we can check on the others?" Tia asked hopefully.

"No. We're just going to have to wait. I'm guessing they'll be here soon. What was in the box, Tia?"

She was taken by surprise at the speed with which the question came, instantly after answering her concern about the absence of her friends. Tia felt a little flustered by it.

"Nothing." She tried to feign her own disappointment in the intonation of her answer.

"What d'you mean?"

Joseph looked a little shocked at her response, but Tia was glad that she'd kept her wits enough to answer so spontaneously.

"It was empty. There was nothing in it," she added. "I tried to ask Mr Randolf, the man who took me to the vault, if there was anyone else who had access to the box, but he told me he couldn't say anything about other clients."

Joseph stood looking at her for a few seconds and she felt the spotlight of his gaze as if it was penetrating her defences, trying to determine her honesty. He turned away and went to the mini bar to get a drink, but Tia caught the look of suppressed anger on his face. The light that came from the drinks cooler threw a sinister blue hue over his features and she wondered what was going through his mind. He was clearly annoyed that the trip seemed to have borne no fruit, though just what he was expecting was a mystery to her. She wondered if he had a hunch about the money she'd seen.

"Want one?"

Tia shook her head, but felt she needed to try to convince him further that she was telling the truth.

"What do you think all this has been about, the earrings and the clues? What was the point if the box was going to be empty?"

She tinged the last question with frustration to make it seem like she'd had enough of the pointless exercise and was posing the question as much to herself as to him.

Joseph popped the top from the beer bottle in his hand and took a drink, but kept his eyes fastened on Tia. She held his stare, hoping that he couldn't read what she was thinking.

Before she was aware of what she was doing she blurted out, "Did my father really send you that picture of me?"

The slight quake in her voice betrayed a little of the emotion that had overcome her in the vault. Joseph continued to stare and she thought he was just going to avoid answering the question, but she refused to give way to the intimidation of his gaze and the thought of Beth's boldness in different circumstances encouraged her.

"Yeah. He sent it to me alright."

Joseph sat down and leaned back in the chair.

"You were friends then?"

"Once... Once we were friends." He paused. "But friends don't betray each other. Do they?"

Joseph reached for the remote and flicked on the TV, using the noise to put an end to any more questions. Tia got the message loud and clear.

~

Lester and Will reached the hotel entrance about twenty minutes after they'd left Beth. The pain of not knowing how she was doing gnawed away at both of them.

"I feel like we abandoned her," Will blurted out, slowing the pace as they arrived at the entrance doors.

Lester took hold of the door handle, but hesitated before pulling it open. He looked at Will and his eyes showed that he was having the very same difficulty.

They went through the reception and the man behind the counter made comment about their friends having just returned, but they were in no mood to engage. They reached the door to the room that Tia and Beth had shared and Will hammered on it.

Suddenly the next door along opened and Tia ran out to greet them. She looked past the two of them. "Where's Beth?" Her question carried a note of alarm.

Will walked straight past her into the room and went to the mini bar, pulled out a bottle, popped the lid and turned to focus on Joseph as he took a drink. Lester put his hand on Tia's shoulder and guided her back into the room, following behind Will.

"She's taken a bullet," Will snapped, spitting the words in Joseph's direction.

Joseph stood and looked at each of them in turn.

Will exploded and threw the bottle in his hand at the wall opposite where it smashed spraying the remaining liquid all over the place. "BASTARD!" he yelled at the top of his voice.

Lester felt Tia physically edge toward him and away from the anger that was pouring from Will's every movement.

"What the hell happened out there today, Joseph?" Will's eyes were blazing as he took a couple of steps towards him. The risk of losing another person that meant so much to him was stirring deep emotions and the injustice of Beth's condition was now focused on the man that led them to New York.

Judging the threat and the violent mood that was simmering in Will, Joseph tried to defuse the situation by slowly easing himself back into the chair. The disarming move took a little heat out of the situation and Will asked the question again, but in a more restrained manner.

"I said, what happened out there today? Who were the guys in that car?"

Joseph held his hands up to indicate he had no idea and shrugged to emphasise the fact. "I don't know, Will." He waited until Will's demeanour calmed a little more. "Where's Beth?" he asked calmly.

Lester saw that Will had no intention of answering the question, so he did.

"She made us go." He rubbed Tia's shoulder. "She told us to 'help Tia'." Lester made eye contact with her and saw the look of pain in her eyes. "There was a man, a doctor or something, helping her. He was trying to stop the bleeding... and she was thinking of you."

The TV was playing in the background, but no one was taking any notice of it until the newscaster started to report an incident in the city in which a number of vehicles had been damaged. Will grabbed the remote and turned up the volume. There were suggestions that bystanders had heard shots being fired. The focus of interest seemed to be that it had taken place near Londen Security International. The speculation was that there might be a connection, but no detailed information was available at that moment.

Will flicked through the channels trying to find other coverage of the incident and stopped when he saw pictures of Londen and the street outside.

We are getting fresh reports about the incident that took place outside of Londen Security International early this afternoon. Londen is the high security safety deposit vault here in New York. Apparently the incident was more serious than originally thought. We have just received a brief statement from an official at the location stating that shots were fired, leading to a vehicle crashing into other parked cars. Early indications are that there were three people in the vehicle, but two of them ran from the scene, leaving a third seriously injured. There's a certain amount of confusion, but we understand that the injured person is a woman. We understand that she has been given emergency medical attention at the scene and is now being moved to hospital. We will, of course, bring you any further information as we get it.

Tia felt her eyes fill. She restrained herself from any movement that might show her feelings, but the tears that started to tumble down her cheeks betrayed what was going on inside. The faces of her three companions showed varying degrees of shock, now that the adrenalin of the drama had begun to wear off.

They'd all walked from that very building *with* Beth, just a little time before. Not one of them could have conceived what the following hours would bring.

Tia slumped down onto the floor and pulled her knees into her chest. She wrapped her arms around her knees and hugged them, trying to ease the horrible feeling in the pit of her stomach. She'd never felt hate like she was feeling as she sat on the floor of that room. The object of the intense loathing was vague, circumstances beyond her control, people she'd never met, situations that had nothing to do with her injured friend.

Tia sat staring at the wall opposite for several minutes, unable to put into words what she was feeling. The others were lost in their own worlds, watching the TV, but displaying serious concern on their faces. "The shoes," Tia whispered.

Lester looked down at her.

"Tia?"

She didn't appear to take any notice of him, so he crouched down beside her. Will looked across at them, realising something was wrong.

"What is it Tia?" Lester nudged her.

"The shoes. They were the same shoes," she repeated.

"What do you mean?" Will prompted. "You're not making any sense."

Joseph moved forward to the edge of his seat.

"The man at Londen, the one who attacked Joseph," she was still trying to recall clearly. "He had the same shoes as the man who was in charge of the people who snatched me. I saw his shoes when I was hiding under the racking."

Lester's face showed that she was not explaining herself clearly, so she tried again.

"When I got away from the people who abducted me and they chased after me down the alley, I slid under some racking to hide. Someone was yelling as they tried to find out where I'd gone. They were the same shoes. He was wearing the same shoes as the man on the street today. They must have followed us here, to try to get me. Why? What have I done that these people would put so much effort into chasing me across the country?"

Tia seemed like she was obsessed as she repeated herself trying to make the others see the significance. "You think it was the same man?" Will quizzed, but his question was usurped.

Their attention suddenly switched back to the TV as an update informed them that the injured woman was being treated for serious, but non-life-threatening injuries. There was a palpable sigh of relief at the news, but the reporters still speculated about what had actually happened.

After several minutes of watching the news briefings, Tia raised herself to her feet and swept her hands over her reddened cheeks to remove the traces of tears that were staining her face.

"I need some air," she said, moving to the door and taking hold of the handle.

"You want me to come?" Will offered.

She shook her head. Pausing, she smiled at him, but it was somehow different, holding Will's attention. She turned away from him, hesitated for a second, then left the room, pulling the door closed behind her. Will continued to stare at the closed door for a few moments before turning his attention back to the coverage on TV.

Once Tia was in the corridor she picked up her pace and ran as fast as she could in her heels and dress, until she was outside the hotel. There was a certain amount of panic in her actions, because she was conscious that this was probably her only opportunity to separate herself from the company of her travelling companions. Torn between her loyalties to those who had helped her so much and what her heart compelled her to do, she cast her doubts aside and was determined to see the man who had gone missing from her life years before. Perhaps he was the only one who could answer her nagging questions about the circumstances that had swallowed her life.

Standing at the side of the road, she was concerned that it would only take a small delay in getting away for her escape to be discovered. That would force some explanation that she was not willing to give and leave her unable to try the same routine again. It was almost like history repeating itself. She'd manufactured her escape and was running in an attempt to get as far as possible before another pursuit got underway.

A taxi came into view and she practically stood in the road to flag it down. He pulled alongside her and she jumped in.

"Jeez lady, there's no way I was gonna get past you!"

"Just drive."

The cab driver shrugged and set off in the direction he was already heading.

"You wanna go somewhere special, or just for a ride, lady?"

"1220 Delaware Road."

The cab started to slow down.

"What are you doing?" Tia shouted in alarm, seeing vital seconds lost.

"Do you want to go to *that* address or *not*, 'cos it's in the other direction."

The cab driver's irritation was clear and she caught the perplexed look on his face in the rear-view mirror.

"Yes. I want to go to that address, but not back past the front of the hotel. I don't care how much it costs. Find another route, but please be as quick as possible."

"Okay," he shrugged and the cab began to accelerate again.

As the cab manoeuvred through the traffic and the road junctions, Tia became conscious that the driver was frequently glancing at her in the mirror. She slid as far to the door as possible to try to get out of the line of sight, but he clearly had an interest in something. Finally, he asked, "Do I know you, Miss? You look familiar."

Tia made brief eye contact with him, but didn't answer. He was not about to give up that easily.

"You famous or somethin'?"

"Not really. Are we far from the address?" She tried to deflect his attention.

~

Will got up from his seat and headed out into the corridor to escape the continuous drone of the news reports. The repetitive TV coverage was delivering no new information, so he decided to go and check on Tia to see that she was okay. Lester and Joseph momentarily glanced at him as he went out, but said nothing.

As Will stepped into the long hallway, he casually glanced in each direction, but there was no sign of Tia, so he walked toward the reception area to see if she was there. It was empty. He began looking through the windows out onto the covered entrance area, thinking she might have gone outside for some fresh air, but could see no sign of her.

"Don't know what you did, but you must have scared her real good." The comment terminated with a loud, intrusive laugh that echoed a little. The guy who'd been on the reception desk when they came back was just returning to his post.

Will spun around to face him. "Excuse me?"

"The pretty lady." He stared at Will as if he should know what he was talking about, but when he registered that Will didn't understand, he elaborated. "The pretty lady who was with you when you checked in. She came running through here in a hurry a few minutes ago. Guess you upset her." He leered suggestively adding inference to his comments.

"Where did she go?" Will demanded. The sudden sharp change in tone surprised the guy at the desk.

"Took a cab, 'bout two minutes ago," he spluttered in response.

"Which direction?" Will shouted, as he headed back to the room.

The guy pointed to indicate, but was a little bewildered by the situation.

Will ran along the corridor and burst into the room making Joseph and Lester jump. The nerves from the event earlier were still tense.

"She's gone. She's taken a cab at the front of the hotel."

Will was already scrambling through Lester's bag to retrieve the laptop. He almost threw it at Lester.

"She's what?" Joseph yelled, as he jumped to his feet in alarm. "Where have you looked?"

Will took no notice of Joseph as he flipped open the computer.

"What are you doing?" Joseph demanded. "We need to find her. Right now!"

"Lester's going to find her," Will shouted.

Joseph looked at the pair of them, his expression showing surprise, then the penny dropped.

"You bugged her?"

Neither Will nor Lester responded to Joseph's question, they were too wrapped up in the need of the moment.

Joseph was suddenly on the case with them. "We'll take the hire car. It's down in the car park."

They all piled out of the room and ran along the corridor to the reception. The man at the desk was alarmed at the group descending on him, but they passed straight through and down the access stair to the first level of the car park.

Moments later the concrete structure echoed with the sound of a roaring engine and squealing rubber as Joseph smoothly manoeuvred the car out at high speed.

"Which way, Lester? Which way?" Will yelled to his friend in the back seat.

"She appears to be going around and back again." The car screeched to a halt at the junction to the main road.

"MAKE A DECISION!" yelled Joseph.

"Right. Turn right."

No sooner was the word out of Lester's mouth than the car hurtled forward to be greeted by a long, irritated blast on several car horns as the drivers swerved to avoid the surprise entry onto the street. Joseph didn't even flinch; he dominated the tarmac with confidence, intimidating the slower moving traffic out of his way. Lester began giving directions as they sped along at a breakneck pace, homing in on their fleeing companion.

CHAPTER 23

The cab pulled up outside a smart house in an area that didn't look like it was part of a city. It was framed by mature trees running the length of the road. Tia passed the driver a fifty dollar bill and told him to keep it.

"Damn. I do know you. You're the magazine..."

The door slammed as Tia left the vehicle, cutting off the cab driver's comment. He figured out where he'd seen her before, but it was of little importance to Tia. She hadn't even heard what he was saying. Her attention focused wholly on the building in front of her.

Her heart was pounding as she stood for a few moments just looking, wondering what the anticipated meeting was going to be like; whether she had even understood the information in the letter correctly. Although she'd been in the vault only a short time before, the whole thing seemed like something she'd watched on TV rather than something she'd actually done.

She tentatively walked along the path to the front door, took a deep breath and braced herself before ringing the bell. There was movement inside the hallway and her heart skipped a beat as the butterflies in her stomach made her feel queasy.

The spy hole in the door was obviously being used to determine who was outside. With a rattle of chains and locks, the door opened a little. Tia felt awkward, not knowing whether she should hold back until someone showed their face or just go in.

She hesitated, but tried to see through the little gap while she waited for something to happen.

Finally the door swung fully open, surprising her, and an elderly Chinese lady stood there with a coat draped over her arm. She stepped outside and made a gesture for Tia to go in. Tia didn't move, not understanding what was required. The lady used her broken English to try to clarify what she meant. "Please. You go in." Then she turned and walked away down the path to the road. Tia stood outside the open door watching her go. When the lady reached the sidewalk, she looked back and again waved her hand to encourage Tia to enter the house.

After waiting a few seconds to watch the old lady disappear on her way, Tia turned her attention to the exposed hallway. On the left side was a door, standing ajar, which opened into a dining area and straight ahead appeared to be the kitchen, at the back of the house. Still unsure if she should go in, she tried to attract the attention of someone.

"Hello?" She waited a few seconds, but there was no response. "Hello?" She tried again.

Stepping across the threshold, she was able to see the full extent of the spacious, unoccupied entrance hall and open stairway that was bathed in light from a central atrium. She cautiously went to the door which opened into the dining room, feeling like she was intruding into someone's private space, then pushed it gently so that it opened fully. The dressed table looked like something from a catalogue. To the right, as she went in, there was a sliding double door that stood open enough for someone to walk through. She went around the table and glanced through the gap into the large living room that had windows at the far end overlooking a private garden.

Stepping through, she was confronted with a figure standing to the side of the room by the fireplace as if waiting to receive a visitor. The light from the window behind him concealed his identity, but only for a fraction of a second. As he walked to the centre of the room, she was rooted to the spot, standing in the gap between the sliding doors, while she watched him. It was the first time she'd seen Carlos Liatzo in years. In that time she had grown from being a dependent teenager to an independent young woman. He had aged, his black curly hair showing signs of grey. His eyes were ringed from lack of sleep. His expression showed joy at seeing her, but that couldn't totally mask the weariness that had drawn lines in his face.

"Sarita." His voice was soft and weak as though the strength had been sapped from his body. The forcefulness that she remembered was gone. "I wanted you to come, but I never dared allow myself to hope that you actually would be able to."

"Papa?" She knew who he was, but after so many years and the letter she'd read, she didn't know what to do. She just stared at the face that had been missing from her life for so long, taking in the alterations brought about by time and who knew what else. They stood staring at one another across the empty room, each taking in the changed appearance of the other, neither knowing what to do next.

In a split second, Carlos's face hardened and his eyes seemed to turn black with anger. He quickly reached inside his jacket to pull out a gun. To Tia, everything appeared to be moving in slow motion.

She screamed out as she suddenly felt an arm reach over her shoulders and grab her from behind. Joseph held Tia to himself and turned her away from the threat of Liatzo's gun, placing himself like a shield between father and daughter.

As Liatzo's gun came up, until it was almost pointing directly at Tia and Joseph, Will burst through the side door from the kitchen and shouted a warning to drop the weapon. If Liatzo challenged, Will couldn't possibly miss. He froze, considering the situation then seemed to shrink in stature, as if giving up a long-standing fight, resigning himself to the fact that he was outnumbered and out gunned.

"Drop the gun," Will shouted again. "Drop it now!"

Keeping his hands visible, Liatzo hesitated before allowing the gun to drop to the floor. There was a thud as the weapon hit the deck.

Will momentarily glanced at Tia who was now standing in front of Joseph, his arm still around her, facing Carlos Liatzo. An expression of alarm on her face made Will glance again.

Joseph's gun was solidly trained on Liatzo, and with Will covering from the side, there was nowhere for him to go. Tia's questioning eyes were fastened on her father, begging for some explanation.

Joseph held on to Tia as she struggled to make sense of the situation. The confusion was overpowering. Why had he gone missing? Why hadn't he contacted her over all that time? What about the letter in the vault? Had he been tracking her movements? How could her father pull a gun to threaten her? The questions bombarded her mind. She brought her hands up to hold onto Joseph's forearm, feeling safe in his embrace.

Will had instinctively gone down on one knee as he threw himself into the room to help Joseph cover all bases. He stood to his feet as he waited for Joseph's cue, eyes fixed on Liatzo, his gun demanding submission.

Tia felt Joseph make a sudden movement. There was a deafening crack right next to her, a gunshot so close it made her jump with fright as she felt the recoil shake her. Will was thrown back through the doorway he'd come through moments earlier. There were loud crashing sounds as he was propelled back into the kitchen by the force of the bullet. Tia screamed in terror as she registered what had happened to Will, but was instantly silenced by the muzzle of Joseph's gun pressed heavily against the side of her head. Liatzo's face showed the horror that Tia felt inside from what Joseph had just done. Tia wanted to scream out; to run to Will's aid; to break away from Joseph's hold, but she could not. The metal tip of the gun felt warm as it painfully pushed against her temple. The smell of cordite was overpowering.

Joseph, holding Tia tightly in his grasp, edged her forward a few steps into the room so they were standing square with Liatzo. Tia saw the anxiety on her father's face as anger flooded his expression at Joseph's ruthless action.

The pressure of Joseph's arm clamped around Tia made it feel like she was being squeezed in a vice. She could hear his heavy breathing close to her face.

"Pretty little thing, your daughter." The sinister voice that had plagued Will and Lester when they broke into Joseph's house was now the curse of father and daughter. "Nice to see you again, *Carlos*. It's been a long, long time. *Too* long. You're a hard man to track down."

Carlos could see the panic in his daughter's eyes, but knew that it only mirrored the look in his own as they stared at one another. Each of them were trapped in the position they occupied, subject to the will of one man, Joseph Charles, a man who'd violently demonstrated his intent.

"You don't need to harm her, Joseph. She's done nothing to…"

Joseph's hand jumped to Tia's throat. She began choking and grabbed at his arm as he applied pressure to prompt a reaction. Carlos flinched as if he was about to try to help Tia, but froze as the gun pressed harder, making her tilt her head further.

"Why don't I need to harm her? You didn't care shit about me, you back-stabbing turncoat. Why should I give a shit about you, Liatzo, or your little Mexican bitch?"

The venom in his eyes sent a shiver down Liatzo's back.

Joseph deliberately nudged the gun again into Tia's temple, making her strain to tilt her head away from it. She gasped out a cry of pain.

Carlos took a step forward out of desperation, but the gun immediately came to bare on him. "You stay exactly where you are, *my friend*." Joseph released the pressure from Tia's throat and waited a second to allow the gagging noises as she drew breath to be clearly heard by her helpless father. Tears streamed down Tia's cheeks as she tried to control the sheer terror that gripped her.

"That was always your problem, Liatzo. You couldn't just follow orders, could you?"

"What we were doing back then was wrong, Joseph. Can you *still* not see that?"

"The only thing that was wrong was that *you* didn't do what was required. I was in charge of that operation and *you* took it into *your* hands to start a mutiny against me."

"We were in another country without clearance from our government, damn it. You were using the resources of our own government to steal money on foreign soil. Did you ever think I would just let that happen without challenging it? The damage you caused has lasted for years."

"Damage *I* caused? You sanctimonious bastard, you three left me for dead. You were supposed to be right behind me in support. You were supposed to be part of *my* elite team. I issued you with orders to follow AND YOU SHOULD HAVE FOLLOWED THEM." The fury burned in Charles's eyes and his face flushed with rage as he waved the gun at Liatzo every time he emphasised his words.

"I should have followed orders? While you massacred innocent people for personal gain? You knew the operation didn't have the sanction of our authorities, but…"

"But *you* screwed it up!" Joseph's expression showed his malicious intent. Tia could feel him shaking as his temper boiled over at the object of his wrath.

"For god's sake, Joseph, what did you expect?"

"YOUR SUPPORT," he snapped.

"To commit a crime?" Liatzo was deliberately trying to hold a measured tone in order to calm the 'ticking time bomb' that held his daughter in submission.

Joseph's eyes were bulging at the impudence of the man before him daring to answer back. It appeared his anger was about to explode when he realised that he was losing control. Tia felt his grip relax a little. The three of them stood in silence.

"I've worked for the government in all kinds of shit-holes around the world." The cold sinister voice returned as Joseph began to justify his actions. "I thought it was about time some of them showed their gratitude for what we've done. God knows we were never going to get anything from our own country. People like you and me are unseen when things go right and unwanted when they don't. It was payback time…"

"At what cost, Joseph?"

"I don't give a damn about the cost… Liatzo." The inference in the way he ended his sentence suggested that all the explaining that was needed was at an end and now it was a time of reckoning. Tia felt a shiver run down her spine as she anticipated what was about to happen.

Joseph slowly turned his gun back to Tia, pressing the muzzle against her head again as he watched Liatzo suffer like the victim of a torturer. She gulped back a sob as her imagination ran a vivid image of what was about to take place. She felt a wave of despair and resignation wash over her as her life was about to be taken.

"NO! Wait." The tone of Carlos's voice and his demeanour seemed less confrontational and betrayed desperation as he could see Tia's eyes pooled and overflowing. She mouthed 'I love you' to her father as he stood helplessly before her. The grip of the man she had trusted held her tightly, his monstrous manipulation of any situation to achieve his evil end was exposed for father and daughter to see and they were at his mercy. But mercy was an emotion that would never reign while this man had control. "Joseph, *please*," Carlos begged. "It's me you want, not her. She's done nothing. It was me that turned against you. Let her go. You have me…"

Joseph sneered at Carlos's attempts to appease him, but that was not going to happen. Too many years had gone by while he tried to track down those who had been disloyal to him. Vengeance had become the driving force of his life. He lived to see the betrayers die and two already had. He was not about to trade the moment of revenge for any sort of reconciliation. It was judgement day and he was going to milk every last drop of 'enjoyment' from it.

"Tell me Tia," Joseph pressed his mouth near to her cheek as he continued, "did you know that he…" Joseph flicked the barrel of the gun momentarily in Carlos's direction to make sure there was no mistake who he was talking about. "He was responsible for the death of your *real* family? Mother; father; brother; three sisters, all shot dead. And Carlos Liatzo pulled the trigger. That's how he came to have a family... you. He killed six innocent people and took you for himself."

Tia squirmed in his grasp in an attempt to pull away from his touch as their cheeks brushed, but he forcefully yanked her closer to him pressing his cheek against her face. "But when it was my turn to get what *I* wanted, he screwed me without a second thought." Joseph smiled as Tia tried to restrain the sobs that welled up from deep within her.

Again her mind flashed to the friends who had helped her and how she had led them to this horrifying situation. They'd all been living their lives in their own way until she became the cause of so much pain. Will had been shot, maybe dead, alone in the adjacent room. She couldn't understand where Lester was while this torture continued, but she had a bad feeling about his absence, and Beth was lying in a hospital bed, badly injured.

"That's not how it was..." Carlos's challenge to Joseph's account made Tia focus on the moment as he tried to reason with their tormentor, but his protest was cut short. Joseph continued in a voice that seemed more appropriate to a story-teller addressing children.

"And now, it's time for daddy to pay for his disloyalty and all the *shit* that he put me through." Joseph pulled away from Tia's cheek and stood upright looking directly at Carlos. "First, with the life of this Mexican bitch you saved."

Tia let out a scream that could no longer be restrained, but Joseph's hand went to her throat again stifling it.

"You killed Steven and Nazim, didn't you?" Carlos shouted in desperation, trying to prevent what seemed inevitable.

The smirk on Joseph's face, as he looked at Carlos, showed the sick pleasure he got from what he'd done and now he had the opportunity to gloat for a few moments.

"I did," he stated emphatically, as if it were some proud achievement. "They had it coming and they didn't even make it a challenge." He bragged over the ease with which he had taken the lives of two men. Tia began to see that he had been at the root of all that had happened to her and her friends. The murdered men in Will's house had been the work of this monster; their reward for failing to get him the bait he needed to catch Carlos Liatzo. The man who attacked him in the street outside of Londen Security International was the leader of that group bent on revenge for the brutal loss of his men.

Joseph sneered. "They weren't quite as smart as you though, Liatzo. Although, I have to admit, that was a neat trick Holden did for you with the ear studs. Tia's friends helped me find that one." He hesitated a moment before continuing. "Come to think of it. That security box probably had this address in it. Didn't it?" He squeezed Tia's throat enough to make her choke again. She nodded as tears streamed down her cheeks. "What else was in there that you didn't tell me about?" He put his cheek next to hers again like they were lovers.

"Money." Liatzo quickly jumped in to answer the question.

Joseph made an exaggerated move to suggest what he was thinking. "Now, shall we figure out at a way to get hold of that money?"

"We can get it if you want to, Joseph," Carlos suggested, grasping at straws, hoping he could stall the situation.

Joseph looked at him for a few seconds and Carlos nodded to emphasise that it could be done.

The gun clicked as Joseph made a deliberate movement to show what he was about to do, enjoying the fact he was stretching out the agony. He held all the cards and he wanted Liatzo to feel helpless.

"I think I'd rather see you suffer, Liatzo… and it starts right here. It's time to say goodbye to your… daughter."

Carlos yelled out in anguish and leapt forward in desperation. The sound of the gunshot in the confined space was deafening. Everything seemed to move in slow motion. Liatzo was stunned by the gun blast and flinched, closing his eyes as he felt the warmth of a liquid hit his horrified face. He instinctively went to wipe over his eyes and as he pulled his hands away to refocus, expecting Joseph to shoot him, he was shocked by the amount of blood covering them.

The horror of what had just happened removed any concern for himself. He would have traded his life for Tia's in a second, but now he had no reason to care for his own. He felt the urge to kill Joseph Charles, even at the cost of his own life.

As Liatzo reached Joseph, he suddenly noticed his glazed eyes staring, wide and shocked.

Joseph's arm slumped to his side and he shuddered. The gun slipped from his grasp and landed with a loud thud. Tia screamed and clawed at her throat as Joseph grasped hold, trying to stop himself slumping backwards to the floor. She pulled at his fingers to release them and instantly threw herself down and away from him, glancing back to see what had happened. She saw Will laid on the floor just outside the sliding doors. He'd dragged himself from the kitchen through the hallway and dining room to get behind where Joseph was standing with Tia and fired a shot upwards seriously wounding Joseph.

Carlos grabbed the gun that Joseph had dropped. He launched himself past Tia to descend with force onto Joseph, whose shoulder and arm were in a mess from the bullet that had disabled him. Joseph's eyes looked like those of an animal caught in the headlights of a car. From being in total control, with people at his mercy, *he* was now the scared one.

"You sadistic bastard!" yelled Liatzo. "How many lives have you wasted to satisfy your bloodlust? Not anymore."

Carlos brought the gun up to Joseph's face.

Tia's reaction was spontaneous, instinctive, "NO PAPA!" she screamed. The little girl that she'd been, leapt out to restrain her father's reckless actions. She reached out and touched his shoulder as he continued to hold the gun at Joseph's head, willing his finger to pull the trigger in revenge. "You're not like him," she whispered. "There's nothing he can do to us now." She held her breath, urging him to make the right choice. Seconds ticked by as he held his position. The internal struggle with the dark thoughts of injustice over the loss of his friends, and almost his daughter, played out in the expressions of his face.

"You're not like him, Papa," Tia repeated, the tone of her voice was insistent and sure of her father's character.

He relaxed a little and she made firmer contact by squeezing his shoulder. The sound of sirens was in the air; the volume increasing rapidly.

Carlos leaned back to connect physically with his daughter who closed in behind him. He felt her embrace for the first time in years and, as he looked at Joseph, he knew that the contact between them held no risk of danger to her ever again.

Joseph coughed and winced at the pain. He struggled to get his breath and took a last gasp at insulting Liatzo. "I always knew you were weak."

Tia increased the pressure of her embrace as she held Carlos back, trying to prevent him from reacting, but he didn't respond to Joseph's provocation. He just looked at the dying man sprawled on the floor who was staring wide-eyed back at him.

"To think I could have turned out like you, Joseph Charles. May God have mercy on your soul."

There was desperation in Joseph's eyes as he saw the last attempt at manipulating Carlos slip from his grasp.

Will groaned from the pain he was in and Tia responded without delay. Stepping over Joseph who was laid incapacitated in the doorway, she went into the next room to try to help. There was a trail of blood along the dining room carpet leading out into the hallway where Will had dragged himself through the house to try to help Tia.

Tia knelt down beside him, trying to ease his discomfort, but felt overwhelmed by the situation. She wanted to say something, but before the words were formed they were whisked away by a loud command.

"POLICE! THROW DOWN YOUR WEAPONS!"

The booming order resonated through the building, but after what had just happened it seemed tame and startled no one. Carlos shouted to reassure the officers that they were safe to enter. The hesitant first few steps were soon replaced by a flood of personnel into the building.

The blur of the following minutes was filled with medical staff and police officers as the wounded were attended to and the shaken were quizzed about what had happened. The last look Tia had of Will was as he was being taken out on a stretcher to a waiting ambulance. They locked eyes for a moment then he was gone. Joseph was being attended to by medics, but their body language painted a grim picture of hopelessness.

As Carlos and Tia were being led out to a patrol car to be taken to the police headquarters, she had a thought. She stopped just as they reached the road where several people had come out on the street to see what was happening.

"Please move to the car, Miss." The police officer urged her forward with a little nudge in the right direction.

"What about Lester?"

"I'm sorry?" The officer prompted her to repeat what she'd said.

"Lester," she said, with some urgency. "He would have been with Will." Tia began scanning the road in each direction and noticed the hire car thirty yards away. It had obviously been left there to avoid being seen when they arrived. "There," she pointed. "That car, it was being used by Joseph Charles. The one with the trunk open." She turned to look at the officer. "There was another man, Lester Donaldson, who would have been with them in that car. Please send someone to check."

The urgency in Tia's voice prompted a quick response once they understood what she was telling them. An officer was approaching the vehicle within seconds. He pulled his gun from its holster and moved in an arc around the side so that he could see through the windows of the car.

The gun went back to its place as he reached the rear of the vehicle and yelled for medical assistance. The flurry of activity shifted to where Lester had been found, but the officer watching Tia wouldn't let her go to see him.

Another ambulance arrived just as the patrol car with Tia and Carlos in it pulled away. She watched through the window at the sight of her friend being attended to by the roadside until the scene disappeared from view. Turning back, she looked at the floor as she wondered about each of the people who had given so much to help her. How could she ever repay their kindness? Their sacrifice? Their loyalty to the end.

She was stirred from her world as Carlos rested his hand on hers. Tia turned to look at him and his eyes showed the emotion of seeing her safe.

"I'm so sorry Sarita. For everything."

She acknowledged his gesture with a worried smile and leant towards him, resting her head on his shoulder.

CHAPTER 24

Will felt a twinge of pain that made him wince as he pushed open the huge door. He hesitated a moment to take a breath and let the discomfort subside before he continued outside to stand on the steps of the New York Police Department. He looked at the traffic passing by and was momentarily lost in his own little world while wondering about who all these people were and where they were so hurriedly going. They seemed so purposeful and determined, emphasising the aimlessness of his own life. It was a feeling that had swamped him in the last few days as he considered the existence he was about to return to. After being driven by the need to find out what was happening to the group of friends he'd been with for several days, he found himself without direction, lost and lonely in a city of millions.

The constant need to be moving on in order to stay one step ahead and the tense nervous energy expended in that process, had worn him out. Days of surviving on little sleep had come back to seek its revenge. He just needed to relax and rebuild his strength after the ordeal he'd been through, but the thought of being alone, back at the house where a horrific event had taken place, was not appealing. Even the garage where he worked reminded him of his lost family.

After being forced to spend time in close proximity with his travelling companions, he increasingly felt bereft of their company. It was contradicted by an urge to escape; to just take off and try to run from the whole experience, but his heart told him there was unfinished 'business' to attend to.

The hospital had discharged him a couple of days earlier, but the police wanted to clear up some of the issues to do with the incident in the house he'd been renting, before they released him totally. It didn't take long for the pieces to begin to fall into place as they questioned Carlos Liatzo and followed up on the activities of Joseph Charles and Vince Kurtis.

The bullet-match to Joseph's gun was made while Will was still being treated for his injuries, so he was in the clear. The murders of Jack Cougar and Raif Bale were the sole work of Joseph Charles as punishment for having lost Tia, again.

Recent events had been very murky, drawing interested parties from all of the law enforcement agencies. Everybody had a theory, but they rarely matched the truth fully. So much was buried, secret, and many had an interest in keeping some of it that way.

The whirlwind of questions and interviews crowded Will's thoughts until he realised he was staring into the distance, lost in his own world. He shook his head, scattering the intrusive memories and fears and focused on the present.

Taking a deep breath, he slowly let it out, as though trying to purge the anxiety from within. A police officer came out of the door beside him and did a double take, but continued on his way without comment. Will suddenly felt conspicuous standing there and decided to leave before they changed their minds about releasing him.

He walked down to the edge of the busy road, adjusting the sling that supported his injured arm then hailed a passing cab. The yellow vehicle swerved into the curb, coming to a stop alongside and he awkwardly climbed in. Pulling the door shut, he sat looking at the official building he'd just left and pondered the hours of questioning he'd endured in the attempt to establish the facts. If anything, he felt more confused by everything. So many things still seemed unclear. His thoughts were abruptly interrupted.

"We can sit here all day, pal, but the meter's still runnin'. D'you want to go somewhere or not?"

The bluntness of the driver took no account of the circumstances Will had lived through, but why should he? What did he know of the way Will's life had been turned upside down?

"I'm sorry. St. George hospital, please."

The cab pulled away sharply and aggressively forced its way into the busy traffic. The sound of car horns shouted the annoyance of vehicles jostling for position, even though the traffic crawled along at walking pace.

'Slow is good', thought Will. "I like slow," he whispered out loud to himself.

"What'd you say?" the cabbie asked.

Will glanced up, catching the driver's look in the rear-view mirror. "Nothing." He smiled then turned to stare through the window at the city landscape passing by. It felt strange to be moving freely through the streets again, without having to consider who was looking or if there was a patrol car nearby.

The cab eventually pulled up at the destination and Will paid the fare. Stepping out onto the sidewalk, he closed the door then stood at the roadside watching as the vehicle gradually merged into the traffic again and finally disappeared from sight. As it rounded the corner, he realised he was daydreaming again and laughed at his inability to focus on the here and now. He turned to look at the huge complex he was about to enter and peered up at the soaring bank of windows that eventually terminated at a slender strip of blue sky.

Wandering slowly inside to the busy reception area, he was engulfed with the bustle of the place. It seemed to all be happening around him, like he was walking through a tunnel that allowed him to see what was taking place, but kept him separate from it all. Again there seemed to be purpose in the hurried movements of the staff as they attended to their duties, hijacking him with another wave of aimless emotion.

He went up two floors and along the corridor until he came to the familiar hospital ward he'd visited when he was being treated. Tapping gently on the door, he cautiously opened it until he was sure it was okay to enter.

"Hey there."

Prompted by the sound of Will's voice, Beth turned to look. She smiled in response to seeing her friend.

"W-i-l-l."

She dragged out his name, filling it with warmth as she said it, and reached out her hand to beckon him over. Will crossed the room to take it and leaned over to kiss her on the cheek. He found it difficult to explain to Beth the comfort he found just being together with her again. It gave him a small sense of family; a feeling that had been so abruptly taken from him a few short months earlier. As he looked at her, it made him wonder why he'd ever let their relationship begin to drift and vowed never to allow that to happen again.

"They say I can go home tomorrow, *if* there's someone to look after me." Beth squeezed his hand.

Will half smiled at her, but one word of her sentence struck him with force. "Home?" He glanced at the ceiling as a reflective expression crossed his face. "Where's that?"

Beth lifted herself a little so that she was sat up more and winced at the discomfort. The sadness in the eyes of her friend was clearly visible to her, his whole demeanour languishing in a subdued place of disinterest in life. The continued contact with people had given him something more than the solitary existence he'd been inclined towards living and she hoped that he wouldn't go back to the same downwardly spiralling lifestyle.

"Have you thought about what you'll do with the garage?"

Will got up from the bedside where he'd been sitting and went over to the window. He stood looking at the traffic passing by below in the busy street as he considered Beth's question. He shrugged as he resigned himself to not being able to give a definitive answer. She wanted more than that from him, so she pressed a little.

"Last time we met, just after your dad..." Beth hesitated and altered her question. "Before all this happened, you were considering selling."

"I was." Will nodded, but didn't offer anything more than confirmation that she was right.

Beth wanted to try to help him take control of his future and she knew she might be treading on toes, but felt it was important.

"And now?"

Will turned to look at her. "And now... I don't know what I'm going to do." He gave a half-hearted smile. "Don't want to go back; not sure how to go forward." He leant back against the window ledge.

Beth smiled at him and tried to lift his spirits with a jokey comment, but it hit the floor like a lead balloon and she apologised for the weak attempt. Will smirked at her.

"Fine pair aren't we?" he suggested.

"You could always come to stay at my place." Beth caught Will's eye as she made the suggestion. She noticed the surprised look on his face and was encouraged that he hadn't rejected the idea straight away. "Well, they told me that I could go home, *if* there was someone to look after me," she repeated.

Will laughed, lifting his arm that was supported in a sling. "You mean one invalid looking after another?"

Beth smiled. "Better that than both invalids struggling on their own." Will raised an eyebrow at her persistence. "You know Boost would like it too, Will," she reasoned.

Will shook his head at her blatant pushing. "Ganging up on me already, what hope would I have if I came?" He turned back to the view out of the window and Beth knew she'd gone far enough for the moment.

"Lester's doing okay," she said, filling the empty space left by him disconnecting from the conversation. "He was a bit concussed from the blow, but said he was doing fine when I spoke to him this morning on the telephone. His mother's pampering him." She laughed. "It's driving him crazy." The intonation in Beth's voice suggested he was lucky to have such a comfort and that she wouldn't mind being driven crazy by Lester's mom as well.

"That's good." Will momentarily glanced over his shoulder to acknowledge he'd heard the news. There was a long pause before he spoke again. "I'd like to see Lester again... Soon."

Beth couldn't help smiling behind his back. There was nothing she wanted more than for the two of them to forget the past and build a friendship.

"What about..." Beth hesitated as she wondered if she should ask, but decided to continue. "What about Tia and her father, Will?"

He shrugged. "They're helping with the investigation. That's all the police ever tell me. I asked where they were. 'They're helping with our investigation', is all they'll say." He shook his head in frustration. "I just wish..." Will's voice tailed off as he shook his head and thought better of finishing his sentence.

Beth watched him as the emotions ran rampant in his expression and he fought against showing them. His efforts were in vain, but she didn't want to draw attention to it and left the room silent until Will spoke again.

"Beth?"

"What?"

Will turned to face her directly. "Were you serious about me coming to stay at your place?"

A beaming smile flashed across Beth's face as she sensed he'd taken the bait.

"Of course. I would *love* you to come." She spared nothing in the feeling she wove into her confirmation.

There was another long pause as Will considered his future and the opportunity being offered. There were many good memories attached to the place where he lived, but the recent ones were very painful to deal with and he knew he couldn't just stay there because of an old workshop that once belonged to his beloved father.

"Perhaps it's time for me to move on; make a new start," he reasoned out loud.

"And Tia?"

Will looked up at Beth and saw in her eyes that she knew more than he had communicated in words. "I really like her. I just wish I could find out..." He didn't finish, but the frustration was clear. He'd tried to find out, but was being obstructed by everyone who could answer his questions. "So when can you leave the hospital?" he asked, changing the subject.

"Can you come and get me tomorrow morning, after the doctor has signed me out? They won't let me leave without someone to accompany me."

"Sure. Then we'll hobble back to your place shall we? Invalids united." There was a twinkle in Will's eye as he threw in his final comment before leaving the room. "I guess I'll have to take up house cleaning as a career."

He laughed out loud as he could hear Beth's few choice words thrown after him.

The following day when Will arrived at ten o'clock, Beth was ready and waiting. They set out on their protracted journey back home, travelling by bus. It would have been more convenient by car, but neither of them were in a fit state to do so and not having to do any driving gave them the opportunity to spend some time talking. With the pressure of the situation that had surrounded them gone, most of the conversation revolved around personal things. Some about Will's father and sister, which was painful, but had a therapeutic effect on Will, who'd bottled up his emotions for so long. Some talk was about their time in the forces, but very little was about what they'd lived through over the past several days. It was all too fresh for them to want to talk about it and there would be time enough for that later.

When they finally arrived back home, the first thing they did was call to see Officer Madeley to inform him that they'd returned and to discuss anything he wanted to know about the events of recent days. He was very helpful and gentle with them both, noticing that they'd been through a tough time. When they concluded their discussions, he asked where they were going from the police station and when they told him they had to collect Boost from Mrs Drake's place before going home, he volunteered to drive them.

For the whole distance from town to Mrs Drake's house, Madeley filled the vehicle with a one-sided conversation. Beth was giving occasional nods to indicate that she was following the discourse, but Will had switched off almost as soon as he got into the back of the car.

Pulling into Mrs Drake's drive, Madeley took the car right to the front steps. The two invalids each climbed from the vehicle in their own awkward way. Boost came bounding down the steps as soon as Mrs Drake opened the front door to greet them. He danced around Will and Beth; his excitement bubbling over at the reunion, perhaps a little too enthusiastically for the walking wounded.

Mrs Drake fussed over Beth like she was a long-lost daughter returned and Madeley was grateful for her generosity with coffee and cake.

When they eventually settled to take their drinks, Beth felt compelled to make some kind of apology. "I'm so sorry that we had to leave Boost without any warning."

"Don't you worry, dear," Mrs Drake interrupted. "We've had a *wonderful* time. Haven't we Boost?" She patted the dog and he responded gleefully to her.

Noticing how withdrawn Will was, Beth thought it important not to stay long, so after ten minutes she determined to make a move.

"I think you're going to have to excuse us, Mrs Drake. I feel so tired from the journey home."

"Of course you do, Beth."

Mrs Drake got up from her seat and went to the kitchen. She came back with some supplies for the weary travellers and made sure that they were catered for before sending them on their way.

Madeley was just as gracious as he drove them to the house and dropped them off, insisting that they should ring if there was anything they needed.

As he left, Will and Beth waved him off with Boost standing watch beside them. Beth leant back against Will, who was standing just behind her. He put his arm around her and was thankful for the warmth of her friendship. The two of them stood in silence, watching dusk begin to settle on the distant hills where they'd driven with Tia only a few days before. So much had changed since then. Beth let out a sigh, turned and glanced at Will, then retrieved the key from its usual hiding place and unlocked the door.

"I don't know about you, but I'm going straight to bed. I feel like I could sleep for a week."

Will smiled. "Do you mind if I sit and watch TV for a little while, before I turn in? I feel tired, but I don't think I'll sleep. There's too much going on in my head."

Beth put her hand on his cheek, but said nothing. The gesture carried all the love and concern that was needed. She pushed the door open and flicked the light switch. What confronted them was the aftermath of a hurried and uncaring search by the authorities who were trying to track them only days earlier.

Beth gritted her teeth and hissed air through them in frustration. She had never kept a tidy house, but the mess was more than she could cope with at that moment.

"The miserable…" Beth threw up her hand to stop Will from making further comment.

"I'm going to bed, if I can find it under the mess." She wandered through the hallway and headed up the stairs without another word.

Will made coffee and took a seat at the kitchen table. He was so lost in his thoughts that he completely forgot to switch on the TV. He sat there for an hour before turning in, but it was a night when sleep was determined to stay far from him. The images embedded in his mind were resurrected in the darkness, like ghosts sent to haunt him. Over and over, he re-lived the tortuous journey as he'd dragged himself through the house in his effort to save Tia from the hands of her tormentor. Always, he would wake with a start, covered in sweat, as he heard the gunshot. Sometimes he would dream that he'd made it in time, but in the nightmares, he saw Tia's limp, lifeless body drop to the floor, her life taken by the hand of a vengeful, bitter man. He would stare at the silvery light that streamed through the gap in the curtains before drifting off to begin living his inexorable nightmare again.

It was a relief when morning finally came as the nightly tussle was set aside for a few hours of relief. Beth became aware of the struggle he was having. Some nights she would hear him shout in anguish at the images that haunted him. She made every effort to keep connected, as Will's inclination to withdraw from company fought hard to take control of him. She drew him into her world out in the workshops as a means of occupying him in a productive way.

It took a while, but there were gradually more times when his spirits lifted and the world seemed less gloomy. They collaborated on different projects and he engaged with enthusiasm, but she would catch him off guard in moments when he was vacantly staring into the distance. She frequently wondered what occupied his mind, until one day, while they were sitting on the steps of the rear porch drinking coffee, she asked.

"What are you thinking about, Will?"

"Umm." He reconnected with the moment and found Beth staring at him.

"I was just interested in what you were thinking about."

"Oh. Nothing important."

"It's Tia, isn't it?"

Will was surprised by Beth's accuracy and hesitated for a second before realising he wasn't hiding anything from her really.

"I can't help it. I was wondering where she is. What she's doing. Why she hasn't been in touch."

"It's funny isn't it?"

"What is?"

"Neither of us knew her for very long, and the circumstances weren't exactly the best," Beth laughed, "but I miss her too."

"I can't get her out of my mind, Beth." Will felt embarrassed at admitting his infatuation, but dismissed his discomfort for the opportunity to tell Beth what he was really thinking. "There was just something about her that…" He was lost for words of explanation.

"It's called love, Will." Beth put her hand on his shoulder. "I could see it."

"You could?"

"At the river."

Will stared at his friend, thankful that she was concerned rather than mocking him.

"I need to find out, Beth, but it's been months since we last saw her. What if she's had to change her identity again? She did it before. You saw all the stuff her father was involved in and the police weren't going to give an inch when I tried to find out. Even when I rang again last month they just pushed me around from one department to the next, avoiding any awkward questions by denying it was anything to do with them."

Beth smiled, seeing the frustration on Will's face, but she had no answers to give and the conversation came to an inconclusive end.

Six months after they'd returned home, Beth was up early one morning, seated at the kitchen table. She'd left Will asleep, having checked on him. They'd had a long week doing repairs to some machinery for a local farmer. It was one rare occasion when she'd got up and not found him already in the kitchen. Boost was fussing, fed up with the sedate lifestyle that had become the norm and wanting some serious exercise. He'd been confined to the house and the yard for far too long.

Just after ten o'clock, Will finally surfaced looking in a little better shape for having slept longer after the late night finish.

"I thought I'd leave you." Beth got up to make him coffee. "I reckon you needed it."

"Umm." Will nodded.

Boost whined as he lay near the outside door, his mournful eyes watching with a certain amount of hopefulness. Beth gave him an exaggerated sympathetic look so that Will couldn't miss it.

"Will, you're going to have to take Boost for a good walk today. He looks miserable, poor thing."

Boost sprang up, aware that he was the subject of discussion.

Will looked at him and smiled. "Alright Boost. I've ignored you, haven't I?" The dog was at Will's side with his tail wagging in appreciation of being noticed. "I'm going to take him on a walk to town."

"Are you sure you'll be okay to do that distance? It's a long way there and back."

"I'm sure. I can always get a taxi back if I need to."

Will fetched a coat and started to put his boots on. Boost was dancing around the kitchen, aware that he was going out. Beth began laughing at his performance, which just encouraged him further.

"I'll see you later." Will grabbed some fruit from the refrigerator, opened the back door and let Boost shoot past him into the back yard.

Beth waved as he disappeared. She went to the front room to watch them go along the drive to the road. Will walked with his head low. Although he was generally okay, there were moments when he slipped into a melancholic state.

Will trudged along the road, heading toward the town, happy to be thoughtlessly following the tarmac. On two occasions cars stopped as people asked if he needed a lift, but he declined, explaining that he wanted to walk to exercise the dog. He couldn't totally avoid Mrs Drake's house though. She saw the two of them passing and called from the front porch. That was enough to send Boost travelling at speed to visit his temporary adopted owner. She asked about Beth and Will chatted for a few minutes, but refused an offer to stay for a while. He just didn't feel like being in company.

It was about an hour before he reached the town and wandered aimlessly through the shopping area with Boost on his leash. It wasn't that he needed anything, but it passed the time just browsing in the windows.

Reaching the far end of the main street, he turned to begin making his way back. Officer Madeley caught sight of him and waved from the opposite side of the road, but he didn't come across to talk and Will felt quite relieved. Madeley was a friendly, caring man, whom the community liked very much, but Will was in no mood to stand around talking. He'd visited Beth's house on occasions and been happy to almost out-stay his welcome.

Near the halfway point, Will paused to look at something in a shop window and as he did he felt Boost tug at the lead.

"Hold on boy." Will patted him as he turned his attention back to the window. Suddenly Boost pulled so strongly that the leash slipped from Will's hand, taking him totally by surprise.

Will shouted after Boost as he ran full pelt twenty yards along the street then veered into an open courtyard where people could sit at tables for coffee. Will raced after him and reached the place to find Boost being fussed by a lady seated at one of the tables. She was wearing a head scarf and sunglasses. Her magazine was discarded on the tabletop in favour of giving her attention to Boost. Will walked up behind her, embarrassed at the behaviour of his pet.

"I am *so* sorry." He bent down to grab the leash and pretended to throttle the dog. "He never usually does this. He's usually so well..." Will looked at the lady as he stood up and it put a stop to his explanation.

"It's no problem," she said. "He's a beautiful dog." Will was rooted to the spot, just staring. She stood, removed her sunglasses and held out her hand. "Hi. I'm Sarita Liatzo."

Boost was standing between them looking up in triumph. Will was motionless for a moment, a smile flickered, then he reached out and shook the offered hand. "Will Harris."

"Pleasure to meet you, Will Harris. Would you care to join me for coffee?" She smiled at him and he nodded in response. He meant to say thank you, but the words just wouldn't come out.

On the table was a wrapped box. The vibrant red paper was embraced by gold ribbon. It shouted, 'Look at me', as the colour contrasted with the white table cloth.

Seeing the extra guest, a waiter came over and Sarita ordered two more coffees. He disappeared to fetch the order and Will watched him as he went back into the coffee-shop.

He glanced at Sarita, but was unsure what to say to her. She looked as beautiful as he'd remembered from the first moment he laid eyes on her in the parking lot of his garage, except that there was a radiance in her face instead of fear.

She loosened the headscarf and let it drop so that it rested on her shoulders, took her seat again and Will followed her example.

She didn't say anything, but simply ran her hand along Boost's golden coat and he responded to the gesture of friendship.

The waiter returned and placed the drinks on the table, but realising that Sarita's coffee cup was still full he asked, "Was your coffee not good? I will make sure you're not charged for it."

"Oh, no it's fine thank you. I'm expecting someone else. I've just spoken to her on the phone, she should be here any moment." She moved the extra coffee in front of an unoccupied seat.

A car screeched to a halt at the parking area by the side of the road, drawing the attention of everyone at the tables. Beth exploded from the vehicle and made the distance to where they were seated in seconds. Sarita stood to receive her, but neither of them said a single word. Beth ran straight into Sarita's embrace and the two of them hugged with such warmth that all the onlookers would have been convinced they were long-lost friends reuniting.

Will watched as they shared the same unspoken joy at seeing each other again. As the hug lingered, he felt a smile creep across his lips. It felt like the first time, for a long time, that the warmth of being near people he cared about had touched him deep in his soul, like the spring sunshine returning after a long, cold winter.

When they finally separated, Sarita indicated for Beth to sit. Beth did as she was beckoned, but deliberately edged her chair fractionally nearer to where Sarita was sitting. It made Sarita bite her lip as though restraining the emotion of seeing Beth show her true affection for a friend that she had genuinely missed.

Sarita took a deep breath and sighed happily at the scene. "I need to apologise to you both that I have taken so long to get in touch, but it was beyond my control. I just had to be patient..." The intonation in her voice clearly conveyed her frustration at having to wait for the reunion. "The authorities needed to do some work with my father to wrap up some issues, things that I have no idea about and don't want to know about. The biggest issue was whether we were safe or if there was an ongoing threat. As it turns out, all the risk, starting with the break-in at the villa in Mexico that prompted my father to move me to the States was the work of

Joseph Charles. Despite the fact that the risk seemed to be coming from multiple sources it was all his doing. My kidnap, everything.

Anyway, I don't want to talk about him except to say that the six months were to assess if there was any further risk and it was determined there is not. The moment they gave the all clear I was on a plane to come here. Father said it could wait one more day. I said not." She laughed at her determination. "He's coming here in a day or two. He wants to meet you both." She glanced across at Will. "He particularly wants to meet you, Will. He insisted that he came in person to express his thanks… Well, I've said too much about that already, so…"

Sarita picked up the wrapped box and passed it over. "This is for you, Beth."

Beth laughed with surprise. Her eyes lit up at the beautifully presented gift. "What is it?"

Sarita smiled with the joy of giving something so small to someone who had given her so much. "You're *supposed* to open it to find out." Her joking, mocking tone made them all laugh.

Carefully pulling the bow, as if reluctant to unravel the perfectly presented box, Beth removed the ribbon and set it to one side. She opened the paper and removed it with the same care, exposing a cream coloured box that she placed on the table. Lifting the lid and pulling back the soft tissue paper inside, she revealed a beautiful black cocktail dress. She paused for a moment, overwhelmed and lost for words, then took the item out of the box, lifting it as though it was the world's greatest treasure.

Will hadn't often seen Beth become emotional, but she was truly choked and simply stared at the dress in disbelief. Sarita and Will waited for her to compose herself and when she thought she could finally get the words out clearly, she said, "Sarita. You shouldn't have." She leant over and they touched cheeks.

"I most certainly should," Sarita whispered in her ear and beamed with joy at Beth's reaction. Pulling away, she looked Beth in the eye and added, "Keisha sends her love. She made me promise that I would take you to visit her when you're free… She also made me promise that I would take you somewhere so that you could wear that dress. So…" Sarita deliberately stretched out the pause to create expectation about what she was going to say and Beth was giving her full attention. "I've arranged for you to go and stay in a five star hotel for a few days. Pamper days, dinner, the works. It's in Florida. They have every facility you can imagine. And… my father has chartered a small yacht for a few days. You fancy a bit of sailing?"

Beth's mouth literally dropped open and her face radiated joy and excitement. Will looked on as the girls bonded their relationship in much different circumstances than those that had initially thrown them together, but Sarita wasn't quite finished. "Lester has promised me that he will go."

"But… you are coming too, aren't you?" The questioning look on Beth's face made Sarita laugh.

"Yes. Are you kidding? I wouldn't miss it for the world." Sarita put her hand on Beth's. She hesitated for a second. "But, *I* need to find a *date*, Beth." The two girls momentarily stared at each other then simultaneously looked directly at Will. Sarita smiled at the questioning look on his face. "And I wondered, Mr Harris…" a questioning look crossed her face, "would *you* do me the honour?"